Everlasting Bad Boys

Everlasting Bad Boys

SHELLY LAURENSTON
CYNTHIA EDEN
NOELLE MACK

BRAVA

KENSINGTON PUBLISHING CORP.

www.kensingtonbooks.com

BRAVA BOOKS are published by

Kensington Publishing Corp.
850 Third Avenue
New York, NY 10022

All Kensington titles, imprints, and distributed lines are available at special quantity discounts for bulk purchases for sales promotion, premiums, fund-raising, educational or institutional use.

Special book excerpts or customized printings can also be created to fit specific needs. For details, write or phone the office of the Kensington Special Sales Manager: Kensington Publishing Corp., 850 Third Avenue, New York, NY 10022; Attn. Special Sales Department. Phone: 1-800-221-2647.

Brava and the B logo are Reg. U.S. Pat. & TM Off.

ISBN-13: 978-0-7582-2850-5
ISBN-10: 0-7582-2850-3

First Kensington Trade Paperback Printing: September 2008

10 9 8 7 6 5 4 3 2

Printed in the United States of America

CONTENTS

CAN'T GET ENOUGH

Shelly Laurenston

1

"*You whore!*"

Ailean the Wicked, veteran Battle Dragon of the Dragon Queen's Armies, third-born son of Afton the Hermit, and one of the *many* from the Cadwaladr Clan, leapt naked and wet from the tub and made a mad dash for the door. Unfortunately, town guards and one blindingly angry father waited for him right outside that door, so he quickly turned and charged hard for the open window.

"Stop him!"

He heard the guards coming into the room, but he didn't waste time looking over his shoulder to see how close they were or bid good-bye to the damsel he'd had his full of the night before. He'd done this enough times in his life to know you never stop and you never look back. Even if you feel their breath on your neck, you never look back.

Several floors up, Ailean dived right through the window, bracing his human body for impact and rolling when he felt the ground beneath him. By the time he pulled himself back to his feet, the soldiers were on the first floor, barreling through the door.

Ailean took off running through the city of Kyffin. An ancient city many leagues away from Dark Plains and Devanallt Mountain, the seat of power for the dragons of Dark Plains. Winding and congested with people, it was easy to disappear in Kyffin.

Unless, of course, you were a completely naked male with dark blue hair. Humans had a tendency to notice that sort of thing.

But he wouldn't be caught. He should have known the woman wanted more from him than a simple tumble for the night. It had happened before. He goes to bed with a woman who promises no commitments and wakes up to a lass whose father wants Ailean dead for "deflowering" his daughter. A daughter the man had planned to sell off to the wealthiest lord looking for a wife.

After all these years there were still some things about humans Ailean would never understand.

And, clearly, they'd never understand him. For Ailean lived life on his own terms. He answered to no one. Not the human lords of this land, nor the dragon lords of his own. He lived as he wanted, fucked who he wanted, and never had a moment of regret about it.

As the years had passed, he'd collected many names. Ailean the Beautiful. Ailean the Killer. Ailean the Bold. Ailean the Wicked, which was still his personal favorite. And, over the last thirty years specifically, Ailean the Whore. Brutal but honest, depending on who you spoke to.

What he didn't plan to take on for a name anytime this millennium was Ailean the Captured by Some Female Who'll Try and Tie Me Down.

No, that name would have to wait for another four or five hundred years. With so many females to taste and enjoy, he had no desire to lock himself in. Why waste all his talents on just one?

Ailean felt the soldiers move closer. He could shift to his true form and destroy them where they stood, but what fun would that be? Besides, he'd kill other humans who happened to be standing around. He had no desire to do that. Not when he enjoyed humans so thoroughly. They had their many flaws, but that was to be expected of any lower creature.

Picking up his pace, Ailean lost the soldiers, at least for a time, when he dashed down a busy street filled with sellers and buyers. He kept moving, charging up a set of steps and inside a building. He immediately recognized it as a school. Perhaps a training ground for sorcerers or those who simply enjoyed learning. He considered himself a "learner," but what he learned he never got out of a simple book. The world taught him all he needed to know.

His dragon hearing picked up the sound of the soldiers heading down the street, so Ailean went up many flights of stairs until he ended in an enormous room filled with books. They were everywhere. On bookshelves, piled on the floor, and on the tables. Students kept their heads down, not even noticing him. Perfect. Nothing had become more tedious than explaining his blue hair. After so many years, simply telling people his poor mother had been cursed while he slept in the womb seemed to quickly end the conversation and had many women going out of their way to prove it didn't matter—which he never minded.

Moving among the stacks, Ailean slid to a stop in the very back, near an exit and another window—in case he needed that as well. Then he caught a scent. It was deliciously familiar. He sniffed the air again. A dragoness. He grinned. Oh . . . he knew that scent quite well.

After more than three decades, he'd never forgotten the owner of that scent. How could he? She'd thrown his own battle ax at his head. Among his kin, that was merely a declaration of neverending love.

No longer thinking of the soldiers searching for him, he let his nose lead him. The library went deeper than he realized, the scent luring him into near darkness among old, dusty tomes he'd never give up a second of his life reading. When he finally stopped, he stared at the human form sitting on the floor. She had her back against the bookshelf and wore the robes of a human acolyte, the brownish-red tint of the cloth suggesting alchemy as the area of study.

Ailean stared at the top of her head, the hood of the robe slipping off a bit to reveal golden hair.

He'd never expected to see her *living* as human. Fascinated, he crouched down in front of her and stared, waiting for her to lift her head up. He wanted to see her face again.

It took her a bit to pull herself out of her book, but eventually she looked up at him. Ailean took in a sharp breath at the sight of her.

Gods of hellfire . . . she really is gorgeous.

She had a pretty enough face and those always-intense gold eyes. But it was those spots splattered across the bridge of her pug nose and onto her cheeks that fascinated him most. Freckles, the humans called them.

And below that . . . he almost sighed. Those lips. They were ridiculously full and the softest pink. He could spend hours enjoying those lips. *Hours.*

Breaking into a wide grin, knowing he was the last being on the planet she'd ever wanted to see again, Ailean said with glee, "By all the gods of blood and death—if it isn't Shalin the Innocent! Did you miss me?"

Oh, gods. Not him!

Anyone *but* him.

The one dragon she'd give anything to have in her cave, in her bed—anywhere she could get him.

But even now, just having him here in the library put her at risk. Especially with him naked.

Ahh, but what a beautiful naked he was.

No. No. She couldn't think like that. Ever. First off, what exactly would she do with him? She'd had lovers before. Well . . . she'd had two. But two nice, quiet, well-schooled ones. But Ailean the Slag . . . well, he was the stuff fantasies were made of. So very tall and wide, all of it sturdy strength and powerful muscle. Whether as dragon or human, he stood much taller than those around him. Then there was that hair. A silky mass of midnight blue she could easily imagine sliding through her fingers, draping over her body. It was long and luxurious and simply . . . och! She was doing it again.

But how could she not? Especially with those bright silver eyes watching her and that adorable grin on those decadently full lips. Even his nose, which clearly had taken considerable abuse as human, made her think all sorts of distracting, I'll-never-be-an-Elder-if-I-keep-this-up thoughts.

Fool, Shalin!

And she was a fool. The one dragon she could never again go near, the one dragon she could never even think of talking to, was

Ailean the Wicked. Also known as Ailean the Whore, Ailean the Slag, and a host of other names, depending on who you talked to.

Why? Why did she have to deny herself the one thing every other dragoness and human female seemed able to enjoy since Ailean had been no more than twenty winters?

Because of that night. That one damn night when he'd become the absolute obsession of Princess Adienna. The dragoness spoke of him constantly. Obsessed over every move she'd heard he'd made. Although she'd never demean herself by tracking him down herself, Adienna still waited for him to return. And every female who had graced his bed before or since—and there had been so very many—became the enemy of this one irrational female.

Adienna said she loved him, but Shalin had a hard time believing love and obsession were the same thing. Would the princess be so "in love" with Ailean if he'd come back to her begging for more time in her bed? If he'd crawled to her on his belly, professing a never-ending love? Or would she have tossed him aside like quite a few others?

But Ailean had done none of those things. He'd run from her bed as though the gods of despair and loathing chased him, and he never came back. In fact, he never came back to Devenallt Mountain again. And every day Shalin prayed to any god who would listen that this would be the day when Adienna would stop talking about him, thinking about him, living for him. But, invariably, at some point, Adienna would find something that would bring her back to that point. Back to Ailean.

Even worse, Adienna blamed Shalin. Especially once the rumors spread that Ailean had left Adienna's bed specifically to search out Shalin.

Shalin almost snorted. If only *that* were true. But she knew better. That night, when Ailean had found her alone in the royal archives deep in the bowels of Devenallt Mountain, that had been nothing more than pure luck. He'd been looking for a quiet escape from Adienna and Shalin had been looking for much needed time alone.

If Adienna hadn't come looking for him, who knows where things would have led. But the bitch *had* come looking for him.

Shalin scented her before Ailean, who'd been quite intent on convincing Shalin to come with him to a human town to find a pub and a meal. "We can spend a bit of time together," he'd said. "Get to know one another."

Looking into those silver eyes, all Shalin had wanted to do was push him to the ground and have her way with him. But that couldn't happen, not with Adienna coming ever closer. Yet Ailean wouldn't listen to her when she tried to explain. He kept cutting Shalin off, trying to convince her he was worth her time. And the more he cut her off, the more frustrated she became.

Her temper was a rarely seen thing. But when she'd heard the flap of Adienna's wings and knew Ailean wouldn't stop talking, proving once again how everyone had a tendency to ignore her, she let a bit of that temper take control and she did the only thing she could think of . . .

She threw his battle ax at him.

In retrospect, perhaps she could have thought of something better. She felt especially bad when it grazed his temple and the blood began to spurt.

Then the rumors took hold.

At first, Adienna paid little attention to them, although her teasing toward Shalin became a little crueler, her venomous tongue a little more pointed. The more time that passed, however, the more Adienna began to turn on her. "*You* are the reason he has not returned," she'd finally accused. "*You* are the reason he stays away from me." Soon the situation had gotten so unstable, Shalin's father met with the Elders and the decision was made to send Shalin out among the humans sooner rather than later. She'd been studying in Kyffin for five years now and not once had she missed the hallowed stone halls of Devenallt Mountain.

Now, nearly thirty winters later, she had the one dragon she could never stop thinking about, dreaming about, or lusting over standing right in front of her—naked.

Of course, he was also the one dragon who could get her killed.

"Ailean," she somehow managed to squeak out. "Good morn to you."

"And to you, Shalin. You look awfully beautiful today."

The fact he could say that and sound like he meant it was probably why so many females fell under his spell. Yet Shalin couldn't be fooled. She had mirrors, did she not?

"Thank you. So why are you—"

"Och!" he cut in as he always did. The dragon rarely took a breath, it seemed. "You won't believe my morning, Shalin. You truly won't. Mind if I sit?"

"Uh—"

"Good. Thanks." He dropped down beside her. All that dragon as naked human male. It took every ounce of her strength not to reach out and touch him. Like that solid thigh brushing against her robe-covered leg, to see how it felt under her human hands. She'd never been with a male as human. She'd heard it could be . . . entertaining.

"So there I am, taking a bath, as she said I could, when suddenly her father comes in."

"Oh, that must have been—"

"Horrible, right. Because she told me that we were alone in that house. But apparently not. I think she wanted me to Claim her or marry her or whatever they call it."

"Even though you're—"

"A dragon, right. She doesn't know that bit, you see. Best to keep her in the dark about that, don't you think?"

"Well—"

"Especially for just a night of entertainment. Why she'd want me as a mate, I have no idea. So what are you reading?"

It took her a moment to realize he'd asked her a question he expected her to answer. *"Alchemic Formulas from the Nolwenn Witches of Alsandair."*

"Is it interesting?"

"A—"

"I don't know how you can read so many books. I get bored after a few pages."

"So," Shalin found the courage to ask, "you've never read the books about yourself?"

Ailean groaned, rested his elbows on his raised knees, and dropped his head in his hands. "Tell me you haven't read those."

Read them? She'd devoured them.

"Well—"

"Because I didn't authorize those to be written."

The books had begun to show up among humans and dragons nearly ten years before. She'd only just finished reading volume three the previous night and word of volume four being available soon had her nearly breathless. Each volume had two editions. One for humans and one for dragons written in the ancient language of their people. A language the humans of this world could never hope to learn with their much weaker minds, ensuring the fact dragons roamed among them freely remained a well-kept secret.

"The books aren't true, then?"

Based on his wince, she knew they were as true as they could be.

"I never said those things didn't happen. I just said I never authorized them being written about." He turned his head and looked at her, those silver eyes hot on her face. "I don't want you to think I run around telling tales about my relationships, Shalin. I can keep a secret quite well."

And how tempted she was to take him up on his unspoken offer, but that would be cutting her own throat. She'd officially be an enemy of Adienna then, and she simply wouldn't risk her life for any male.

"I—"

"Perhaps I could tempt you away from your interesting book with promise of a delicious meal at one of the nearby taverns?"

Shocked, Shalin gripped the book in her lap tightly. He wanted to take her out? In public?

What should she say? *I'd love to? How about dinner in my room? Forget that, let's go for it right here, right now?*

Instead what she heard herself stuttering was, "I . . . I can't."

"Can't or won't?"

"Both." She shot to her feet, the book still in her hands. "I have to go."

He stood and towered over her as no human could. "Don't go, Shalin. Spend the night with me."

She should be insulted. He'd just left another female's bed and now, still naked and wet from the woman's bath, he'd asked Shalin to warm his bed. But this was Ailean the Whore. He wasn't doing anything out of character. She actually felt kind of proud he'd asked her at all. Although she knew that to be pathetic. And she'd never admit it out loud.

Shalin focused on the book in her hands. "That's very kind of you, but . . . but I . . . I—"

Big fingers lightly gripped her chin and tilted her face up to his. "Gods, Shalin. You do so tempt me."

She nearly melted at his words. Melted right into a big puddle at his feet.

"Ailean, I—"

Shalin stopped talking when she realized guards stood behind him.

"There you are," one of them said, slapping his hand down on Ailean's shoulder.

Ailean gave a short snort. "And such a good job finding me, since I've been standing here for the last twenty minutes."

With a snarl, the guard motioned to the others and large steel manacles were locked onto Ailean's wrists.

"Don't look so, Shalin." Ailean grinned. "I have every intention of coming back for you."

Shalin opened her mouth to say something, but no words would come out. He'd rendered her completely speechless. But since he really didn't let her get a word in edgewise, this wasn't exactly an incredible feat. Holding the book close to her chest and pulling the hood of her acolyte robe down over her face, she nodded, turned, and fled.

The city guards handed Ailean the pair of leggings he'd left behind. Ailean pulled them on, the steel manacles on his wrists clanking against the chains as he did so, while the guards asked him questions about his intentions toward the lady. He'd had none except for what they'd done the evening before. But when they demanded to know if he was aware he'd bedded a virgin, Ailean had laughed outright.

At that point, they led him downstairs to the great front doors of the school. As he walked out into the bright morning, he saw

Shalin standing on the front steps talking to an aged human male who wore the robes of a master.

Although she nodded and made noises as if she paid attention, Ailean knew Shalin was fully aware of his presence.

"Shalin."

Shalin stopped talking to her teacher and, with a nod, faced Ailean. "Yes?"

He glanced at the guards who grudgingly allowed him to step closer.

"I am sorry."

Shalin frowned. "Sorry? Sorry about—what are you doing?"

"Doing what I've been dying to do since I saw you in the royal archives."

Before she could even think to ask what that might have been, Ailean's manacled hands gripped the front of her robe and yanked her close, forcing her to rise on her toes. She gasped and then his mouth was on hers. Startled, she automatically slammed her fists on his shoulders and, if he were actually human, she might have crushed him where he stood. But with a Battle Dragon it was like hitting a mountain. His head tipped to the side and she felt his tongue slip between her lips and into her mouth. She drew her tongue back but his only followed until it had the poor thing cornered. Then it stroked and stroked and Shalin's human body heated, everything beginning to ache, demanding the dragon finish what he'd just started.

But as she reached for him, Ailean abruptly pulled away. He stared down at her, his eyes wide in shock.

"I never thought . . ." Ailean shook his head, looking confused. Finally, he said, "I promise, Shalin, I will be back for you."

Not sure she understood, she asked, "Back for me?"

"It might be a bit, though." He took several steps back, holding up the chains and manacles that had been clamped to his wrists, only now he held them in his hands. "And, uh . . . sorry. Think of it as retribution for that bloody ax."

Ailean dropped the chains and gave her a wicked smile and wink seconds before he took off running.

Watching him bolt down the street, that big grin on his handsome face and the town guards right behind him, Shalin could do nothing more than laugh. Even as the school masters took her back inside the school to calm her "hysteria" after her brutal "assault," she continued to laugh and laugh as she never had before.

2

"Wake up, brother."

Ailean felt the bed lift when his brother's big foot kicked it. His big, cold, lonely bed.

It had been nearly a full moon since he'd had a female in his bed. The father of the woman whose name he could no longer remember still searched for him, so Ailean had taken up residence in his home. A castle buried in a valley between the Taaffe Mountains of Kerezik. He knew he could find a female—many females—to share his bed, but he didn't want that. He wanted to go back and get Shalin. He knew from that kiss alone the name "Innocent" had been wrongly given. Until things calmed down a bit, however, he'd have to wait to go back to Kyffin. But not much longer. He didn't think he could wait much longer.

"Go away, Arranz," he grumbled, turning his face away to bury it deeper into his pillow.

"You did this," his brother replied in that calm way he had that barely hid a veneer of ruthlessness Ailean appreciated during a time of war. "You need to fix it."

"I did what?"

"Shalin the Innocent."

Realizing his brother wouldn't leave, Ailean rolled to his back but still did not leave his bed. "What about her?"

"You've caused her much trouble, brother. And you have little time left to go and protect her."

"What are you talking about?" No one believed she'd helped him, did they? He would have taken her with him that day if he thought for a second she'd be in any danger. "Are you telling me the city guards are planning to punish her for what happened?"

His brother, a silver dragon nearly three decades his senior, dropped into a chair across from him. "City guards? This has nothing to do with them. It's your princess I speak of."

Cringing at the mere mention of her, Ailean snapped, "That viper is not *my* anything."

"Someone told her you two have been together. You were seen kissing the little gold outside that human school she attends. The princess seems to think you love Shalin."

"Love her?" With a laugh, Ailean shook his head. "I don't know where that fool Adienna got that idea but—"

"She's sold her, brother."

Ailean's grin slowly faded. "I'm . . . I'm sorry. What?"

Violet eyes stared at him. "She's sold her. To old Tinig."

Sitting up, Ailean growled, "The Lightning dragons? She's sold her to the Lightning dragons?" Their greatest enemies and some of the most dangerous warriors.

"Tinig has nineteen sons." Like the humans of that desolate place, those in the Northlands bred few females. Instead they stole them from wherever they could find them. "Adienna sent word she had a female to sell. He was reluctant when he heard she was no great beauty, but when he found out Shalin could read and write, he doubled his offer, and they settled on a price."

"And you're telling me Shalin is all right with this?" If so, then he needed to speak with her. He wouldn't allow her to leave her people over this ridiculous situation.

But Arranz shook his head. "Shalin does not know, brother. But I have a lover in the court. She told me all this. She's always liked Shalin and thinks this is unfair."

"Of course this is unfair!"

"Then you best get up. The Lightnings are coming for her. I've heard they near Kyffin as we speak."

Ailean tossed off his bedcovers, rage singing through his veins. "How could Adienna do this? Shalin is her friend."

"That beast has no friends. I warned you, brother. I warned you not to involve yourself with her."

"I know. I know. Don't you think I know?" he said, yet again, as he temporarily dragged on leather leggings so he wouldn't walk through his castle naked. The humans always seemed so flustered by that. "It was barely one night. And trust me, it was not up to my usual standards, because I couldn't wait to get out of there."

"You bruised that mighty ego of hers. If you'd crawled back to her on your knees, this wouldn't be a problem. But you ignored her like you do all the rest."

"I don't ignore the rest. I ignore her because she makes my skin crawl."

Together the brothers strode from Ailean's bedchamber and down the hall. As they made it to the top of the stairs, the second oldest of the brothers rushed up. "There you are. Have you heard?"

"Aye."

Bideven shook his head. "What did you do to that poor dragoness?"

"Nothing."

Bideven had always been the meddlesome worrier of the three, which was why they sometimes called him "Biddy"—which he hated.

"I don't understand all this," Ailean continued. "It was a kiss."

"A kiss in front of everybody in Kyffin, including one of Adienna's spies. Seems she's had Shalin watched for years. She's been sure you two were lovers, but she'd had no proof—until you kissed her."

"And, brother," Bideven added, "you seem to forget that rumors have swirled around you and Shalin since the morning after you lay with the princess."

"Rumors? What rumors?"

Arranz shook his head. "How do you remain so oblivious to all that is around you?"

"Skill."

"The rumor," Bedevin continued, "that you left the princess's bed to track down Shalin."

"I didn't track her down. I stumbled upon her when I was making my escape."

"And that she threw an ax at your head to protect her innocence."

"That's not what happened. Although I must admit, the rumors are much more interesting."

As was their custom since they were young, Ailean grabbed hold of one brother, Bideven, in this instance, while the other deftly turned and opened one of the windows carved into the stone wall.

"Ailean! Don't you—"

Using both hands, Ailean chucked his older brother out the window.

Bideven didn't hit the ground below—for once—and instead shifted midair. "Bastard!" he snarled while hovering outside the window they'd chucked him through.

"You need to learn to be prepared at all times," Ailean stated simply before Arranz closed the window.

"Whatever the truth, Ailean, your princess believes much differently."

The brothers quickly walked down the stairs, heading toward the Great Hall and the courtyard.

"She's not *my* anything, so I wish you'd both stop saying it."

They made it out into the front courtyard. The two suns hung low and bright as the wintertime inched toward them.

"You know if you interfere, Ailean, you risk the wrath of the royals."

Ailean shrugged as he easily stepped out of the way of Bideven's swinging tail. "I don't care. It's like father used to say: it's one thing to fuck up your own life—"

And with a smile the brothers finished the words together, "—but shit all to fuck up another."

Shalin, sitting in a field no more than several hundred paces outside Kyffin with her back comfortably resting against a large tree, studied closely the parchments she'd brought with her. Deciphering ancient text remained one of her top skills and one she was woefully behind on. Lately she'd found herself easily distracted with thoughts of a kiss so blindingly intense, she often couldn't focus for hours.

Now, however, she'd begun to get back into the swing of things. She had no choice. Ailean had not returned for her and that was best. Time with him would only get her killed. So she threw herself into her work, hoping she'd eventually forget all about him.

So completely lost in the moment, she didn't know she wasn't alone until she heard a low voice say, "You read?"

She looked up and saw three males in front of her. They all wore black capes, the hoods pulled over their heads. Shalin's nose twitched. They were dragons in human form. Fully dressed.

Her nose twitched again—but not dragons of Dark Plains.

She forced a smile, trying to remain calm. "Aye."

"That is a skill we value, dragoness." The tallest of the three crouched in front of her. She could now see his face and he was . . . beautiful. She'd always heard the Northland dragons were anything but. They lived in a hard, brutal land and their faces, their bodies, showed that clearly. This dragon bore scars, but nothing that detracted from the natural beauty his body possessed.

But Shalin was no fool. Although the tenuous treaty had been agreed upon at the end of the last war, the North dragons were still considered dangerous enemies of Shalin's people and had been for hundreds of centuries. They had no overall ruling body and instead lived in kin-related fiefdoms. Again, just like the Northland humans. And, like the land they came from, they were a brutal lot. Cruel—many said heartless—and Shalin would concur, based on what she'd read.

"Sweet dragoness, how would you like to come to a land where you'd be appreciated for your intelligence as much as your beauty?"

She had to admit, that sounded wonderful. Although her "beauty" had never been much revered in Dark Plains but education was hard to come by in the Northlands and they searched for females who could help with that. Just being a beauty meant nothing to the North dragons.

"That's very kind, but I don't want to leave my home."

"We waste our time, brother," one of them snarled. "Let us just—"

The dragon's words were cut off when his brother stood and spun so quickly, all the other could do was stumble away.

"We discussed this, brother. It is my rule you follow on this trip."

While the brothers argued, Shalin slowly stood. She knew something was wrong here, she simply didn't yet know what.

But she knew no Northland dragon would be this far south without a reason.

The hairs on the back of her neck began to stand, and Shalin quickly called up spells she could use if necessary.

The brothers seemed to come to some sort of silent agreement, and the one she'd been speaking to all along faced her again.

"Sorry for that, Shalin. My brother knows not when to keep silent."

Shalin gave herself a moment of calm. She felt the bark of the tree against her back. She could hear crows over her head, talking to each other as they did. She smelled the earth beneath her bare human feet and the warm suns over her head.

When she knew her voice was steady, she asked, "How do you know my name?"

Sharp blue eyes watched her closely. "We've come for you, Shalin the Innocent. To take you to your new home." He said it kindly, but Shalin knew if she ran they'd simply drag her back to their lands in chains.

"Let us show you what we can offer someone like you." He took a step closer and she had to lean her head back to look at him. "I'll do all in my power to make sure you never regret coming with us."

Shalin swallowed hard, her gaze trapped by his.

"Brother," one of his kin said with a chastising tone, "you know the rules. We all get a chance to prove ourselves to the dragoness."

"I have not forgotten," he murmured while staring at her mouth. "I forget nothing."

He stepped back from her and held out his hand. "Come, Shalin."

Still staring into his eyes, she realized she reached for him. Her hand slipping into his firm, dry grasp . . .

And like that, he was gone.

She watched the dragon knocked across the field by a blast of flame so hot it almost singed off the front of her dress.

"Battle Dragons!" one of the brothers warned too late and then they began shifting to their dragon form.

Shalin escaped into the woods, knowing if she didn't move fast, she could easily be crushed before she could shift. She burst through the trees into another clearing. With a thought, she shifted from human to dragon and took to the air. She'd barely gotten off the ground when another set of strong dragon arms wrapped around her from behind, blocking her wings from fully extending.

"Got you!"

She went to spit out a spell until she saw midnight-blue scales on the arms that held her. Shalin looked over her shoulder and started in surprise. "Ailean?"

"I can explain everything."

What kind of greeting is—

Her eyes widened. "This is your fault, isn't it?"

"Why assign blame here?"

"Wait. What?"

"No time for answers, dragoness. We have bigger problems at the moment."

Northland dragons bursting from the clearing and heading straight for them proved him right.

Ailean pushed her away. "Fly, Shalin! Toward Kerezik. Go! *Now!*"

Shalin did as ordered, turning away from Ailean—barely noticing that the dragon had on his battle armor—and heading toward the land of Kerezik. Although what waited for her in Kerezik, she had no idea.

The first blast of lightning hit him dead in the chest, knocking Ailean back a hundred feet. Thank the gods for his battle armor. The breastplate protected him from the power of their attack. At least until they went for his head.

They sent out another blast and Ailean spun to his left. As the purple bastards took in breaths to assault him again, he unleashed a line of flame, hitting the one in the front. The dragon flew back right into the range of Arranz, who hit him with a breath of flame that shoved him into one of his kinsmen. Bideven swooped up from underneath and took aim at the weakest spot on any dragon, the underbelly. While Ailean's armor protected him from that, the Lightning dragons wore no armor. Probably because they'd felt safe coming into Dark Plains territory at the behest of the princess.

Too bad Ailean had never been known for following the dictates of anyone but himself. Hence why his time in active duty in the Dragon Queen's Army had been short-lived. He was too good a fighter for them to take his rank completely, but he was only called to battle when they needed him. Otherwise Ailean had been too much trouble to tolerate among the general rank and file.

The Lightning dragons screamed in agony as Arranz circled around them, his battle sword drawn. "Go, little brother. We'll follow."

"Are you sure?"

"Go!" Arranz ordered before unleashing another blast of flame. Ailean turned and followed Shalin.

Not far from Kerezik, Shalin waited until the blue dragon passed beneath her. Ailean hadn't told her everything, and waiting until he'd come up with a satisfactory excuse didn't sit well with her. Besides, she was angry and felt the need to take it out on someone.

Eyes narrowing, she dived into Ailean, crash-landing on his back.

"What the—"

"What did you do?" she demanded, grabbing handfuls of his hair and yanking.

"Ow! *Have you lost your mind?*" Ailean bellowed, angering her more for some reason.

"What did you do? I know this is your fault!"

She yanked again, knowing how much Ailean the Wicked prided himself on his hair. True, it was shinier and more beautiful than most, but that only made Shalin want to rip every hair from his head!

Ailean headed toward the land below them but, tricky bastard dragon that he was, he waited until the last moment before flipping onto his back. Shalin slammed hard into the soft lakeside dirt, the weight and speed they'd been going pushing her until she slammed into ancient trees half-circling the lake.

Yet even after all that, Shalin still refused to release his hair.

Ailean scrambled off her, not wanting to crush her. She was small for a dragoness and he was bigger than many dragons. Add in his armor, and he could easily crush her.

But still . . . *his hair!*

Yet when he went to stand, he realized she still held on to his hair with both claws and kept yanking. Not only did it hurt, but he could feel hair ripping from his head.

Mad cow!

"Release me, Shalin!"

"Not until you tell me what you did! I'll rip every hair from your enormous head if I have to!"

To prove it, she did just that, strands of hair tearing right from his scalp.

Snarling, Ailean slapped at her claws. When that didn't work, he grabbed hold of her wrists and slammed her forearms to the ground, using his weight to pin her into place. Startled, she released him, but he knew she might go for his hair again if he didn't calm her.

"Shalin, stop this. Now!"

"Tell me what you did, Ailean the Whore!" she spat into his face. "Tell me!"

Sitting back on his haunches, he released her, holding up his claws. A placating gesture. Seemed the little innocent had quite a temper. "Just . . . calm down."

"I won't calm down," she promised, scrambling back to her feet and away from him. "Just tell me."

"Someone told Adienna about the kiss I gave you outside the school. She seems to believe you've betrayed her."

The rage went out of her, replaced with confusion.

"I don't understand. What do the North dragons have to do with Adienna? Or with me for that matter?"

"We can talk about this later." He wanted to get her back to his home, where he knew she'd be safe.

"No. You'll tell me now."

Gods, where was the mouse he was used to? The shadow who silently followed Adienna? The female calmly ordering him around was far from the Shalin the Innocent he'd heard about all these years.

"Fine. Adienna sold you to the Lightnings."

"She . . ." Shalin sat back on her haunches and stared at him. "She sold me?"

"Aye. To old Tinig. I've fought him in battle. I took his eye. It just made him look crazier."

Taking in a deep breath, Shalin nodded. "She sold me."

"Shalin—"

Shalin held up a claw to silence him. "And you," she looked directly at him. "You took me from the Northerners."

Ailean nodded solemnly, completely comfortable with his role as hero and rescuer. "I couldn't let this happen to you, now could I?"

Years later he'd admit—he never saw that tail coming.

Covering his jaw where the sharp tip of her tail had slashed him, Ailean glowered. "Is there a reason you did that?"

"You brought war to our people and you stand there looking *smug*?"

"*I* brought war?"

"Yes. You." She shook her head, turning as she did. Ailean took a step back to avoid that tail. He wasn't frightened, but he wasn't stupid, either. "I have to go back," she finally said and looked as if she were seconds from taking flight.

Ailean grabbed hold her arm. "What are you talking about?"

"I have to go back, Ailean. It hasn't been that long." She glanced up at the sky to confirm. "And if your brothers haven't killed them yet, I can fix this."

He knew from her words and her expression what she planned to do. Sacrifice herself for the greater good of her people.

"You'll fix nothing, Shalin."

She tried to walk away from him. "Ailean—"

Ailean yanked her back, harshly, making sure he had her attention. He did.

"You'll. Fix. Nothing."

"Get your claws—"

He gave her a hard shake. "Listen well, Shalin. I've created this, but I'll fix it. But I'll be damned if I let you sacrifice yourself because of that mad bitch."

"She's not mad, Ailean. She's mean. Meaner than you or I."

"I don't care."

"You have to know she won't stop. She won't stop until I'm gone or dead. I think gone is better."

"So you'll . . . run?" The word was foreign on his tongue. Male or female, young or old, his Clan never ran.

"Why not? I'm quite speedy. And I have this odd love of having my neck attached to my body."

With a growl, Ailean turned, dragging her behind him.

"What are you doing?"

"We're going to my home, if I have to drag your pretty ass there myself."

"But won't your family be there?"

Finally, his full anger snapped and he turned on her. "*You think you're not safe with my family?*"

Now Shalin held her claws up in a placating gesture. "That's not what I mean at all."

"Then what do you mean?" he demanded.

He watched her gather her courage before saying, "You'll be putting them at risk, too. Adienna will stop at noth—"

Amazed she seemed more concerned with everyone but herself, Ailean calmly cut in, "If Adienna crosses my family, she'll soon learn how little her royal title means."

"Ailean—"

"We're not discussing this any more. You'll come with me."

Her mind turned. He could see it, see her trying to figure anyway out of this. Her gold eyes furtively glanced around, desperate, but he only had to flash a fang to make it clear how far he'd go.

"Fine," she said with an absurdly tragic sigh. "I'll come with you. But . . . my father. He's *not* safe."

"I've already sent two of my cousins' mates to protect your father."

"Only two?"

"Trust me. These two . . . your father will be fine."

"Knowing my father, he'll want to go to the queen. To see if he can fix this."

"And they'll go with him when he's ready. His own personal guards. No one will get near him."

Shalin sighed again, and Ailean knew he'd won. At least he'd won this particular argument. He sensed other fights wouldn't be so easy.

"I'll go with you."

Ailean forced himself not to grin. He sensed she wouldn't appreciate it and his scalp still stung. "Thank you." With that, he took several steps back from her and extended his wings in preparation to take flight, but stopped a moment, compelled to make something very clear.

"Shalin?"

She'd just unfurled her wings, ready to follow, when she looked up at him.

"There's something you should know."

She merely tilted her head, waiting for him to continue.

"I am sorry this happened, and I'll do what I can to fix it—but I'm not sorry I kissed you." He winked as her eyes widened in surprise. "She'll not make me regret that."

3

Shalin had so many things that annoyed her at the moment, she wasn't sure what topped her list.

Perhaps the dress she had to wear? A brazen dark red that was much too big for her, since it belonged to one of Ailean's cousins. Big enough that she constantly tripped over the hem and couldn't seem to keep both sleeves on her shoulders at the same time. Every time she adjusted one side, the other slid off and every male eye in the house seemed to focus right on her.

Or perhaps the fact she wasn't in a lovely cave. No, she was in a . . . a . . .

Shalin glanced around and barely contained her annoyed growl.

She was in a castle. A bloody castle. What dragon willingly lived in a castle? A nice enough castle, to be sure, but a *castle*. If she shifted and spread her wings here, she'd take out a good portion of the Great Hall.

Or perhaps that, because she was in this castle, she had to remain human—all the time. When they'd first arrived, Ailean had actually shown her to a bedroom . . . with a bed in it! A bed he expected her to sleep on!

Now, true enough, she'd been living among humans for quite some time, but that had been different. A necessity. The sacrifice she'd been willing to make to further her knowledge. But to live this way on purpose irritated her.

And although all those things annoyed Shalin to the point of distraction, she'd begun to realize that what annoyed her most of all, what had her teeth grinding, her hands tightly clenched in her lap so she wouldn't unleash her claws, and kept her gaze focused on the floor to stop herself from showing the growing rage and annoyance in her eyes . . .

What annoyed her—was *them*.

Not just Ailean's brothers. Or an uncle or two. But *all* of them. The entire Cadwaladr Clan from within a league. And, even worse, they never shut up. She'd never heard anything like it. Like a tree full of hungry crows, but with much more rough language and abrupt changes of topic. Now Shalin understood why Ailean cut her off so often . . . they all did it to each other constantly. If one wanted to be heard among this brood, one literally had to scream.

Since Shalin didn't scream, she merely kept her hands in her lap, her head bowed, her eyes on the floor, and her mind as far away from this place as she could imagine. While they all shouted at each other, Shalin flew in the bright bronze skies of Alsaindair. She'd only gone once to the desert lands with her father, but she'd never forgotten. And the desert dragons themselves had fascinated her. The same colors as the dragons of Dark Plains but there was a shiny bronze overlay to their scales she absolutely adored. They'd looked like jewels to her, and she'd been fascinated by their history and language and lifestyles.

So focused on her own thoughts, it wasn't until someone gently tapped her shoulder that she realized they'd all finally gone silent. Yet she sensed that was only because they were waiting on her to say something. What exactly, Shalin had no idea.

Clearing her throat, she looked up and found them all watching her. Good gods, what exactly had they asked her?

"I'm sorry, I—"

"Now, no need to apologize, lass," one of Ailean's aunts told her while patting her hand. "This isn't your doing, now, is it?"

Before Shalin could respond, the entire room erupted into angry shouts about Adienna, and Shalin lost the thread of conversation yet again.

Frustrated, Shalin pulled her right dress sleeve onto her shoulder. Of course, that only meant the left fell off the other side, hanging low on her arm. Knowing he watched her, Shalin glanced over and, as she suspected, Ailean stared at her from behind several rows of his kin. He smirked and raised an eyebrow. If she could have reached him, she would have slapped his face.

She wished she'd aimed her tail lower. Perhaps cutting his vocal chords would have eased her growing resentment.

Enjoying that vision more than she should, Shalin let her gaze slide back to the floor and back to the images of her flying.

Flying anywhere but here.

"You'll need to leave her be, Ailean."

Surprised, Ailean glanced at his aunt. One of his mother's bloodline. When his mother had died, his Aunt Briaga had done what she could for Ailean and his brothers, when not dealing with her own offspring or in battle.

"What are you talking about?"

"You and the innocent. Stay away from her."

"Why?"

His aunt gave him that look she used to when he'd bang his head into walls to see how long before he could actually break through. "Look at her. Poor, shy little thing."

"Shy? Her?" He watched Shalin for a moment and saw how his aunt could make that mistake. Sitting there with her back straight, the dress she wore slipping off all the best places, but still managing to look innocent and untouched, hands in her lap, eyes downcast. But Ailean was no longer fooled by Shalin the Innocent. "She's not shy."

"Och! Deniela, tell him." One of his father's many sisters, Deniela had two things to her name. Her lethal way with a battle ax and that she was the mother of the Cadwaladr Twins.

"Tell him what?" Deniela asked, chewing on what better be dried cow. Ailean forbid the eating of humans on his territory. He'd already had to clear up a few things for Shalin when she'd casually asked, "Is she dinner?" as one of his servants had walked by with two water buckets from the kitchens. The buckets hit the floor, and water went everywhere.

And then there had been the hysterical screaming . . .

That was when Shalin realized the humans in his territory knew exactly who and, more importantly, *what* he was. That had confused her, which he had to admit, he enjoyed doing. The look on her face was comical and adorable all at the same time.

Briaga leaned across Ailean and said to Deniela, "Tell him he can't be bothering the little dragoness. Look at her up there."

"Och. I know. Isn't she a sad little thing."

"What are you two looking at?" Because all he could see was the viper who ripped the hairs from his head. And the discovery of some bald spots did nothing but make him want to return the favor to the little royal.

Deniela pinched Ailean's arm lightly and it took all his strength not to scream out in agony. "You stay away from her, Ailean the Blue. Look at her. Poor wee thing."

"Oh, come on! She attacked me, you know?"

"Aye," Briaga agreed. "Threw that ax at you to protect her innocence."

"That is not what happened, and that's not what I'm talking about. Just today she attacked me. Pulled hair from my head."

"Why do you lie to me?" Deniela laughed. "We both know I'm smarter than you. That wee thing would never attack you, so stop making up stories. Don't you feel bad for her?"

"No!"

"Ailean! I expected more from you." She leaned in closer and whispered louder, "Look at her face. That deformity."

"What?" Ailean looked at Shalin. "What are you talking about?"

"Those horrible things on her face."

"Oh, no, no," Briaga explained, incorrectly, "that's just mud. She needs a bath."

"It's neither. It's freckles."

"Then I was right. Deformity."

"And you know," Briaga whispered, "she's probably a virgin. And you, Ailean the *Slag,* are not the dragon for virgins."

"What does *that* mean?" And was Shalin a virgin? Ailean shuddered a bit. He didn't entertain virgins. Much too much responsibility for his liking.

"She must be. How else would she get such a name?"

"Especially living at court," Deniela muttered, pulling more dried beef out of the little carry bag she kept tied to her sword belt. "All the fucking that goes on there."

"So you just keep your claws and your cock to yourself, Ailean the *Whore*," Briaga warned him, "or I'll be pulling your father out of his cave to deal with you and he'll be none too happy."

He definitely wouldn't be happy. For other dragons—a normally unsocial group—to call Ailean's father Afton the Hermit said a lot. Still, it was better than his earlier name. Afton the Murderer. But there had been a reason for that. A very good reason.

"Fine. I'll stay away from her." At least while she was at his home, under his protection, since that could easily be misunderstood. And how hard could it be? Once this had all been straightened out and Shalin went back to her school and Kyffin, he could finish what had been started that night in the royal archives. "But you two hags leave me be."

He covered his head with his arms as soon as he said the words, laughing while both his aunts slammed fists into his head. He didn't appreciate the kidney shot from Deniela, though.

Sneaking away had been a lot easier than Shalin thought it would be. No sneaking really involved; she simply stood up and walked out. So engrossed in their own disturbing conversations, none of the others even noticed her leaving.

Thank the gods.

She really didn't know how much more she could take. Her first thirty winters it had been only her, her father, and mother. Thirty winters of reading, quiet contemplation, and soft-spoken discussion on any topic from politics to religion. Her parents had taught her how to think, how to reason. They'd taught her how to survive without lifting a weapon. Good thing, since she was as hopeless with a weapon as Ailean was with a book. That thrown battle ax being nothing more than a lucky shot.

But the Cadwaladr Clan didn't really have quiet contemplation or soft-spoken discussions. There was nothing soft or quiet about these dragons.

Now, all Shalin wanted was some time to herself. Blissful silence. But would she ever find it?

"Need some help, m'lady?"

Shalin looked at the sturdy woman before her. One of Ailean's servants but, Shalin had quickly noticed, none of them looked downtrodden. She'd never seen servants who seemed happy and comfortable with their lot in life. Simply going about their day without misery.

"Yes . . . uh . . ."

"Madenn, m'lady."

"Shalin. Just Shalin."

"As you wish."

"I know this may be a tall order, but is there anywhere that I can . . . some place I can . . ."

"Get some quiet?"

Shalin almost dropped from gratitude that the woman so immediately understood her. "Yes."

"Just the place." She held one finger up and quickly went into the kitchens—with a clan this large, Shalin wasn't surprised Ailean needed more than one. When Madenn returned, she had a basket of warm scones, a chalice, and a wine-filled pitcher. "This way."

Madenn silently led Shalin down a winding path of hallways. The castle was enormous and Shalin wondered how Ailean could afford it. The Cadwaladr Clan was not born of wealth or title and had no inherited riches the way most of the royals and nobles did. Anything they had, they stole from humans. But Shalin couldn't imagine Ailean attacking some unsuspecting caravan.

"Here you are, luv," Madenn said while she pushed a door open with her foot. She'd gotten comfortable quickly and Shalin didn't mind. "Will this do you?"

Shalin sighed in absolute pleasure as she stepped into the well-lit and dust-covered library. "Aye. Very much."

"Thought it might. Ailean's kin—well, they're not much for reading, are they?"

Grinning, Shalin said, "So they won't be down here, is your point?"

"Luv, I don't think they know the castle has one, much less where this room is. You should be fine here for quite a bit. Especially when they make battle plans. They can do that sort of thing for hours."

Madenn placed the scones and drink on a long wooden table. "I don't have any cooked meat for you yet, but I'm guessing the scones will hold you for a while."

Slowly walking down one row of shelves, looking at each title, Shalin said, "You know what I am. What we all are."

"Aye. I do. We all do."

"But you've never told."

"We never have, we never will. But it's a long story and not one I'm much in the way of telling at the moment. Besides, it's more Ailean's story to tell than my own. I wasn't there, ya see."

Shalin grabbed a book she'd never read and pulled it off the shelf. "I understand."

Madenn walked toward the door, but before she left, she added, "We protect Ailean and his kin as he's protected us and ours. Our loyalty is deeper than any you'll find and well-earned."

Sensing some kind of warning, Shalin turned to look at Madenn, but she'd already walked out the door, silently closing it behind her.

The chant for food started when the suns set. It turned to catcalls and loud screaming until the servants began bringing out the platters of hot food and placing them on the tables.

"Where's Shalin?" Ailean asked Arranz, who only stared at him. Blankly.

"You lost her?"

"We didn't lose her. She's around somewhere. We'll look after we eat." Of course Arranz said that around a mouthful of food.

Afraid she might have gone off to handle all this on her own, Ailean searched the castle for her.

He went to her room first but found it empty. He went down to the small dining hall in the back of his home, thinking she might have gone there in search of food. But he found that empty as well, except for a few of the dogs playing on the floor.

Ailean walked into the kitchen, getting more desperate by the second.

"Something we can help you with, Ailean?" asked Madenn. An older human, she'd worked for him since she'd been a young girl, as had her mother and her mother's mother. He liked Madenn very much. She made him laugh.

CAN'T GET ENOUGH / 33

"The lady I brought home today? Have you seen her?"

"Last I saw her, she was in the library."

Ailean tilted his head to the side and stared at Madenn. After a long moment's pause, "I have a library?"

Madenn snorted. "Aye, m'Lord," she replied, not bothering to hide her laughter. "With books and everything!"

"Truly?" He grinned now that he knew Shalin was safe and not sacrificing herself for the dragon nation. "I never knew."

"As I'd guessed."

"Fascinating." He started to walk away, then gestured to the door. "Uh . . . can you point me . . ."

With a good-natured shake of her head, Madenn walked with Ailean out to the hall, giving him quick directions. "Once you're in that part of the castle," she finished, "go down the hall, all the way to the end, turn left, and the very last door on the right."

"Thank you."

"Welcome."

Ailean followed Madenn's directions and, as she suggested, he found Shalin in the library. Still wearing that dark red dress and barefoot, she sat on the floor, completely engrossed in a book. She probably had no idea how late the time had grown.

Even more fascinating, she had one of the new batch of black-furred puppies asleep in her lap. When Ailean had taken over this land, he'd begun to breed the animals to create bigger, more battle-ready dogs. They were wonderful pets and companions but could easily tear the limbs off a good-sized man. And had when the situation called for it.

"Shalin?"

"Mhhm?"

He couldn't help but grin. "Shalin?" he called again.

She finally lifted her head. "Yes?"

"It's time for evening meal."

"Evening . . ." She turned her head toward the window. "Oh. It is dark."

"Aye. It is. And I'm starving." He held his hand out for her. "So let's go feed, then."

"No." She waved him away. "I'll be fine until later."

"You will?"

"Aye."

"If you're sure . . ."

"Of course." She ran a hand down the puppy's back while staring at her book. "This little one will tide me over until I— oiy!" she barked when Ailean reached down and grabbed the puppy from her lap. "He's mine!"

"Not if you're planning to eat him."

"What else would I do with him?"

"He's a pet, Shalin. A companion animal. If you wish, you can keep him as such. But if you're planning to eat him—no."

"That's unfair."

"On my territory we don't eat dogs."

"You have the most ridiculous rules. You do know you're not human, yes?"

"I'm well aware of that, Shalin."

The puppy, now awake, yawned and tried to scramble out of Ailean's arms and back to Shalin. When Ailean held him tight, he began to cry and paw at his hands.

"You're hurting him," Shalin accused, quickly getting to her feet.

"You were going to eat him."

"Give him back to me," she ordered as only a royal could.

Ailean moved away from her grasping hands. "Only if you give me your word you'll not eat him."

"Fine. I give you my word."

"Good." Ailean shoved the puppy back at her and Shalin snuggled him close. "He seems to like you. I'd hate for that affection to be betrayed."

"It won't be." She giggled when the puppy licked her face and nipped her nose.

"Then he's my gift to you."

Shalin looked at him in surprise. "A gift? For me?"

"Of course." He reached over and stroked the puppy's head, smiling when the little bastard tried to bite his finger off. "While you're here, I'll show you how to care for him."

"No one but my father and mother has ever given me a gift before." She smiled, and Ailean wondered if he'd ever seen anything so beautiful. "Thank you."

He cleared his throat and stepped back from her, wondering why he had this sudden, almost overwhelming desire to give her everything he owned and fuck her beyond reason. He'd never felt both tenderness and lust at the same time for anyone and he didn't much like those feelings now.

"Let's go in and eat. You can bring the puppy."

With the puppy and the book she'd never released still in her hands, she peered up at him. "I don't spend much time with others, Ailean. I mostly keep to myself."

That surprised him a bit. "But all that time in Devenallt Mountain with Adienna . . . ?"

"I just followed. No one ever expected me to do or say anything." She gave a devious little smirk. "Very few at court find me very interesting. And I've found if I stay unbearably boring long enough, they wander away and stop talking to me altogether. I like when they don't talk to me. Before I went to school in Kyffin, I could sometimes clear a chamber simply by entering it."

Ailean laughed, tugging her forward until her bare feet touched his boot-covered ones. "Tragically for you, I haven't been bored yet. So I know how fascinating you truly are."

"And you'd know that how? You never let me finish a sentence."

His own smile fell at the innocent barb. "Are you saying I talk too much?"

"Well—"

"Because I don't. I don't talk too much."

"All—"

"I have things to say, sure. But it's not like I can't shut up if I have to. Because I can."

"O—"

"And do! When I have to."

Shalin stared up at him once again, her mouth closed.

"Well?" he demanded. "Answer me."

"You're right. You don't talk too—"

"Exactly! Now come on. You can even bring your book if you like and read at the table. This lot will never even notice."

It was like watching wild animals feed with much snarling, growling, and food stealing. But to make it uniquely theirs, there was also much laughing, taunting, and yelling. Shalin said nothing because she really didn't have to. With Ailean on one side of her having either a running argument or an animated conversation with his brothers—she didn't know which—and his infamous twin cousins on the other side, yelling at different family members across the room, Shalin didn't have to say a word. Instead, she devoured her delicious food, hand-fed the puppy comfortably ensconced in her lap and, much to her delight, read her book. That she would have never done at court. Ever. She'd have been forced to keep up some boring patter to entertain whatever noble sat beside her or she would have had to listen to Adienna softly mock everyone in the room.

Truth be told, Shalin hadn't had a meal this lovely since she'd lived with her father. He'd always brought work or books with him to their evening meal of a freshly butchered cow or two. They'd eat, read, and barely speak and were both quite comfortable doing so.

The hour had grown late and she'd devoured half a cow's worth of ribs before she finally lifted her gaze from her book.

"What you reading, then?" one of the twins asked.

"It's a book on the Northland pirates. The ones who come down along the coast and raid the small towns there."

"I heard about them. Oh, I'm Kyna by the way. This is Kennis."

Kennis greeted Shalin with a grunt, since she had a mouthful of food. Shalin had never met the twins before, but like every other dragon in Dark Plains, she'd heard of them, the pair having cut a bloody swath through the enemy during the last battle against the North dragons. They were feared as much by their own people as by their enemies.

"So go on," Kyna insisted, "tell us about the pirates."

Shalin glanced at the book and shrugged. "Well, there was this one story that was kind of interesting about how one of the raids went horribly wrong." Shalin leaned in a bit and proceeded to tell the cousins what she'd read, adding in some additional details about the town and the Northland pirates that she'd read in other books. Since the twins never looked bored the way most others did when she spoke for longer than a minute or two, she kept talking.

"He knew, then," she said.

"Knew what?" Kyna all but demanded.

"He knew he either had to cut her throat or watch his men die."

It was the silence Shalin noticed first. Neither Ailean nor Ailean's kin were ever quiet. Yet for a brief moment she thought that only she and the twins remained. But when she glanced around, she gave a little start of surprise. They were all watching her. If she hadn't known she had Ailean's protection, she'd have feared for her very life, the way they all watched her.

Then, finally, from the back of the room someone snarled, "Well . . . go on, then!"

"Aye," one of his many—*many*—aunts demanded. "Finish the story."

A chorus of "ayes" followed and Shalin briefly debated making a run for it.

"You best finish," Ailean murmured near her ear. "They'll tear this castle down around us until they get what they want. Besides," and the smile he gave her nearly had her melting in her chair, "I'm dying to hear the end as well."

Realizing she really did have their undivided attention and that she didn't much mind, Shalin continued. "But for the captain neither of those options worked for him. But if he was going to save them all, he'd have to move fast . . ."

The dinner ended and his family went off on their own, heading out to check Ailean's territory or simply enjoy the quiet night before the storms came. Storms were blowing in from the east, but it was the rainy winter season in Kerezik, so no one was particularly surprised or worried.

Ailean silently watched Shalin head up the stairs to her room, the puppy in her arms.

"Don't even think about it."

Ailean turned away from the tantalizing sight of Shalin walking away to that of his twin cousins, Kyna and Kennis.

"Don't think about what?"

"Now that is an innocent face, isn't it, Kyna?"

"That it is, Kennis. That it is. You'd never think he has nefarious plans for Shalin the Innocent."

Ailean rolled his eyes and laughed. "I do not have any plans for anyone."

"Not sure I believe that, cousin. Who can resist a female with the moniker 'the Innocent'?"

"Your lack of faith in me, Kyna, hurts." He held his hand to his chest. "Deep inside."

His cousins, two of the greatest Battle Dragons he'd ever known, laughed and each punched one of his arms. He gritted his teeth, trying to ignore the pain.

"They have a point, though, brother."

Forcing himself not to rub where the twins had hit him, he focused on Bideven, who stood over him. "What are you talking about?"

"You with a fresh, untried female under your roof. I'm concerned."

Ailean pushed away from the table he'd been leaning against and stood tall. "Concerned?"

"Aye, brother. Concerned. Shalin the Innocent is not like your other—"

"Whores?" Kyna added helpfully.

"Aye. She's not."

Ailean felt his rarely used anger growing. "I never said she was."

"But I saw how you looked at her."

"I have eyes. I was looking. It doesn't mean that I'll—"

"Take advantage?"

"I don't take advantage. I've never had to before."

"She's naive, Ailean. Sheltered. She's never been away from her library and her books before."

"And?"

Kyna stepped between the two brothers who were now toe to toe. "And she might misunderstand or expect more. More than you're willing to give. No one wants her hurt. Least of all you, I'm guessing." She rested her hand on his chest. "You have the biggest heart of us all, Ailean. But sometimes you make the mistake that everyone thinks like you. Or us. She's not like us. She's cultured and that, isn't she, Kennis?"

"Aye. Cultured and soft."

Kyna brushed her hand against Ailean's jaw. "Breakable, Ailean. So be careful what you do."

He took his cousin's hand, kissed the back of her knuckles. "You've a good heart yourself, little cousin."

She smiled, seconds before she slammed him hard across the face with her free hand. "Don't try and sweet-talk me, you wily bastard." But she grinned just the same.

"We're off, then," Kennis informed them all, heading toward the door. "We'll go up north a bit, make sure there's no other surprises from the Lightnings. We'll be back later tonight."

"And if you find more of them?" Ailean asked. "More of the Lightnings? What will you do then?"

Kyna grinned as she followed after her twin. "Then we'll have more horns to add to the ones already on our den walls, won't we?"

Ailean turned back to Bideven, but his brother did no more than sniff in disgust before storming off.

"What is wrong with him?" Ailean snapped, knowing Arranz stood behind him.

"Don't know. He's been strange all day. So are you going to fuck her?"

Ailean sighed and walked off.

"It was just a question."

4

It really galled him that his own kin thought so little of him. Thought he'd take advantage of Shalin or any female merely to sate his lust without a care for the female. He didn't need to take advantage of anyone and it insulted him anyone thought he would.

Passing Shalin's door, Ailean heard her cooing to her new puppy. Her scent had him pausing a moment. She always smelled so . . . delightful. Enticing.

His knuckles almost struck the door before he stopped himself.

Gods, I am weak.

Before he did something foolish, Ailean went to his bedroom, stripped, and got into bed. He ignored his desire to crawl back down the hall and scratch on Shalin's door like that puppy. He'd leave her alone. He would.

An hour into that chant, and the knock on his door came.

He ignored it, hoping she'd believe him asleep.

"Ailean," Shalin whispered urgently through the door. "I need you!"

When he still didn't answer, she began banging on the door.

"Hold on," he snapped, getting out of bed and wrapping a fur around his waist. He snatched the door open, ready to order her back to her own bed when he saw tears streaming down her face. "Gods, Shalin. What is it?"

She grabbed his hand. "I think he's dying!" Then she dragged Ailean toward her room. Once she got him inside, she dragged him around her bed where her puppy was hunched over.

"Do something!" she demanded, her panic tugging at his heart.

Ailean crouched next to the pup and said, "Well, luv, there's not much we can do."

Shalin looked at him with something close to abject horror. "You're just going to let him die?"

"No. I'm going to let him bring back up whatever he's been eating."

And that's what the little bastard did.

They both moved back, disgusted.

"Oh, that's vile!" Shalin gasped, covering her nose and mouth.

"That it is." Ailean glanced around until he found a few rags piled in a corner. He grabbed them and quickly cleaned up the mess while the puppy whined softly and crawled into Shalin's lap.

"He's still sick."

"His stomach ails him, is all." He took the rags out into the hall and dumped them where the servants could find them in the morning. When he came back in, closing the door behind him, he found Shalin staring down at the pup like she feared he might gasp his last breath at any moment. "Shalin, he'll be fine. You just have to watch what he eats."

Ailean washed his hands in the wash bowl before walking back to her side.

"Why don't you get some sleep?" he asked her, sitting beside her on the bed.

"What if he dies while I sleep? I'll never forgive myself."

It took all Ailean's strength not to roll his eyes. He knew she meant every word. "He won't die while you sleep, Shalin. He merely ate something that didn't sit well with him. You've no need to fret so."

"He's mine. My responsibility. I'll sit with him until he's better."

"No. You'll get some sleep." Ailean took the pup from her lap. "I'll stay up with him so you can rest."

"That isn't fair." She smiled and stood, taking back the puppy. "We'll stay up together."

"Uh . . ."

But he didn't have much choice, since she crawled into the center of the bed and sat down, her legs crossed so her ailing puppy could rest right in the middle. She patted the space across from her and Ailean reluctantly moved there, desperately clutching the fur covering against him.

They sat silently for several minutes, until Shalin said, "I enjoyed dinner tonight."

"Good. You, uh, blended in quite nicely."

"Did I?"

"Aye. They all like you. Oh, and I got word from the ones protecting your father. He's fine and safe."

Shalin briefly closed her eyes. "Thank you. I worry about him so."

"Why? I've never met him, but I've always heard he's well-respected."

"He is. Very well-respected, especially among our scholars. But, he can be a little . . . a little . . . " She suddenly smiled. The softest, warmest smile Ailean had ever seen. "He can be a bit befuddled at times."

"Is that why he's not an Elder?"

"He and the Elders don't see eye to eye on much. He never understands why anyone has disputes if they're not related to something scholarly. He'll argue for hours over some tiny historical fact or another, trying to prove his point, but he won't fight for his territory. And without much prompting he'll just give you his gold. He doesn't understand why our people can be, as he likes to put it, 'so bloody violent all the time.' Eventually even he had to admit that being an Elder was not for him."

Ailean began to relax, realizing he wouldn't leave her this night. She seemed to need him, although her puppy was just fine. Besides, he enjoyed her company more than he could say. "And what about you?"

"What about me?"

"I've heard it told you intend to be an Elder one day."

"Intend and will are two different things. I've a far way to go before I hope even to be considered."

"But it's not what you want, is it?"

And the way her entire body jerked at his question, causing her puppy to whine in annoyance before snuggling back to sleep, he knew he was right.

"Why would you ever think that?"

"Because I see no excitement in your eyes when you talk about it."

Excitement? In her eyes? Was that even physically possible? "What?"

With a yawn, Ailean leaned back on the bed and Shalin felt a little guilty for not letting him go back to his room. But between her sick puppy and the fact she liked having Ailean around—especially when all he had on was that fur covering around his hips, giving her a delicious view of that chest—she had no intention of sending him away.

Could she do it, she wondered. Could she lure Ailean to her bed? True, she had him in her bed, but could she make him want her? Even she had to admit she'd never been known for her seduction tactics. And she couldn't bring up the courage to simply pounce.

"When you talk about a library or being alone, your eyes light up. Or when you were telling that story to everyone downstairs. There was excitement in your face and your voice that wasn't quite there when you discussed becoming an Elder one day. Looked more like you were going to the gallows."

"That's not true. I . . . I'm just tired. I'm not very enthusiastic about anything when I'm tired."

Although Ailean was a bit correct. The thought of becoming an Elder almost made her queasy. All the politics. All the centaur shit. She'd rather bury herself in a library than face that life on a daily basis. But she'd promised.

Because she didn't want to think of it any more, Shalin asked, "And what about *your* father?"

Ailean stared at her while he put one arm behind his head and Shalin immediately became fascinated with the way his muscles bulged from the action. *Gods, he makes a beautiful human.* "You know my father, Shalin."

"I know *of* your father. Can't say as I met him. Afton the Hermit."

"He's had other names. In the past."

If a dragon lived past his first hundred winters, he or she would start to gather many names over time. It was nothing to be ashamed of, yet Ailean appeared . . . troubled. "Like?" she prompted.

"Afton the Cruel. Afton the Murderer."

"Oh." Shalin pushed her hair behind her ear and she briefly noticed Ailean's eyes followed her hand while she did it. "Your father is *that* Afton? I always thought the Hermit and the . . . uh . . . Cruel were two different dragons."

"No. Just one." Ailean's gaze moved to the ceiling. "He wasn't always like that, you know. He didn't earn either of those names until after my mother died."

Now, that she understood. More than most, she was sure. "My father was lost after my mother died. Inconsolable for a while, and completely lost. She was equally brilliant, you see, and understood him so well, but much less befuddled. She kept everything organized and logical. Now when I go to visit, I find him under desks, behind desks, searching through piles of gold that turn out to be nothing more than brass coins merely painted gold." She shrugged at Ailean's smirk. "He can never tell the real from the fake. And I don't think he bothers to try."

"How did she die?"

"As only one of *my* parents can. She went out for a snack and picked up a bull instead of a cow. Its horn lodged in the roof of her mouth, piercing it. Nothing any healer did could fix it, and eventually she caught a brutal fever and died."

"How old were you?"

Shalin thought a moment. "Barely thirty winters. Young." With the puppy asleep, she rested her elbows on her knees and her chin on her fists, focusing on Ailean. "And you?"

"Eleven winters."

"Och. You were a babe, Ailean. I'm so sorry."

Ailean stared hard at the ceiling. "It was my fault, you know."

"Your fault? How could it be?"

"Because I didn't stay put. My father took my brothers hunting and I wanted to go with them. So I followed."

"At eleven winters? Could you even fly?"

"Barely. So of course my father told me to go back home. I did, but I was so low to the ground—unable to get any real height—soldiers spotted me and they thought I'd be fun to hunt." He suddenly closed his eyes. "They had me, too. Cornered. About half a battalion's worth."

"For a hatchling?" Sometimes humans truly disgusted her.

"And then she came. A battle dragon like all the other females of her line. She decimated them, but one of them . . . one of them had good aim. He wounded her, and though she saved me and destroyed them all, she couldn't save herself."

"And your father went on to become Afton the Cruel."

"Aye."

"Did any humans survive?"

To her surprise, Ailean opened his eyes and smiled. Truly, the most beautiful thing about him had to be that smile. "Some. You see, my father was gone for days, but three human females found me. All sisters. One a healer, one a barmaid, and the other a servant in the duke's castle. For three days they stayed with me. The healer, a witch, she tried to help my mother, but there was nothing to be done. So they made sure I ate and soothed me when I cried. Then my father came home. When he didn't find us in the cave, he tracked us down. He almost killed the women until I stopped him, told him what happened. He left the villagers alone after that. They'd suffered enough, you see. The Duke, his men, they took the villagers' food and used their women, sometimes even the young ones barely old enough to breed themselves. They left untold numbers of babes of their own lying around but they never claimed them. But that duke and his soldiers—they didn't survive my father's wrath."

"So that's how your father got his name."

"Actually . . . no. No one thought he was cruel then—just angry. Then word spread that the duke was dead and others came to claim the land as their own. But my father always met them first, and he'd kill them all. He was still angry, you see. If it moved, he killed it. Eventually they all stopped coming and my father went into his cave and rarely came out. My uncles, my aunts, they all taught me and my brothers how to fight, how to survive." He glanced at her and shook his head. "No, Shalin. No one among my kin ever blamed me. At least not as much as I blamed myself."

"You were a babe," she reminded him fiercely, annoyed he'd even think otherwise.

"I should have stayed put. I didn't. And she died, all because I couldn't fight for myself."

"Fight for yourself? Ailean you were too—"

"Don't say I was too young. A dragon can never be too young to learn to protect himself. Not in this world. My sons and daughters will be able to fight from hatching."

"Ailean, isn't that a bit of a tall order?"

"No. My brothers and I came up with a training method that will get them started early. My hatchlings will be prepared for *anything*."

Shalin felt for the future hatchlings of Ailean the Wicked. They wouldn't have easy lives. Then she frowned for a moment when she wondered who exactly he'd fall so in love with he'd settle down and have hatchlings with. But she quickly pushed the feeling away when she realized it was none of her business.

"Did all this happen here?" she asked, trying to distract herself.

"Aye. Madenn's kin were the ones who stayed with me. Her great-great-grandmother and aunts. My father wanted nothing to do with any of them. Although he spared them, he still felt nothing for them. My brothers could go either way, but I knew these people needed protection. Human males can't stay away from unclaimed territory for long. It's like this overwhelming need they all have to conquer anything they've even heard about."

"So you stayed."

"Seemed natural, really. I'd already spent so much time with them and they never told my secret. Eventually the entire village knew about me and no one said a word."

"But didn't you hate them? The humans?"

"For the actions of a few? No. Doesn't seem fair to do that."

He had to be the first dragon Shalin had ever heard say something like that.

"You look tired," he suddenly told her.

"No. I'm fine." And to prove it, she yawned.

Smiling, Ailean turned on his side and picked up the puppy

from her lap, laying the little fur ball lengthwise on the bed. Then Ailean patted the mattress. "Come on now. Stretch out here."

"But, the puppy . . . " Yet she was already stretching out on her side, facing Ailean, the puppy between them, her eyes rapidly closing. The day had caught up with her so quickly.

"He'll be fine," Ailean murmured, and she felt him take her hand. "And tomorrow, Mistress Shalin, we'll discuss his diet."

5

Ailean didn't know what woke him up first. The two suns shining in his eyes—or the paw repeatedly slapping at his head.

Yawning, he glared at the little monster trying to claw him to death. "Oh, now you're feeling fine, aren't you?"

He yipped in answer and that's when Shalin murmured in her sleep.

That's also when Ailean realized Shalin was asleep on his chest.

Slightly terrified, Ailean desperately tried to remember if they'd done anything the night before. He didn't think so and, when he looked down at her, she still wore the red gown from yesterday and the fur covering he'd brought with him still lay between them.

He let out a breath, but still didn't know what had come over him. He might not have touched her, but all the things they'd discussed . . .

Ailean never talked about his father with anyone but his brothers, and those two never mentioned the old dragon unless necessary. Ailean definitely never discussed his mother and what happened that awful day. His own kin knew never to mention it. Nearly a century ago, one cousin drunkenly brought it up after a family hunting party and lost both his horns when Ailean snapped them off.

But Ailean had told Shalin pretty much everything. Gods . . . why?

The puppy yipped again and Shalin's head snapped up from his chest. "Wha—where—?"

"You're safe, Shalin," he told her, seeing the confusion and panic on her face. When she looked at him, her panic seemed to pass and she smiled at him with real warmth.

"Good morn, Ailean."

"Good morn to you."

She turned a bit to look at the puppy, but she seemed more than comfortable cuddled up to his chest. "And look at you, Lord Terrify Me."

The dog yipped again and Ailean said, "You best let him out, Shalin. Or there'll be more mess to clean up."

"Let him out?"

"Just open the door. He'll find the rest of the dogs."

"All right."

He thought she'd roll away from him, but instead, she moved across him to get to the edge of the bed. Ailean gritted his teeth and willed his body not to react. It had to be one of the hardest things he'd ever done and he'd gotten in a fight once with a giant octopus.

"Will he come back?"

"I'm sure. He's bonded to you, Shalin." And he knew how the little bastard felt. Ailean knew if he left this moment, he'd probably come back, too.

"Come on, then, you little terror." Shalin picked the dog up and walked to the door. Ailean heard it open and then Shalin's strangled, "Uh . . ."

"What's wrong?" He rolled to his side, raising himself up on one elbow, and looked toward the door. "Shit," he barely had a chance to mutter before Bideven pushed past Shalin and stalked in, Arranz and the twins right behind him.

"You dirty bastard. Couldn't keep your hands off her, could ya?"

Ailean slid off the bed and stood in front of his kin, the only thing holding up that fur covering his hand.

"I'm not quite sure what it has to do with you, brother."

Bideven moved toward him but Shalin calmly stepped between them. "He never touched me."

Arranz sighed. "Shalin, love, could you move? You're in the way of some lovely violence."

Giving no more than an annoyed sniff, she didn't respond to Arranz and instead said again, "He never touched me, Bideven."

"Then why was he here?"

"I needed help with my puppy."

Arranz and the twins started laughing and didn't seem inclined to stop while Bideven's accusing gaze shot daggers at Ailean.

"You bastard!"

Shalin rested her hand against Bideven's chest. "Stop this now."

"Shalin, you're an innocent about this sort of thing—"

Ailean didn't realize he'd snorted out loud until they all looked at him.

He glanced at Shalin and shrugged. "Sorry."

"—and his intent," Bideven finished. "We're just trying to protect you."

Shalin folded her arms over her chest. "Do you think so little of your own brother?"

The confusion on their faces would be something Ailean remembered for ages.

"What?"

"Do you think so little of him? That he'd take advantage of me. Force me."

"I never said—"

"Is that truly what you expect of your own kin? I thought the Cadwaladr Clan loyal to each other."

"We are."

"I haven't seen it. Not when you barge in here and accuse your own brother of being all manner of lizard."

"I never meant to—"

"Then you should apologize."

"Apologize?"

"Yes."

"You can't be—"

Shalin's foot began to tap and Bideven growled. "Fine. I apologize."

Patting his shoulder, Shalin ushered Bideven and the rest out. "Now don't you feel better?"

"Not really," Bideven shot back, but Shalin had already closed the door in his face.

Ailean stared at Shalin. "That was . . . *brilliant!*"

Shalin held her finger to her lips while she bent over silently laughing. "He'll hear."

"Good!" Ailean watched her walk across the room. "How did you do that?"

She shrugged before falling back on the bed, her grin wide and happy. "Years of court life, my dear dragon."

It happened so fast, Shalin thought a wizard must be involved. But no. It was simply rainy season in Kerezik and that meant sudden darkness and sudden storms.

Well, she thought, *that might at least keep the beasts from the door for a little while.* Lightning dragons, from what she'd read, didn't much like traveling in this sort of weather. Not only did they possess lightning within them as her people possessed flame, but they attracted lightning. Which could make for painful, if not lethal, travels during storm seasons in the different regions.

Running a comb through her freshly washed hair, she looked at the courtyard beneath her window. Not surprisingly, very few of the human servants were about and the few that were quickly scurried toward one of the many buildings so they were out of the rain. Then she saw him, marching through the rain, not caring that his clothes were getting soaked.

Ailean stopped and spoke to a large, burly human. She'd guess the woman was the local blacksmith, based on her dress and the size of her arms. Laughing at some joke of his, the female placed her hand on his forearm, and Shalin's eyes narrowed dangerously.

With a quick hug, the blacksmith walked away and Ailean continued on to his destination. She watched until he walked into the stables.

Stables?

"Yum . . . horse."

Ailean gently brushed his favorite mare's coat and softly hummed. Black Heart liked when he hummed.

He loved doing this. It was one of those things he could do and still focus on something else completely. Like why his family had suddenly lost their collective minds. Never before, in his nearly hundred and fifty years, had they ever cared about what he did or who he did it with. But now, suddenly, he had the lot of them trying to push him away from Shalin as if they thought he'd purposely hurt her.

Could involving himself with Shalin only lead to hurting her more than anyone else because she truly was innocent? He hated the thought of hurting her and hated the thought of never lying with her even more.

So focused on his thoughts and feelings—something Ailean rarely paid attention to for more than three seconds at a time—he didn't notice Black Heart's growing nervousness until she bucked suddenly. Ailean placed his hand on her flank, felt the tensing muscles. He crooned to her softly while he slowly, carefully stood. It wasn't like Black Heart to be so jumpy around him. He'd ridden her and many from her line into local battles when he'd fought as human. She'd never balked before, although she could smell what he was.

"What is it, girl?" he asked softly. "What has you so nervous?"

"Is she for tonight's meal?" that sweet, innocent voice asked.

And Black Heart kicked at the stall door, forcing Shalin to back up.

"Hmm. She may be tough of hide, Ailean," Shalin said in all seriousness. "She'll be hard to chew."

Ailean quickly stepped in front of Black Heart before she could knock down the stall door. "Ssssh," he sang softly. "It's all right."

Once he had her relatively calm, he glanced over his shoulder at Shalin, forcing himself to ignore how beautiful she looked in another one of his cousin's gowns, this time a deep blue. Like before, it was too big for her and kept falling off her shoulder, giving just enough to tantalize and tease but still hold everything back. "She's not dinner, Shalin."

"She's not?"

"No."

"Then what are you doing with her?" she asked, honestly confused.

"Grooming her."

"For what, if we're not going to eat her?"

"Because I like to."

"Oh." Shalin looked down the long rows of stalls. "What about that one?" She pointed at Dragon's Gold. "She looks like she'd be tasty and enough for two."

Dragon's Gold, only a few feet away, jerked back and kicked her stall door.

"Shalin!" he snapped, startling her attention back to him. "We don't eat horses here."

"You don't?"

"No. These are working animals. Just like the dogs."

"Aren't you running out of food options?"

He couldn't help but chuckle. "We make do."

"I see."

She wandered off, glancing into each stall.

Ailean took a moment to brush his hand over Black Heart's snout. "It's all right, girl. It's all right."

Black Heart clicked her teeth together and motioned with her head. Ailean looked up in time to see Shalin open one of the stalls and step in.

"Gods, Shalin! Not that one!"

Ailean shot over the stall gate, not able to take the time to open it, and charged after the dragoness. He stumbled to a stop when he found her petting the enormous pitch-black horse inside.

"I can see why you enjoy this," she murmured. "It's quite soothing." She looked up at him. "What's his name?"

"Nightmare."

"Hmmm." She ran her hands through the horse's long mane of hair. "He's not as clean as the others and his mane's a mess. Why?"

Ailean smiled at the accusation in Shalin's voice and crossed his arms over his chest. "That's because no one else has ever been able to get near him except to give him a little food and water. He's known for having broken more ribs, arms, legs, and heads than any other horse in my province. He's mean, cranky, and foul-tempered. No one trusts him and we think he enjoys hurting people. Hence the name Nightmare."

At his words, Shalin shrugged. "He seems to like me well enough."

"That he does."

"I'll clean him myself, then."

"Shalin, wait—"

"It's not fair. All the others tended to and not him." Shalin grabbed a bucket and headed out to get water. "I know what it's like to feel like an outsider among your own," she said so softly he almost didn't hear her.

"I'll take care of him," she said again before disappearing out the stable door.

Ailean watched her go. It still astounded him Shalin was born a royal. She never acted like it.

And perhaps Nightmare wasn't as big a bastard as they'd all originally thought if Shalin found some good in him. Ailean almost believed that too, until Nightmare reared up on his hind legs and brought his forelegs down on Ailean's chest, sending him flying back into an empty stall. A human might have been killed, but—like Black Heart—Nightmare knew exactly what Ailean was and how much he could take.

As Ailean tried to get his breath back, Shalin reappeared with a bucketful of water and one of the stable boys to assist her. She glanced down at him.

"What are you doing?"

When he didn't answer, mostly because he still couldn't, she shook her head. "So lazy, Ailean the Wicked."

6

It took her several hours to groom the horse to her particular standards. In the time it took her to do one, Ailean and the stable hands had done all the others. And while she groomed the horse, her puppy ran around and around until he'd drop wherever and sleep. Only to snap awake a little while later and do it all over again.

In all honesty, Shalin had never been so entertained before while doing absolutely nothing. She and Ailean never really spoke unless they asked each other specific questions, and yet she thoroughly enjoyed his company.

"You doing all right over here?"

She smiled as she ran the brush through Nightmare's mane, yet again. It took her hours to get all the brambles and things out of it, but it was worth it. "Aye."

"It shines."

She patted the horse's neck. "As it should."

Ailean pulled open the stall door. "You missed dinner."

Surprised, Shalin looked up. "I missed dinner?"

He nodded. "You've been out here hours. Didn't you notice you're the only one left in here?"

"I guess I missed that." Her fingers slid easily through the horse's mane. "Such a simple task and yet so . . . soothing."

"Are you hungry, Shalin?"

"I am."

"Then come. Madenn has food for you."

Shalin stroked Nightmare's forelock, which fell across his forehead. "He's a fine horse, Ailean."

"He's your horse now." When Shalin only stared at him, Ailean shrugged. "No one else can handle him, Shalin. No one else wants him. I tried to sell him once and he nearly bit the man's hand off. You are the only being who has ever been able to get this close to him. He's chosen you, so you might as well accept it."

"I can't take your horse."

"He's not my horse. He hates me. He's always hated me. And to be honest, I hate him, too. It's a mutual hate."

"I don't understand you."

"You sound like my kin. They never know what to make of me, either." He held his hand out. "Come on, then. He'll still be here in the morning."

Shalin nodded and patted the horse's neck. As she walked out, the puppy charged past her and out of the stables.

"Where does he disappear to?"

"To play with his brothers and sisters. He'll return when there's food."

Ailean locked the stall door, and together they walked out of the stables.

"The rains stopped," she said, feeling the need to say something.

"Hours ago. You really do get lost in what you're doing, don't you?"

He didn't sound mocking, merely curious. "There's always noise and such at Devenallt. In order to get any work done, I've had to teach myself to shut it all out. To focus only on what's important."

"That's a fine skill. No wonder you handle my family so well. You simply ignore them."

Shalin laughed. "If it works. But I'm sure you have the skill. When you're in battle."

"In battle I become aware of everything. I can't afford to shut anything out except my own fear."

"You don't seem afraid of anything, Ailean."

"I have fear. Anyone with sense has fear. You simply have to focus it where it'll do the most good."

"That first night we were here, your kin talked of going to Devenallt Mountain."

"They did."

"To—if I remember correctly—raid it."

"Aye. That was what we in the family call a Twin Battle Plan." At Shalin's frown, Ailean elaborated. "Anything that requires us to go into the most impenetrable fortresses in the land and kill everyone not friend is called a Twin Battle Plan. Because the twins are usually the ones who suggest it."

"There's a reason they've never been invited to Devenallt Mountain, isn't there?"

They paused at the steps leading into the Great Hall. "The Twins make the royals nervous. They're short on temper and long on bloodlust. The royals want them to fight their battles but they live in fear of having them around. Since my cousins care nothing for politics, they stay away. It makes no difference to them."

"Does anyone among your kin care about politics?"

"Only Bideven. But only enough to help when any of us get into trouble."

"And you?" she asked, smiling up at him. "Do you care about politics?"

"Not even a little." Big fingers brushed across her cheek. "Dirt," he explained.

With a nod, Shalin walked into the Great Hall, desperately trying to ignore the way her skin tingled where Ailean had touched her.

Ailean paced the length of his room again. Since he'd knocked the wall out of three rooms to create it, this was no short trip.

For two hours he'd tried to sleep. For two hours he'd tossed and turned and masturbated until he feared his hand would fall off. Yet nothing could alleviate the burning, clawing need he had at the moment.

And Ailean wished with all his heart that this need was merely sexual. That all he wanted from Shalin lay between her thighs. But he wanted more than that. He wanted to sit and talk to her again. He'd never been so at ease with anyone not blood, and he never had to yell over her to be heard. She listened to him and that meant more than anyone could realize.

"This is ridiculous," he told the air. "I'm a grown dragon. I can do as I like." And they would only talk. Like they had the night before.

Confident in his intent, Ailean stormed to the door, snatching it open—and froze.

"Good evening, brother," Arranz said calmly. He sat in a chair just outside Ailean's room, cleaning his weapons.

"What are you doing?"

"Just . . . keeping watch."

"Keeping watch outside my room?"

"This hallway, brother. Danger is everywhere. Even you. You're in danger, too, Ailean. We have to be ever vigilant with you as well as Shalin." Arranz looked at his brother, all innocence and naïveté, which Ailean knew for a fact was nothing more than centaur shit. "But Ailean, where are you off to so late? Is there something you need, brother? Something I can get you?"

Ailean's eyes narrowed and Arranz grinned.

"You have money on this, don't you?"

Arranz went back to wiping his weapon down. "How you think of me, brother. As if I'd bet hard-earned gold on something like this."

Snarling, Ailean stepped back into his room and slammed the door shut. He hated his kin.

Hated. Them.

Shalin jumped when a door slammed. Biting her lip, she charged across the room, sliding to a stop in front of her own door and placing her ear against it. She listened but could hear nothing that would lead her to believe Ailean made his way to her room.

Damn the gods! Why were they torturing her so? Putting her in arm's length of her greatest desire but keeping it just out of reach.

And the gods did not give her the kind of bravery that would allow her to march out of her room, down that hall, and to Ailean's chamber. To demand he take what she offered.

Instead she waited in her room like a frightened mouse, hoping someone would put the cheese before her.

Gritting her teeth, Shalin paced back to the window, the puppy stumbling behind her.

Would her life always be this unfair? This brutally cruel? Would she *ever* get what she truly wanted or would she always yearn for what she could never have?

"Do the gods have some vendetta against me, little one?" she asked as she picked up her puppy and held him close. "Some vendetta against my ancestors that I'm unaware of? Or do they simply enjoy toying with me?"

Since Shalin came from a most boring line of dragons, she felt quite confident that the gods merely toyed with her.

"Bastards," she muttered before heading to her bed.

7

Shalin had not slept well. She'd pretty much done everything but sleep. She'd read. She'd tossed and turned. She'd played with the puppy until he fell asleep. Now all she wanted to do was spend some time with her horse.

She walked down the stairs and into the Great Hall.

"We need to get you a dress that fits," Arranz said in lieu of a proper greeting. "And some boots."

"Are you done?" And her clipped words had Arranz staring at her.

"Is there a problem?" he asked.

"No. Not at all. Feel free to comment on anything. My hair all right with you? My face? Anything else I can fix to your satisfaction?" When he didn't answer, Shalin looked at the rest of the Cadwaladr Clan. "Truly. Feel free while I'm standing here to comment on anything you like. No?"

Unable to stop sneering, Shalin grabbed a loaf of bread and walked out to the courtyard.

Ailean walked into the Great Hall. He passed by his kin, the lot of them nearly filling the room, grabbing a loaf of bread from the table. Before he went outside, he stopped and asked, turning back to his kin as he did so, "I need to train. Anyone up for—"

In the ten seconds since he'd started to ask his question, all but three of his kin remained. The twins stood.

"We'll—"

"Sit down," their mother ordered. And they both obeyed. She remained the only being on the planet who had full control over them. "What's going on with you two?" Deniela asked Ailean.

"What are you talking about?"

"That sweet, innocent dragoness—"

At Ailean's snort, Deniela's eyes narrowed, and he held his hands up, indicating she should continue.

"She was in a foul mood and I'm blaming you."

"How is it my fault?" Although deep in his soul, he prayed it was his fault. He shouldn't be the only one not sleeping.

"She's an innocent, Ailean. Don't play with her."

"I haven't. And she's not an innocent."

"She's probably a virgin."

"Don't be daft."

"Have you asked her?" Deniela demanded. "Maybe you should before you set your sights on dirtying her up."

"I have to say, *Aunt* Deniela, that I don't appreciate you suggesting her being with me would *dirty* her up."

When the old cow only stared at him, he walked out.

Shalin glanced up and that's when she saw Ailean staring at her—again. She'd found him doing it several times since he'd walked in to groom the horses a few hours before. Finally, unable to stand it anymore, she asked, "Is something wrong?"

"No. Why do you ask?"

"Because," she said, focusing back on Nightmare, "you keep staring at me."

"Sorry." But he didn't stop staring.

"Ailean," she finally said, "you haven't done anything wrong." In fact, he hadn't done a damn thing and she'd gotten tired of waiting for him to.

"I know that."

"Then why do you look like you've ravished me and left me pregnant like some human?"

"No, I don't." He finally grinned. "There'd be much more running away involved."

She petted Nightmare's neck. "I appreciate your family's desire to protect me, but I don't need them to protect me from you." She forced a smile. "I'm sure when this is all over we'll be the best of friends."

"Friends?"

Shalin's lip curled. "Is there a reason you snarled that?"

"Are you a virgin?"

Rearing back a little, Shalin wondered at the abrupt change of conversation. Her anger sliding away from her in seconds. "Sorry?"

"You heard me."

"I . . . uh . . ."

"Yes or no."

"No. But I'm not sure it's—"

"You sure?"

"Am I sure? Am I sure I'm a virgin or not?" She stepped away from Nightmare. "Is there something wrong with you? Mentally?"

"Yes. Or. No."

"Yes. I'm sure that I'm not a virgin. I haven't been one for quite some time although it's none of your damn business."

"No reason to get snappy. It was a simple enough question."

"I don't get snappy. Now if you'll—"

"Ever been with anyone while human?"

Shalin let out a long breath. "Why is this conversation getting stranger?"

"Answer me."

"You want me to answer you? Fine." Placing her feet in between the slats of the stall gate, Shalin rose up so she could look him right in the eye. "Here's my answer. No. I've never been with anyone while human. But after reading those books about you, I've always thought if there was anyone who could show me how good it could supposedly be, it would be you. Little did I know at the time that you were *insane!*"

Ailean carefully wiped off the bit of spit that hit his eye when she'd hissed that last part at him. "Good, because—"

"Ailean?" the human female said from the front of the stables.

Shalin realized it was the blacksmith from earlier and she growled, causing the woman to step back.

"Uh . . ." the blacksmith stammered, ". . . you said you wanted to see the blade as soon as it was done." She held up something long and wrapped in soft cloth. "I have it here if you'd—"

"Yes, yes. I'll look at it now."

"You're leaving?" But he hadn't finished what he'd been saying! *Good because what? Good because what? Dammit!*

"I'm not flying to the suns, dragoness. I'll be back."

And he thought she'd still be here?

He walked away, heading toward the blacksmith and Shalin jumped down from the stall door. She looked at the horse. "Would you like to teach me how to ride?"

In answer, Nightmare slowly lowered himself enough for her to easily mount him.

"Oh," she sighed, "if only they were all like you."

Once he'd approved the blade, Ailean walked back to the stables. His body almost vibrated with the thought of getting inside Shalin. Teaching her exactly how enjoyable a human body could be. To be the first to do so.

Still, that little voice of doubt wouldn't shut the hell up. Constantly asking him if he should do this with someone he'd sworn to protect. Would that turn him from Ailean the Whore to Ailean the Right Bastard?

Ailean stepped in front of Nightmare's stall and stared blindly inside.

When one of the stable boys walked past, Ailean asked, "Where's Mistress Shalin?"

"She took Nightmare out a few minutes ago."

He turned on the boy and yelled, "*And you let her?*"

"Well . . . she didn't actually ask my permission."

Ailean snarled and went to Dragon's Gold, his fastest mount. It wasn't that Shalin had walked away from their conversation. It was that she'd rode away with that demon horse. It was one thing for her to feed him and groom him, but riding that big bastard was another matter altogether. If he threw her and she landed the wrong way, her human neck could snap.

He saddled and mounted his horse quickly and took off after Shalin, using her scent to guide him. It didn't take him long to find her. Typical dragon. She'd gone to the lake. To water. Something his kind were elementally drawn to.

"Have you gone mad?" he demanded, dismounting before the horse had even stopped.

She'd already dismounted and stood staring out over the lake at the next coming storm. He, too, could see the dark thunder clouds approaching, which fit his mood quite nicely.

"He could have killed you."

"Well, you know us virgins. We just run off half-crazed."

"I can't believe you're still upset about that."

"Upset that you were discussing my intactness with your kin?"

"It wasn't like that, Shalin." Well . . . not *much* like that.

She waved him off. "At the moment, I really don't care."

Ailean gently swiped a hand down her back. "Are you all right?"

"I'm fine. I've just . . . " She let her hands fall at her side. "I've just never seen that before."

He followed her line of sight before returning his gaze to her face. "You've never seen storm clouds?"

"Of course I've seen storm clouds. I've just never *seen* storm clouds."

"Perhaps we should get you inside, Shalin."

"Don't be dull," she said before walking away from him.

"I beg your pardon?"

"You heard me. I don't want to go inside. Nothing is wrong with me."

Ailean entertained the idea she might be right until she took off running and did a somersault—for no apparent reason.

"In fact," she announced, "I feel *amazing*. At least a hundred years younger."

"Shalin, you're not old."

"No. I just feel like it most days." She suddenly did a handstand and Ailean briefly closed his eyes and groaned. He couldn't help himself once he realized she was completely naked under that dress.

"Shalin—"

"You know," she flipped forward and landed on her feet, "I don't *do* anything. I go where they tell me. Do what they tell me." She put her hands on her hips and said, "I almost handed myself over to the Northland dragons because I thought it was the right thing to do. I'm tired of living for others."

"Then don't."

"Don't?"

"Don't. Gods know, I don't."

"It's easy for you. No one expects anything from you."

"Thank you."

"I mean . . ." Again she waved her hand like she was waving away a fly. "Why lie? I meant what I said. All they expect from you, from your kin, is to kill on command. That's your skill. Your gift to our people. When you're not killing, they really don't care what you do."

"But you . . ."

She laughed, but there was no humor in it. "From me, they expect much."

"Your life is your own, Shalin. That's the true beauty of being dragon. Even our gods know not to demand much of us."

"It's not the gods I care about disappointing."

"Your father?"

She nodded. "I love him too much to ever want to hurt him. Failure—*my* failure—would hurt him."

"But, Shalin—your father's not here. And, based on those clouds, he won't be here for quite a bit. So, perhaps you can allow yourself a chance to just be. For once." He grinned. "Who knows what you'll discover about yourself?"

She frowned a bit. "I guess I can do that."

"You guess?"

She snorted. "I don't know how to throw all caution to the wind like you do, Ailean."

"Then isn't it time you learned?"

"How do you—"

"You just do it. You simply see what you want and you go after it. That's what I do. Trust me, Shalin, there's no one here who will hold you back."

"Truly?" And she looked afraid to hope.

"Truly. You may not always get what you want. But I've found it never hurts to at least have tried."

Shalin nodded. "All right, then."

Then she took off running—right at him. He barely had a chance to stumble back before she slammed right into his chest. If he hadn't been hit with so many other unexpected things over the years, he'd never have been able to stay on his feet.

Shalin wrapped her arms around his neck and her legs around his waist. She stared into his eyes for a long moment before she said in no uncertain terms, "I want you to fuck me, Ailean."

She couldn't tell if he looked horrified, appalled, or merely stunned.

Shalin swallowed and gave him a way out. "You can say no, of course. I don't want you to do anything you don't want to—"

"Shut up, Shalin."

Ailean closed his eyes, and she could hear him gritting his teeth. He looked as if he was in physical pain.

"What do you want from me, Shalin?"

That seemed like an odd question, and he seemed so angry, she decided retreat might be her best option. "Nothing, Ailean. Nothing." She tried to pull out of his arms and he yanked her back. That's when she felt his erection pushing against her sex.

"You don't understand me. What do you want from me, Shalin?" She shook her head, still unclear what he meant. "Are you a romantic, Shalin? Do you need the soft light of candles and the gentle touch of your lover?"

"Uh—"

"Normally, I could give you anything you'd want. I'm known for my versatile skills. But I can't promise that right now." He pushed a wind blown lock of her hair behind her ear. "I've wanted you too long to be much of a sensitive lover. All I can promise you at the moment is a rough ride right here in the dirt. If you don't want that, then walk away from—"

"Put me down, Ailean."

He looked so disappointed, she almost felt guilty for how happy that made her.

With a curt nod, he carefully placed her on the ground and she stepped back. "Give us your shirt."

"What?"

"Your shirt." She motioned to the linen shirt that fit him perfectly but would hang on her like one of his cousin's dresses. "Give it to me."

Not sure why she wanted it, he still reached back and grabbed up the shirt with both hands, dragging it over his head. He handed it to her and she took it but stopped a moment to simply stare at him. Gods, he had a nice body. And he wasn't even naked yet.

Clearing her throat, she shook the linen shirt out and placed it on the ground. "Until you've actually had dirt up your bum, you really can't appreciate how uncomfortable that could get."

She stood, brushing off her hands. "Now make sure to get me there." She pointed at the shirt. "You know, when we actually get to that point."

He seemed to struggle between wanting to glare at her and smile. "Did you hear a word I said to you?"

"Quite clearly. I have excellent hearing." She moved closer to him and Ailean's body tensed. "I appreciate the warning, though. It was very sweet of you to give me the option to run away . . ."

Ailean's hands were fisted at his side while he eyed her. She had the feeling he would not make the first move. He needed her to prove that she wanted this.

Wanted this? Gods, she *needed* this. Perhaps her only chance at getting something she really, truly wanted that had nothing to do with anyone or anything else. No matter how temporary, she needed this.

Now Shalin stood so close to him their bodies nearly touched. She raised her hand and let her fingers skim along a jagged scar across his upper chest. Ailean's big body trembled beneath her exploring fingers, and she felt a surge of confidence and lust she'd never known before.

She moved her fingers to another scar, this one on his shoulder. And while her fingers toyed with that, Shalin leaned in close and licked Ailean's nipple. His entire body jerked so she did it again. The fists at his side relaxed.

Shalin laid her hands flat against his chest while she licked his other nipple. Ailean groaned and it reverberated through Shalin's body, making her feel hot all over, her skin itchy. She wanted to strip and rub herself all over him.

Big, strong fingers speared through her hair, and Ailean pulled her head back. His eyes roamed over her face and she tried hard not to shrink back from his examination. She was used to shadows. She liked shadows, liked blending into walls. But Ailean and his kin wouldn't let her. She tried to hide and they only pulled her back out again, but not out of cruelty. Not as a way to hurt her.

And that was why she kept her eyes on his. Because she wasn't afraid to meet his gaze, to challenge him as he was challenging her. He looked for fear, and she'd show him none. Not now, not ever.

Ailean groaned once, and then he kissed her. And Shalin knew she'd made the right decision.

She wanted him. And not in some shy, innocent way, begging him to lead. When he kissed her, she met him with as much passion as he felt. Her tongue met his, bold and demanding. Her hands slid up to his shoulders and around his neck. She raised herself on her toes, tipping her head to the side to get a better angle. For a dragoness who'd never been with a male as human, she seemed to know her way around. He truly thought she'd be lost without her tail.

Shalin's small hands reached for his leather leggings, tearing at them, trying to get them off. Her passion for him making her as rough as he'd threatened to be. Ailean pushed her hands away, so he could deal with her dress, doing his best not to rip it in the process. It was so large, it took no effort to push it off her shoulders and down her body. Once the dress cleared her arms, Shalin went right back to removing his leggings, sliding them over his hips. As she lowered them, she went along, crouching in front of him, her lips leaving a delicious trail down his naked hip and thigh.

His cock sprang free of his clothing, clearly begging for her mouth. And when she licked her lips, Ailean knew he had to get control of this situation or come before it even truly started.

"No," he said simply before digging his hands back in her hair and yanking her to her feet. He pulled her tight against his body and took her mouth again. Only now it was flesh against flesh and nothing had ever felt so wonderful to him. Gods, there had been so many others, but none like Shalin.

He didn't understand it. Maybe it was that innocent honesty. No lies or deceits. No seduction. Simply knowing what she wanted and making it clear. Now it was his turn to know what he wanted and to make it clear.

Ailean released her hair and slid his hands under her ass. Lifting Shalin up, he dropped to his knees and placed her on the shirt she'd laid out, careful not to slam her head into the ground.

Moving down her body, he kissed and licked her flesh, pinning her to the ground with his hands against her waist. Sliding between her thighs, Ailean pushed her legs apart and nuzzled her sex until she growled and grabbed hold of his hair.

"Don't pull," he warned.

"I'll pull every hair from your head if you don't—if you don't—"

"If I don't what?" He gently ran his finger along the already wet slit, her body jerking from the light touch. "If I don't what? Tell me."

He grinned, waiting to see her struggle with the words. But his little innocent grabbed his hair as firmly as any soldier during battle, yanked his head up, and snarled, "Fuck me with that tongue, Ailean the Whore, or I swear by all the dark gods you'll be bald before nightfall."

Ailean pulled back a bit and for one horrible second she feared he'd walk away, leaving her to teeter on this precipice. Her fear almost had her begging until Ailean smiled. His hands slid under her backside and lifted, her legs going over his shoulders. She watched his face disappear between her thighs. His tongue slid inside her and Shalin's eyes crossed.

To say this dragon had talent would be a gross understatement. This wasn't a talent. This was a gift from the gods.

Blindly, she dug her hands into the soft soil around her, panting as Ailean's tongue stroked and flicked and teased her beyond anything she'd ever felt before. While his tongue played there, his nose helped out in other areas until Shalin shook beneath him. She could feel the explosion coming, her breathing harsh and uncontrolled. Then, while keeping her legs on his shoulders, Ailean's arms slid under her hips and around her waist to her chest. His fingers took firm hold of her nipples, pulling and rolling until Shalin's climax crashed into her. Her screams of re-

lease echoing around the lake, the horses nearby restlessly pawing the ground.

Shalin's hands dug into Ailean's hair and held his head in
place, her back lifting from the ground as another wave cut
through her, ferociously stronger than the first, her screams turning to pitiful cries.

After several moments, her grip on him weakened, and Shalin
dropped back to the ground. Before she even had a chance to get
her breath, Ailean was there, on top of her, his hands now in her
hair, his lips against her neck.

"Shalin . . . I'm sorry . . . I can't . . ."

Shalin knew what he needed. It was what she needed. She
opened herself to him and said, "Don't wait, Ailean. Please."

He didn't. He entered her with one brutally hard thrust. Shalin
gasped seconds before his mouth covered hers and he drove into
her again and again, giving her the rough ride he'd promised. She
didn't care. She loved every second of it, holding him tight as he
took her.

His lips moved from her mouth and down her jaw to her neck.
She felt his teeth press against the skin and then he bit down,
sending her flying over the edge again as he climaxed with her, his
body pinning her to the ground as he emptied himself inside her.

Ailean couldn't move. *Wouldn't.* Why should he when he'd
never been so comfortable before in his life?

Cool hands stroked his back, his hair; her soft voice sighed in
his ear.

"Are you all right?"

Ailean laughed in surprise. No one had ever asked *him* that
before. "I'm fine." He lifted up a bit so he could look into her
face. "And you?"

She tried to hide her smile but she snorted, which started her
laughing with him.

"I'm doing quite well, thank you," she finally managed.

"Good." He kissed her neck and felt the first drops of rain on
his back. "Damn."

She ran her hand down his cheek. "We better get in. I got ill
once while human—" her eyes rolled, "—took me days to recover."

Ailean chuckled. "Well, we can't have that, now, can we?"

Slowly, he pulled out of her, both of them groaning when he did. Unfortunately, once Ailean was out, all he wanted to do was get back in. Steeling his resolve, Ailean stood on shaky legs and reached down to help Shalin to her feet. She gripped his forearms and he sensed her legs were as shaky as his.

Making sure she could stand without him, Ailean then grabbed Shalin's dress and carefully pulled it over her head. "Will you be all right to ride?"

"Of course. Nightmare takes very good care of me."

Ailean grunted, suddenly feeling jealous over a bloody horse.

"He should still have a saddle," he said while pulling her arms through the armholes of the dress.

"I'll not put a saddle on him, Ailean."

"But, Shalin—"

"Is he mine or not?"

Ailean raised an eyebrow. "I certainly don't want him," he informed her before pulling on his clothes.

"Then he's mine to manage as I see fit."

" 'Then he's mine to manage as I see fit,' " he mimicked back to her in a high-pitched voice that had her slapping at his shoulders in a pitiful attempt at an assault.

Laughing, Ailean grabbed her around the waist and pulled her close again. "You have quite the temper, don't you?"

"Don't sound so mocking. I do have quite the temper. Few, though, make me angry enough to show it."

"I'll have to work on that. I'd like to see you truly angry."

Shalin's face fell and she looked a little . . . terrified. "No, Ailean. No you wouldn't."

Before he could ask her more questions, the skies opened up and rain poured down on them. Quickly setting the dragoness aside, Ailean pulled on the rest of his clothes and boots.

While he did, he watched Shalin merely crook her finger to get Nightmare to trot over to her side. Without any further prompting, he lowered himself so Shalin could mount him easily.

"Meet you back at the castle?" she asked, using Nightmare's hair for reins.

"We'll be right behind you." He whistled for Dragon's Gold.

"Stay on the path and head straight home, Shalin. I don't desire searching for you in this downpour." Ailean placed his hand on her thigh. "Oiy."

"Yes?"

"No kiss?"

Leaning down a bit, she kissed him and Ailean felt no cold blowing in from the storm. He only felt warmth and desire, his hands reaching for her automatically.

"No, no," she laughed. "We have to go." Shalin sat up straight, her hand stroking his cheek. "Thank you for today."

He grinned at her, completely unaware that his clothes were already soaked through. "And are you leaving this afternoon?"

Shalin looked up at the sky. "In this storm? Of course—"

"Then we're not done. We can thank each other another day. For now . . ."

"For now . . . what?"

"For now we'll need to find a way to avoid my family's involvement. Unless you're hoping what we do every day turns into a nightly topic of discussion at dinner."

"Gods no!"

"Between us then?"

She surprised him by looking impossibly relieved and he didn't understand the bit of resentment that caused. Usually he adored the ones who wanted to keep their involvement between the two of them rather than spreading so many rumors it turned into another edition of those damn books.

"Yes. Between us."

"Then ride and I'll see you back at the castle."

Smiling, she pushed her soaking golden hair off her face and said to Nightmare, "Go."

And to Ailean's shock, the beast did just as she'd asked.

What power did this female possess over wild animals?

"Well, she has no control over me, Dragon's Gold." When the horse snorted at him, he glared until she looked away.

8

A meal had never been so delightful for Shalin. Especially with so many others around. But none of Ailean's kin bothered to note or question the two of them putting their horses up together or quickly going off their separate ways. Instead they were too busy arguing, because apparently that's what they did when trapped in close quarters for any length of time. Any length of time being about five minutes, because it really hadn't been raining that long.

So Shalin spent the rest of the afternoon in the library. The entire time she had a book open, but she never actually read it. She couldn't focus. Not when she kept thinking about Ailean and what they'd done that afternoon. And the fact that he wasn't done with her. Perhaps they could meet again at the lake tomorrow. Or someplace else on his territory out of his kin's line of sight. On her ride earlier in the day she'd noticed a nice little cave built into a small mountain. A perfect place to spend some time alone.

But that would be tomorrow and she still had to get through the night. Still, not too hard when it involved the Cadwaladr Clan. What she never expected, though, was for the twins—who sat on either side of her so they could keep her laughing through the entire meal—to turn to her and say in unison, "So tell us another story."

The room immediately fell silent at their request and all eyes were on her.

"Me?"

"You told us one before. Didn't she, Kennis?"

"Aye. That she did, Kyna."

"It can't be hard, then, to tell us another."

Without even thinking about it, her eyes focused on Ailean at the other end of the enormous table. She knew he could see the panic in her face, but instead of rushing to her rescue, he simply gave her a warm smile and winked at her.

And like that . . . her panic melted away.

Swallowing, she asked, "Humans or dragons?"

"Och," Kyna said with a wave of her hand. "We know all the dragon stories. Give us some human ones."

"Uh . . . all right." She thought a moment. "There's the story of the blind warrior who challenged an entire army to get back the woman he loved."

His family sat enthralled by Shalin's softly spun tale. Yet he felt like a right bastard because he couldn't stop thinking about her naked. And coming. Naked and coming. He had to see her like that again.

Ailean had never known himself to be so enthralled by anyone. He'd lusted, panted even, but never been enthralled. He wasn't exactly sure how to handle enthralled. Although he knew what he *wanted* to do, but he felt pretty confident Shalin would tear his balls off should he simply grab her up and take her to his bedroom to finish what they'd only just begun by the lake.

The room erupted into laughter from something she said and Ailean tried again to focus on her words and not the way the green dress she'd put on before dinner draped over her curves, or the way her body loosened up the more comfortable she became while telling the story, or the way her breasts rose each time she took a deep breath. He really had to stop focusing on her breasts.

Knowing he had to do something or risk everyone in the room noticing his lust, Ailean tried focusing on his breathing and thinking about the new cattle he'd recently purchased and the weapons he'd ordered. He tried thinking of *anything*, but nothing worked.

His gaze kept moving back to Shalin, sitting there in front of his kin, appearing so innocent and shy—he knew better now.

Gods! How much more could he take?

He forced himself to see where in the story she might be, perhaps she neared the end . . . but he quickly realized the blind warrior of this story had not yet gone blind! Since Shalin's audience seemed more than happy to let her ramble incessantly about some not-even-blind-yet bastard, Ailean had no choice but to sit and wait until the evening ended.

Oh, but then he'd get what he so desperately needed.

"No, no. Books are not for chewing." Shalin dragged her tenacious little puppy off one of the books she'd found carefully stacked in a corner of her room. The books hadn't been there when she'd changed before dinner, so she could only guess Ailean had them sent up for her. The gesture made her smile. "We need to get you something else to chew on."

She glanced around the room. "Here. Use this chair." She crouched down and unleashed him on Ailean's furniture. It had seemed like a good idea until she watched the puppy go after that chair leg like she went after grazing cows. She reached for the hungry little demon again when she heard a soft tap at her window.

Looking carefully through the thick glass, Shalin didn't see anything. But the soft tap came again. This time she put her hands against the glass to keep out the glare from the torches and pitfire and leaned in close.

"Are you going to open the window—" a voice snarled at her, making her jump back several feet "—or just keep staring at me?"

She took a deep breath before she snatched the lock back and pulled the window open. "You scared the life from me!"

"I couldn't figure out what you were doing."

"Trying to see you." She blinked. "I still can't see you." She leaned out the window only to bump into Ailean's snout. "Oh!" It took her a moment and then she exclaimed, "You're a chameleon!" Which meant he'd been able to blend into the night and the building perfectly. Unless one was right on top of him, they'd never know until it was too late. It was a rare gift among the dragons of Dark Plains.

"Must you shout that?" he whispered. "My kin don't know."

"Why?"

"Because it irritates them when they don't know how I get past their defenses. And their irritation brings me such good humor. Now, are you going to let me in or make me stay out here in the cold?"

Shalin placed her hands where she knew his head to be and leaned forward, trying to see the rest of his body. "Ailean, this is simply fascinating—and stop sniffing me!"

"I can't help it." His snout pushed through the window and nudged her groin. "You smell so good."

His moaned words had her stumbling back into the room and, after a moment, Shalin watched the dragon shift from nearly invisible to clearly visible and human. He flipped himself into her room and she quickly looked away from the sight of all that lovely nakedness. Drooling would do nothing but embarrass her.

"What is that vicious animal of yours doing to my furniture?" Shalin turned in time to see the chair tip forward because the puppy had eaten through one of the legs.

"Oh!" She picked up the puppy and turned the chair around so it leaned against the wall. "Bad puppy!" she chastised, but he seemed much too happy to care about her harsh tone. "Your teeth seem unnaturally strong for someone so young."

"I bred them that way."

"I see. I'm sorry, Ailean," she said, turning to face him. "I'll get you a new—oh!" He stood right behind her, all naked and warm and sinfully delicious. "Chair! I meant to say, I'll get you a new chair."

"Later." He took the puppy from her hands and set him down. As soon as those little paws touched the floor, the puppy ran right back to the chair and, Shalin thought with some despair, the remaining legs.

Ailean's hands slid into her hair, massaging her scalp while his firm lips skimmed across her cheek, her jaw, down to her throat. Teeth nipped at flesh while hands began to purposely move. Pushing her dress off while brushing here, touching there.

Shalin groaned when teeth nipped a bit of flesh hard enough to bruise.

"They lied, you know," he muttered, walking her back to the bed and going down with her on it.

"Lied?" She found it hard to concentrate when he kept nipping at her with his teeth before laving the same area with his tongue. "Who lied?"

"Whoever named you 'Innocent.' They lied." He rose over her, his hips between her thighs. As if he belonged there, he slid inside her and Shalin let out a gasp of pure pleasure.

"Trust me," she panted, her hands gripping his shoulders, "it was better than my other options."

His first stroke was slow. The second equally so, only he'd moved a bit. The same with the third and fourth, moving a bit each time.

Frustrated, she demanded, "What are you doing?"

"Figuring out what you like."

She frowned. "Figuring out what I—oh, oh, *gods!*" Shalin's torso arched, and she barely had time to bury her face against his shoulder and moan desperately into his neck.

"Aye. That's the one."

He didn't have to sound so smug. Until he did it again a few more times and Shalin realized he could sound any damn way he wanted to.

Ailean kissed her, his mouth slowly moving over hers, his tongue exploring. Lazy was the word for it. Lazy and wonderful.

"I can make you come like this," he murmured. And she knew he wasn't boasting. Any moment, she'd come all over him. "But I'm not going to."

His rhythm changed and Shalin's eyes opened wide in panic. "What—wait—*why?*"

"That would be boring, wouldn't it? Making you come the same way every time."

She desperately grasped his face between her hands. "Please. Feel free to bore me. At least this time. Or, if you're so inclined, the rest of the night. I *like* being bored."

Ailean grinned. "You're funny."

"Ailean—"

"Sssh." He took her hands in his own, pushing them to the bed, one on either side of her head. He nuzzled her cheek. "Trust me, luv." Now he nuzzled her jaw. "I'll get you there," he whispered before nipping her earlobe, hard. "When I'm ready."

Ailean gritted his teeth and stared up at the ceiling. He tried counting to ten. Thought about the weather and tried to focus on the storm that had come back to life outside this room.

But nothing, absolutely *nothing*, could distract him from Shalin's mouth on his cock.

She lifted her head, releasing him with a "pop" sound that made him shudder.

"Is everything all right?"

Ailean fisted his hands in the fur coverings beneath him. "Yes, Shalin, everything is fine."

"Are you sure?"

He glared down the length of his body at her. She'd been doing this to him for the last hour. Keeping him on edge, torturing him, really. And she knew exactly what she was doing. She kept that innocent expression on her face but Ailean knew all that innocence for the lie it truly was.

"Yes. I'm quite sure."

"Well . . . if you're sure." But she rested back on her heels. "Although I'd hate to disappoint you."

Ailean closed his eyes, tried the counting thing again. It still didn't work.

"Shalin."

"Ailean."

"Everything you're doing is perfect."

"Perfect? Really?"

His eye twitched. "Yes. However—"

"However?"

"However, you must keep going in order for it to remain perfect."

"Ohhhh. I didn't realize that."

"I think you did realize that." And slowly, he sat up, going on his knees. "I think you know *exactly* what you're doing to me, Shalin the Not Really Innocent."

Laughing, she backed away from him. "I don't know what you're talking about."

"Yes, you do." He reached out, snatching her around the waist and yanking her close. "You're a cruel, vicious vixen." He kissed her hard. "Admit it."

Her arms went around his neck and she relaxed against him. Nothing had ever felt better. "You're right." She kissed his jaw, his throat. "But I can make it up to you."

"Think you can, do you?" But she was already making his eyes cross simply from kissing a line across his shoulders.

"Well, Ailean," she said in his ear after she'd kissed her way back up, "I think I can definitely try."

And who was *he* to stop someone from at least making the effort?

They'd fallen asleep with Ailean cuddled up behind her, his arms tight around her waist. And he was still like that when Shalin felt the first thrust as he took her from behind.

Gods. Insatiable. This dragon was insatiable. And she absolutely loved it.

"It's almost dawn," he murmured in her ear while he used one hand to pull her hair off her neck. "I'll have to go soon."

"I understand."

"Unless you want me to stay."

She did want him to stay. But she didn't want to end up in one of his books. Another Ailean the Wicked conquest for the annals. No thank you.

"No. Go." She gripped his thigh, digging her small nails into the ungiving, hard muscle. "But come back. Tonight."

One hand slid down to her sex, his fingers stroking her, while his other hand roughly grabbed her hair. Holding her, he took her harder, his cock hitting that wonderful spot inside her that he had found earlier. This time he didn't stop, this time he didn't change his rhythm. Instead he kept up the pressure, the harshness of it until Shalin's entire body shook in his arms.

"I'll be back, Shalin," he growled against her neck. "You won't be able to keep me away. Understand?"

She couldn't answer, not with that climax ripping through her.

"Understand?" he pushed.

Shalin nodded and buried her face into her pillow so she could muffle her cries. Then Ailean pulled out of her and flipped her onto her back. He drove into her again, another climax washing over her.

"I love looking at you when I fuck you," he told her plainly, each harsh thrust extending the life of her climax until she feared the intensity of it would tear her apart.

Ailean kissed her as he came inside her, his shout of pleasure lost in her mouth.

When he finally pulled away from her, he covered her sweat-soaked body with furs and kissed her cheek.

"I'll see you tonight, my little innocent."

She tried to say something meaningful to him but all she could manage was a rather undignified grunt.

9

Ailean had barely stumbled into his own bed when his brothers knocked on his door and walked in without actually
waiting for him to tell them to.

"What?" he barked, his forearm covering his eyes from the
now-invading light of the two suns blasting through his window.

"The old dragon is on the move," Arranz informed him, dropping down on the foot of the bed.

"Where?"

"Devenallt Mountain. He's arranged for a meeting with the
queen."

"And he's still protected?"

"Of course."

"Don't give me that look. If anything happens to Shalin's father, she'll never forgive herself and I'll never forgive myself for
making her unhappy. And we all know I hate when I'm miserable."

"What's wrong with you?" Bideven asked, his eyes watching
Ailean closely.

"Nothing. I'm tired."

"The twins will take her to their home if you don't want her
any more."

As much as Ailean wanted to simply respond, "Hell, no!" he
knew that would be a mistake. Instead he gave a long suffering
sigh. "No, no. She's my responsibility."

"If you're sure," Arranz told him, and Ailean could hear the smirk in his voice. Later, he'd toss him out the closest window for it.

"Aye. I'm sure."

"So . . . are you a witch?"

Shalin swallowed the porridge she'd spooned into her mouth. "No. I mean . . ." She sat back and thought a moment, trying to answer Kyna's question. Questions she'd had to ask herself a long time ago. "I know spells. Many. But I wouldn't call myself a witch. I don't have that kind of elemental power."

"What are you studying, then?"

"Alchemy."

"That's turning brass to gold, yes?"

Shalin laughed. Everyone wanted to change things to gold. "I don't think of alchemy that way. Changing one thing to a complete other thing doesn't make sense to me. I think of it more like taking a branch and making it a tree. Expanding on what it already is."

"That's boring."

Shalin nodded. "It is. But you could also make a dagger a sword. A sword a lance."

"Imagine that, Kennis," Kyna said before diving back into her porridge. "Imagine how deadly we'd be in battle."

"I've heard you already are deadly. They talk about you at Devenallt Mountain."

The twins shrugged and continued to eat.

"What makes you such good warriors?" Shalin asked casually, enjoying a conversation that had nothing to do with scholarly endeavors or throne politics.

"We like to kill," Kyna replied simply.

Shalin choked up her porridge, barely covering her mouth in time to stop it from flying across the table.

"You all right?"

She nodded.

"And we hate to lose," Kennis elaborated.

"I see." Shalin cleared her throat. "Don't think I've heard any other warriors put it quite that way."

"I doubt they enjoy the killing as much as we do. Our mates, they say we have the bloodlust. Can't really argue with them, can we, Kennis?"

"No. We really can't."

It amazed Shalin there were two dragons out there brave enough to be mates of the twins.

"You take Ailean. He loves a good battle and he'll kill when he has to, but I don't think he enjoys it."

"Unless someone pissed him off, eh, Kyna?"

"Exactly, Kennis. Then he enjoys it as much as we do. But when the war ended, we found other wars to join and he came back here. To his horses and his . . . uh . . ."

Shalin smirked. "His women?"

Kyna gave a little wave of her hand, clearly deciding not to go down that road. "Only we fight as human in these wars."

"So you spend most of your time as human, too?"

"Not as much as Ailean. 'Course, don't think anyone does."

"That's true," Kennis agreed.

"We do like it. Doubt we could live this way forever, though."

Kennis made a face. "Och! Never."

"Is it true you plan to be an Elder?"

Shalin tensed at the sudden change of topic. "Aye."

"You don't seem like an Elder."

"Well, I'm too young at the moment. Another three or four hundred years at least."

"Even then." Kyna pushed her empty bowl away, as did her sister. Always the same, those two. They moved the same. Talked the same. Nearly everything synchronized. It was . . . strange. Especially because Shalin felt the twins did it all on purpose.

"Even then what?"

"Even then you don't seem like an Elder. Is that what you really want?"

For one hundred and forty-nine years, no one had asked her that before. Now she'd been asked twice. She looked down at her half-empty bowl of porridge, suddenly feeling no hunger at all.

"They say I'll make a good Elder. Fair."

"That's not what I asked you, luv."

Shalin pushed her bowl away. "I promised her."

"Promised who?"

"My mother. I promised my mother I'd become an Elder."

"The dead one?"

Two pairs of eyes locked on Kennis and she winced. "Sorry. That came out wrong."

"How does that come out right?"

"What my sister means, Shalin, is how can you base your future on something you promised someone who has long left this world for another?"

"Honor. That's how. I promised her."

"What about what you want?"

"I didn't say I didn't want to be an Elder."

Kyna shook her head. "That's not what we mean, Shalin. And you know it." But before Shalin could press them on what they did mean, the twins abruptly pushed back their chairs, and stood. "We have to train."

"Something wrong?"

"Not at all." Kyna patted Shalin's head and Shalin realized she'd have a lovely headache from that "gentle" touch. "We just realized how late the day is and more storms coming."

Shalin didn't like the twins' abrupt ending of their conversation, but she decided to ignore it, since they were too frightening a pair to push about anything.

She slipped out the book she'd stowed away under her chair and flipped it open. She didn't know how long she was reading before she sensed someone had sat next to her. Glancing up, she smiled. "Good morn to you, Arranz."

"And to you, mistress. Everything all right?"

"Fine."

He leaned in a bit and whispered, "I was wondering, Shalin, if you could help me with something."

Other than reading, she had absolutely nothing to do. "Of course."

Ailean stomped down the hallway toward the kitchens. He needed a new rag and Madenn's skills to stop the bleeding on his arm. But he abruptly stopped in the middle of the hallway and took several slow steps back.

He looked into the room that held all the maps and documents necessary for when they made battle plans. He glared.

Arranz sat at one of the tables, his feet up on the thick wood, his hands laced behind his head. Shalin stood before him in a dress Ailean had never seen. Even more annoying—she'd been posing when he walked in.

"What in all the hells is going on?"

Shalin gave him a quick, shy smile that had his entire body burning. "Arranz wanted to see this dress on me to see if it would look nice on his lady friend."

"Lady friend?"

"Aye," his brother answered, smugness personified. "She's a tall human. About Shalin's size and I wanted to make sure the dress would look good before I gave it to her. Since it looks divine on Shalin, I'm sure it will do wonders for my friend."

Shalin blushed and nervously combed her hair behind her ears with her fingers. "Stop it, Arranz."

"Aye," Ailean growled. "Stop it, Arranz."

"I only speak the truth, sweet Shalin." It annoyed Ailean even more that his brother ignored him. "But now that I look at you, I don't have the heart to take that frock back."

Frock? Ailean had seen and purchased enough dresses over the decades to know a casual frock and a dress made for a woman. And this dress, off-white with gold thread weaved through, had been made for Shalin.

"I can't keep it, Arranz. It's too fine."

"It's perfect for you."

Too perfect.

"Arranz, if this is about the other morn . . ."

The other morn? What about it?

"No reason to bring that up, Shalin. You'll keep the dress and tonight we'll pull the tables back and dance."

Shalin's eyes widened and she stepped back. "I don't know how to dance."

"I'll teach you."

Over my dead carcass . . .

"Arranz, students of the Magickal arts don't dance. Instead we walk around giving disapproving looks at such activities."

"Really? Can you show me?"

Shalin leaned forward a bit and drew her brows down.

Arranz laughed. "I've seen that look."

"I believe you and all your kin have seen this look."

"You're not with some stodgy acolytes, Shalin. You're with the Cadwaladr Clan, and you'll dance."

Arranz swung his long legs off the table and stood. "Brother," he said as he passed Ailean.

"Bastard," Ailean muttered back.

Once he knew his brother had walked a good bit away, Ailean stepped farther into the room and closed the door with his foot.

"You don't like this dress on me, do you?"

"What?"

"The dress. You don't like it." Shalin smoothed the front down, and Ailean knew she loved the dress.

"You look beautiful in that dress."

"Then why are you—what happened to your arm?" She rushed over to him, and he turned from her. "Ailean?"

"You'll get blood on your dress."

"Don't be foolish." She rushed around him and latched on to his arm.

"Shalin—"

"Let me see." She lifted the cloth and frowned. "Gods, Ailean, what happened?"

"That demon beast you call a horse did this."

"Nightmare?"

"Who else?"

"Why? What did you do?"

"What did I—" Ailean pulled his arm away from her grasp and took a few steps back. "This is *your* fault, wench."

"I beg your pardon?"

"Beg all you want. This is your fault. You've bewitched the males here and now they've all gone mad." Him included, because all he could think about was tearing her lovely new dress from her body and burying himself inside her until the two suns burned from the sky.

"You're insane, all right. But it has nothing to do with me."

Slapping the bloody rag back on his still bleeding wound, Ailean snarled, "Stay away from my brothers, Shalin." He stormed to the door and yanked it open. "That is *not* a request," he informed her before marching out in search of Madenn—and Arranz.

* * *

Shalin must have sat on that table with all the detailed maps for an hour, her mind blissfully blank for once. But she didn't understand . . . was Ailean jealous? Of his own kin? *About her?*

It didn't make sense. None of this made sense. She looked down at the gown she still wore. She'd never had anything so fine. Before her time in Kyffin, Shalin had spent little time as a human, so there'd been no need for dresses. And as an acolyte at the school, she wore the requisite robes. So a dress this beautiful and regal was something she never thought to have.

And why had Arranz given it to her? It would have made sense coming from Ailean because of their . . . uh . . . tryst? No, that word didn't seem quite right. Not any more. Liaison? No. Too fancy for the way she and Ailean . . . uh . . . fucked, as Ailean loved to say.

Perhaps this was simply some sibling rivalry that had nothing to do with her. And she refused to see anything beyond that. She knew her heart to be a fragile thing and she'd encased it in ice long ago. She'd not thaw it now.

No. She'd simply enjoy this . . . this . . . *thing* for what it was.

Resolved, she stood and turned in time to see Arranz fall by the window, landing hard on the ground. Convinced that his seemingly hard head could handle such a drop, she went out to check on her horse. But she still chuckled when she heard Arranz yell, "*You blue-haired bastard!*"

10

"What exactly did you do to my horse?" Shalin accused him lightly as she dropped into a chair next to Ailean and watched his family and many of the humans who lived on the territory dance. What had sounded like a simple little get-together after their evening meal had turned into a large party. Not that Shalin minded. She liked parties, although she never really participated before. She usually sat in a corner and watched. It seemed, however, that sort of thing wasn't allowed among Ailean's kin.

"Me? That evil bastard bit me."

"You must have done something. It took me ages to calm him down and I had to feed him by hand."

"Och!"

"What?"

"You are so easy, Shalin. He's trained you like you've trained that puppy. Only he's done a better job of it."

"What does that mean?"

"Nothing."

He'd seemed miserable all night and she didn't understand why.

She turned in her chair, her knees grazing his leg. "You should dance."

"I don't want to dance."

"Dance, Ailean. I'm sure any of these ladies would love to

dance with you." The glare he gave her had her rearing back. "What was *that* look for?"

"For someone so smart you can be so . . ." He bit off his next words and growled, looking away.

"If you're going to be like this, I'll go." She went to stand up but Ailean's hand clamped onto her arm.

"You want me to dance? I'll dance."

Then he stood and dragged her with him.

"Wait! Ailean!" She'd danced with both his brothers and several of his male cousins, but she'd been horrible at it. In fact, she'd been quite grateful for their jovial attitude regarding her lack of skill. "I can't—"

He turned and yanked her in close. "*You can dance with my kin, but not with me?*"

Her eyes widened at his growled words. His family, dancing around them, seemed quite oblivious.

"I'm not good at it."

"That didn't stop you before."

"Because I don't care if I make a fool of myself with them."

And like that, Ailean's anger seemed to evaporate. He grinned, placing one of her hands on his waist and gripping her other hand tight. Pulling her close against his body, he said, "Trust me, Shalin. I'll teach you."

"You won't laugh?"

"At you? Never."

Even though a fast jig played, Ailean started off slow, taking her carefully through each step. He kept her spirits up and when she was moments from quitting, and before she even realized it, they'd danced around the floor as if they'd been dancing together forever. Fast music or slow, Shalin handled all of it as long as she stayed in Ailean's arms.

She'd lost track of how long they'd been dancing when Kyna patted her shoulder. "We're going up, luv. Care to come with us?"

Shalin looked around and realized they were one of the few couples left. Others were enjoying late-night meals or had already left.

Shalin pulled out of Ailean's arms, hoping to control her human body's weakness of blushing.

"Of course. I didn't realize it was so late." She smiled up at Ailean. "Thank you for the lessons."

"My pleasure, Shalin."

Hoping he'd still come to her room later, Shalin followed the twins up the stairs.

Ailean went to Shalin's window as he had the night before. As dragon, but using his camouflage skills to hide his presence from anyone, even another dragon, who might be watching. She'd left the window open for him this time and when he pulled himself through, she stood with her back to him, a fur covering wrapped around her.

"Shalin?"

She didn't face him when he called to her, but instead asked with horror in her voice, "Ailean, I found chains and a metal neck collar in the small closet back here. Why are they there?"

Ailean winced and gritted his teeth. He'd forgotten to clean out this room before Shalin took it and Arranz had unusual . . . tastes.

He took a deep breath and prayed she'd believe the truth—although he couldn't promise he would have if the roles were reversed. "Shalin, you need to believe me when I say that Arranz—"

"Because I took them out of the closet and stupidly tried them on." She finally turned to face him, her head bowed, completely naked under the fur that she parted just enough to tease. Naked, that is, except for the metal collar locked around her throat and the chain hanging from it. "And now I can't get them off."

Slowly, so slowly he thought he'd explode right there, she raised her eyes to look at him. "Do you think, Ailean the Wicked, you can help me with this?"

Ailean let out a breath and walked toward her, watching as she dropped the fur covering to the floor.

"Aye, Shalin the Innocent," he growled, reaching out and taking firm hold of the chain hanging from the metal collar. "I do believe I can help you."

Winding the chain around his hand, he tugged her close. "But first, I need your help."

Looking shyly up at him through her lashes, she said softly, "Anything you want, m'lord. I am yours until the chain comes off. Until then, until you release me, I am yours to do with as you will."

"Then I need your help with this intense ache I have." He tugged down on the chain and, with a small smile, Shalin slowly went on her knees in front of him. "I need you to give me relief, Shalin."

Shalin gently ran her hand down the length of him, her small smile growing until she fairly leered at him. "Oh, it'll be my great pleasure, m'lord," she said, before she took him into her mouth with one deep swallow.

"You have to tell me," he said softly.

Shalin, who'd found a comfortable position with her head on Ailean's flat abdomen while his fingers combed through her hair, glanced away from the window and at him.

"Tell you what?"

"Who, Shalin?" And he smiled in disbelief. "Who in all the bloody hells named you Innocent?"

With a chuckle, Shalin kissed his stomach, loving the way the defined muscles jumped at the touch of her lips. "Adienna." She chuckled at the surprised expression on his face. "Adienna named me Innocent."

"Why?"

Shalin repositioned herself a bit so her chin rested high on his stomach by his ribs and her right arm wrapped tight around his waist. "Because I kept rejecting her cast-offs. She kept tossing these dragons at me with these little comments as to how they were as lovers and why I should try them out. As if she were giving them a go first for my benefit. When I rejected one of Ceanag's sons—I forget which one—she started calling me 'innocent.' And I decided not to argue the point."

Ailean ran both his hands through her hair as he so often did and gazed into her face. "But you didn't see me as a cast-off?"

Her eyes narrowed and she saw the look of concern on his

face. "I won't say she didn't want you from the beginning, Ailean. But I can assure you that her knowing I wanted you so badly made it extra special for her."

When he only stared at her blankly, she admitted, "She knew I wanted you. And she made it her mission to get you. And afterward, every time she obsessed about you or talked about the night you shared, she did it to make sure she hurt me. Adienna likes to see others in pain."

Ailean took a deep breath, let it out, and said, "I'm sorry."

Shalin shook her head. "I don't need you to be. I'm completely aware of how enticing she is. Of how much others desire—"

"No," he said softly, cutting her off. "I wish I could tell you I wanted her because I had to have her. Because I desired her so much. But it was really because I couldn't believe a princess could want me, the low-born."

"I hate that term. It's cruel."

"But how we're viewed. I went to her bed that night for every wrong reason there is and as soon as I got there I regretted it more than I thought possible. I always felt like these past years with her obsessing over me was some sort of punishment for not doing what I normally do."

"Which is?"

"Fuck the ones I want." He laughed, but it was bitter. "I didn't even fuck her. I brought her pleasure but that night I found none myself. I pushed her until she passed out, and then I ran like some startled kitten."

"You wouldn't be the first who ran," Shalin said. "Although you may be the only one who didn't come back out of fear. I do think you may finally be free, though. I'd heard a bit before the North dragons arrived that the queen has chosen a mate for Adienna. And Adienna is none too happy about it."

"I feel sorry for the poor dragon sharing his life with her for the next six hundred years. I'd rather swallow glass."

Before Shalin could respond to that, Ailean gripped her shoulders and pulled her up until they were face to face. "I'm sorry, Shalin."

"Stop it. There's nothing to—"

"I should have done what I'd planned to do that night, but I was stupid." His hands went from her shoulders until they cupped her face. "It was you I was going to see that night. You I was walking toward. Then someone stopped me, I don't remember who, and asked me some questions. When I turned back around, you were gone."

Shalin stared at Ailean as that night came back to her with stunning clarity. Finally, she gave a soft laugh and shook her head. "That bitch." She stroked his chest with the tips of her fingers. "She came to me that night, telling me to track down one of her personal guards. I searched everywhere. Every cavern, every chamber. After more than an hour I returned and found her guard already there. But the two of you were long gone. That explains why her friends were snickering at me the rest of the night, but I didn't pay it much mind. They did that a lot, anyway."

Ailean pulled her head down a bit and kissed her forehead. "I should never have listened to her. She told me you ran from me. That me, my reputation, scared you. And, like a fool, I believed her."

"She's very good at making a body believe whatever she tells them. Trust me when I say I won't hold it against you. However," she kissed his jaw, his throat, "that doesn't mean you shouldn't make it up to me."

Ailean roughly grabbed her rear and pushed her up his body until her breast hung over his face. His tongue flicked against the nipple, making Shalin gasp until he took it into his mouth and she groaned.

He sucked and teased until Shalin gripped his head and held him tightly to her. That's when he flipped her onto her back, him on top.

"I promise, Shalin," he said, his mouth already moving to the other breast. "I'll make it up to you all night long."

Ailean looked down at Shalin again. Asleep, she had her head resting against his chest, one arm around his waist, the other fisted against his shoulder. Her legs were intertwined with his and she slept peacefully, positive she was safe in his arms. She trusted him when she trusted no one else but her own blood kin.

How did he let this happen? How did he let her dig her way into his heart and became mistress of it all? But she had, hadn't she? His little dragoness.

Yet, what now? Once this all got straightened out—and he was sure the queen would do what was right—Shalin had her life to return to. Her school. Her future as an Elder. Although it didn't seem like she truly wanted any of that. Did she really want to sit through painful, dead boring council meetings over fights for territory between dragons? Did she want to live her life in Devenallt Mountain? As an Elder, she'd be required to live there at least part of the year.

Yet after spending all this time with her, it looked to Ailean as though Shalin wanted nothing more than to be left alone to read.

If she promised her nights to him, he could give her that time alone and so much more. Gods, there was so much he *wanted* to give her if only she'd let him.

The little dragoness brought him so much joy. And not merely in his bed. While he knew he made her feel physically safe, she had yet to realize that she made him feel safe too. Safe talking to her, being with her. She made him laugh one minute and lust for her the next. And sometimes she broke his heart because she felt so alone. He could see it on her face, the way she watched his family. Her expression torn between envy and annoyance.

Yet Shalin still hadn't realized what had become so clear to Ailean. She fit into his life, among his kin, perfectly.

She was the one he'd been waiting for all this time and neither of them had known it.

Ailean stroked her hair and smiled when she growled softly in her sleep.

"Who knew?" he asked the puppy staring at him from the end of the bed, the giant bone Shalin had given him slobbered over but uneaten and resting by his tiny paws. "Who knew I'd fall in love with Shalin the Innocent?"

11

"How long are you going to pretend we don't already know?" Kyna demanded, dropping into a chair next to him.

Ailean didn't bother looking up from the hot porridge and bread he shoveled into his mouth. Shalin had already gone out to the stables and he wanted to meet her out there before he got in some training later that day.

"Already know what?"

"About you and Shalin. We guessed it before, but the party last night only confirmed it."

"It's no one's business until we decide it is. Stay out of it." He reached for another loaf of warm bread, tore it in half and gave a piece to each sister. Kennis thanked him with a grunt as she dived into her own porridge, but Kyna wasn't so easily distracted.

"Come, Ailean. Really. Do you think it's fair to toy with her?"

"I'm not toying with her."

Kyna snorted. "Then what are you doing? Planning to have hatchlings with her?"

Ailean finished his porridge, grabbed another loaf of bread, and stood. He smiled down at his cousin. "That's exactly what I'm planning."

Enjoying the way the twins froze in shock, Ailean went out to the stables.

* * *

Shalin ran the brush through Nightmare's mane again and stepped back. "How about some braids today?"

"Because you're a big *mare* of a stallion, aren't you?"

Glaring at Ailean over the stall door, she corrected, "*Warrior* braids."

"For him? He's never been in battle."

"How do you know? You only found him a few months ago." She stalked up to Ailean and shook the brush at him. "And if I want to give *my* horse warrior braids, I'll damn well do it. Understand?"

Turning away from him before she got an answer—because she knew she wouldn't get an answer she'd like—she still heard the sudden grunt of pain and spun back around.

Ailean rubbed his head—and the lovely hoof print in the middle of it—and glared daggers at Nightmare.

"Oh, Ailean." But even as she went to him to comfort him, she still couldn't stop the laughter. "Are you all right?"

"As if you care."

"I care." She placed her feet on the slats of the gate and stood until they were eye to eye. She kissed his forehead and did her best not to laugh in his face. "I'm sorry. He's very sensitive."

"He's mad, Shalin."

"He's mine," she reminded him. "You promised him to me, did you not?"

"Yes. But I might be willing to temporarily change my rule on eating horse in Kerezik."

Nightmare moved forward but Shalin held up her hand. She knew she was the only thing standing between these two beasts getting into an ugly fight.

"Stop it. Both of you. Honestly, it's like dealing with two young ones."

"He started it."

Disagreeing, Nightmare slammed his front hoof down.

"I said stop this." She motioned to the partially eaten loaf of bread in Ailean's hand. "Give me some of that, would you? I'm taking Nightmare for a ride."

"Alone?"

"Yes. Alone."

"I'll go—"

"You said you have training and I'm only going to the lake. Besides, Nightmare will take care of me."

"That does not bring me ease."

"Bread," she ordered, holding out her hand. He tore what remained in half and gave it to her. "Thank you." Shalin kissed him, her tongue slipping between his lips to tangle with his own. They both groaned and Shalin realized she'd have to pull away or Ailean would take her right here in the stables. Not that she would have minded, but still—it seemed a tad inappropriate.

"We won't be long."

"Meet me in your library later."

Shalin blinked. *Her library?* "Yes. All . . . all right," she stammered, stepping down from the gate and unlocking it. She walked out and Nightmare followed.

"Be careful, Shalin."

"I will." She smiled before she took Nightmare out the less used exit at the back of the stables. She took him that way since he had a tendency to bite and kick anyone he passed.

"You like that horse better than me, don't you?" Ailean called after her.

"Sometimes . . . yes!" she replied and got a little nuzzle for her trouble. "And take care of the puppy!" Although her puppy seemed more than happy to spend his time during the day with the pack of dogs who had free rein of the castle grounds and surrounding forests, only to appear suddenly at her feet during mealtimes, clearly expecting to spend that time in her lap with food at his disposal.

Once she'd awkwardly mounted Nightmare—she really would have to learn to do that a bit better—he immediately took off at a full gallop. She didn't mind; she liked how it felt. Together they made a quick turn around the grounds right outside the castle before heading out to the lake. Once there, Shalin dismounted just as awkwardly and fed him apples from the leather pouch she'd tied around her waist. While she did, she chatted with him and petted his head and neck.

Eventually she held up the last apple and said, "I'll give you this apple . . . if you promise to stop hitting Ailean in the head with your hooves."

The horse snorted and turned his head away.

"Oh, come on!" she laughed, until he startled her by charging back a few feet before turning around.

Standing in front of her, Nightmare rose up on his hind legs and Shalin prepared herself to shift.

She stepped beside Nightmare and the twin males examined her from head to toe. They were fire dragons, but she didn't recognize them.

"He's protective," said one.

"Aye. That's good," said the other.

She placed her hand on Nightmare's neck to calm him. "Who—"

"Is Ailean about?" one of them asked abruptly.

"Castle."

They nodded and walked off. One decided to push the other, so the other pushed him back. Then there were headlocks and fists thrown—all while they kept walking.

"They're like that—*constantly.*"

Shalin turned at the new voice and grinned.

"Daddy!"

Ailean dived for his blade, but Kennis slammed her lance down in front of it and raised an eyebrow. "You'll need to be faster than that, cousin."

He hated training with the twins. They were brutal and fierce and bloody mean. But he and his brothers knew—if they could hold their own with the twins, they could defeat anyone else. Kennis and Kyna were, by far, the greatest warriors of their clan and the most deadly of the Battle Dragons of Dark Plains.

Still, training with them was never fun.

He sensed but never heard Kyna as she moved up behind him and brought her lance toward his head. Kennis went for the legs.

Before the twins could even fly, they'd taught themselves how to fight in tandem. With fourteen older brothers, they really had no choice. They could use almost any weapon, but favored the lances they'd designed and helped forge themselves, which could adjust to their smaller human size or extend when they were in dragon form.

Ailean maneuvered back, reaching for the lances but below the always-sharpened steel tips. Yet, like him, they sensed it and quickly adjusted, Kennis now going for his head and Kyna going for the legs.

He ducked the blow aimed for his head, but Kyna took him out at the legs, dumping him on his back.

Each slammed a foot against his chest and grinned down at him. "Sloppy, sloppy," Kennis chastised.

"Perhaps he has something—"

"Or someone."

"—on his mind, eh, sister?"

"I say we put him out of his misery."

"Good idea."

Together they raised their battle lances and Ailean cringed. They'd never kill him, but one never knew what damage they would decide to do.

"Oiy! Female!"

Kennis lowered her weapon and turned. When she saw her mate, she squealed, dropped her lance, and charged toward him, throwing herself in his arms.

"Don't make me come get you," Kyna's mate warned.

She snorted at Ailean. "Lucky for you." Then, like her sister, she dropped her weapon and charged her mate, landing in his arms.

Ailean raised himself on his elbows and stared at the quartet. How Kyna and Kennis had found their true mates with another set of twins, he had no answer. Especially when sets of twins were as rare among his people as white dragons.

"Oiy," he said to the males. "What are you two doing here? You're supposed to be watching old Baudwin."

"We did and we are. We left him by the lake with his daughter."

Ailean stood, and Arranz, still bleeding from the head wound Kennis gave him, and Bideven, still limping from one of Kyna's blows, walked over to him. "What about that?"

"What about what?"

"Her father. Here." Arranz gave a little smirk. "You going to tell him what you've been doing with his daughter the last few nights?"

"I find it amusing you didn't think we'd know," Bideven sardonically sneered.

"That old dragon may be weak, but a father is a father. He won't like what you and Shalin have been up to."

"I'm not too worried." Ailean wiped blood from the wound over his eye.

Arranz snorted. "Oh. You're not?"

"No. Once he finds out I love her and we're going to be together forever, he'll be fine."

Ignoring the shocked expressions on his brothers' faces, Ailean headed over to the well for fresh water.

"Ailean," Bideven rushed up behind him and asked, "have you actually mentioned any of this to Shalin?"

"No." He shrugged. "Why should I?"

Shalin hugged her father again before stepping back. She really saw his age when he was in human form and it hurt her heart. She knew she only had another hundred years with her father. Maybe two, if lucky, but no more. Her parents had waited until very late in their lives to have Shalin and although it never really bothered her, she also knew it made her different from all the other dragons who grew up with parents young enough to take them on long flights and teach them the proper way of hunting and fighting.

But Baudwin the Wise only hunted up that which stood right outside his cave. And although he could give detailed histories on every war that had taken place among the dragons *and* humans, he was a worthless fighter himself.

None of that mattered to Shalin, though. Her father meant everything to her. Always had.

"I'm so glad you're all right, Father."

"And I you." He pulled back, examining her carefully. "You don't look any the worse for wear."

She smiled. "No. I'm just fine."

And that's when her father's sharp brown eyes narrowed. "Are you?"

Clearing her throat, she said, "Oh. Yes. Just fine. We should go." She walked around him to get to the clearing.

"Go where, Shalin?" he asked in that calm way of his. "Do what? And shouldn't we have those two oversized beasts with us?"

Turning around, Shalin chewed on her lip. "I guess." She nodded. "You're right, of course."

"And aren't you interested in what the queen has to say?"

It took Shalin a moment to remember she hadn't been on Ailean's territory merely for sexual satisfaction. And if she hoped to conceal what happened between her and Ailean from her father, she'd better act more like she cared.

"Oh! Of course. Yes. What was the decision?"

"No decision. Not until the council meeting."

"A . . . a council meeting?"

"Calm yourself, Shalin. I see the panic in your eyes." He rubbed a soothing hand against Shalin's back. "The queen and Elders wish to have the case presented in front of all the court. And to everyone's surprise, the Northern dragons have put in a demand for the deal struck with Princess Adienna to go through as planned."

Shalin crossed her arms in front of her chest. "To everyone's surprise because who would want me?"

Her father shook his head in confusion. "What are you talking about? I mean surprising because we all assumed the Northerners would simply try to take you rather than follow the usual rules of etiquette. That's usually how they do things." Baudwin sniffed. "Barbarians. The lot of them." He nodded at his daughter. "That oldest one seemed much more civilized than his brethren. I assume it was his decision to put in the claim. I believe he truly likes you."

"Well, I can read," she said on a chuckle.

"Of course you can. You're my daughter." Her father glanced around impatiently. "Where do you think those two bickering ninnies went?"

"Drive you mad, did they?"

"Don't misunderstand me, daughter. I will appreciate until my dying day their protection. Truth be told, I knew with all certainty they would kill anyone or anything that moved within a dragon's tail of me. But the constant chatter—" He shuddered. "—it drove me to distraction." Which was her father's quiet way of saying if he could have killed them both . . .

"I should take Nightmare back anyway. I'll get them and bring them back here."

"Nightmare?"

She motioned to the horse. "Nightmare. My horse."

Her father frowned. "You named your midmeal? Shalin, you know better than to—"

"No, no. He's not . . ." she cleared her throat. "They don't eat horses or dogs here, Daddy. They're considered pets and working animals."

Her father made a small gesture with his hands. "I can't . . . they're just . . . the entire Cadwaladr Clan simply confuses . . ."

Shalin kissed her father's cheek. "I completely understand. And for that reason I won't mention the puppy Ailean gave me."

"Puppy?"

Shalin laughed. "I won't be long."

She walked off and Nightmare dutifully followed behind her. She led him back to the stables and to his stall. She made sure he had ample food and water. She rubbed her hand down his muzzle. "Now listen to me. I want you to let them feed you. Please. I have to go away and—" she swallowed "—and I won't be back. So I need you to take care of yourself and to let them take care of you. I've already had a word with that stablemaster."

Leaning forward, she kissed his muzzle and stepped back. "I'll miss you."

Then, before she did something horrifyingly human—like cry—she walked out the back door.

And right into Ailean.

Legs braced apart, arms folded over his chest, he stared down at her with one brow raised.

"They warned me you would simply try and leave and I didn't believe them. But you were, weren't you?"

Shalin sighed. "Don't you think that's for the best?"

"No, Shalin. I don't."

"I fear if my father sees us together, he'll know. And we both agreed this would be kept between—where are you going?"

But she knew exactly where Ailean was going and what he most certainly planned to do.

Ailean could hear her charging up behind him, demanding he stop and talk to her. But he had nothing to say to her. He knew exactly what she'd been planning to do and it made him blindingly angry even to think about it.

So he marched on until he arrived at the clearing by the lake. The old brown dragon stood as human, staring up at one of the trees. He seemed to be studying the birds. Why anyone would do that was lost on Ailean, but at the moment he really didn't care.

"Lord Baudwin?"

The older dragon turned, looked up at him, and took a hasty step back. "Ailean the Wicked? Gods. Did your mother perform spells before your hatching to get you that size?"

Ailean blinked. "Not that I know of."

"You are simply gargantuan! I thought those twins you sent were big, but you . . . simply frightening."

"Well—"

"How do you get around as human? Does no one question someone of your size lumbering around?"

"I don't lumb—"

Shalin pushed her way between the two males. "Father, we have to go."

"Where are those large fellows? Aren't they coming?"

"No. We'll go without them."

"Like hell you will," Ailean snapped.

"Don't," Shalin warned, "get in my way, Ailean."

The old dragon glanced between the two. "Is there something I should know?"

"No!"

"Yes!"

Baudwin sighed. "Somehow I sense I won't like this, will I?"

"I need to speak with you," Shalin said softly before walking away from her father.

Ailean followed and when she felt they stood far enough away, she said, "What are you doing?"

"Don't you know?"

"You have to know this is over. You must."

"That unhappy with me?"

"Of course not." She'd never been happier. But she had to be realistic as well. Passion and multiple climaxes did not a future make. And she had to think of her future. She had to stay on this path. "We both know I had a wonderful time here, but we also knew it would end."

"Why does it have to end, Shalin?"

"You're mad if you think I'll become one of your regular trysts."

"That's not what I—"

"I go to see the queen and the Elders today to get their ruling," she cut in. It horrified her when the thought of having *any* time with Ailean sounded better than none. The fact she'd sunk so low as to even consider spending her life as one of the females he regularly dropped in on when in certain towns made her stomach turn. She deserved better than that. "What happens from now on is no longer your concern. I appreciate everything you've done, and it will never be forgotten, but we both knew it couldn't go any further. So please, don't make this any harder than it has to be."

She'd kept it direct and calm, never once raising her voice or losing her temper. Considering how angry she was, she felt extremely proud of herself.

Suddenly, Ailean asked, "Do you love me?"

Startled, Shalin took a quick step back. "What?"

"You heard me. Do you love me or not?"

"What kind of question is that?"

"A simple one. Yes or no, Shalin. Do you love me or not?"

She forced herself to remain perfectly calm, perfectly in control. "No."

Ailean snorted. "You lying cow."

"I beg your—"

"Fine. I'll tell your father the truth myself."

Shalin grabbed Ailean's arm. "Don't you dare!"

"I'll make it quick," he said casually. "I promise."

He started walking, heading over to her unsuspecting father as well as the two males who'd been protecting him, Ailean's brothers, and the twins who'd just arrived. A veritable audience!

"Ailean, I'm not joking!"

"Nor am I. I understand why you're nervous. So I'll handle it."

It was his calm, casual tone. His relaxed nature. As if telling her father they'd been sharing a bed for days was something of no real concern.

Shalin jumped in front of him, slamming her hands against his chest. "You're not understanding me, Ailean. You're not to tell my father anything."

He leaned forward a bit and whispered loudly, "Don't you think he'll notice?"

"Notice what?"

"That I've Claimed you as my own. He'll definitely notice after the first hatchling."

Somehow, she still managed to control her temper—but it was definitely getting harder to do so. "You won't be Claiming me. Not you."

"Why not me?"

"Do you really need me to give you a list?"

"*A list?*"

"Don't yell, Ailean. Simply accept it."

"Like hell I will. You love me, why won't you just admit it?"

"And why won't you admit I only wanted one thing from you, I got it, and now I'm done?"

She saw it for only a moment, a flash deep in his eyes, the grim set of his mouth. She'd hurt him. But the part that wanted to soothe him, to see him smile again, she ruthlessly battered into submission. She'd shake this dragon from her tail even if she had to make him cry.

But Ailean didn't cry. He didn't argue. He did slightly flinch, but it was so small only she would have noticed it.

Without another word said between them, Ailean gently gripped her by the shoulders and moved her out of his way.

Shalin watched him walk over to her father and knew he'd ignore her wishes. Like everyone else, he assumed she'd be compliant. Adienna certainly thought so. She thought Shalin would quietly go off with enemy dragons to live in the North until she became ancient. And what made Shalin wince was the truth of it. Before Ailean and his brothers showed up, she had been taking the Northerner's hand. Without a fuss, she would have gone with them even as her heart screamed for her to fight, to flee. To at least try to stop them.

So, perhaps it was no great surprise Ailean thought the same of her. Like everyone else, he thought she'd comply. Bend to his will for her "own good."

To get what he wanted, he was willing to embarrass her in front of her father while his kin stood and watched. Then years later they could joke about weak little Shalin and how her futile protests were ignored. The pain of it ripped through her, leaving her shaken and angry. So angry, she could barely see or hear.

In that instant, something inside her snapped—and there'd be no going back now.

Ailean stood only a few feet away from the old dragon when Shalin suddenly stepped in front of him. The cold expression on her face surprised him. Wait. Not cold. Icy. An icy rage.

The instincts he'd honed in battle and war screamed at him to step away from her, but he didn't understand why. This was his sweet Shalin. And she'd simply have to understand this would be better in the long run. They were meant to be together and there was no use in fighting it any longer. Besides, Ailean had no patience to wait for her to realize it.

Ailean reached for her to again move her out of his way and, hundreds of years later, he'd refer to this as "one of the stupidest things I'd ever done."

In one fluid moment, as her father and his kin quickly scrambled out of the way, Shalin turned and her human body shifted to dragon. As she did, the razor-sharp tip of her tail lashed out and ripped across his human throat, slicing it from ear to ear.

Ailean's hands wrapped around his neck and he dropped to his knees. Blood flowed between his fingers and dripped onto the forest floor.

"Shift, you fool!" Shalin's father shouted. "Shift now!"

Ailean did, calling up the ancient spell and shifting right where he kneeled. His scales quickly covered his body, preventing him from bleeding to death right there.

As his body changed and tried to right itself, he watched Shalin motion to her father and take off from the clearing. Confusion on his face, the old dragon followed.

"Gods, Ailean!" His brothers stood on either side of him now in dragon form, trying to figure out the best way to help him while the twins tried to go after Shalin and most likely kill her in the air. But their mates held them back until Ailean, shaky from the loss of blood, stood.

He couldn't speak, not with his vocal chords sliced in half and still trying to mend, so he motioned to the twins' mates to follow Shalin and her father. To keep them safe. They understood and did as he bade. While his cousins continued to rant and swear blood oaths to Shalin's death, Ailean placed his blood-covered claws on each of his brothers' shoulders.

They'd grown up together. Fought together. Killed together. He didn't need words for them. Never had.

They knew they'd be going after Shalin themselves.

And then, Ailean would settle all of this.

12

Shalin waited outside the queen's meeting chamber. Soon she would have to enter and plead her case. Unfortunately, she really didn't care.

"I'll speak for you, Shalin."

She shrugged. "As you wish."

His claw brushed her cheek. "Look at me, daughter."

She did, but she quickly tried to turn away, unable to bear his gaze. But her father's other claw came up and gripped her other cheek.

"Do not turn from me."

"I'm so sorry, Father." Tears began to flow and she couldn't stop them. "I know I've disappointed you."

"Och! What is this? How have you disappointed me?"

"Ailean," she said simply.

"Because you tried to kill him?"

"No." Her tail nervously swished across the stone floor. "Because he and I . . . um . . ."

"You and he what?"

"I'd prefer not to spell it out, Father." Although she had no doubts their story would become known throughout Dark Plains before the next full moon.

"Spell it . . . oh. Oh!" He absently patted her head before brushing nonexistent crumbs off his chest. "Yes. Of course you did, dear. You're not made of stone and he is quite a virile speci-men."

Only her father could make it all sound so . . . medicinal. "And you're not ashamed of me?"

"Ashamed of what?" He quickly combed his claws through his gray and brown hair. "What were we talking about again?" he asked. It wasn't that he was confused, merely not interested. But when this was all over and settled, then he'd want to discuss it in complete detail and she didn't look forward to it. Nothing was worse than her father turning to her after a day, a decade, or even a century, after something she'd thought had long gone away and suddenly demanding, "Wait. What just happened?"

Stepping back, he motioned to her eyes. "Dry those tears, lit-tle one. This queen detests weakness. And when you are called, come in with your head high. Understand?"

She nodded. "Yes, sir."

"Good."

"Baudwin the Brown," one of the heralds called out.

Her father patted her cheek and gave her a quick smile before entering the meeting chamber.

Once his tail disappeared after him, Shalin took several sooth-ing, calming breaths and wiped the tears from her eyes and cheeks with the backs of her claws.

Her father was right. She needed to get her emotions under control, but it would not be easy after that rage she'd let loose on Ailean. Unlike many of her brethren, Shalin kept her temper under control with a will of iron. In her mind, to show rage was the same as showing sadness, which meant showing weakness. She'd learned during her time at court that to show emotion of any kind merely gave Adienna what she needed to destroy those who crossed her.

Then Ailean came along and he had this uncanny ability to get all sorts of emotions out of her—irritation, affection, rage. Even worse—love.

"As lovely as I remember," a voice said near her. She turned and blinked. It took her a moment to recognize him in dragon form, though the purple hair and scales were clear enough. But it was the eyes. Such a startling blue. Simply beautiful.

"Are you here to drag me away while I scream and cry?"

He laughed. "No, no, dragoness. That had been my father's idea. He still follows the old ways. I have, however, come here today in the hopes of convincing you to come with me of your own free will."

Now Shalin laughed. "I barely know you and you expect me to become your mate?"

"No. But I would love for you to come with me so I can show you my home. It's a rugged land, but you'll find more beauty there than any other place that you've seen."

Shalin looked away. "And if I don't come? There will be war amongst our people?"

The herald called to the dragon and, with a sigh, he headed toward the meeting chamber. "That I do not know. My brothers have different ways of dealing with females." He glanced at her over his shoulder. "They may not stop until there is war."

He entered the chamber, and she watched his tail disappear inside. For the first time, she noticed that the tip wasn't purple like the rest of him, but more like burnished silver. She sensed he sharpened it. Smooth and charming he might be, but a predator just the same.

Many long minutes passed until the herald returned. The green dragon stared at her. "Shalin the Gold. You have been summoned."

Ahh, yes. The Gold. When you entered the royal meeting chamber, the name you had earned over time was stripped so no one was above another.

Knowing she'd have to face Adienna, Shalin briefly closed her eyes, refusing to panic. Then, she raised her head proudly and walked into the meeting chamber where they all waited.

Ailean and his brothers landed at the entrance of Devenallt Mountain. He allowed Bideven to lead the way, knowing his brother knew the world of politics better than he or Arranz. All three brothers were dressed in their battle armor, but that was for show and rank rather than actual fighting. Although he'd do whatever necessary to get what he wanted.

"This is the meeting chamber," Bideven whispered.

With a nod, Ailean headed toward it.

"Ailean, wait. You can't just go in there!"

A large green dragon, a herald most likely, stepped in front of the chamber's entrance. Ailean grabbed him by the snout, yanked him away, and entered. As he'd been trained to do, he quickly took in everything around him so he could act accordingly.

The Elders sat on a dais built out of solid rock. The queen sat on a separate rock protrusion but hers was neither higher nor lower than the Elders. Although she was queen, the Elders still held great powers among the dragons of Dark Plains. Only during a time of war did the queen's decisions outrank the Elders', simply because they didn't have the time to vote and debate when lives were in jeopardy.

On the far side of the chamber he saw one of the purple dragons who'd originally come for Shalin. A good, solid fighter and strong, he'd be a worthy opponent. But when it came to Shalin, Ailean would tear the purple beast apart scale by scale to keep her.

The bastard sat with an audience made up mostly of royals . . . and Adienna. The smugness on her face made Ailean want to rip off her head himself. But his main concern was Shalin.

She stood alone, in the middle of the chamber in the center of a rune design etched into the cave floor. She held her head high and stared at each Elder without flinching. He felt unbridled pride watching her. She'd give him hatchlings to be proud of.

"Shalin the Gold," said Elder Cilydd—he had to be nine hundred years old if a day and, last Ailean heard, very nearly blind— "we've made our decision on this matter."

The herald strode up behind Ailean with his brothers right behind him. Ailean reached back and batted the green dragon out of his way and grabbed Bideven's shoulder and dragged him forward.

He motioned to his brother and Bideven only stared, so Ailean slammed his fist into his shoulder, hard enough to break something.

"All right. All right. Don't hit me."

Bideven stepped forward. "Elders. My Queen. I must interrupt these proceedings in the name of Ailean the Blue."

Ailean slammed his brother with his claw and Bideven hissed at him. "In this chamber all monikers are stripped save for the one given to you at birth. Now would you shut up and let me handle this?"

Forcing a smile, Bideven turned back to face the Elders and the queen.

The queen looked over at the brothers. "I've known Ailean the Blue many years, Bideven the Black. Can he not speak for himself?"

Bideven cleared his throat and glanced at Ailean. All Ailean could do was shrug and Arranz agreed with a shrug of his own.

"Actually, my Queen, he cannot. At this time." Another throat clear, and this time a furtive glance at Shalin, who refused to look at any of them. "His throat was cut while human and it still heals. It will be a few more hours or even days before he'll be able to speak without pain."

The queen's body went rigid and her eyes lashed across the hall to the Lightning dragon.

"Is this down to you, Theodoric?"

"Not I, Queen. Nor my kin—that I'm aware of. I sent them back to the Northlands yesterday."

"Then who did this to Ailean?" She looked around the chamber and finally settled her clear blue eyes back on Bideven. "Who, Bideven?"

Bideven scratched the back of his neck with his tail and stared down at his claws. "Uh . . . well, my Queen . . . uh—"

"I cut his throat," Shalin suddenly piped in, grabbing everyone's attention. But it was Ailean she now stared at and, with a viciousness he never heard from her before, she added, "And I'd do it again at the asking."

The room fell deathly silent and Ailean raised an eyebrow. Something Shalin took as challenge. Gasping, she stormed toward him but Arranz stepped between the pair.

"Now, now, hatchlings," his brother chided with obvious amusement, "let's be calm here."

"This is your fault," Shalin snarled over Arranz's shoulder. "*Your* fault. I wouldn't be here if it weren't for you."

Frustrated that he couldn't speak, Ailean grabbed Bideven by his hair and dragged him forward.

"Ow!"

He hit the black dragon on the shoulder and gestured at

Shalin. Looking between the pair, Bideven shrugged. "What do you want me to say?"

Gritting his teeth, Ailean pointed at Shalin, pointed at himself, made circles in the air with his claw, and slammed his fist into the palm of the other.

Bideven's eyes grew wide. "Am I supposed to understand any of that?" he demanded.

But Shalin gasped and stepped back. "*I'm* being unreasonable. How can you say that? I'd told you to leave my father to me, but you wouldn't listen. *Like always!*"

Ailean slapped his claw against his chest, pointed at the ground with it, and then slashed both arms across each other, accidentally hitting Bideven in the snout.

"Ow!"

"Ho, ho!" Shalin barked. "Do you actually expect me to believe that? Or to base my whole future on that load of centaur shit?"

Ailean flashed his fangs and smoke curled from his snout.

"Don't you dare threaten me, Ailean the Slag!"

Resting his fists on his hips, Ailean slammed down his back claw, accidentally crushing Bideven's claw in the process.

"*Ow!*"

"No," Shalin answered with a haughtiness he'd never noticed before. Damn royals. "Absolutely not."

He brought his tail forward to make his point, accidentally slapping Bideven in the back of the head and shoving his kin forward.

"*Owww!*"

"That's enough." And then the queen was there, gently lifting Bideven's massive head, examining his wounds. "Much more of this conversation and your brother will be dead before the two suns set."

She gestured Bideven and Arranz away and stood between the pair. Enormous, and one of the rare white dragons, Queen Ganieda towered over Shalin while meeting Ailean eye to eye. "I have to tell you two that all of this complicates things. When your father came to me, Shalin, this was all very simple. Simple because what happened to you was and is unacceptable. Dragons don't sell dragons. I don't care if you're a lower-born, a royal, or future heir to the throne." Glittering blue eyes cut across the room to a glaring princess. "It was something that was understood, but now the Elders and I have been forced to put that down in writing so there is no mistake ever again." The queen sighed. "And once that decision was made, well, all need be done was track you down and let you know you could safely return to your life among the humans. Return home to your father. Or, if you so wished, and as Theodoric of the North so humbly offered, go with him into the Northlands and see if you could find your mate there. The choice, of course, was yours."

She took several steps away from the pair before turning back to face them. "Now, however, things have changed, haven't they, Ailean the Blue?"

He nodded, his eyes locked with Shalin's. Without a word, without moving, the greatest battle took place between them. The greatest and the most important.

"You wish to Claim her as your own, do you not?"

Ailean gave one determined nod in agreement.

"No!" The word rang out over the chamber, but it wasn't Shalin who spoke. She'd only shaken her head to let him know she'd rather eat stone than be his mate. It was from the princess.

She pushed past the other royals into the middle of the chamber. "I demand to speak," she snarled.

Her mother chuckled. "Denied. Your mate has already been chosen for you."

"I have not agreed—"

"You'll do as I say or regret that I ever gave you life," the queen hissed. "Your future mate waits for you. Go to him. Now. And on the next full moon, he'll make you his own."

"You can't make me—"

Ailean grabbed Shalin by the arm and yanked her against him as a line of flame lashed by, hitting the princess in the chest and sending her flying back across the chamber. Then Queen Ganieda, in a rarely seen full rage, stormed forward. She grabbed the heir to her throne by the neck and lifted her from the floor.

"You dare tell *me* what I can and can't make you do? You betray your friend, break our laws, and bring the potential of war down on our heads, and you think you have rights to tell me *anything*?"

Adienna gasped and slapped at her mother's claw, but the dragoness was simply too powerful. Even Ailean would have thought twice of challenging Ganieda. But he would have—for Shalin. For Shalin he'd take on an entire army of Lightnings and even his own kin.

"And you do all this," the queen continued, "for a male. A male who never loved you and never will. Now," she threw her daughter across the chamber to the exit, "go to your chosen mate before I can no longer control my temper."

Palpable rage radiating from her, Adienna dragged herself to her feet. The onetime friends locked eyes, but Shalin never backed down. She never looked away.

Then Adienna's gaze moved to Ailean and although he expected to see the same rage, he saw nothing but an obsessive longing that unnerved him more than the rage could have.

Without another word, the princess left, and the queen let out a disgusted sigh and shook her head. "Honestly. These hatchlings today."

She turned back to face Ailean and Shalin. "And as for you two—"

"My queen," one of the Elders gestured to her and she went to him. The queen and the council whispered amongst themselves while Shalin snatched her arm out of Ailean's grip and stepped away. She glared at him and didn't seem to appreciate when he blew her a kiss and winked at her.

"I agree," the queen finally said and turned to face them all. "I have one question for you, Shalin the Gold. Did you give yourself willingly to Ailean or did he have to seduce you into his bed?"

"What does that have to—"

"Answer me, dragoness." Shalin gritted her teeth and the queen smiled, showing many rows of bright, white fangs. "You've already seen how I handle my daughter's impudence. Do you really want to test me as well?"

Shalin glanced once at her father before looking away and answering, "Willingly."

"I see. Then yes, we have no choice but to follow the law regarding this. Ailean the Blue has until the next full moon to mark you as his own. Shalin the Gold will stay on his territory until that time. If she is not marked by the full moon, Ailean, you must leave her be. Is that understood?"

Ailean nodded and he could see it in Shalin's eyes. She had no intention of letting him mark her . . . ever.

"That being said, Shalin the Gold, Ailean can use anything in his, shall we say, *arsenal* to convince you to remain with him forever. Except, of course, violence or the threat of violence against you or your kin." Suddenly Shalin's father moved up behind the queen and whispered to her. She frowned in confusion and added, "Or against your . . . dog?" Shalin's father whispered something else, "Or against your . . . horse?" The queen blinked and shook her head. "You have a dog and horse?"

Shalin nodded, her head down to hide the rage Ailean could feel like he could feel the cold wind whipping through a hole in the cave wall.

"As pets?" Shalin nodded again. "How . . . fascinating." Although the queen sounded more disturbed by it than fascinated. "That is the decision of this council," she walked back to her dais. "We wish you both good luck." She smiled again, her rows of fangs twinkling from the light of the pitfire nearby. "I sense you'll both need it."

Livid beyond all reason, Shalin stormed to an exit that would take her from Devenallt Mountain. That's where Ailean caught up with her, grabbing her arm and pulling her around.

She slammed her two front claws against his chest and pushed. Of course, she might as well have pushed the mountain instead, for all the good it did.

"I hate you, Ailean the Slag. I'll always hate you and I'll never be your mate!"

She tried to pull away, but he held fast. He swallowed and she saw him wince from the pain. She ignored the pang in her heart that ordered her to soothe him. To take him to a healer and help control the pain. She ruthlessly tamped that desire down as ruthlessly as she'd cut his throat in the first place.

"Shalin, wait." His voice, always low, sounded like the hardest gravel and she knew each word caused him immeasurable pain. "Please."

"No. I'll come back to Kerezik as I've been ordered, but I'll not stay in your bed or even in that blasted castle. But I'll be on your territory until the full moon. Then I'll be heading back to school, and I never want to see you again."

She yanked her arm away and walked to the edge of the exit, ready to take flight.

"I'll come for you, Shalin. I don't care if you're on my property or living in a desert cave in Alsandair. I'll not give you up. You're mine. I am yours. Face it."

Shalin didn't even turn around. "The only thing I have to face is that I'll be paying for the foolishness of leaping into your well-used bed for decades to come." With a sigh, she glanced at him over her shoulder and the look in his eyes nearly tore her heart from her chest. She ignored it. "Leave me be, Ailean," she forced herself to say. "I'm sure there are thousands of females who'll happily warm your bed. Someone more suited to you and your life—for it is not me."

Shalin let her wings stretch out, but before she took off, she felt compelled to add, "And I wouldn't shift to human anytime soon. You'll only bleed to death if you do."

Without another word or another glance back, she pushed off from the edge and headed back to Kerezik.

Ailean stood at the edge until his brothers arrived. Without bothering to look at them, he managed to ground out, "We need to find a healer."

"I know," Bideven answered. "My snout is still bleeding."

Rolling his eyes, Ailean snapped, "Not for you, you big baby."

"You really do love her, don't you, brother?" Arranz asked, awe in his voice.

Ailean nodded rather than answering. With every spoken word, pain ripped through him.

Arranz grinned. "Then we'll help you, Ailean. We'll get you your dragoness." Abruptly looking off, Arranz stroked his chin. "In fact . . . I think we should round up the entire clan." When his brothers only stared at him, he shrugged. "Trust me, Ailean. We may be low-born Battle Dragons, but we'll do whatever necessary to help one of our own. If you want that royal . . . you'll get her."

Ailean smiled, loving his brother more than he ever thought

possible. He placed his hand on Arranz's shoulder and Arranz did the same to him.

"If you two are done having this moment of brotherly bonding, I am possibly bleeding to death here."

Ailean gave a small shrug at Arranz before using his tail to ram Bideven in the back, shoving the poor bleeding—and now screaming—bastard out of the cave.

He hit the side of Devenallt Mountain three times before he could catch flight.

"He's going to get you for that," Arranz warned.

"Perhaps," Ailean said, ignoring the pain so he could get this out. "But it was so worth it."

13

It started the first morning she woke up in that cave she found on Ailean's territory. Big and roomy, she'd nearly crashed into it, immediately falling asleep in the first chamber she found. She'd been more exhausted than she realized and slept a good twenty hours. She awoke when something indescribably small and adorable nipped at her snout and climbed up onto her head.

He'd brought her the puppy.

A few hours later she found Nightmare in one of the caverns with lots of hay and water.

The next day books began to appear. All sorts of books. Many she'd read. Quite a few she hadn't. She'd find piles of them in chambers, lined up against walls. Everywhere.

Then his kin came to visit. His aunts first, in teams of two or three.

"Just talk to him," they'd say.

"You know you love him," they'd accuse. "Why are you fighting this?"

Her favorite comment of the day? "I heard you were smart. You couldn't be that smart."

After the aunts, the uncles and male cousins arrived the following day. But they said very little and mostly brought flowers or cows before hastily leaving.

If only the same could be said of the female cousins. They came back and stayed for hours. They talked. They cajoled. They outright threatened. Except the twins. They never spoke to her and instead sat on the edge of the cave entrance sharpening their weapons. Every once in a while, they glared out over the land. Their silence hurt the most because Shalin had grown so fond of them. But unlike the rest of Ailean's kin, they clearly had "not forgiven you for the whole slashing throat incident," as Ailean's Aunt Briaga put it.

By the fourth day, and as the full moon neared, they all stopped coming. Leaving her alone to fully realize exactly how much she missed Ailean. Gods, and she did miss him. With her very soul she missed him.

Determined not to focus on the acute ache in her heart, Shalin shifted to human later in the day and put on one of the dresses the aunts had left for her, since the cave could get quite chilly for human flesh. She groomed and fed Nightmare, appreciating the way he kept nuzzling her, trying to cheer her up.

Once done, she didn't bother to shift back and instead walked to the cave entrance and sat down, her legs hanging over the edge. She stared out over the land. It was quiet. Not like the busy streets of Kyffin, where it was never quiet unless it was a religious holiday or a public execution was taking place.

Shalin didn't know exactly when Ailean sat down beside her but she wasn't really shocked.

"I'm surprised to find you as human, Shalin."

She gave a little shrug. "It's easier to tend Nightmare."

Glancing at him, she saw that his wound had healed but it had left a nasty scar behind. Would take a decade or two for that one to fade.

"Are you all right out here? Need anything?"

Shalin couldn't help but smile. "Hardly. I've had quite the influx of your kin stopping by with gifts."

"Good. Madenn sent up some food for you as well. It's cooked, though."

"That's fine," she said casually, although she'd already scented the food and her mouth had begun to water. Nothing like fresh meat she'd torn open herself, but she'd learned to enjoy the herbs and seasonings the humans used to enhance their cooked meats and fish. She'd definitely begun to miss it.

Not that she'd ever admit that out loud.

"Thank you for bringing my puppy and Nightmare."

"I had to." He chuckled. "Big bastard wouldn't eat and nearly stomped one of the stableboys when he tried to groom him. And the puppy whined incessantly when he couldn't find you at evening meal."

As if sensing they spoke of him, the puppy yipped and charged forward, but Ailean easily caught him before he slid right out of the cave. "You ever going to name this little one?" he asked as he placed him back on the floor and patted him back inside.

"Name him?"

"You have to name him, Shalin. We can't keep calling him 'puppy.' Especially once he gets to be about two or three hundred pounds."

Ailean slid his hand under hers, big fingers intertwining with her smaller ones.

"I've missed you, Shalin. I've missed you so very much."

She closed her eyes, trying to block out the sound of his voice and the words. But she didn't have the heart to shake his hand off. She liked how it felt against hers.

Ailean leaned in close and nuzzled her neck. "Let me stay the night, Shalin."

"I—"

"I promise I won't Claim you until you want me to."

She snorted. "So sure I'll want you to?"

"Not sure. Hopeful."

He kissed a trail down her neck to her shoulder, tugging the dress down a bit so he could toy with the flesh beneath.

"If I let you stay," she whispered, already losing the battle, "you know it won't mean anything."

Ailean reached around, sliding his hand into her hair and gripping the back of her head. He forced her to look at him. "We both know that's a lie. But if it makes you feel better this night, I won't argue." His gaze traveled to her mouth. "Gods," he moaned, "I've missed you, Shalin."

Shalin opened her mouth to speak, to tell him to go before she lost any more of her heart to him, but before she could get the words out, he kissed her. And, as always, her human body nearly burst into flames from the passion of it.

She couldn't fight him. Not when she'd missed him so much.

So she released herself into that kiss. At least for the moment, she let go the anger and stubbornness and simply unleashed the desire she'd been bottling up for days.

Gods, he truly had missed her. Just the feel of her mouth on his or the way she pressed her body into his. Whether human or dragon, she always fit him perfectly. For days he'd been longing for her, following his kin's dictate that the time wasn't right. His aunts were insistent. "When a dragon pushes a dragoness, he ends up very lonely . . . and very bloody."

Without prompting, Shalin straddled his waist, her knees on either side of him. She dug her hands into his hair and kissed him with as much need as his own.

Desperate and unable to wait, Ailean pulled the skirt of her simple peasant dress out of his way and entered her in one powerful thrust. He found her wet and hot, more than ready for him.

Shalin wrapped her arms around his shoulders, buried her nose in his neck, and it all felt so perfect. Ailean didn't move. They simply held still like that.

When Shalin began to shyly kiss his neck and jaw, Ailean pulled back a bit to look at her. "Tell me what I did wrong." When she only stared at him, he said again, "Tell me what I did wrong and I'll do whatever necessary to make it right."

Her gaze lowered until she seemed firmly focused on his neck and she admitted, "You didn't listen to me. I'm ignored by everyone. I never thought I'd be ignored by you as well."

"I didn't ignore you."

She gave an adorable little snort and looked away from him completely.

"I didn't ignore you," he said again. "But I was fighting for my life. For our future. I knew if I'd let you go, you wouldn't come back."

Those bright golden eyes suddenly locked on him and he could see the bitter anger in them. "Isn't that my right? To choose my own lovers, my own mate? Or do you wish to control that, as Adienna does?"

"Don't throw her at me, Shalin. That's not fair and you know it. Don't you see or are you so blind? I would have broken any law, destroyed any army, done *anything* to keep you as my own."

"Why?"

"Why what?"

"Why are you so determined to 'keep me'? Is it because I'm sweet and innocent like the puppy? Or solid and reliable like Dragon's Gold? A good work horse to breed you sons?"

And it was at that very moment, before he could stop himself, that he laughed at her.

Snarling in outrage, Shalin tried to scramble out of his arms, but he grabbed her around the waist and kept her right on his lap and his cock.

"Oh, no, you don't. You'll not run away from me again until we're done here. Until you hear everything I have to say."

"Then say it and let me go."

"Fine, then. You're not sweet, Shalin. Oh, I know you fool everyone else into thinking you are, but I know better. And you? Like Dragon's Gold? More like that beast you love sitting in his chamber plotting his next attack."

She gasped in anger, but his grip merely tightened on her waist, holding her still.

"You're just like him, you know. Just like Nightmare. Exactly. He, too, stands by appearing placid and mild. Then, when you get close enough to touch him, he proves how dangerous he truly is. Just like you. Nor can I call you a reliable work horse since I never see you actually working, lazy sow."

"Ailean!"

"Anytime I look for you, I always find you in the library reading. I'm relatively certain three hundred years from now that's exactly where I'll find you still." He chuckled again. "You're the most dangerous kind of dragon, Shalin. Like the sand dragons, you blend into your environment and you wait. You wait until the very last second, until there's no hope for escape or mercy, and then you strike."

Shalin shook her head, confused. "If I'm so horrible—"

"I never said you were horrible. I said you were dangerous."

"And a lazy sow!"

"You are a lazy sow," he taunted back. "A spoiled royal, expecting everyone to serve *you*." And he punctuated that "you" by slapping her ass . . . rather hard.

Startled into action, she reached for his face with fingers bent into human claws but Ailean easily caught her hands and forced them behind her back, laughing the entire time.

"You're a bastard!" she hissed.

"A mad bastard, according to my kin." He blinked and with false shock said, "Why, Shalin? You're getting even wetter! Enjoy that slap, did you?"

She screamed and fought to pull her arms away.

"Gods," he gasped. "Like a vice. You like a bit of a struggle too, I see. And," he added before kissing her throat, "you like when I won't let you go."

"Lies," she moaned, melting against him. "These are all lies."

He moved up her throat, across her chin and cheek. He held her arms crossed behind her back but his fingers continued to stroke her skin, teasing her.

Ailean rocked up into her while he pulled her body down. Shalin threw her head back, the feel of him inside her nearly more than she could bear.

"Kiss me, Shalin," Ailean panted. "Kiss me now."

She looked at him then, but didn't understand what she saw. What she knew he was trying to tell her with his expression alone. Yet even though she didn't understand, she was still drawn to him as she'd never been drawn to another. And, she feared, as she never would be again.

Shalin kissed him and the power of it tore through them both. Holding her arms tighter, Ailean slammed her down as he pushed up, the rhythm of it bringing her to climax within seconds, her surprised screams disappearing into Ailean's mouth. He groaned in absolute pleasure and kept going, kept taking her. She exploded a second time, reduced to nothing more than whimpers and soft mewling.

Finally, when she didn't think she could take much more from him, he brought her down hard and held her in place as he climaxed inside her. His face buried against her neck, he groaned and gasped as his pleasure seemed to roll on and on, yanking her over the edge a final time. She nearly passed out from the intensity of it and could do nothing more than let her body go limp against his.

Ailean released his grip on her arms and Shalin brought them forward, too weak to do much of anything but drop them around his shoulders.

"Oiy," he said softly. "Lazy sow."

She knew she should be insulted but she was simply too tired to argue with him at the moment. "What?"

"There's another reason I like to keep you around."

"And that is?"

"I love you."

Shalin tensed at the words, but Ailean's hands rubbed her back, soothing her. "Sssh. No need to panic. I just wanted you to know everything for when you make your decision.

"I'll stay the night," he added.

Arms around him, Shalin laid her head against his shoulder and nodded.

14

Shalin awoke early to the puppy scratching at her head. She dragged herself up and gave him water and food. She checked on Nightmare, who seemed to be enjoying his solitary life quite well. She gave him some fresh water and hay before pulling on another little frock left by Ailean's kin. Once dressed, she set off to find Ailean.

It had been a long and delightful night with the dragon. He hadn't let her get much sleep but she didn't really feel the need to complain about it. Besides, after their night, she'd come to a decision. But there was one thing she had to do first, and she wanted to let Ailean know.

Eventually she tracked him down by the cave entrance. Still human as well, he stood naked at the very edge, staring out over the land. She walked up to him and immediately knew something was wrong.

"What is it?"

Ailean nodded toward the east.

She looked and immediately her heart fell. "I see lightning."

"And not a cloud in the sky."

Shalin let out a little sigh. "I guess Theodoric's kin didn't abide by his decision."

"I had a feeling they wouldn't."

She nodded. "As did I." Shalin began to pull off the dress,

preparing to change and not wanting to ruin it, but Ailean stopped her.

"No."

"Why not?"

"If you shift, and they catch up to you, they'll take at least one of your wings. Stay human as long as you can." He took her hand and dragged her back inside. "Take Nightmare back to the castle."

"No." She stopped, and he turned to face her. "If I go there, they'll only follow."

"They'll go there anyway. I need you to protect the castle and my people."

"Me? How can I protect them?"

"Think of something," he said plainly, again dragging her toward where they'd bedded for the night and where Nightmare was standing. "You've read enough books. You must have some ideas."

He stopped long enough to open the gate built into the cavern walls and let Nightmare out. Shalin quickly grabbed the puppy, but Ailean shook his head.

"He'll be safer here."

She nodded and placed him back on the ground. Ailean again grabbed her hand and pulled her out of the chamber and down deep into the catacombs, Nightmare right behind them. It took some time, but eventually she saw a shaft of light and she finally knew how he and his kin had been getting in and out of this cave. Which quickly brought her to another realization.

"This was your mother's cave, wasn't it?"

"Aye. I was born here." And close to where his mother had died.

Once outside, he released her hand and she mounted Nightmare's back and took firm hold of his mane.

"You know your way back?"

"Aye."

"Then go. Protect our people, Shalin."

Ailean slapped Nightmare's rump, forcing her horse to sprint off into the forest.

* * *

Ailean waited until they were far enough away, then he shifted and grabbed hold of the outside cave wall. He easily climbed it until he reached the top. Then he lay flat against it, using his gods-given skill to change his coloring to blend into the rock face.

He waited, and it wasn't long before four of them came into sight. Ailean closed his eyes, his other senses taking over. Their scent moved closer, but Ailean waited until he heard their wings and felt the air around him move. When he knew they'd passed him, Ailean rose up into the air and grabbed one, his arm wrapping around the Lightning's throat. The outsider roared and his comrades turned to face them. That's when Ailean unleashed a ball of flame that forced them back. While he had the moment, Ailean flipped the smaller dragon in his arms upside down and used his talons to rip apart his soft underbelly.

Ailean had only just reached inside the screaming dragon and yanked out his intestines when a harsh bolt of lightning hit him in the shoulder. He dropped his prey and slammed into a tree, the leaves surrounding him, momentarily confusing him. Once he'd pulled himself out, another Lightning waited for him.

Before Ailean could react, the bastard unleashed a bolt of lightning aimed right at his head. Ailean began to move out of its way when a glint of metal momentarily blinded him. He jerked to the side and his vision cleared. One of his aunts hovered in front of him, her large shield up. The lightning hit it and bounced off, slamming back into the sender.

"Go!" his aunt yelled. "I've got them. Go!"

Nightmare tore through the forest while Shalin held on to his mane and kept low. She did know the way back, but she didn't need to.

The horse kept close to the trees, using them as cover, and kept away from the clearings. But no matter what they did, unless they wanted to go days out of their way, they'd have to cross the clearing near the lake.

And, as Shalin had predicted, as soon as Nightmare made it out of the forest, he had to scramble to an abrupt halt. They dropped from the sky, stretching out in a line from the lake, and across a good portion of the clearing. They didn't attack. They didn't want her hurt.

They wanted her to shift, hoping she'd panic and try to go over them. The glint of their sharpened weapons told her exactly what they'd do. With one wing, she wouldn't be going anywhere and then they could carry her wherever they'd like. She'd read that's how they kept dragonesses they stole, but Shalin had always hoped those were merely lies told by their enemies. Now she saw there was truth to it. And although Theodoric obviously had hoped for more from his kin, some of the old ways were simply too hard to give up when desperate. For although they could sate their lust with a human, they could never breed with one.

"Dragoness," one said, and the voice sounded familiar. She remembered him.

"You're Theodoric's brother."

"Aye. Erdmann. Twelfth oldest."

Shalin didn't even want to know how many they had in total to warrant that answer.

"Theodoric won't be happy with what you've done here today," she told him.

"Not at first. But once we battle for the right to be your mate, he'll understand."

"Ailean will come for me." And she knew it to be true. She knew it with all her heart. "He'll destroy all of you to get me back."

"We smell him on you," one of the others remarked. "But I'd bet gold he hasn't marked you. So how attached could he be?"

A few of them moved in a bit closer, slowly trying to surround her. Nightmare stood perfectly still but Shalin could tell by his tense muscles he knew what was happening; he was just waiting for the right moment.

"It doesn't matter, Shalin the Innocent, if he comes for you," Erdmann told her softly. "The queen of this land will never send an army out to bring back one dragoness. And if he comes alone, he'll die alone."

Slowly, Shalin smiled. She'd heard nothing, she'd always remember that, but still somehow she knew. "Ailean the Wicked needs no army to bring me back—and he *never* fights alone." Her smile grew wide. "He has his kin."

Moving as silently as the smallest mouse, Kyna landed on Erdmann's back, bringing her tall steel shield down with her. She slammed it into his neck, slamming him to the ground. The sharp end of her shield rammed into the purple scales with such force it ripped through them and into the flesh until it was buried in the dirt and Erdmann's head thudded to the ground.

Kennis landed on the back of another dragon and buried her lance in his spine.

Kyna looked over at Shalin and Shalin no longer saw anger. At least, not toward her. "Go!" Kyna ordered, jumping off Erdmann's still flailing body as the blood from his neck continued to spay across the clearing.

Nightmare must have understood Kyna because he took off with no prompting, running under and around the battling dragons as more of Ailean's kin dropped from the skies, weapons in hand, and ready to kill.

They tore back to the castle and burst through the courtyard gates as bells rang in warning, and Ailean's human soldiers prepared for battle, the servants scrambling for someplace safe to hide.

Nightmare slid to a halt right in front of Madenn.

She let out a breath when she saw Shalin on the horse's back. "I feared—"

"I know." Shalin reached down and grabbed a soldier trying to dart by. "Get the gates closed—now."

With a nod, he took off running as Shalin slid off Nightmare's back.

"What good will that do?" Madenn demanded. "They'll simply fly over it."

"Leave that to me. Get everyone—" Shalin cut herself off as she grabbed Madenn around the waist and yanked her out of the way, the bolt of lightning hitting where the woman had been standing.

Shalin pushed her away, staring up at the sky. "Go. Now."

Moving quickly to the center of the courtyard, Shalin finally shifted. Going on memory alone, she drew a circle of ancient symbols in the dirt. Once done, she looked around desperately until she spotted another soldier.

"Your shield," she shouted at him. "Give it to me." He tossed the metal shield at her, and Shalin caught it easily, placing it carefully on the ground inside the circle.

Lightning danced around her, but she knew none would hit her directly since they couldn't afford for her to be hurt. She kept her wings tucked in close to her body and focused all her energy into the shield. As it pulsed to life, she slammed her claw down on it and the metal flattened, turning to liquid. She chanted a recently learned spell and the liquid disappeared inside her hand. It tore through her. Through her organs and veins, tearing up through her lungs.

Shalin raised her other claw, palm up, and liquid burst out and up, heading toward the sky. It exploded over the castle and the courtyard, creating a solid metal bubble over all she visualized. A shield now for the entire structure.

She heard roars of anger, then screams as unleashed lightning bolts slammed back into those who sent them.

"By the gods," she heard Madenn whisper.

For some reason that made Shalin chuckle—just before everything went black and her head took out the front of the castle where she landed.

Ailean held the head while Arranz held the back claws and Kennis happily chopped away at the neck. Once they separated head from body, they let it drop.

It hadn't taken long, wiping out a small army of Lightning dragons. Well, it would have if he'd been fighting with the queen's army. There were rules to follow and those who gave orders to listen to.

But a family free-for-all, as his father liked to call it, usually ended pretty quickly. Although it was quite enjoyable while it lasted.

Glancing around, he saw that his kin had it under control, so he motioned to Arranz and Bideven. "Back to the castle. We need to—"

Ailean abruptly stopped talking. His head tilted to the side as he stared out over the trees toward his home.

"What's that?" he asked his brothers, pointing at the silver thing glinting from the early afternoon sun.

"I . . . I have no idea," Bideven responded. And since he was the smartest of them all, if he didn't know, none of them knew.

Panic flooded through him and Ailean charged forward, heading toward the castle. As he neared, he saw several Lightning dragons lay on the ground. They weren't dead, but they were unconscious.

His brothers were on either side of him, Kyna and Kennis hovering behind him.

Slowly, he moved around the foreign thing above his castle. It fit snuggly against the gate surrounding his castle. A perfect fit. Eventually, not knowing what else to do, Ailean leaned forward a bit and rapped on it with his fist. It was metal. Solid metal.

"What in all the hells is this?"

Arranz tapped his shoulder and pointed to the middle of it. "Brother . . . isn't that your crest?"

It was. The crest his human soldiers wore on their shields and surcoats.

Ailean laid his claw flat against it, and the solid metal suddenly wobbled a bit before dropping away completely. Stunned, he watched the metal shrink and change back into the small human shield it once was, landing with a loud clatter at the clawed feet of Shalin.

"Oh, gods!"

He quickly landed beside her, his brothers and the twins right by his side, Nightmare anxiously pawing the ground near her left shoulder.

"Shalin?" He pushed her hair from her face, leaned in close and said loudly, "*Shalin! Can you hear me?*"

She winced. "Don't scream."

Ailean let out a breath and glanced back at his kin. "She lives."

In answer to that, Shalin coughed and a piece of metal flew out of her mouth, landing near the shield. Arranz picked it up and held it next to a small open hole toward the base.

"Look at that . . . it fits."

"That's it." Kyna stood. "I'm going out beyond the castle gates to kill the rest of the Lightnings. That I understand. This—"

she motioned to the shield Arranz held "—I don't." She took flight, her sister right behind her.

"Shalin . . . what did you do?"

"Did what you told me to. I protected our people."

Ailean gave a small smile. "Yes, luv, you certainly did."

But she didn't answer. She'd passed out again.

15

Shalin woke when she heard arguing. She rolled her eyes. *Can they never get along?*

Glancing around, she realized they had her back in the cave. She lay on a huge pile of furs, a large pitfire nearby, and the disgusting taste of metal still in the back of her throat.

She pushed herself up until she could sit back on her haunches. The cave shook as the arguing between kin became more . . . insistent.

Shalin didn't know what they were arguing about and she didn't care. Instead she focused on finding a bit of parchment and a quill.

Shaking blood out of his eyes, Ailean slammed his fist into one brother's face and used his tail to toss the other across the cave floor.

Bideven jumped up and charged and Ailean lowered himself, waiting for the hit.

But Kyna stepped between them, grabbing both brothers by the hair and shaking. Ailean would have to admit—it hurt.

"Stop it. Both of you." She shoved them apart while Kennis helped Arranz to his feet. "Is this about Shalin?"

Ailean frowned, confused by the question. "No."

"Then what are you three up to?"

The brothers all shrugged. "We were bored," they said at the same time.

Disgusted, Kyna paced away from them. "That's brilliant."

"What's wrong?"

"She's gone," Kennis informed them.

"What do you mean she's—" Ailean pushed past them and walked into the chamber they'd put her in. All that was left—a piece of parchment.

"I'll be back," Bideven read over Ailean's shoulder.

"Is that a promise or a threat?" Arranz asked.

Ailean crumpled the parchment in his hand at the same time he expanded his wings, sending both of his brothers flying across the chamber.

Shalin walked into her father's work chamber and smiled. How could she not when she found the old dragon on his knees and under the enormous wood desk he used to work on? His tail lazily swung back and forth while he dug through books and muttered to himself. Her heart swelled at the sight of him. Even *that* sight. Gods, she loved him so much.

"Father," she said softly, as not to startle him. But he jumped anyway, slamming his head into the desk.

He moved out from under it and smiled at his daughter. "Shalin!"

"Hello, Father."

"What are you doing here? Is everything all right?" He walked closer to her. "You look tired?"

"North dragons came for me."

"Oh, dear." He leaned in a bit, his face solemnly sincere. "I feared as much. Do you need me to protect you?"

Shalin snorted, and her father smirked. "Thank you very much, Daughter."

Covering her snout, Shalin shook her head. "Forgive me, Father. I didn't mean—"

He waved her words away. "We both know I'm no warrior."

"But you'd die to protect me."

"Of course." He hugged Shalin. "You mean everything to me." He kissed her brow. "Sit and you'll tell me why you're here."

Her father motioned to a spot closer to the pitfire.

"Now I have some delicious wine here somewhere. If I could just remember where I put it."

Shalin smiled. Her father misplaced everything. It used to drive her poor mother insane.

"Ahh. Here." He grabbed two goblets and what looked to be a very old bottle of wine before he sat down across from his daughter.

"Are you hungry?"

"Not really."

"Like your mother with that. Won't eat when something worries you." He pushed the filled goblet closer to her with the tip of his claw. "Drink then talk."

She sipped the wine. "It's very good."

"I found it just the other day. I think I put it away three or four hundred years ago." He shrugged. "Or maybe it was last week. I never remember."

Her father sipped his wine and said, "So what is it, Shalin?"

"I've made a decision."

"About Ailean?"

She nodded. "He told me he loves me."

"And do you love him?"

"I do."

"Then why the hesitation to admit you want him as your mate?"

"Father, they call him Ailean the Whore."

"Aye. They do. They also call him Ailean the Deadly. Ailean the Powerful. Ailean the Decimator, which is my personal favorite. He has many names you can be proud of." Her father thought for a moment. "If you're a dragon," he added for good measure.

"But there are so many of them, father. There's Ailean, his two brothers, an untold number of aunts and uncles. Cousins. And the twins. I'm not used to so many around me."

"It's time you had kin of your own, Shalin. You've never been like your mother and me."

That surprised her more than she could say. "I haven't?"

"No. Don't you think a father knows? You were lonely. And

bored. When the queen asked for a companion for her daughter, I sent you there thinking it would be good for you to get out and meet others. I had no idea the princess was a vindictive little bitch, though."

Shalin almost spit up the wine she just drank. "Father!"

"It's true. If I'd known how bad she was, royalty be damned."

"It was a good experience. I've had access to books and knowledge I never would have, had I not been part of the court."

Her father smiled at her attempts to soothe him. "And you've become quite the diplomat as well."

Shalin laughed. "I guess I have."

"The Cadwaladr Clan needs that, Shalin. They need *you*. Ailean needs you."

"He does?"

"Gods, lass. Are you that oblivious?" She couldn't believe her father, of all dragons, had the nerve to actually say that. "He's lost his heart to you, Shalin. Make no mistake."

"And I've lost my heart to him, Father. That's why I've decided to stay with him." She placed the glass down and ran her claws through her hair. "But—"

"But what, Shalin? What has you so worried?"

"I promised her. Promised I'd become an Elder and I doubt I can do that if I'm the mate of Ailean the Whore. His reputation alone will—"

"Promised who?"

"Mother. Before she died. I promised her."

Her father stared at her for several long moments, then said, "She's dead, Shalin."

"Father!"

"She is. I miss her every day, but she's dead. And I will be soon enough. Will you go on living for me as well? Long after I've gone?"

"I don't want to disappoint her."

"It's impossible to disappoint the dead. You made promises to a dying dragoness when you were barely fifty winters." Actually thirty, but why argue with him now? "Still a hatchling, in my estimation."

"And you, Father?" she asked the question that bothered her more than anything. "Will I disappoint you?"

"Disappoint me? If you don't become an Elder? I'll be more disappointed if you don't allow yourself some happiness."

Annoyed that her father saw some things so clearly, she muttered, "I never said Ailean made me happy."

Her father laughed, his old voice cracking. She remembered when it was strong and clear, ringing out through the cave chambers.

"If he didn't make you happy, you wouldn't be worried about staying or going. You would have already left. Sweet the world may see you as, Daughter, but I know better. And so does that frighteningly large dragon you love, I'd wager. You always get what you want in the end. Not only that—" Her father took her goblet and poured what was left of her wine into his glass. "—you bring out the best in each other. There are some who bring out the worst, but you and Ailean . . ." He nodded. "A good, solid match."

Shalin threw up her claws in exasperation. "I've tried to kill him. And I've tried to pull the hair out of his head. Actually, I've tried to kill him twice—although that first time was a necessity."

"And both times, I daresay he most likely deserved it. But you're dealing with the Cadwaladr Clan now, my love. They don't want the weak in their bloodline. Every time you fight him, challenge him, you make him yours. And, if I thought for a minute he meant nothing to you or he was a bad match, I'd tell you to send him a very stern letter and get back to your studies. But he means everything to you, Shalin, and we both know it."

She sighed in resignation. "True."

"And think of it this way—among that family, you'll always be the smartest."

"*Father!*"

"Yes, dear?"

"So you're just going to sit here? And wait?"

"Yes," Ailean stated to Bideven—yet again. "I'm just going to sit here and wait."

He thought when he began sharpening his swords and spears, his brothers and cousins would leave him be. No such luck.

"And what if she doesn't come? What if she stays in her school?"

"Then she'll have made her decision."

One of his cousins angrily tapped a finger against the Great Hall's worn wood table. "I say we tear the school down stone by stone until she agrees to come back to you."

Ailean held his blade close to his face and studied the edge, examining it for any nicks or jagged edges. "And why would I do that, cousin?"

"So she'd understand her place belongs with you."

"Should I cut off one of her wings too, so she can't escape? Then we can be just like the Lightnings."

"I never said—"

"No. You didn't. But you might as well have."

"The full moon is tonight, brother," Bideven pointed out—yet again.

"Yes. I'm well aware of that fact."

"And if she doesn't come tonight, Ailean? Or any night? Then what will you do? Find another?"

"There is no other, Arranz. We both know that."

"Then perhaps our cousin is right. Perhaps—"

"No. This is her decision to make. I ignored her wishes once before and she cut my throat. And that I'd happily risk again, but I won't risk losing her."

As one, all of the kin cluttering his Great Hall began shouting at him, telling him what they thought he ought to do. Most of it involving violence against anyone who would possibly step between him and Shalin.

But Ailean's patience waned, and in one movement, he stood and brought the blade of his favorite broadsword down on the thick oak table, splitting it into two.

Not surprisingly, that brought immediate silence.

"Now," he said calmly, "I'll ask again. Does anyone else have anything to say?"

"No," they all said as one.

16

It took Shalin a bit longer to get back to Kerezik, since her father decided to drink a bit more than was good for him and she had to stay to ensure he didn't pass out. But she had a few hours before the moon would rise. Enough time for something to eat and some time to talk to Ailean before tonight. Before he made her his.

She landed outside the castle gates and shifted. A guard standing outside immediately handed her a robe. What she found fascinating was that he wouldn't look at her.

"Something wrong?"

"No, ma'am."

"All right." She pulled the robe on and tied it at the waist. The gates immediately opened and she walked inside. It took her only moments to realize that, although they all nodded to her in greeting, no one looked her in the eyes.

Madenn met her on the stairs, a basket of warm bread in her hands. "Don't worry. They'll get over it."

"I scared them."

"A bit. But they're grateful. Give them time. Our ancestors were scared of Ailean in the beginning as well."

Wincing at the state of the front of Ailean's castle where her head had crashed into it, she asked, "Is Ailean in his room?"

"No," Kyna told her from inside the castle walls where a makeshift door had been erected. "He's not here."

Patting Madenn on the shoulder, Shalin walked into the Great Hall. "Where is he, then?"

"Out with his brothers. He should be back soon."

"You just left," Kennis accused.

"That's between me and Ailean."

"Fair enough."

Shalin nodded at the two and walked toward the stairs. She had her foot on the first step when she was propelled forward. She never hit the stairs, though, as hands gripped her tight and pinned her arms behind her back.

Looking over her shoulder at the twins, "What do you think you're doing?"

"Handling this."

The pair forced her up the stairs as Shalin tried to shake them loose. "You can't do this!"

"We can," Kyna told her.

"We are," Kennis confirmed.

"We know you two. You'll talk and talk and the full moon will pass. That won't work for us."

"*Work for you?*"

"Aye. And don't screech so. Makes me head ache. Don't it, Kennis?"

"That it does, Kyna."

"I'll shift," she threatened. "I'll shift and take this whole blasted building with me."

The twins stopped walking. Kyna moved right up next to her and said against her ear, "And kill all these lovely humans? Would you really do that, Shalin the Innocent?"

"From protector to murderer in the beat of a heart," Kennis said with a smirk.

Shalin glared at them. "I hate you both."

"Hate us today. Love us tomorrow," Kyna laughed while she and her sister shoved Shalin through Ailean's bedroom door.

Ailean walked out of the stables and into Madenn, who was about to walk in.

"What?" he grumbled.

"Still in a bad mood, I see?"

"And it's getting worse. What is it?"

Madenn gave a small smile. "She's back and—oh!"

Ailean kissed her forehead and ran off toward the castle. He was up the stairs and heading toward his room when the twins stumbled out, laughing hysterically. But when they saw him, they immediately stopped, which had his eyes narrowing in suspicion.

"What have you done?"

Kyna and Kennis passed him, both patting his shoulders.

"Just helping," Kyna said on a giggle.

"But you better get in there," Kennis added.

"Before she tears the walls down around us."

Then they took off running.

Ailean walked to the door and opened it. His first thought was, *When did I get a headboard?*

Shalin heard the door open again, but when she looked over her shoulder, it wasn't the twins.

"Oh, gods," she groaned, then again desperately tried to get loose of the leather bonds the twins had tied around her wrists and to the headboard that, according to the twins, had only been put up that afternoon while Ailean was away.

And she thought the North dragons had laid in wait for her.

"Well, well, well," Ailean said jovially, closing the door behind him. "Look what we have here. A gift for Ailean!"

"I'm going to kill *all of you*. It will be my mission in life."

Bad enough they'd tied her up at all, but they'd bound her wrists so close to the wood headboard that she faced the wall. And although they'd tossed a fur over her, she still had her ass sticking out to the world—and to Ailean!

"Now, now, my sweet, *innocent* Shalin. No need to get so testy."

Shalin closed her eyes as Ailean slowly pulled the fur off her body.

"I do have the *best* family," he groaned.

"Ailean—"

"Do you know why the ancestors began marking each other while human?"

"I—I never really thought . . ." Ailean's hand brushed down her back to her thigh. "I have no bloody idea," she laughed, reveling in his touch. The way his fingers stroked her.

"Damn." And he laughed with her. "I was hoping one of us would know."

The bed dipped as Ailean moved in behind her. He brushed his head against her back, his hair trailing along her skin like the finest silk, his lips against her spine.

"Where should I mark you, Shalin?"

He'd already stripped and the heat from his naked body nearly seared hers. His hands landed on either side of her own, his big body braced over hers.

Ailean pressed his hips forward and Shalin groaned at the contact.

"Tell me."

"I don't care," she finally admitted.

"The breast?" One rough fingertip circled her nipple, toying with it. "Or perhaps the neck." He kissed her on the back of her neck while his hand moved lower. "Perhaps your belly or something lower . . ."

Shalin pushed back against him. "I don't care where, Ailean," she panted out. "Just make me yours."

Ailean briefly buried his face between Shalin's shoulder blades and let what she'd said wash over him. She wanted him as her own. She wanted him until their ancestors called them home.

"And Ailean?" she said softly. "I do love you."

That was more than he could stand. More than he could ever hope to handle.

Rising up, he dug his hand into her hair, turning her head so he could kiss her, plundering her mouth with his own. Their tongues tangled and stroked until Shalin pulled back.

"Don't make me wait. Not a second longer."

He didn't. Kissing his way down her back, Ailean gripped her breasts with both hands. He massaged them and toyed with the nipples, loving how hard they were against his fingers.

Ailean kissed her lower back where her hips met her ass. He released one breast and used that hand to stroke her pussy, already wet and hot and all his.

Then, when he had her writhing, had her begging, he dragged his tongue across her lower back. Shalin gasped and groaned in pain even as her body shook under his, even as her pussy gripped his fingers. He stroked her clit while his tongue continued its journey across her lower back.

"Gods," she moaned desperately, her body shaking. "Ailean . . ."

"I love you, Shalin," he told her as he pushed her over the edge, the mark of his Claiming burned into her flesh. "I'll always love you."

"I know," she sobbed before she came all over his hand.

Then Shalin was his.

Reaching up, he untied her bonds, determined to keep the leather thongs for later. Ailean grabbed Shalin's hips and flipped her over while pulling her down on the bed and under him. He kissed her and pushed his cock inside her, gasping at how hot and tight she was.

He wiped the tears from her cheeks with his thumbs and rested his forehead against hers. "I love you."

She smiled, her hands cupping his face. "Finish it, Ailean."

Ailean started off slow, taking his time so he could enjoy every second. He kissed her as he drove into her, wanting to touch every part of her. Shalin's legs wrapped around his waist, her grip on him near-painful.

"Gods, Shalin," he told her, "you feel so good."

He took her harder, deeper, until Shalin climaxed again. He came with her, his head thrown back, his own body shaking in release.

Gasping, exhausted, Ailean collapsed on top of her. He grinned when he heard her grunt, laughed when she started hitting him.

He rolled onto his back, bringing her with him. "I only needed a moment to relax."

"You're as big as an ox," she growled at him.

"I was recovering," he said before he pulled her close and started kissing her throat.

Shalin giggled and pushed at his shoulders. "I thought you were recovering!" she squealed desperately.

Grinning, Ailean pushed her to her back, "I recover quickly."

"I don't."

"Guess we'll have to work on that," he sighed as he sunk [sic] into her again.

*　　*　　*

Shalin stared up at the ceiling in the dark bedroom and wondered how late it was. She'd lost track of time hours ago. Ailean simply didn't give her time to think about anything but him.

"Ravenous beast," she whispered softly, smiling.

"You called?" Ailean asked, reaching for her again.

"No!" she squealed, slapping at his hands. "Rest! I need rest!"

He snuggled in close. "Fine. Another ten minutes."

"Very generous."

"Keep that tone and it goes to five."

Ailean's arms were wrapped tight around her, keeping her warm and safe.

"Where did you go this morning?" he asked, one hand stroking her forearm.

"To see my father." She turned her head and looked at Ailean. "He means too much to me not to have talked to him before—"

"There is nothing to explain to me, Shalin. I understand." And he did. She could see that in his eyes. "You know, Shalin, there's this nice little cave not far from here, close to my mother's. If we fixed it up nice, think he'd mind living there?"

"It—it depends," she stuttered in surprise. "Knowing my father, we could probably move him and all his things without him ever complaining as long as we don't disturb his current work."

"We'll do that, then. I worry about him. He's older and alone. I know you'd feel better with him closer."

Letting out a shaky breath, Shalin said, "That would mean much to me, Ailean. Thank you."

"Nothing to thank." He kissed her temple, her cheek. "Family is family, luv."

He stared at her intently and said, "Rest is over, Shalin."

"That was not ten minutes."

"Too bad."

She batted at his hands and slipped out from under him. "Wait. Wait. I want to see."

She scrambled off the bed and went to the tall mirror in the corner of the room. She had to wipe off all the dust first since it seemed never to have been used and probably belonged to the humans who'd once lived there.

Turning so her back faced the mirror, she looked over her

shoulder at what Ailean had burned into her flesh. "Huh," she said in surprise.

"What's wrong?"

"It's so small." It truly was. A lounging dragon burned into her lower back. The point of its tail aimed right above the cheeks. Over the years she'd seen and heard of some very elaborate Claimings. Brands covering an entire arm or leg, sometimes an entire back or chest. One day, she'd mark Ailean as her own as well, but not right away. It was a male thing and she didn't bother trying to understand it.

"You don't like it?" He stood in front of her, his hands on her waist and leaning over her shoulder to take a better look.

"No, no. I do like it. Very much. It's just so . . . so . . ."

"So . . . what?"

"Subtle."

He glared down at her. "Your point being?"

"Nothing."

"You don't think I'm subtle?"

"I didn't say that." But the laughing wasn't helping, either.

"Your rest is over, dragoness."

"I'm not done—"

"Later," Ailean told her, walking her back to the bed until he could push her on it.

But as Ailean moved over her, they both stopped and stared at the window.

"What is that?" she asked.

"You don't want to know."

Slipping out from under him again, Shalin walked to the window and pushed out the thick glass encased in a metal frame. In shock, she stared down into the courtyard.

"Told you," Ailean said, now standing behind her, again looking over her shoulder.

They all stood out there, all the Cadwaladr kin, cousins, aunts, uncles, and brothers of Ailean. Now her kin. Ale in hand, they all stood outside the window—singing.

For the life of her, she'd never be able to tell a soul what they'd been singing—it was unintelligible—but she knew it came from their drunken hearts. And gods, they were so very drunk.

"Congratulations, you two," Kyna called up.

"We're so happy," Kennis added, sobbing for no apparent reason.

"Does this mean we're royals too?" another cousin asked.

"Let's fly to Devenallt Mountain and ask the queen!" cried his aunt Briaga. "Who's with me?" She didn't get far, though. She fell backward seconds later. Out cold.

Shalin grinned, trying not to laugh instead, until one of Ailean's uncles called out, "The royal there . . . she's got nice tits, eh?"

Ailean kissed Shalin's cheek and let out a sigh. "Welcome to the family, luv."

She looked down at her chest and back up into his beautiful face. "Thank you?"

Epilogue

"Oiy, brother!" The bed went up and crashed back down. "It's time."

Shaking his head and yawning, Ailean dragged himself out of bed. "Good. I want my mate back where she belongs." Under him. Over him. As long as he was in her, all was right.

"So selfish," Arranz chided.

"I'm not the one been complaining about no stories at mealtime, you whiny bastard."

Ailean tugged on a pair of leather leggings and walked past his brother and out into the hall. At midday, the house was its usual busy self. Servants and young ones under foot, along with kin who'd dropped by for whatever reason. He walked past one of the bedrooms and saw one of his younger sons in human form leaning out the window, flirting with one of the local girls.

Arranz smiled and stepped back as Ailean snuck up behind the young dragon. He stood behind him a good five seconds and the little fool, so busy trying to seduce the blacksmith's daughter, didn't even realize he was behind him.

Grinning, he slammed his hands against his son's back, sending him flipping out the window. So stunned, the little bastard didn't even shift to dragon and instead landed on the hard, unforgiving ground. Although the girl moved fast enough out of the way. Not too bad for a human.

"You need to learn to pay attention, boy!" Ailean yelled down, earning a snarl and a curse that would have his mate yanking someone's tail in reprimand.

Brushing his hands together, he walked back into the hallway and to his brother.

"I'm surprised your children haven't tried to kill you in your sleep, Ailean."

"They hate me now, but they'll learn to appreciate me when they go into battle."

The brothers went down the stairs and across the hall. Ailean took flight as soon as he made it outside, and he arrived at his destination in minutes. He walked into the brightly lit cave, now decorated with torches and tapestries along the walls. Shalin had made the space her own and he was happy to have life in it again as it had when his mother breathed.

And this time, the cave was always protected. Shalin and their offspring were always protected, even when he was leagues away. He never worried for their safety because his kin made sure he never had to.

Ailean walked past a new batch of puppies, direct descendants of Shalin's first dog—whom she never did get around to naming. A few more steps brought him past the cavern where she kept her favorite horse. Right now that meant direct descendant of Nightmare whom Shalin called Dragon's Heart but whom everyone else called Insane Bastard.

Ailean found Shalin in the hatching chamber. With gentle flame, she blew on the egg and brushed it with her claw while holding a book with the other. After eight sons and daughters already, the whole process seemed to have lost most of its allure for his Shalin.

"Well?" he asked, walking in.

"Give it time," she said without raising her head from her book. "You're too impatient."

"I miss you," he growled and Shalin smiled, finally looking up at him.

"And I miss you, you old bear. But only a dragoness can protect her egg properly."

"What does that mean?"

"It means yelling at your own that they need to get a move on because you're bored is not how the life-giving process works, my love."

"That was one time."

"You're much better once they're out of the egg than while they're in it. But barely."

The shell cracked and Shalin grinned, motioning him forward. He'd missed the last three because he'd been off in battle against the Northland dragons. But he'd been very glad to be here for this one.

He stood over the egg and watched as a small black fist punched through the shell. He went to remove more of it but Shalin slapped at his claws.

"Leave it be, Ailean. They must do this on their own."

He sighed impatiently and stared. A few more punches. Several long pauses. And then the top of the shell broke off. Ailean leaned over even farther and looked in. Pitch-black eyes nearly covered by pitch-black hair glared up at him.

"Is he supposed to frown like that?"

Shalin leaned over like her mate. "He's serious, is all." She leaned in a bit closer. "And I'm not sure he likes you."

Ailean smirked. "Thank you."

The hatchling finally looked away from him and at his mother. The glare faded to a much more neutral frown and Shalin reached for him.

"Let's see you, little one." She lifted him up and said, "A male."

"Another one? We need more daughters."

"Must you complain? I've given you nine all together. Four of them daughters. You're lucky you got any hatchlings at all."

His son wrapped around Shalin's neck, his long black tail looping around her arm.

"Maybe this one will be a scholar, eh?" Ailean said hopefully.

"I don't think we should hold our breath for that anymore."

Ailean leaned in close to get a better look at his son. "What will we call him?"

"I don't know."

The dragon turned and glared at his father and then unleashed a puff of smoke that, when he was older, would be a deadly ball of flame.

Coughing, Ailean stepped back. "Little bastard."

Shalin laughed out loud, no longer remotely shy after so many years around his kin. "Ailean," she chastised. "Be nice. You're probably scaring him."

"This one doesn't look scared of a damn thing." A good warrior he'd make with his horns already growing in. Although Ailean did hold out hope that at least one of their offspring would be more reader than born killer. At least for Shalin's sake.

"I know what we can name him," he finally said, once he brushed the soot off his snout.

"It better not be 'little bastard.' "

"No. No. That name your father always liked. What was it?"

Nearly a decade ago, Shalin had lost her father and it had devastated her. And although she'd gotten through it as they all knew she would, Ailean still knew she missed the old brown dragon every day.

Shalin looked at her son. "Bercelak. He always liked the name Bercelak."

"Aye. That's the one." They'd already named their oldest Baudwin, so Ailean thought they could use one her father had liked. "What do you think, little bastard? Bercelak the Black fit you well enough?"

"Stop calling him little bastard."

"He is a little bastard."

Glaring at her mate, she pulled her son off her neck and into her arms. "Would you like that, my son? To be Bercelak the Black?"

Still too young to answer, the small dragon instead studied his mother intently. Small black claws petting her cheeks, down her snout. She nuzzled him and Bercelak nuzzled her back.

"Aye," she finally said. "I think that name fits him well." She hefted Bercelak in her arms. "He needs to sleep now and, later, he'll feed."

She turned to walk toward the pitfire and that's when the little demon lashed at Ailean with his tail, almost taking out an eye. The glare he gave his father over his mother's shoulder told Ailean all he needed to know about this one.

"You'll stay?" Shalin asked as she stretched out by the fire, her son tucked tight into her arms.

"Aye. I will." Ailean settled in behind her and kissed her neck. "Now tell me what's wrong. You're worried. I hear it in your voice."

"With Adienna on the throne now? Of course I'm worried." But she still tangled her tail with his own—gods, he loved when she did that. Whether as dragon or human, Shalin made every moment they shared perfect.

"Don't be. They'll all be ready when the time comes. Especially this one. Look at that angry face, Shalin. He'll take care of himself just fine."

"Aye, Ailean," Shalin teased, rubbing the frown lines on her son's forehead, "but besides us, who will ever love him with such an angry frown?"

"Who says I love him?"

She slammed her elbow into his stomach so hard he could only gasp. And, for the first time, the little bastard grinned.

"I'll find him someone," Ailean vowed through gritted teeth, watching as his newest son fell asleep against his mother's shoulder.

"Think he'll ever find what we have?" she whispered, her voice sounding drowsy, her body relaxing against his.

Holding his family close to his heart, Ailean whispered back, "We can only hope he'll be that lucky."

SPELLBOUND

Cynthia Eden

1

She summoned him at midnight. The witching hour. Power swept through every inch of Serena Tyme's body, pulsing, growing, and the words of the spell poured from her lips, faster, *faster*.

Her arms shot above her head, and the air crackled with magic. Thunder roared and lightning flashed across the cloudless night sky.

Her eyes squeezed shut, just for one fearful moment, and when her lashes lifted, *he* was there.

The relief that rushed through her body had her trembling.

Then he spoke. "Nice body, sweetheart." Voice deep and rumbling like the thunder. Golden eyes drifted over her skyclad form. Heat flared in those depths, then, voice slightly rougher, he snarled, "Now why don't you tell me who the hell you are and *where the fuck I am.*"

Serena drew in a deep breath and watched the man's eyes dart to her chest. Jeez. Men. All alike—mortal or immortal—they always got distracted by a pair of breasts.

But she hadn't called him across space to ogle her. She crept forward, keeping an anxious eye on him. She knew how much power he possessed, far more than a mere hereditary witch could hope to control. The sooner she explained things to him, the better.

After all, it wasn't an easy task to summon the devil.

The fire she'd built flared higher. Not her magic, *his*. Serena reached for her black robe, belted it quickly.

"You didn't have to dress," he muttered, and his powerful legs were braced apart, arms resting easily at his sides. "But I am *waiting* on my answers."

His tone implied that he wasn't a happy waiting camper. She really hadn't expected him to be, though. She licked her lips, cleared a throat gone dry from chanting and the—flames and said, "M-my name's Serena Tyme. I'm a witch and—"

He grabbed her then. Moved far too fast for her to follow, even with her slightly enhanced senses.

The circle she'd drawn should have held him in place, at least for a few minutes.

But it had failed.

Oh, damn.

His hands locked around her upper arms. A hold too tight to break, but not fierce enough to hurt, not yet. But the threat was in his steely grip, and in the eyes that blazed down at her.

"I know you're a witch." The flames were reflected in his golden stare. A stare that burned brighter every moment. "No one else could have forced me here. Dammit, tell me—"

Her chin lifted. "Look, I'm *answering* your questions, OK?" He'd wanted to know who she was, and well, question one was now answered. As for the second question ... "You're in Atlanta, Georgia." When those eyes of his narrowed, she added, in a questioning tone, "The U.S.?" The guy spoke with no accent, and she had no idea where he had been when her spell had grabbed him. Although the where didn't really matter to her. All that mattered was that he stood before her now.

She saw a muscle flex along the hard, square line of his jaw. Black brows fell low. The brows were a perfect match to the slightly too long, night-black hair that brushed the collar of his shirt. "*Why* am I here, witch?"

Ah, this was the tricky part. She took a moment, letting her gaze dart down his body. He was dressed as any man would have been. Loosely buttoned black shirt. Jeans. Ragged boots. Oh, yeah. He looked normal. Could have been the guy next door.

If the guy next door happened to be the most powerful paranormal being known in the *Other* world.

For, despite what most folks thought, paranormals *did* exist. They lived right alongside the humans. Demons, vampires, and witches like her—they were everywhere. But the humans, well, sometimes they had a hard time seeing what was right in front of them.

But she could see exactly who, or rather *what,* was in front of her.

The man before her had many names. After all, if the legends were true, he'd been roaming the earth for centuries, and he'd continue to roam and fight and raise hell long after she was dust.

Cazador del alma. Soul-hunter. Destroyer.

The rarest of the paranormals, *cazadores* were produced from the mating of witches and all-powerful, level-ten demons—the terrors of the demon world.

Cazadores were gifted with the full powers of a hereditary witch, the full powers of a demon, *and* the soul-hunters, well, they could live forever.

All the better to hunt.

She stared at him, unable to stop the nervous tremble that shook her body.

Hell, when she'd been a kid, her parents had told her that he was the boogeyman.

The immortal who came after the *Other* when they crossed that fine line between right and wrong. Because a *cazador* had more than just witch and demon powers. He was the immortal who could also steal a life away, with but a simple touch.

"Always be good, Serena." Her mother's husky voice echoed in her mind. *"Because the cazador, he comes after witches when they're bad."*

Oh, yeah, the threat of the big, eternal badass had kept her on the straight and narrow for years.

His fingers tightened around her arms. "Are you trying to piss me off?"

Serena blinked. "Uh, no. Really—I—" Oh, hell, what had he wanted to know? Damn, but she was tired. And scared. And so weak.

The first binding had hurt her more than she realized. She'd barely managed to focus enough power for the summoning spell.

When his fingers moved, just a bit higher on her right arm, and he brushed the still tender flesh, she winced.

"Why. Did. You. Summon. Me." Gritted from between his clenched teeth.

Ah, yes. Simple enough answer for that one. "Because I need you."

He glared down at her and she realized his features *could* have been handsome but weren't—no, they were far too hard. As if they'd been carved from ancient stone. Too-sharp cheekbones, nose too long, high brow. Thin lips. Skin a darkened gold—made only more so by the flickering light of the flames.

As she stared at him, that hard mask slackened—just for a moment—and disbelief flashed across his face as he said, "You know what I am."

Of course. Would she have gone to the trouble of bartering for a dark spell if she hadn't?

"You know what I am, and you still summoned me." He shook his head as if he couldn't believe she'd actually called for him. "I bring death." He freed her. Stepped back. Clenched his hands into fists. "I'm not some kind of idiot demon that you can screw around with, sweetheart. I'm—"

"A soul-hunter." Soul-eater. OK, that was the less-than-respectful term. Her voice was soft but firm as she continued, "I *know*. I also know that you're exactly what I need." The others in her coven had said that she was crazy. That she was courting the devil.

Summoning him didn't mean that she could control him, and the *cazadores*, well, they were damn unpredictable.

In fact, until the menacing guy before her had appeared, she'd actually wondered if *cazadores* were just myths. She'd never actually met anyone who'd known a *cazador*, and certain paranormals had sure been crossing that good/evil line at will lately.

Which brought up just why she needed her hunter.

"What is it that you need from me?" The words were a rumble of sound that seemed to shake through her body.

"I need you . . . to save me." The mark on her arm burned with remembered pain. "And to do your damn job and kill the bastard who is after me." Not just her, but her entire coven.

If the *cazador* didn't help her, well, they'd all be dead before Halloween, just a few terribly short days away.

Serena was *not* ready to die. Not without putting up one hell of a fight, anyway.

Because she was one witch who wasn't about to burn easily.

Luis D'Amil shook his head and stared in disbelief at the shapely witch before him.

Dammit. One moment, he'd been sitting in his favorite bar in Cozumel, and the next, he was in the middle of a forest, facing a naked woman.

A woman with a lot of power.

A woman who'd dressed far too quickly.

The witch had ripped him across time and space—hell, the least she could have done was let him look at those pink-tipped breasts a while longer.

The witch had *gorgeous* breasts. It'd been far too long since he'd seen breasts that—

"Are you going to help me?" she demanded, and her voice held a tight, hard edge.

Luis sighed and gave up the tempting image of her bare flesh. "No." He crossed his arms over his chest. "Now do your magic, and get me the hell out of here!" He had a bottle of tequila waiting on him.

Her mouth dropped open. Good lips, he couldn't help but notice. Sexy. Red and full. Just the way he liked 'em. Nice little heart-shaped face. Pretty. Cute nose, even if it did turn up a bit. High cheeks. Wide eyes. Green eyes. *Cat eyes.* Those eyes seemed to glow at him. And her hair . . .

Wild. A thick, curling black mass that skimmed her shoulders. The firelight burned brightly around them, making the red highlights lurking in the darkness of her hair flare to life.

But even if the flames hadn't burned, he would have been able to see perfectly. It was the *cazador's* way.

Made the hunting easier.

His witch was all curves and soft skin. Not too thin—good, he'd never been attracted to a woman he couldn't hold tight. Lush breasts and hips and legs that—

"Didn't you hear me?" she nearly shrieked at him and Luis winced. "I said I need your help. Someone's after me—"

"Then go to the cops. The *Other* are everywhere these days. You'll be able to find a paranormal to help you."

"I don't trust cops."

"No, you don't trust *human* cops."

"I don't trust *any* of them." Said with absolute certainly. Ah, so his witch had experienced a bad run-in with the law, eh? "I've seen cops on the take," she muttered, "humans, *Other*—they can all be bought if the price is right." She exhaled, shaking her head. "Besides, no crime has been committed yet. Even if I went to them—and I'm *not*—what would I say? Someone's trying to bind me? Like they'd care!"

Someone's trying to bind me. Luis stiffened.

Witches were bound all the time. Some willingly because their powers were too much for them to handle. And some, well, *not* so willingly.

Long ago, the binding spell had only been used for protection. To bind those who would do harm. To stop the negative forces and to bind them safely. But the spell had been perverted by many over time, and the old ways were long gone.

"The cops can't help me." She glared at him. "Shit, isn't your job to catch the *Others* who go bad? To stop them from killing?"

Sometimes it was. Sometimes his job was just to clean up the blood left behind and make the humans forget the chaos they'd seen.

"Please." Her voice dropped, and for an instant, Luis swore he saw a flash of tears in her eyes. "I *need* you. My coven—someone's trying to destroy us."

He swallowed, memories flooding through his mind. No, no, this couldn't be—

Serena pulled aside the top of her robe, baring her upper chest, the tempting swell of her breasts. Then she twisted, bringing her right shoulder forward and he saw . . .

The first binding mark.

A long, angry red slash cut across the top of her arm. A slash that could have been made with a red-hot knife.

But had really been made by magic.

"It takes three to bind," she said, but he already knew that.

His mother had been a damn strong witch, and she'd taught him all the magic she knew, both light and dark. "Some sick bastard is out there. I don't know who he is or how he's doing this, but he's binding the members of my coven, one at a time."

A bound witch was a weak one. Perfect prey.

So very easy to kill.

Almost as easy as a human.

"Half of the coven fled when the first mark appeared on their flesh. I don't know how long the others will stay. They're scared, *I'm* scared, and I don't know what the hell to do."

She fixed her robe, tightened the belt, then closed the space he'd put between them. Serena reached for his arm. Her fingers felt so soft against his flesh.

Her scent teased his nostrils. Roses. Lavender. A sweet, light blend. One that reminded him of innocence. Youth. A time long past for him.

Poor little witch. She thought the danger was hiding out there in the night, stalking her.

She didn't realize that the real threat was standing right in front of her.

One touch, just one. If he focused his power, he could drain her dry in an instant.

By the time she gathered the breath to scream, it would be too late.

Soul-eater. Yes, he knew that was what many called him. Because he didn't just hunt. He took. Drained his prey dry until nothing was left but the shell of the body.

No soul. No power. No life.

Because he took everything.

"Three years ago, this same thing happened in LA." Her nails were long and sharp. Red. The hand that clasped him shook. "I wasn't in the coven that was marked, but my aunt—she was." Pain echoed in her voice and he saw the faintest quiver in her lips. "My aunt raised me, *cazador.* Took me in when my parents died." She shook her head. "I was eleven, she was seventeen— *and she raised me,* all those years, all by herself."

The pain was deeper now.

"Then she got marked. I couldn't help her." Rage with the pain. A hard fury. "I couldn't help any of them. The witches in her coven were bound by a force they couldn't fight. Then one by one, they were killed."

His gut clenched. Hell, yeah, he knew about that case. He'd been fighting his ass off in Brazil at the time, because a pack of panther shifters had laid a trap for him and he'd been forced to eliminate them.

One shifter's soul after another.

"Some of the coven tried to run, but it didn't do them any good. They all still *died.*" She drew in a ragged breath. "When the rest of the witches in LA found out, they were scared as hell. Most of the unbound ones cut out of the city—"

"Like you did?" Why else would his little witch be all the way on the other side of the country?

"I couldn't stay in LA without Jayme. I couldn't live in her house, day after day, when she was gone." Serena shook her head, and a twisted smile curved her lips. "Besides, I thought I'd be safe here," she muttered. "And for a while, I was." Her lips, the ones that he really wanted to touch, firmed as her smile disappeared. "Then the asshole showed up here and started marking *my* coven—the only damn family I have any more."

Ah, the coven. To hereditary witches, a coven tie was deeper than blood. The coven was power, security, trust. Life.

"You have to stop him." Serena's pointed little chin lifted into the air. "If you don't, then I'm dead."

He stirred at that, as a wave of tension rolled through him. Why should he care if one more witch—or even a dozen—passed to the next realm? There were others who would take her place.

And yet . . .

Her eyes. There was just something about them. So deep. Greener than the fields near his mother's old home.

Those eyes . . . *innocence.*

No. There was no way the witch was an innocent. Too much knowledge filled her voice, and she'd used the darkest of spells to rip him away from his promised drink.

And the promised fuck that had been waiting for him.

"I will do anything," the witch said, and the desperation on her face and in her words was undeniable. "*Anything,* if you help me and my coven."

Ah, the pleading. He'd heard it before. Too many times to count. Normally, that shit didn't do a thing for him.

Her eyes. What was it about them? The woman was no virgin, not with that ripe body. He could smell her power in the air, and the lush scent of her body.

Sex.

No, not innocence in her eyes, Luis realized.

Hope.

How long had it been since he'd seen that?

"There are thousands of others in this world who could use me," he told her, keeping his voice hard. His hands were fisted because damn if he didn't have the urge to draw her close. To press her tight against him and feel those breasts against his chest. "But I'm not a savior." He'd tried that route once, and fucked up admirably. No, saving wasn't really his bit.

Seeking vengeance, sending monsters to hell, yeah, that was more his deal.

"Help me!" Her nails dug into his skin. For an instant, he imagined the two of them together. A dark room. Rumpled sheets. Her nails digging deeply into his flesh. "I have power, I can give you *anything*—"

Again with that magic word. *Anything.*

A dark, hungry temptation flickered through him. *Because I am my father's son.*

It had been far too long since he'd lain with a witch and tasted the magic on her tongue and sipped the power from her body.

Anything.

Those green eyes . . .

He lowered his head toward hers. She was so small, her head barely came to his shoulders. She didn't back away when he closed that distance. Her eyes widened, but she held his stare.

A fire there. Burning inside her.

He'd always liked to play with fire.

"Are you trying to put me under a spell, witch?" A possibility. Her magic was more focused, even with the first binding mark, than any other witch he'd ever met. The hunger he was feeling, the stirring in his groin, it could be a trick.

Sure, a succubus was far better at laying a sensual trap than a witch, but with the right spell, Serena would still manage to turn him on.

Had managed to turn him on.

He'd been aroused from the first glimpse of her pale skin. As soon as the fog cleared and he'd seen her, he'd wanted to fuck her.

Not a usual response for him.

Killing, yes, that was normal.

But wanting to fuck on first sight, not so typical.

Unless a spell was involved.

Serena licked her lips and the sight of that pink tongue nearly made him groan. "I-I only had enough power left to summon you. I c-can't hold a lust spell now."

He stared into her eyes and let his own power out. *Truth.*

One of his handy talents. A soul-hunter held the power of truth. He could hear lies—the words twisted, grated in his ears. He could discern truth with but a light push of power.

Before he killed, he liked to make certain he was executing the right monster.

He inhaled softly and caught her breath. Tasted her fear and her need.

The witch would do anything to save herself and her coven.

Luis realized he should probably admire that.

But he didn't.

Because the hunger he felt for her was growing too strong. His decision was made in that instant. A choice that came fast and wild—just like the need he felt for the curvy little witch. "I'll find the one after you." It wouldn't be easy. The hunts never were. The psychotics were always smarter than they appeared, twisting and turning and leaving a tangled mess for him to sort out. "But it *will* cost you."

That hope flared even brighter in her gaze and her whole face seemed to light up. Not pretty, *beautiful.* "My coven will—"

"Not your coven, sweetheart." He wasn't interested in the others. No, he only cared about the witch who'd drained her powers to summon him.

And then offered the man feared by all *anything.*

"What do you want?" No fear. Good, because he'd never wanted fear in his women.

"You."

She shook her head. "I don't understand." But the dawning realization was in her eyes and her voice pitched too high in his mind. *Lie.*

Luis didn't call her on the falsehood. There would be time for that, later. Just as there would be time for much, much more. "You will, witch. *You will.*" Because he wasn't just talking about sex. A few hours of mindless pleasure.

He wanted all of her. Body and soul.

The hunt was on.

2

Exhaustion flooded Serena's body, but she walked doggedly forward, putting one foot in front of the other and focusing as hard as she could on not falling face-first onto the ground. She'd barely managed to cleanse the earth and break the remnants of her spell before the last of her power deserted her.

"Uh, is walking around naked out here a real good idea?" The *cazador* spoke from behind her.

She didn't stop. Couldn't, or she just might do that face-first routine. "Look, hunter—"

"Luis." Soft. "Luis D'Amil."

Now she did pause, glancing over her shoulder. This was almost worth a fall. "Where are you from, Luis?" Luis—that was a Spanish name, and it fit with the Spanish designation the hunters had long ago been given. But D'Amil—

"Once upon a time, I grew up in the area you know as Spain." His lips twisted into the faintest of smiles. "As the legends say, many of my kind hailed from that rich land."

Rich in magic. Always had been, but . . . "You don't sound Spanish." His voice was deep and dark, and completely devoid of any accent.

A shrug. "Witch, I've been everywhere on this earth. Languages, accents—after a few hundred years, they all blur."

"But you have to . . . live . . . somewhere now. I mean, you do have a house, or an apartment or *something*, right?"

A shrug. "I travel. There are safe places for me to stay."

I travel. OK, big euphemism for stalking prey. She swallowed. "I didn't . . . ah . . . take you away from your family or anything, did I?" Serena hadn't even thought of that. Oh, damn, but what if he had a wife who was frantic because her hubby had up and vanished? But the guy had just propositioned her. Well, she was ninety percent sure he'd propositioned her, and the jerk had better not have a wife at home who—

His smile died. "I have no family left." Cold. No, *arctic*. Then, "My mother died in the Burning Times."

Oh, shit. *The Burning Times.* Those horror-filled years when witches had been hunted and hundreds, no *thousands* had been put to the flames. She shouldn't ask, really shouldn't, but . . . "Your father?" A level-ten demon was the only sire for a *cazador*, and level tens were all but immortal themselves.

In the demon world, there were several levels of power. The weaker demons were generally considered levels one through three—they barely had powers above a human's inherent psychic gifts. But the big, dangerous bastards who were ranked as level tens—well, those were the guys who could bring true meaning to the old phrase, "Hell on earth." Get them angry enough, and folks around the level tens would literally fry.

"My father died after her. He trusted me to save her. I didn't, and he couldn't live without her," he bit off the words. "See, witch, I'm not a savior—I couldn't spare my mother from the flames."

Her lips parted. *What do I say?* "I-I'm sorry, Luis." And she was. She knew just how much it hurt to lose a loved one to the fire.

He kept talking, as if he hadn't heard her—and maybe he hadn't. "I tried to save her. When I learned what the villagers had planned, I tried to help her. But I was too far away and couldn't get to her fast enough." His eyes narrowed. "And we all know just how fast witches burn, don't we?"

The image of her aunt's charred body flashed through her mind.

Serena swallowed back the bile that wanted to rise in her throat.

"Still sure you want my help, witch?"

Taunting, but she could hear the echo of pain in his voice.

Pain for the family he'd lost. Perhaps the *cazador* wasn't so very different from her after all. "Absolutely."

He was her best bet.

Her only chance. "I'm sorry about your family, Luis, and you may not believe me—but I *do* understand."

The wind blew against her cheek. He stared into her eyes, and after a moment, his shoulders seemed to relax, just a bit. "I do believe you."

Well, that was something.

"But don't waste your time feeling sorry for me. I don't need your pity."

Her brows shot up. "Sympathy isn't the same thing as pity." *Jerk.*

"I need neither from you."

"And just what is it that you need?" she demanded, but she knew, dammit, deep down she knew—

The smile that curved his lips had her heart slamming into her chest—and her nipples tightening beneath the robe.

Dangerous.

"I'll show you exactly what I need. Very soon." A darkly sensual promise.

She just bet he would. Serena cleared her throat. *Enough.* Keeping her shoulders straight, she turned and resumed her march.

She felt his stare upon her with every step that she took. Heavy, hard and—

"You didn't answer me, little witch." Answer him? What had the question been? She paused, and then, when the rest of his words sank in, she almost snorted. Little, her ass. Her abiding love for chocolate and all things dessert meant that she generally stayed out of the "little" category.

He snagged the back of her robe, and Serena stumbled, barely catching herself. "Wait! Stop!"

"Aren't you concerned about wandering around naked?" He grated, and there was a different note in his voice. Anger?

Shoving a lock of hair out of her eye, she muttered, "Not really. This is coven land. No one but us should be out here." If any human intruders tried to cross the protected land, well, they'd find themselves turning and inexplicably walking the other way—fast.

Oh, the power of a good spell.

His hold on her loosened. "And we'll return to your house . . . with you unclothed?"

The guy was obsessed with her nudity. "I've got clothes in the car, OK?" She wasn't a flasher. Just a really desperate woman.

"Good." He *finally* released her.

"Glad you approve." Arrogant ass. But an arrogant ass that she needed.

They trudged the rest of the distance in blessed silence and Serena soon saw the glorious sight of her beat-up Chevy and—

Luis grabbed her, locking his fingers around her wrist and moving in a whirl to stand before her.

"What—"

"We're not alone." The shoulders before her were tight with tension.

As his response sank in, her eyes widened. But she hadn't sensed any danger. Even weakened, she should have felt a premonition of warning.

Rising to stand on her toes, Serena peered over his shoulder. Then she saw them.

Robed figures. Four. No, five of them. Walking from the woods near her car. Black hoods drawn over their heads.

"Don't get in my way," Luis ordered. "I'll take them down, stay back and—"

"*No!*" OK, maybe her scream came too loudly.

But the hunter didn't even flinch.

She pushed against his back. "Luis, they're my coven!" What was left of the coven, anyway.

The women walked toward them. Serena scrambled to Luis's side, a nervous knot tightening in her stomach. One by one, the women drew back their hoods. First, Susan, the stylish matriarch who didn't look a day over fifty, but who Serena knew was actually pushing seventy. Patricia was next, her cloak falling away to reveal her long, straight black hair and her perfect, dark cream skin. Patricia's twin sister, Pamela, tossed back her hood almost in unison, exposing her delicate features and her close-cropped hair. Then Sasha, the youngest member of the coven, shoved back her covering. Sasha was barely nineteen, but, like Serena, she had grown up hard in a big city. The girl was tough as nails.

The last face to be revealed was that of Vanessa Donnelley, a fiery redhead Serena had met shortly after moving to Atlanta. Vanessa worked for Dr. Emily Drake—or, as the paranormals in the city called her, the Monster Doctor. The psychologist only treated the *Other*, and Serena was pretty certain that by the time this whole mess was finished, she'd have to pay the good doctor a visit.

Susan didn't look at Luis. Her horrified stare went straight to Serena. "What have you done, sister?"

Condemnation. She should have expected it but, "I'm trying to save this coven." They were all marked. They knew that death was coming.

No sense running. *Why couldn't they see that?* Serena wondered, as her hand rose to brush against the always wild locks of her hair.

"I-is this him?" Sasha asked, eyes wide as she stared up at Luis.

Serena glanced to the left. Saw Luis smile. "What do you think, witch?" he murmured.

The women flinched.

"You've destroyed us," Susan whispered, but the words carried easily on the wind. "The *cazadores* aren't to be trusted. You know that—you know the stories. They turned against the council years ago, slaughtered innocents—"

"Careful, lady, you're about to piss me off." His words were easy, but the power suddenly pulsing in the air was hard.

Susan fell back a step. Hmm. Fell back, or was pushed? Before Serena could decide, the elder witch stiffened her shoulders and said, "He'll demand a price from you, from *all* of us."

Luis laughed. "Serena already knows my price, and she's agreed to pay." A shrug. "I have no interest in the rest of you."

Pity flashed across Susan's face. "What did you do, Serena?"

The only thing she could.

"I'm hunting now." From Luis. "I won't stop until I find the one after your coven."

"And then?" Vanessa's voice trembled. Normally so tough, but now, she was afraid. As were they all.

"Then I'll make him disappear. Permanently."

Soul-eater.

"We're leaving," Patricia muttered quickly. "Getting out of town until—"

"Won't do you any good." Luis crossed his arms over his chest and stared down at her. "He's got your power trail, that's how he's binding you, *all* of you. He has something personal, and he can track you now, no matter where you go."

Yeah, Serena had been telling them all the *same damn thing*. But when the *cazador* said it, well, the witches gulped and whispered. And their plans changed.

"Tell us when you find the bastard." Susan lifted her silvery mane proudly. "We will help you." The glow of magic lit her body.

Luis shook his head. "I don't need you to help me." He waved a mocking hand toward them. The witches were standing between them and Serena's car. "I just need you to get out of my way . . ."

The witches moved, fast.

As Serena hurried toward her car, she was given one last warning.

"Be careful, Serena, once you use the dark magic, there's no going back." Susan's eyes flickered with power. She knew that the summoning spell Serena had used wasn't on the light spectrum. No, it tipped the scales sliding into the darkness—as did any spell that utilized force on the unwilling.

Dammit, she hadn't wanted to use the summoning spell—it had been her only option. Dark magic scared the shit out of her. When she'd been performing her spell, she'd heard the whispers of temptation from the damned. The lure of the ancient power.

But she'd resisted the whispers.

Done her job—and gotten her *cazador*.

There had been no choice. She lifted her chin. Squared her shoulders and heard her mother's voice whispering through her mind, "*The cazador, he comes after witches when they're bad.*"

Well, it looked like he was already after her.

But just what he planned to *do* with her . . . she was a bit afraid to find out.

His little witch needed more clothes. The black T-shirt and too-tight jeans barely covered her body, and he kept getting a teasing glimpse of the smooth flesh of her stomach.

The *tattooed* flesh of her stomach. A five-pointed star enclosed her navel, and a glittering gold hoop flashed from the center of her belly button.

Luis didn't even bother acting as if he weren't staring at her flesh. He'd been so busy admiring his witch's breasts earlier that he'd missed the tat and the piercing.

A pity, because the gold was damn sexy on her body.

Was she holding any more secrets on her flesh? He would discover them all—very soon.

She braked in front of a small ranch house. One on a perfectly normal-looking street. One that had small, blooming purple flowers along the sidewalk.

Her fingers clenched around the steering wheel. "I'm not going to just wait around while you hunt."

Her words had his brows rising.

She turned to him, jaw locked. "You're not gonna shut me out of this, do you hear me? I *summoned* you, and that means I have some control over you. You're not gonna shove me in some corner while you go off and hunt alone."

Ah. He almost smiled at her fierce words. Almost. Instead, he moved fast, catching her shoulders and pulling her against him. "Time for the rules here, witch." Her lips were parted in surprise. It always amazed him that even the *Other* were surprised by the speed of his movements.

"R-rules?" Her eyes were wide and so damn green. He could stare into those eyes for hours.

He drew in a deep breath and caught her scent. "Yeah, rules." Although, really, there weren't many. "First rule, no one controls me." *Ever.*

Her mouth opened ever more. "But—"

He kissed her. Took her mouth with his tongue and his lips like he'd been fantasizing about for the last half hour. And, damn, but the witch tasted good. Sweet, hot. Fucking incredible. Her tongue moved against his, tentatively at first, as if she were almost afraid to respond.

He didn't want her fear.

His arms wrapped around her, his embrace becoming more like that of a lover. Her breasts pushed against him and the feel of her nipples pressing into his chest made his cock swell. He stroked her with his tongue, holding on to his control, courting her, *not* demanding . . . but he needed her response.

Her willing response.

A moan built in the back of her throat. The sound shot straight to his erection, made the lust double. Then her fingers were on his flesh, digging into his shoulders.

Those nails. Hell, yes. Pushing into the skin as she held on tight.

And she kissed him with the same ravenous hunger that he felt.

Their mouths became rougher. Hands more demanding. The heat in the car ratcheted up about twenty degrees.

His fingers slipped down her arms. He wanted to touch those fucking perfect breasts. Feel the nipples. They'd more than fill his hands. He'd caress her, squeeze her, then get those gorgeous nipples in his mouth so that he could suck and lick and make her moan again.

But Serena flinched and he froze.

Not pain. From her, he didn't want pain or fear.

Only pleasure.

Slowly, he pulled back. Realized that he'd touched her binding mark. His finger stroked the flesh just under the jagged line, silently soothing her.

Her breathing panted out, and so did his.

More.

His gaze darted to the dark house behind her.

"You . . . didn't have to do that."

Luis blinked. "Trust me, sweetheart, I did." He would do a hell of a lot more once he had her safe and beneath him in a bed.

"What do you want from me?" she whispered, and the sound of her husky voice was like a silken stroke right over his throbbing arousal.

Everything—and that was what he would take.

"The summoning spell didn't give you any control over me." The minute he'd stepped out of her circle, her control had vanished. If she thought she'd be able to manipulate him, well, the lady was dead wrong. Best to get that cleared up right now.

Long ago, a council of *Other* elders had been created to keep the paranormal peace. They'd made the mistake of thinking they could control the *cazadores*, too.

As far as Luis knew, no members of that illustrious council still lived.

Not that he was particularly concerned with what had become of them all. Once he'd learned that the majority of those assholes had ignored their own so-called peace rules and slaughtered humans—he'd stopped caring about their lives then.

And begun focusing more on their deaths. He'd hunted down several of the killers, despite their pretense of authority.

"The summoning spell brought you here." A satisfied smile curved her lips and drew him from the past. "That was what I wanted and—"

"No, what you wanted was to live." His words had her smile vanishing. "And I'll do my damned best to see that you do."

For a price. He didn't say the words this time, because his witch already knew.

Before she could speak, there was a loud screech of sound, and something pounded against the windshield of her car.

Something small. Black. With claws.

Fuck.

He turned his head and glared out the windshield, meeting a pair of shining yellow eyes. "That damn well better not be your familiar."

The sensual spell between them had shattered. Serena turned away, fumbled with the lock on the door. "He's not," she said. "Just a stray who wandered up a few days ago." She climbed hurriedly from the car and didn't bother glancing back at him.

His nostrils flared. The scent of her arousal carried easily to him. Like a shape-shifter, he had very advanced senses. Smell, taste, sight, sound, and touch—they were all substantially heightened for him.

He could smell the rich cream from his witch's sex.

She wanted him.

Good. That would make things easier.

When he got out of the car, Serena stood waiting near her small porch, one delicate foot tapping, and the cat, a too-skinny, long-haired beast, had his tail wrapped around her legs.

She lifted her keys. "The poor thing looks like he's starving. I'm going to let him inside and find some milk or something for him."

The cat let out a satisfied purr.

Luis frowned.

His magic didn't work with animals. He wasn't a charmer and in all of his years, he'd never taken the soul of an animal-talker. Charmers generally weren't on the lists of fatal badasses who needed to be put out of their misery. Since he'd never taken one's power, that meant Luis couldn't communicate with beasts, but . . .

But he *felt* a whisper of dark power hanging around the cat.

Serena opened her door and the cat ran in front of her, tail up, darting down the darkened hall as if he owned the place.

Serena stepped forward.

"Wait."

Her curls bobbed as she glanced back at him and he could see the shadows of exhaustion under her eyes. His witch had been fighting a dark foe on her own for too many nights.

But not any longer.

"I don't want you anywhere near that cat," he said.

A surprised laugh burst from her lips. "You can't be serious!"

But he was.

Brushing by her, and greedily inhaling her scent, he headed after the feline.

Behind him, Serena tapped a button, and the overhead lights flickered on.

The living room was to the left. Oversized couch. Cozy fireplace. Candles. Spell books.

And paint. Brushes. Easels. The heavy scent of the paint filled the air.

So his witch was an artist. Interesting. And, judging by the paintings that sat on the two easels, she was very, very good.

A castle filled one canvas. Heavy grays. Dark blues. A fortress under siege, battling the wind and rain and the night.

The second painting was of a woman. A portrait. A beauty with hair as black and curly as Serena's, but with green eyes that shone with light and happiness.

He hadn't seen happiness in his witch's eyes.

The cat nosed around the easel positioned near the window. Brushed its fur against a brush that lay all but forgotten on the floor.

A personal item would be needed for the binding spell. Something Serena had touched. Something from her home.

He growled. The sound was a perfect match for a wolf, not a man.

The cat jerked his head up, arched his back and hissed.

Luis bared his teeth.

The furball took off, running straight toward him, and Luis was ready. He grabbed the beast by the scruff of his neck and lifted him high into the air.

Yellow eyes blazed at him.

"Uh, what are you doing to the cat?"

He didn't answer Serena. All of his attention was on the beast.

Usually humans were the only ones who mistakenly thought animals were harmless.

A witch should have known better.

"Tell your master I'm coming for him," Luis snarled, "and that he'd better start fucking running."

The cat's whiskers shivered. Then the feline twisted and fell from Luis's hands. He landed on all fours with a soft whisper of sound. The front door was still open, and he ran toward it, hissing.

Luis didn't bother chasing the animal. He had the creature's scent. The cat wouldn't get away from him.

Serena slammed the door shut, locked it. "I-I don't understand. I didn't sense evil from him—"

"He's linked with a charmer, sweetheart." Had to be. "The cat's been visiting you, probably all the coven, and providing the charmer with the link he needed to *know* you." A string, a piece of hair— the cat could have taken anything small back to his master. In order for a binding spell to work, a personal possession was needed. The cat had been a perfect thief.

She shook her head. "But charmers can't bind witches. They don't have that kind of power."

On that note, she was dead right. "The guy's not working alone." It was the conclusion he'd reached as soon as he recognized the taint of power lingering around the cat. Which meant . . .

"There's not just one asshole out there trying to take down your coven." No, not just one.

A smile lifted his lips. Ah, damn but he loved a challenge.

"We've got to go after them! Let's go follow that cat and—"

"No."

Her mouth tightened. "I thought you were *helping* me."

"I am." He strode toward her. "You're dead on your feet. I'm getting you in bed."

Her breath jerked. "You're—no, you're just trying to go off on your own—"

He shook his head and touched her cheek. Such soft skin. So smooth. "I'm not going to leave you."

"I don't trust you."

Good. "You're tired. If you're going to hunt with me, you'll need your strength." It would take some time for her to recover from the summoning spell.

Her lips tilted. "Y-you're going to let me hunt with you?"

He'd never let another accompany him, but in the past, he'd gone to seek vengeance. Not to stop the crime.

Since it was her life, it was the least Serena deserved.

So he nodded.

A relieved laugh burst from her lips, the sound high and sweet. Nice.

"I thought you'd be pissed as hell at me for forcing you here, but you're—"

"I am." *Pissed as hell.* Yes, a fairly apt description.

The smile faded from her lips.

"Don't forget who I am, not for a moment," he told her. She needed the warning, and he wouldn't give her another. "I agreed to help you, but I am most definitely *pissed as hell* at being yanked thousands of miles across the globe. You didn't have my consent, witch, and I don't take lightly to those who would seek to control me."

I summoned you, that means I have some control over you.

Her words lay between them.

Her throat moved as she swallowed. "Can you—can you really kill with just a touch?"

His hand was on her cheek, because he wanted to keep stroking that flesh. Slowly, he trailed his fingers down the side of her face.

Down the elegant column of her throat. His fingers wrapped around her neck. "Yes." One simple touch.

But he didn't have to give just pain and death. He could also give pleasure. He'd give that to her, when the time was right.

"Are you afraid of me, Serena?"

Her eyes held his. So steady. So deep. "No."

Lie.

The one whispered word grated in his mind.

"Pity." He meant it. His hand rose slowly, cupping her cheek, and his head lowered toward hers. Her lips were parted. "Do you want me to kiss you again, witch?"

"Yes."

Truth.

His mouth took hers. Claimed it. Tasted the sweetness on her tongue and greedily took everything that her tender mouth had to offer.

He'd have her naked soon. Beneath him in bed. Taking him deep inside of her.

Her body was supple against his. Her thighs shifted and he fought to control the impulse demanding that he reach down and search out all her secrets.

Such tempting female flesh. Waiting for him.

He wanted her breasts. In his mouth.

His tongue brushed over hers. Thrust into her mouth.

So good.

Her hands seemed to scorch his flesh. Even through the thin fabric of his shirt, he could feel the heat of her touch.

If only they were naked, he'd feel her, *everywhere.*

Not now.

Dammit.

Luis forced his head to lift. Serena's cheeks were flushed, her eyes sparkling, her lips red and swollen from his mouth.

"You want me." Luis said the words because he wanted no pretense between them. When he was between her thighs, thrusting as hard and deep as he could, he didn't want her pretending the sex was just some sort of sacrifice for the safety of her coven.

The price for the coven's protection would be met later.

The sex—that was just between them. A need he hadn't expected, certainly never imagined that he would feel for a witch who'd tried to control him.

He could smell her arousal, the lush perfume of woman filling his nostrils and making his cock twitch.

He waited for her denial. None came.

The witch wasn't going to give him the speech about how she was a good girl, one who didn't sleep with strangers.

Because good girls didn't use dark magic.

"That's what you want from me, then? My body?" Still so calm. Too calm.

"I'm gonna be taking a lot more than just your sexy flesh, Serena." She'd learn what he wanted, soon enough. "Besides, don't you want my body?" If there was anything he'd learned about witches, it was that they were sensual creatures. It was partly due to the magic that constantly streamed through their bodies. All of that glorious, rich power.

Sex was necessary for witches. Not as necessary as it was for sex demons, but witches mated often.

With Serena's power running low, she'd need the brief boost she'd get from a hard climax of pleasure.

And the thing about witches . . . they had a reputation for always leaving their lovers well satisfied.

The succubi usually only cared about their own pleasure.

Not so for a witch.

"You know I want you." Her words came slowly.

Truth.

"I shouldn't," she said, and her breath feathered over his face. "It's the wrong damn time and you're sure as hell the wrong man."

His brows shot up.

"If I wanted to play with a devil, there are any number of demons I could find in this town for a fix."

A growl worked in his throat. He didn't want to think of the witch with another. Not when he hadn't even come close to possessing her yet.

"No other," he ordered, and meant it. The lust between them was unexpected as hell, but Luis had never been the sharing type. He'd have Serena, and no being—human or *Other*—would touch her while he was near.

"And no other for you," she said, her words holding the same edge of possession that his had.

"Agreed." The response was instantaneous. He wanted no other.

His right hand still held her chin. He squeezed gently then slid his hand down and let his fingers curve around her neck once more. Beneath his touch, he felt her pulse beating far too fast.

Serena's hunger matched his, but her strength didn't.

Not now.

"I won't hunt without you," he told her again. Then, "Don't be afraid . . ."

Her eyes widened. "What? Why are you—"

"I'll be here when you wake."

Understanding dawned too late in her gaze.

Exhaling slowly, he blew a stream of magic right at her.

She sagged against him, her body limp as sleep claimed her. He pulled her close.

And thought about the magnificent twists of fate.

And how very, very easy it was to kill a witch.

After all, his mother had burned so quickly . . .

"*Anubis.*"

The black cat hissed and arched his back as Julian Kathers crouched before him. Julian listened intently, a frown forming along his brow, then, "*Dammit.*"

The warlock who sat on the other side of the room arched a brow. "Trouble, charmer?"

Julian stroked the cat's back, trying his best to calm Anubis. The cat was shaking, scared to death.

With damn good reason. "A soul-hunter's in town."

For the first time in the fifteen years that Julian had known the warlock, fear flickered over Michael Deveaux's face. "Bullshit."

Anubis hissed again.

"He's with one of the witches." Fucking bad news. The witches—they were easy enough to pick off one at a time, after they'd been bound, anyway. And he sure did enjoy the sight of a witch bitch burning, but—

But the *cazadores* were a different game.

He'd never gone up against one of them. Didn't have the power to face one.

Did the warlock? Julian's heart pumped fast at the thought. Maybe. *Maybe.* A wild laugh sprang to his lips, but he bit it back. *I'd love to see a cazador die.*

Maybe the bastard would beg. Plead. He loved it when prey pleaded.

Made the death so much sweeter.

Fuck, but he should have been born stronger! Not as a damn worthless charmer who could only talk to strays. Those fucking witch bitches in his old neighborhood had taunted him, using their magic to make every day of his life so damn miserable, one spell after another.

But he'd shown them. *He'd shown them all.*

A witch's screams were so sweet, and the flesh of a witch smelled so very good when it burned.

The laugh he couldn't hold back any longer broke from his lips.

The warlock had swiped a hell of a lot of energy from the witches over the years. *Yes*, maybe he could do it—

Another laugh. The cat shook beneath his petting hand.

The warlock rose, the light of a nearby lamp reflecting for a moment in his golden hair. "The hunter saw the cat?" His voice was calm, even.

No fear—of course not. *Because he knew that he could take the cazador bastard.*

Excitement had Julian's heart drumming even faster.

Anubis arched his back again and his whiskers twitched.

"The hunter was with the witch—the black-haired one, Serena—at her house. He followed the cat inside."

Anubis *meowed.* A high, plaintive sound.

"What did the damn feline just say?" The warlock demanded, voice snapping as he stalked toward them.

"The *cazador*—he said he'd be coming." *And that I'd better start fucking running.*

But Julian hadn't run from anyone, not since he was sixteen and those witch bitches at his school had thought it would be funny to chase him after class with one of the stone gargoyles that *should* have forever stayed resting on the roof of the old building next to his high school.

They'd known he was *Other,* so they'd felt confident in playing with him. The bitches never would have worked tricks like that on humans.

For the longest time, he'd heard their laughter when he closed his eyes at night.

Then, after he'd hooked up with the warlock, he'd been able to hear only their screams.

"He'll have the cat's scent." The momentary heat that had flared in the man's voice was gone. He walked around Julian, keeping a careful distance from Anubis.

The warlock had never liked his cat, Julian knew that.

But he'd sure used Anubis every chance he got.

Such a perfect pet. So good at sneaking into the homes of witches.

Witches always had a soft spot for black cats.

Fools.

"We can be ready for him," Julian said, confidence and the thrill of the kill filling him. "Let the hunter come, we'll gut him and—"

Snap. Julian's words ended. His hand stopped stroking the cat.

Anubis jerked back, tiny teeth bared.

Slowly, the warlock lifted his hands from Julian's neck.

So easy to kill charmers, Michael thought. *Almost as easy as killing humans.*

The best part? He hadn't even needed to waste a drop of his magic.

"One problem down," he muttered, and smiled at the cat. The soul-hunter could trace the cat's scent all he liked now—he'd just find death waiting for him.

Lifting his hand, he motioned for the cat. "Here, little kitty . . . come to me . . . so I can send you to hell with your master . . ."

The cat turned and ran, jumping up onto the window ledge and then diving into the night.

Michael laughed.

The cat had been smarter than the charmer.

Not really surprising.

So, the witch, Serena, had summoned a soul-hunter. Interesting.

Resourceful.

Usually the witches just ran and hid when the first binding mark appeared on their flesh.

Hmm. The witch had to be strong. Most couldn't use a summoning spell even at full power, much less initially bound.

Good. It had been far too long since he'd taken a strong witch's magic.

He stepped over the body. Headed for the door. He'd face the *cazador* on his own time . . . and at a place of his choosing.

But first, first he had to finish the witches.

Because he'd need every last drop of their power to kill the soul-hunter on his trail.

Fortunately, he knew just which of the coven members he would mark for first death.

The lovely Serena.

3

She woke to find him standing at the foot of her bed. Dawn had yet to creep across the sky, so he stood, clothed in the shadows and darkness. His golden eyes glittered at her, lit with a heat that reflected his dark hunger.

Lust.

Serena sat up slowly. She was still dressed, just missing shoes, and a sheet had been pulled over her body.

She licked her lips, staring up at him. The silence in the room was thick and heavy and she waited . . .

Luis crept around the bed, and the carpet muffled the sounds of his footsteps. Closer, *closer* . . .

Her heart hitched faster, but she didn't speak, not yet.

He neared the side of her bed. Stopped and gazed down at her with those burning eyes.

So much need.

Was the same desire reflected in her own stare?

It had been so long since she'd been with a lover. So long since she'd let down the wall around her and trusted another to be close to her.

You can't trust him, a soft, niggling voice warned.

No, she couldn't.

She *shouldn't*.

But she did want him.

Her last lover had left over a year ago. Gotten tired of her secrets. Human, he'd sensed she was holding back on him, but Serena had never felt ready to tell James the truth about herself. She'd been afraid he would run.

Then, one day, she'd come home to find a note waiting for her. And no James.

After a few days, she'd stopped missing him.

Would the same thing happen when her hunter left? When his job was done, would she be able to write him off as easily?

When Luis's hand brushed over her cheek, she jumped.

"I want you." His voice, so deep, almost guttural, growled from the darkness.

Just the sound of his voice, hardened with hunger, had her breasts tightening, nipples pebbling.

She'd never been with a man as strong as he was. Her lovers had generally been mortals, except for the bear charmer and the fox shifter, and—

"Don't think about anything right now . . . but me." His fingers slid over her flesh. Caught her chin. Tipped back her head and—

He kissed her. Pushed his tongue past her lips and took her mouth just as he'd done before.

And, just as before, her blood began to heat, desire to uncoil, hard and fast, within her. Her hands caught his shoulders, held on tight.

Magic.

Passion.

Power.

It was all there in his kiss, and she wanted it—wanted him.

For the first time in twenty-nine years, dammit, she decided to take what she wanted.

Serena's lips widened, and she met him, tongue to tongue, mouth to mouth, kissing greedily, rising to hold him tighter.

Fuck being the pristine one. Holding out for love—well, that had never worked so well for her.

Going for the wild, mad ride of pleasure—she'd just see how that worked out.

Besides, death was on her trail, and she wanted to make certain she lived as much as she could.

Every. Single. Moment.

"I want you." He gritted the words against her mouth. Her lashes lifted and she found Luis staring down at her.

A rush of sensual power flooded through her veins and Serena heard herself respond, in a voice gone husky with matching desire, "Then why don't you take me?"

In the next second, she was flat on her back in the bed. Luis was over her. Her hands were pinned in the bedding. His legs tangled with hers. The thick length of his arousal pushed against her.

Yes.

This was what she wanted. Wild. Fast. Hot. Hard.

His mouth blazed a path down her neck. Lips branding. Tongue licking. And his teeth . . .

Serena shuddered when the edge of his teeth grazed her flesh.

Her sex tightened and cream flooded between her folds.

She twisted beneath him, wanting to feel his naked skin against hers. "Dammit, too many clothes—" The words tumbled from her lips as she drew in ragged breaths.

He freed her hands as he reared back. His long, strong fingers caught the edge of her shirt. Jerked it over her head. The garment disappeared, tossed somewhere in the room—she had no idea where and didn't care.

She'd put on a bra when she'd dressed. Now his fingers went to it, fumbling quickly with the front clasp. Then he was touching her, pushing the lacy cups aside and running those rough fingers over her flesh.

A moan fell from her lips. Her fingers found his shirt front, jerked it open and sent buttons flying across the bed.

His hands cupped her breasts. Teased. Fingertips caught her nipples, caressed, then his dark head lowered.

The warm, wet lap of his tongue sent a shock wave through her.

"*Luis!*" Her nails skated down his chest. Power was in the air around them. Energy vibrating against her skin.

There was magic for a witch in sex. The renewing power of life, the blissful wonder of pleasure.

Just what she needed.

No, *he* was what she needed.

He pulled her breast into his mouth, laved her with his tongue. Suckled.

Her sex contracted and she arched her hips, rubbing against the bulging length of his arousal.

Flesh to flesh. That was how she wanted him—and how she would have him.

Her hands gripped his upper arms. Tested the muscles, then caressed the hot flesh of his chest as her hands began to trail down his body. His strong abs rippled beneath her fingertips. Damn, but the man was like some kind of perfect freaking statue.

Not a man.

More.

He freed her breast, lifted his head. "Serena . . ."

Such hunger. Raw lust.

She loved the way he said her name.

Her fingers caught the top of his jeans. Unhooked the button, eased down the zipper with fingers that shook with eagerness.

"Are you afraid?" He asked the question, his voice as demanding as the hands that were now stroking her flesh.

"No." Right then, she couldn't get close enough to him. Afraid? *Only that he'd stop.*

Her vision wasn't shifter strong, but she caught a glimpse of his smile. The flash of his teeth.

"Good answer."

His hand slipped down her stomach, hesitated over her belly button. "I want to kiss you."

Hadn't he already? What—

He shifted his body, pulling back and bringing a cry of protest to her lips.

Then his mouth pressed against her stomach. His fingers eased open the top of her jeans, and he licked her. A long, slow lick right along her belly—and along the piercing she'd gotten as a birthday present just last year.

Her heels dug into the mattress and her thighs clenched around him.

"I can smell you," he whispered, the words merging with the darkness. "So damn sweet."

Her arousal. She knew instantly what he meant, and the knowledge that he knew of her hunger only made her sex cream more.

"Get rid of the jeans," she ordered, and meant hers, his. She'd never been one for too much foreplay—she loved the act of sex too much. The slide of bodies. The hard thrusts. The joining.

She wanted to join with Luis. To mate.

A growl shook his body and an answering moan rose in her throat. When his fingers pushed the denim completely off her hips and his breath fanned over the front of her panties, she arched toward him, ready—

White hot pain lanced her, burning, cutting into her upper arm, the agony so intense that she contorted, tears trickling down her cheeks.

"Sonofabitch!"

Luis stilled at once. "Serena?"

She clenched her teeth, trying to choke down the pain. It felt as if someone were cutting her arm. Driving a knife all the way to the bone and carving her flesh.

Not again. Goddess, no, not the second mark.

"Fuck!" The cry was Luis's. He jerked away from her and shot from the bed. Chanted a spell of protection.

A spell that would do no good.

The lights flashed on in her room. Burning far too brightly. A burst of air tousled her hair.

The pain began to recede. Throbbing now, in time with the rapid beats of her heart.

She squeezed her eyes shut, needing to block out the light, and not wanting to look at her arm.

Because she knew exactly what she'd see.

A second mark meant her powers would be even more limited, dammit.

Who was doing this to her?

A feather-light touch upon her shoulder had her screaming, her eyes flashing open.

Luis stared at her, his face tense. Looking so fierce—as fierce and deadly as he'd appeared when she first summoned him.

"Are you all right?"

No. She was most damn definitely not *all right.* Her life was spiraling out of her control. Some sick bastards were screwing with her and her coven, and a second binding mark meant her time was running far too low.

"When did the first mark appear?" Luis demanded.

Serena pulled in a slow breath. The passion she'd felt so deeply moments before was gone, erased by a tide of pain.

And rage.

"When the Blood Moon took the night." Had it really been just a few nights before when the full moon had risen so powerfully into the sky?

And the first mark had appeared.

Steeling herself, Serena finally dropped her gaze to stare at the flesh of her upper arm. Already, the binding cut looked like a scar. Four inches long. The flesh raised, angry red.

Only one more mark to go, then the spell would be complete. She would be as helpless as a human.

Luis's fingers hovered over the mark, as if he wanted to touch her, but was afraid.

"It's a warlock, you know." He said the words softly.

Serena's gaze was on her arm. "I know." The throbbing continued. The aching flesh pulsed as she stared at the skin. *A warlock.*

In the *Other* world, those who practiced their power in good faith—following the rule of *to harm none,* were termed witches or wizards.

But a witch who crossed that line, or a wizard who harmed innocents, well, then that person was given a new designation.

Warlock.

Shunned by the coven. Expelled from the magical community. Alone to work the dark magic.

She'd known, of course, for only another witch would be able to work a binding spell. Demons didn't have the power. Djinn couldn't strip a witch of her magic.

No, it took one of her own to work spells like this.

A fact that made the betrayal all the harder to bear.

His fingers brushed over the marks. She sucked in a sharp breath, expecting the burning pain to flare to life again but—

But she felt a cool balm on her skin. The throbbing eased. The redness lightened.

Her eyes widened.

His head bent toward her and he pressed a kiss to the second wound, then the first.

The pain vanished.

Serena stared at him, stunned. He was the bringer of death, not a healer. "How the hell did you do that?"

He looked up at her through his lashes, his mouth poised over her arm.

A spark of remembered need had her shifting and realizing that she was mostly nude and that if she'd had but a few minutes more before that bastard had struck—

Well, she wouldn't have been thinking about pain.

"I don't just bring fear and terror, you know." Another kiss, then he eased away. "I can also ease pain or . . ." His gaze dropped to her bared breasts. "Give pleasure."

Oh, yeah, she'd gotten a firsthand sample of that *pleasure*. And she wanted more. Serena swallowed and jerked on her bra. She'd sure as hell like to just lie back with Luis and get a few more samples, but . . . "W-we've got to go after them." The warlock and his charmer. "If the warlock marked me, he could be trying to mark the others—we have to go!"

Luis gave a grim nod but asked, "Are you certain you're up to facing him?"

Like she was going to back down. "This is my life he's fucking with so, hell, yeah, I'm ready."

"Then we'll fight now." Again, a dark heat flashed in his eyes, "And later . . ."

We'll fuck.

Yes, they both knew exactly what would happen later.

Damn. Damn. Damn. He was going to make the bastard pay. He'd hunt him down, no, hunt *them* down, and make them beg for mercy.

Then he'd kill them.

Luis knew he was after a team of killers. Had to be a charmer working with a warlock. No way the charmer who controlled the black cat would be able to bind the witches on his own.

The memory of Serena's pain-filled cry echoed in his mind. His hands clenched and magic snapped in the air around him.

Oh, yeah, those bastards would pay in blood.

He'd been seconds away from tasting the sweet cream between her thighs, then some assholes had fucked up his plans *and* hurt his witch.

Luis couldn't wait for the fighting to begin. He was definitely in the mood to kick ass and send a few deserving paranormals straight to the next world.

"Stop!" He gave the order when Serena's car turned the corner of Ruthers Lane.

The window on his side of the car was down. He'd been following the trail of the black cat—using his enhanced sense of smell to catch the feline's scent. He'd also been tracking the taint of the dark magic that had hung heavily on the cat—a taint that, to his eyes, appeared as a fine mist in the air. A mist that led him straight to the small shop at the end of Ruthers Lane.

"Turn off the car," he said.

Serena obeyed instantly. "Is this—is the warlock here?"

He wasn't sure, but the cat had been there. The cat had gone inside the antique shop that boasted the sign, HIDDEN TREASURES.

Dawn had come, the sun rising and chasing away the shadows. They were on a small business street, one lined with curiosity shops and galleries. One that would soon be teeming with humans.

They'd have to move fast.

Luis turned to Serena, "Let's—"

She shoved open her door and hopped outside.

He blinked. OK, so his witch was ready to kick ass, too.

She'd changed her clothes before they left. Slipped on a long blouse that covered her arms and that stomach he loved to see. She was wearing jeans—jeans that hugged the rounded curves of her hips and thighs. Her small feet were encased in snug, black leather boots.

Serena had even managed to find him a shirt, a fact that pissed him off. Why the hell would his witch have men's clothes handy? And she hadn't conjured them—they'd been hanging in the back of her closet. She'd muttered something about her ex leaving the items behind.

The bastard had better not be coming back to claim the clothes—or Serena.

Luis climbed from the car and glanced around to make certain no human was nearby. The last thing he needed was a nosy mortal catching sight of his battle.

Or of him.

Satisfied that the humans hadn't yet come to play, his hand lifted, and he pointed toward HIDDEN TREASURES. The shop's windows were dark, and a CLOSED sign hung haphazardly against the front door.

His nostrils twitched as he caught a darker, pungent smell on the wind.

Hell.

"Luis?" Serena called his name softly.

"Death's waiting, sweetheart." No mistaking that dank scent. "Stay on your guard."

She gave a grim nod.

And he led the way toward the scent he knew too well.

4

The door was locked, but one quick jerk of his hand made the cheap lock shatter. He yanked open the door and heard the squeal of an alarm. His gaze darted around the room, locked on the small black box with the blinking red dot.

Luis grabbed a nearby candlestick, one that was a perfect polished silver to his eyes, and threw it, sending the candlestick hurtling end over end toward the alarm.

When it smashed into the box, blessed silence filled the air.

So much for going in quietly, but, then, he'd never really been the quiet type.

Besides, for one of the bastards he was chasing, the noise wouldn't matter. Not much could wake the dead.

"The cops will be coming," Serena said, her voice carrying just to his ears. Cautious witch. "The alarm will have been connected, the security service will alert them—"

"Then we'd better move, fast."

A *hiss* sounded from the back of the store. An all too familiar sound.

Damn cat.

He hurried forward, saw the small beast pacing in front of an old, scarred door.

The cat arched his back at Luis's approach and bared his teeth.

"Out of the way, pussy." Not in the mood to deal with the feline, Luis flashed his own teeth.

The cat turned and ran back toward the entrance of the shop.

"Luis . . ."

Serena stood behind him. So close he could feel the warmth of her body.

He lifted his hand, touched the door. Then sent the wood crashing to the ground with one hard punch.

Sometimes enhanced strength could be a real bonus.

His gaze fell on the body. The still man with bright red hair. The fellow whose neck was twisted and whose eyes were wide open.

Never saw death coming.

Because he'd trusted his killer.

Serena sucked in a sharp breath. "Oh, goddess, is he a human?"

"No." A quick scan showed that no one else was in the small room. Luis crouched beside the body, reached out his hand—

"*Meow.*" The black cat ran back into the room and pressed against the dead man's side.

Luis exhaled. "It's the charmer." The asshole who'd been working with the warlock. Dammit. *The kill should have been mine.*

"I don't understand." He glanced up at her. Serena's face had gone pale and her eyes were staring fixedly at the body. No, at the bastard's twisted neck. "W-why is he dead? If he was working with the warlock—"

The cat's head prodded the charmer's side as he tried to get his master to wake.

"Not gonna happen," Luis muttered to the small creature and rose to his feet. "The warlock knew I could trace the cat back to his master."

Her gaze jerked away from the body. Understanding dawned on her face. "Then, once you had the charmer, you could have tracked the warlock."

As easy as connecting the dots.

Or, it should have been.

But the warlock had decided to cover his ass and throw a dead body in their path.

Serena swallowed and lifted her hand to her throat.

Ah, hell. "Is this your first body, witch?" How many corpses had he seen in his time? Hundreds? Thousands? The sight of the dead no longer fazed him.

But Serena was another matter. "Not my first." Her brows pulled low. "My aunt—I found what was left of her."

The urge to go to her, to hold her, rocked through him—and what the hell was up with that?

He was *not* the comforting type. The killing type. The fucking type.

Not comforting.

The witch was screwing with his head.

Luis found himself taking a step forward, blocking the dead body. "Nothing can be done for the bastard now."

In the distance, a siren wailed.

Serena shook her head, and some of the color seemed to return to her cheeks. Her gaze darted around the room. "We've got to get out of here," she muttered. "We've got to—" She broke off. Her eyes widened and then she was nearly running across the small room, her hip thumping against the side of a desk as she skidded to a halt.

"Serena?"

"This is Vanessa's." She lifted a long, blue hair ribbon. "She had it in her hair last week." Her fingers reached for a swatch of fabric. "And Susan was working on a quilt just like this—*dammit!*" She dropped the fabric. "The bastard has us all right here!"

Actually, he had to have even more of their belongings stashed somewhere else. In order to continue the spell, he had to hold one personal article from each witch. No way would the guy have left all his treasures behind.

The wails of the sirens were getting closer.

Serena swore, then started to frantically grab all the witches' possessions.

"What are you doing? We don't have time—"

"And if the cops connect any of this stuff to the coven? We'll be screwed!"

She was right. So he started helping her, fast. Their hands were overflowing when they ran from the store.

Fate was on his side, for once, because the street was still deserted. Good. He wouldn't have to waste any magic on the humans.

They hurried to the waiting car, tossed the materials inside and—

A police cruiser hurtled around the corner. Brakes screeched and the lights above the vehicle flashed in a blur. Two officers jumped out, guns drawn. "Freeze!" The command came in unison.

Serena stilled near the driver's side door of her car. "Shit," she muttered and glared at the cops. "This isn't what you think—"

"We're not here," Luis said, walking toward them, pitching his voice low and calling on the powers he'd been given by his father.

A level ten, the strongest of the demons—and those who could most easily control the minds of humans.

The guns lifted higher. The cops' hands shook. "D-don't m-move." The shaky order came from the guy on the right, the one who looked like he was barely twenty-one.

"*Luis.*" Serena's horrified voice.

Horrified—because she was used to living in her safe coven world, a world where the good rules said not to hurt humans.

Well, he wasn't going to hurt these two, unless that option became absolutely necessary.

He really did try to spare the innocents when he could.

It was those who deserved his fury that he unleashed his power upon. And let the fire rage.

But he would make the humans forget, with a quick compulsion sure to drive the memory of him and Serena forever from their minds.

"You didn't see us," Luis told the men softly, as Serena swore behind him. "When you arrived on the scene, there were no other cars in the vicinity."

The young kid's eyes bulged. He swallowed, once, twice, then his gaze shot to Serena, and the gun moved to aim straight at her chest.

"*Drop the weapons!*" Luis snarled, heart lurching as something he'd not felt in centuries reared its head.

Fear.

Fuck.

The weapons hit the ground with a clatter.

Luis turned his head and glared at Serena.

She blinked. "What?" Then she looked over her shoulder, as if expecting to see some kind of threat.

She was the threat, to him.

Dammit. The danger his mother had warned him of.

A weakness.

He ground his back teeth together. This wouldn't do. Not at damn all.

With an effort, Luis turned his attention back to the cops. "You didn't see us," he repeated, forcing the compulsion deeper. The kid was stronger than the slightly balding guy behind him. Could be the rookie even had a touch of psychic power.

But there was no way either of the humans were strong enough to resist him.

Another paranormal, yeah, because the *Other* could resist his compulsion. Serena would be able to because of her witch blood.

But the humans before him didn't stand a chance of fighting him.

"Get in the car," he told Serena, not wanting to push his luck. He didn't want to risk a shifter or charmer cop pulling up on the scene.

She didn't move.

By the grave of—

"The cat," she said, and bit her lip. "We can't just . . . leave him alone with that dead body."

His eyes closed for a moment. Witches and their damn soft spots for animals. Had to be a leftover trait from the heavy familiar days. "Fine!"

Luis jabbed his index finger in the rookie's direction. "There's a cat inside. A furry, skinny-as-hell stray."

The officer waited.

"He's yours now."

A nod.

"Satisfied?" He threw the question at Serena as he ran around the car. More sirens were sounding, probably because he'd heard someone from the station trying to contact the officers on their radio during his compulsion, and the men hadn't responded as requested.

"For now," Serena agreed as she climbed into the car. She revved the engine. Then Serena threw the car into reverse, shot backward, narrowly avoiding a hard slam into the side of the cruiser. She shifted gears, twisted the car into a tight turn, and floored the gas as she roared down the road.

A touch of admiration filled Luis as she got them out of the about-to-be-swarmed neighborhood in less than thirty seconds.

Nice.

His witch had secret talents.

"Are you, Luis?" Her voice floated to him.

His gaze jerked to her face, locked on her profile.

"Are you satisfied?" she asked.

The flash of fear he'd felt moments before returned.

She was too vulnerable.

And he'd just found her.

"Fuck, no," he snapped, and her gaze flew to his.

He leaned closer to her, wrapped his fingers around the supple flesh of her thigh. Damn but she felt good.

She'd feel even better naked.

"Drive faster, Serena."

A shiver worked over her body, then her gaze darted to the rearview mirror. "Are the cops behind—"

"No one's behind us." His fingers inched up her leg. Paused near the juncture of her thighs. He swore he could feel the heat from her sex burning through the fabric.

Her breath jerked in. "Then w-why?"

He pushed his fingers between her legs. Stroked the crotch of her jeans and shoved the bitter memory of fear from his mind. "Because it's time for us both to be satisfied." His fingers strummed against her, and a red flush brightened her cheeks.

The engine rumbled as her foot pressed down even harder on the accelerator.

She'd been too close to death. His witch had felt the icy breath of the specter when she entered the dusty storage room. She needed to fight the fear and the anger that churned in her.

And passion, lust—well, for him, they'd always been perfect weapons.

Time for him to take his witch.

* * *

When her car screeched to a stop in front of her house, Serena wasn't thinking about dead bodies any more. She wasn't thinking that a dead man's eyes could hold such shock, and she wasn't thinking that death felt cold . . . far too cold. She'd thought of all that before. Back in that horrible storage room.

No, as she jumped from the car and she and Luis hurried up her steps, she wasn't thinking about death any more.

She thought of *him*.

Luis's touch. His body. The pleasure he'd give her.

The pleasure that would block the fear of the waiting cold.

The door slammed closed behind them.

His hands settled on her hips. "How fast can you get naked?"

Ah, now wasn't that a question she'd never heard before? Excitement had her blood pumping, and Serena pulled away, turning to face him as she cocked her head and asked, "How fast can you?"

In a blink, he was naked, his clothes having vanished with but a wave of his hand.

Gotta love that magic.

Her gaze dropped to his chest. She loved his chest. So strong, with all those rippling muscles. His stomach was flat, the abs damn perfect.

His hand lifted, and his fingers grazed over his erection.

Oh, *yes*. The man was *built*. His cock bobbed up from a thatch of dark, curling hair. Long and thick.

Moisture gleamed on the broad head.

He was ready for her.

Good, because her panties were soaking wet for him and her nipples were so tight they ached.

Her magic might be limited by the binding, but she still had a few tricks of her own. She waved her hands over her body, and her clothes and shoes disappeared.

Yeah, sometimes, it was good to be a witch.

When the devil wasn't after you.

She pushed the thought away as quickly as it rose. For just a few minutes, she wanted pleasure.

Not fear.

His eyes heated as he looked at her. The gold gleamed so brightly. His cock swelled even more.

They didn't have to worry about birth control, a nice little *Other* perk. Witches completely controlled their cycles, and as for *cazadores* . . .

Immortals never caught illnesses of any sort.

He was the safest partner she'd ever had.

And the most dangerous.

He reached for her.

Shaking her head, she caught his hand in hers. "I want a bed." She wanted cool sheets, soft mattresses, and him. Thrusting as hard and deep as he could between her thighs, until the hungry ache in her sex had been assuaged.

"What my witch wants . . ."

She expected more magic. Wondered just what he was truly capable of doing. Could he move them by spell alone to her room or would he—

His arms wrapped around her and he pulled her up against his warm chest. His mouth crushed down on hers, tongue thrusting deep and she tightened her lips around him, sucking lightly. She loved the man's taste. Dark and rich and—

She was on the bed.

He sprawled over her, mouth still locked to hers, and he pushed her deep into the mattress. His legs—*the man had thick, muscled thighs that she'd love to ride*—angled between hers so that Serena was spread wide for him. Her sex was open and wet and so ready that she knew he had to catch the scent of her arousal.

He tore his mouth from hers. Lifted up to gaze at her body. "Fucking gorgeous," he growled. Then took her breast with his mouth. Licked. Bit. Sucked.

Made her moan.

His fingers—she *loved* those clever fingers—parted the folds between her legs. His thumb pressed over her clit, and Serena nearly came off the bed.

"Easy . . ." A dark rumble.

But she didn't want it easy. Not with him. Hard, fast, *wild*— that was how she wanted it.

And how she would take it.

Her nails dug into his back. Her thighs lifted and wrapped around his hips. "Hard." The demand snapped from her mouth.

His head jerked up. His mouth was wet, glistening, his lips parted.

She scored her nails down his back. Pressed her hands into Luis's taut ass. "*Wild.*"

His face hardened. "Then that's what I'll give you . . ."

The fingers that had caressed her sex stilled.

A wave of anticipation had her trembling.

Luis pulled back, dislodging her legs, and he brought his left hand up and curled the fingers over her thigh. When his gaze dropped to her sex, she knew what he was going to do.

And she couldn't wait.

His shoulders pushed between her legs. His breath fanned over the dark curls that shielded her feminine core.

Then he drove two fingers deep into her creamy opening.

Every muscle in her body stiffened.

She opened her mouth to cry out, but the sound broke on her lips when Luis pressed his mouth against her. He locked his open lips over her clit. His tongue teased, tasted.

Drove her *wild.*

His fingers thrust, moving in a fast rhythm. First just the two, then a third large finger lodged inside of her.

He licked her, swirling his tongue over the straining button of her desire, then lapping up the moisture that pooled between her legs as the lust grew and grew.

Serena felt the edge of his teeth, a light graze that had her freezing, then all but whimpering with pleasure when his tongue licked between her folds.

Her heart thudded in her ears and sweat slickened her body. The sunlight trickled through her blinds, and she watched Luis, unable to look away from the sight of his dark head between her thighs.

Her sex squeezed around him, clenching tight with every thrust of his hand. Her nipples stabbed into the air, her thighs trembled, and the promise of release beckoned, just seconds away.

"*Luis.*" He was driving her crazy. And damn him, he was holding the control. Every single bit of control.

Time to break that control, time to—

His fingers withdrew—shit, just when she was close—then he drove his tongue inside of her.

The mounting tension erupted. Serena squeezed her eyes shut and her head jerked back as the powerful spasms shook her.

Pleasure was power.

A secret every succubus and incubus knew.

And one that the witches used for their own gain.

Her eyes flashed open, and her lips parted on a sigh of satisfaction.

The magic of the release filled her body and as her sex clenched in powerful contractions, Luis moved. Rose above her. Pushed the head of his cock against her opening.

"Time to get wild, witch."

He slammed into her, the force of his thrust strong enough to send the bed sliding back against the wall.

More than ready for him, Serena arched her hips and whispered his name.

His cock filled every inch of her sex and stretched muscles gone sensitive from her climax. He was big, thicker than she'd thought, and he felt *amazing*.

Once again, her legs clamped around his hips. As he began to move, rocking harder, driving deeper, she held on as fiercely as she could.

And enjoyed the ride.

Their mouths met. Tongues thrust as hips jerked. Breaths panted. Their hearts raced. The spiral of lust built, *built*.

His hands fondled her breasts. Teased the nipples and had her squirming beneath him.

When he rose, pulling that delicious cock nearly out of her, her head lifted. Her fingers traced his nipples, then she licked him, loving the slightly salty taste of his skin.

They rolled, twisting and turning as they fought for release. For a pleasure that was just out of their grasp.

Serena settled on top of him, legs on either side of his hips, sex clamped around his cock, feeling every inch of his arousal pulse inside of her.

His hands were on her hips. Holding too tightly, but she didn't care.

She squeezed him, clamping down hard on his erection. Then releasing her muscles with a hiss of pleasure.

His teeth ground together.

Another slow squeeze.

Now she had the control.

"Witch." Gritted. An accusation.

One she'd never deny.

Bending over him, she licked his nipples, drawing out the slow movements of her tongue, then glancing up at Luis from beneath her lashes.

His eyes glittered.

In the next second, she was on her back again. Her legs splayed over his shoulders and he thrust fast, hard, and she was—

Exploding. A white-hot pulse of release ripped through her as Serena climaxed. Her whole body shuddered beneath him and the cry that burst from her lips seemed to echo in the room.

Lights danced before her eyes. Magic.

Pleasure.

Still, he thrust. Deeper.

The bed was a mess. Sweat coated their bodies.

Flesh to flesh. Sex to sex.

He swelled within her. Another wild inch, so thick now that the friction of his thrusts sent a stab of pleasure through her with each move of his body as aftershocks reverberated in her core.

"*Serena.*" He drove deep. Froze. His gaze caught hers. For an instant, the molten gold of his eyes faded to pitch black.

Demon eyes.

The hot jet of his release filled her.

The air in the room heated, brushed against her skin.

Pleasure is power. For the hunter, as well as the witch.

He shuddered against her, held tight in the grip of his own climax. Her arms wrapped around him, and she clung to his stiffened muscles.

When the pleasure finally eased for them and their heartbeats began to slow, Serena stayed just where she was.

Right before she drifted to sleep, she could have sworn that their hearts were beating in perfect tune.

As if they were one.

204 / Cynthia Eden

* * *

Her aunt was in the middle of the circle of protection.

But the circle hadn't protected her.

Jayme Michaels lay on the ground, her long, curling black hair cascading around her face.

Serena ran to her, fear shaking her from the inside out.

No, no, not Aunt Jay. She was the strongest witch Serena had ever met. No one could harm her, not human, not Other.

Whoever was after Aunt Jay's coven, they wouldn't get to her, they couldn't have—

Her aunt's head was twisted. Her neck broken.

Her eyes were open. Her lips parted in surprise.

Serena skidded to a stop just outside of the sacred circle.

No, no, this wasn't right.

Not her aunt, not—

Serena awoke, jerking straight up in bed. Sunlight hit her hard in the face, and she turned away—

Only to have her gaze land on Luis's sleeping face.

The sight of him wiped away the fog from her dream.

No, not a dream. *Nightmare.*

She sucked in a deep breath. Her aunt hadn't looked like a broken doll when Serena had found her body.

The fire had already gotten to her and destroyed her beauty by then.

Another deep breath.

The dream had come because of the body they'd found—she knew it. Pleasure had only been able to push aside the darkness for so long.

Her hand reached for Luis. Hesitated.

His task was to stop the one after her. He would kill the warlock.

But she would not be useless in this battle.

As she'd been in the fight to save Aunt Jay.

Her fingers curled into a fist.

Her powers wouldn't return full force until the binding was removed, and that blessed event wouldn't happen until the warlock drew his last breath. Death—either the bound victim's or the spell caster's—was the only way to remove a dark binding.

Fortunately, she wasn't completely without magic—thanks in part to the furious pleasure she'd taken from Luis.

She would not be helpless.

Luis would destroy the warlock.

It would be up to *her* to find him.

Serena eased from the bed. Grabbed a light silk robe and belted it across her waist. The day was vanishing; already the clock told her it was long past noon.

Night would hold dangers, perhaps another binding.

The dark ones were always stronger at night.

Time for her to hunt *now*.

Carefully, she crept across the room, not wanting to risk waking Luis. He wouldn't like what she planned to do with the vestiges of her magic, but that was just too bad.

Her power, her life.

The door closed behind her with a soft click.

Luis waited a moment. Listened to the faint footfalls as Serena disappeared down the hallway.

Then his eyes opened.

He drew in the scent of woman and sex.

His cock was already erect. Just from the lingering traces of her sweet fragrance in the air.

What mischief was his dangerous little witch up to now?

He'd give her a few minutes, then he'd find out exactly what spells she was crafting so secretly.

Serena should have realized that after their mating, there would be no more secrets.

The soul-hunter had found the perfect soul that he wanted to take.

And she was just down the hallway.

5

Serena placed the items she and Luis had taken from the antique store in the middle of her living room. She'd pushed the furniture back moments before, the better to work.

Her fingers were steady as she positioned the candles around the witches' possessions. North. East. South. West. She lit them with a wave of her hand.

She'd sat her scrying mirror down near the sofa. She picked it up, aware, as always, of the icy feel of the mirror in her hands.

Serena walked back toward the candles. Put the mirror at her feet. She drew in a deep breath, raised her hands high above her head in the goddess position, and began her spell.

"Show me the one who used his spell,
To bind the witches I know too well.
Show me the man—show me the one
Whose magic I seek to have undone.
As I will,
So mote it be."

A simple spell. One that she wasn't certain would work. But the warlock had made a mistake. He'd worked magic on the items before her, and the dark magic left a faint taint. A touch of darkness.

A touch that would reflect him, *if her spell worked.*

The candles flickered around her.

Serena's glance fell to the mirror. She watched as the surface darkened, as if black clouds were sweeping over the face of the mirror. Then moving faster, faster as the wind blew.

Air brushed over her face. Sent the edges of her robe flapping back.

Her body trembled as she poured her magic into the spell, forcing the image to sharpen.

She wouldn't be able to last much longer.

Show me the one I seek.

The clouds thickened in the mirror. Pressed closer. Slowly began to form the face of a man.

Blue eyes stared up at her. Clear and sparkling. Dimples winked at her from the sides of his curving mouth. His blond hair blew, as if he, too, felt the breeze stirring in the closed room.

Dammit. Why did evil always seem to hide behind a pretty face these days?

"Got you, bastard." Luis's voice growled from right behind her.

"Not yet," Serena muttered, memorizing that face. She'd never forget him. "But we will."

The candle flames died. Serena's arms dropped to her sides. Her gaze was still on the mirror and on the man who laughed up at her.

Luis's hands wrapped around her waist and he pulled her tightly against him.

The grinning warlock slowly vanished.

Asshole, we're coming for you.

"He has more, you know." Luis picked up the tattered cloth that Serena had assured him several times was actually a swatch of Susan's quilt. "He wouldn't have left everything behind. If he had—"

"He wouldn't have been able to put the second bind on any more of the coven, I know." Serena ran an agitated hand through her curling locks. Damn, but he loved her hair. The wild curls. The soft, silky feel of the tresses under his fingers.

"Vanessa and Susan were both hit by the jerk this morning. So he *has* to have more of a stash." She jerked on her shoes. She'd dressed moments before, though he rather wished she'd just stayed in that silky blue robe. He liked the way it exposed the tempting swell of her breasts.

Serena had been practically pulsing with rage since her spell. "The bastard's out there. You saw him—he's out there, *laughing* at us."

Because he mistakenly thought he held the power. *Fool.* "We're just waiting for the night, Serena."

She slanted him a frowning stare. "Why? Isn't that supposed to be *his* time?"

Her shirt had lifted when she started running her fingers through the hair that *he* wanted to touch, and Luis had to fight to hold her stare and not let his gaze drop to that glittering belly of hers.

"Luis? Are we just going to be some kind of damn sitting ducks for this psycho?"

"No." He crossed his arms over his chest. Hell, who did the lady think she was dealing with here? An amateur? "The night is *my* time, Serena. Mine more than any other being you'll ever meet." Vampires might have mistakenly thought they ruled. Demons could skulk in the shadows all they wanted, but *he* was the one who drew power with the setting of the sun.

Soon it would be time to use that power.

Her eyes sharpened with interest and her hand dropped. "What's our plan?"

Our. Well, she had summoned him, and he'd given his word that she could hunt.

But that had been before he'd learned what pain sounded like on her lips.

"We have two options, sweetheart."

Her foot tapped.

"As soon as night falls and the demons and vamps crawl out to stalk the city, *we* stalk them." It would be easy enough to catch the stench of the vampires—most of 'em smelled like decay and rot. As for the demons, well, being part demon meant he could stare right through the veil of glamour that cloaked the majority of his kind. And he'd be able to smell 'em, too.

"And, uh, when we catch them?" She looked *and* sounded hesitant.

Probably because, unlike him, she didn't spend the better part of her nights stalking the psychotic demons most wanted to pretend didn't exist.

But it never seemed to matter how many of the assholes he stopped. There were always more out there.

And Serena—she was proof of just how damn little good he could really do in this shit screwed world. If she hadn't summoned him, he would have stayed in Mexico, finished his drink, had his fuck, then gone off to hunt the level-nine demon who'd been spotted in the area—the one who'd made a recent habit of hurting humans.

While he was hunting that bastard, Serena would have died. *Serena would have died.*

There just weren't enough hunters in the world any more. Too few to begin with. Too few left after the strongest, sickest paranormals had targeted his kind decades ago.

Maybe it was time for new blood.

His gaze caught Serena's.

"What do we do when we find the vamps?" Her nose wrinkled. "I hate the way those bloodsuckers are always staring at my neck."

Yeah, he could understand that. Luis made a mental note to give serious pain to any vamps unlucky enough to be caught ogling Serena's gorgeous neck.

He cleared his throat. "When we find 'em, we make 'em talk. A warlock strong enough to bind an entire coven—he'll be known by someone." *Something.*

They just had to look in the right place.

Or, in this case, the wrong one.

The wrong side of town. The dangerous side. The side most humans inherently knew to stay away from when the sun set.

A deer could sometimes sense a hunter.

Luis had learned in his lifetime that humans could all too often sense the *Other* that would prey on them.

Not that the sensing usually did much good for them.

"Make 'em talk," she repeated slowly. Her head tilted, the curls danced. "Are we going to have hurt someone?" Not particularly concerned.

Because she'd been hurt.

"Maybe a little," he allowed. *A lot.* But he'd be the one doing the hurting. Serena would keep her lily-white hands clean.

She nibbled on her lips. Fuck. Did the woman not understand just how badly he *still* wanted her?

Her tongue swiped out.

His cock jerked.

Business.

Well, business *should* come first. But there were several more hours until dusk . . .

"What's our second option?" Serena asked.

The lust cleared a bit. He didn't like option two. Not a damn bit. "We wait for the third bind. Let the bastard think that he's broken your coven, and when he comes . . ." He shrugged, tried to look careless when he was starting to care too much, too quickly. *The way my father had fallen.* "I'll be waiting for him."

She backed up a step, and her shoulders hit the wall. "You— you mean you'd use me as bait."

Not the choice he wanted, but, if they couldn't track down that blond warlock, it might be their only option. "I wouldn't let him get to you, Serena." A promise.

"I'd be a sitting duck!" She shook her head frantically. "One more bind on me, and I'm—I'm—"

"Human." Or as close as a woman like her would ever come to that fate.

"Yes, dammit! And we both know that if a bound witch dies while her powers are locked up inside of her—"

The witch's killer took her powers at the moment of passing. "I wouldn't let him get to you," he repeated.

Serena didn't look particularly convinced and her doubt—it pissed him off.

Luis stalked toward her. She was already trapped against the wall. She'd trapped herself, so it wasn't like there was room for the witch to run. He crowded her deliberately, though, brushing his body close against hers. His arms rose, caged her, as his hands pressed against the white wall behind her head. "Do you trust me, witch?"

She'd let him into that tempting body of hers just hours before. Let him take her with the hot passion that still burned him.

And made him ache for her.

Serena hesitated.

A ball of anger unfurled in his gut. It was the answer he should have expected, but—

He wanted her trust.

As much as he wanted her.

His head lowered over hers. "Do you trust me?" he repeated as he caught her scent, inhaling deeply.

"I-I don't know." *Truth.*

The anger flared brighter. "So you trust me enough to fuck, huh, sweetheart? But you don't trust me with your life—is that the way this game works?" Damn, was it because of his mother? Because he'd failed before, did Serena not think that he could keep her safe? "I'm not gonna leave your side, witch—I won't leave you like I left her." He'd been on a hunt. Going after a djinn who'd slaughtered half a village. He hadn't realized his mother was in any danger. He'd thought she was safe and—

"Luis, no, I didn't mean—"

"Forget it, sweetheart." He shoved the memories of his past away and focused only on her. "Know this—I *will* keep you safe, whether you trust me or not. I'll protect you *and* do my damn job of eliminating the warlock."

"Luis, *I'm* the one who summoned you, remember? That means—"

"Jackshit."

Green eyes narrowed and tension tightened her body.

"You summoned me because you wanted a guard dog, and that's what you got, Serena. A fucking killer dog who would take anyone and everyone down before they had a chance to hurt you." He meant it. No one was going to sacrifice his witch.

No one.

Her lips parted and, hell, a man could only take so much temptation.

His mouth crushed hers, taking her. *Good enough to fuck.* Well, if that was the case, then he'd just go ahead and take his pleasure with her.

She was wearing a skirt now. A short, black skirt that teased the tops of her thighs and made his cock pulse with arousal.

Luis drove his tongue into her mouth and pushed his left hand between her spread thighs.

Her gasp was swallowed by his mouth.

She twisted, pushing against him, and her tight nipples stabbed into his chest.

The witch wanted him. He'd caught the scent of her arousal even when she'd glared at him with sparks of anger in her green eyes.

When he touched the crotch of her soft cotton panties, his fingers felt her wet heat.

No preliminaries this time.

He was pissed with her for doubting him. With the blond asshole who was hunting her.

And he was hungry—for her. Her body. Her damn soul.

It was his nature to hunt. To take.

He wanted to take her more than he'd ever wanted anything in all of his centuries.

Serena's hands were on his shoulders. Not pushing away, pulling him closer, and her mouth was wide and hungry on his.

Trust me enough to fuck.

The growl in his throat sounded just as he ripped her panties away.

"Luis!" She jerked her head back, gazed up at him with eyes gone dark with need.

Her folds were slick and swollen, heavy with the same lust that hardened his cock. He pushed his finger into her tight opening, loving the feel of her clenching sex around him.

She'd feel even better around his cock.

"Not here, we can—"

"*Here.*" They were in the middle of her kitchen, and her blinds were up, windows wide open.

He didn't really care.

His fingers retreated, drove deep once more, and her head tipped back against the wall on a hard sigh.

Then she started to ride his hand.

A flush rose up in the open vee of her shirt. Darkened her neck. Stained those glass-sharp cheeks.

Gorgeous.

Her breath quickened as he watched her. Her movements jerked faster.

Sexy witch. Sensual as a succubus.

His.

He drew his fingers away from her, and had to bite back a fierce smile of pleasure when she shook her head in protest.

Her eyes were on him as he lifted his fingers to his lips and tasted her. A long, slow lick.

She swallowed.

"Later, I'm gonna have more of you, sweetheart." *Later,* she'd be spread beneath him again and he'd lick her until he'd had his fill of her rich cream.

But for now . . .

His hand dropped to the front of his jeans. He popped open the button, eased down the zipper, and pulled out the cock that was twitching for the feel of her hot, tight sex.

"Put your hands on me," he ordered and his voice came out like a snarl. No help for that. He was living in a red haze of hunger right then.

All for her.

Her hands slid down his body, soft as a butterfly. Slowly, she wrapped her fingers around his arousal.

Serena squeezed him, then pumped his straining flesh with a long stroke, from root to head.

Again.

Again.

It took all of his control not to come in her hands.

He grabbed her hips, aware that his hold was too tight, too rough, but not able to ease his grip.

No damn way.

Luis lifted her, pinning her back even harder against the wall. Her legs were up, her sex open, and her hands still pumped him.

Fuck.

"Guide me in," he growled. "Take me deep inside, Serena. Let me watch you . . ."

Her skirt was bunched at her waist. The folds of her sex were flushed pink and glistening.

Damn, but he wanted another taste.

Her fingers tightened around him.

His hips thrust forward helplessly as sweat slid down his back.

Serena guided the head of his cock toward her body, straight toward the tight opening that quivered for him. When he felt the first brush of that creamy, hot flesh along his erection, Luis clenched his back teeth.

Control wasn't going to be lasting much longer.

Every instinct he possessed screamed for him to thrust forward—as hard and deep as he could go.

But he wanted to watch her. Wanted to watch as his cock slid slowly into her straining core.

"Luis . . ." His name came on a breath.

Ah, hell—

He slammed balls deep into her.

And immediately felt Serena's sex begin to spasm around him as she came.

His spine prickled. Her contractions were silky, strong, squeezing him even better than her hand. He pulled back, drove deep.

Retreated. *Her creamy grasp was so strong and—*

He plunged deep.

Heard her strangled cry of pleasure.

Felt the bite of her nails on his skin.

He wanted her to come again. With him.

Her legs locked around his hips and he pumped into her, driving as fiercely as he could for the rush of release that he knew was waiting.

The ripples of her sex continued. She moaned and shuddered against him. "Luis. Luis. *Luis!*"

He felt the second climax hit her because the pleasure hit him, too.

Semen jetted from him, spilling deep into her body as he came, pumping and thrusting and holding on to her with all of his strength.

The power of his release had his knees trembling, his breath rasping out, and the room shaking around them as his magic and power surged through the kitchen.

The release went on, the pleasure filling every pore in his body. He emptied into her, hungrily drinking in the ragged sounds that tore from her lips.

Pleasure is power.

Power for his witch.

Power for him.

His gaze met hers as the spasms began to ease. Her lips were blood red. A tear tracked down her cheek.

Then her mouth curved and her hand released its fierce grip on his shoulder to slide down his chest, stopping right over the heart that raced for her.

"Again."

And the already swelling cock inside of her was only too happy to oblige.

After all, only a fool would deny a witch's demand.

She yanked off his shirt. Her mouth locked on his nipple, and he thrust deep into her wet heat.

Luis had never thought of himself as a fool.

Night found them on the streets. Walking in the darkness on the side of town that most didn't even realize existed.

Buildings stood as battered shells. Boards lined the windows of the closed shops. A few burning garbage cans spit flames into the sky and chased a bit of the darkness away.

In the distance, a drum pounded in a furious, driving beat.

There were clubs in the city. Places that the *Other* frequented. They were close—close enough for Luis to smell the blood in the air.

The blood that would lure the vampires.

They weren't heading to the clubs. No, their prey wouldn't be inside.

The monsters they sought were *on* the streets. Waiting. Planning. Hunting.

Just as he was.

"Dammit, didn't we have this whole talk already about using me as bait?" Serena muttered, slanting him a simmering glance.

She stood just under one of the few street lights that actually worked. Her arms were crossed over her chest, her booted feet spread apart.

He stood a few feet behind her, body pressed tight to the cold brick wall and completely hidden by the shadows.

"We both agreed you weren't going to be bait for the warlock." She wouldn't be, unless that dark choice became absolutely necessary.

But he would protect her.

He wouldn't fail again.

"Then why the hell am I the one standing out here all defense-less with come-and-get-me written on my forehead?"

Simple. Because the woman looked like perfect prey in the dark sweater that cupped her gorgeous breasts and in the jeans that clung all too well to her great ass and legs.

"It's easier to get the *Other* to come to us this way." Or, rather, to her. The ones he was hunting, they'd love to get their hands on a morsel like her.

Deceptively innocent, with her wide eyes and nervous hands, she'd bring the bastards right to her.

"Aren't they gonna sense you?" she asked. "Demons *can* sense each other, you said it yourself—"

"No one will sense me." Not even a level-ten demon would be able to pick up his power trail. "Don't forget, sweetheart, I'm not a full-blood demon."

He thought he saw her shiver. "So everything I've ever heard about you—it's true, isn't it? Your kind—*cazadores*, born of witch and demon, you're immortal."

"Yes." A blessing and a curse.

Everyone else died. It was so hard to watch the people he loved slip away.

Easy to watch the assholes he stalked pass from this earth, but when it was the others, like his mother—

"How many of your kind are there, Luis?"

Too few. "Less than there were a hundred years ago." Luis re-alized he hadn't seen another of his kind in what—five, ten years?

Too busy killing.

And fighting to stay alive.

Just because a being had been graced with the ability to live forever, well, that didn't mean some smart bastard couldn't come along and figure out the secret to his death.

Everyone and everything could die, but the real trick in this world was figuring out just *how* to kill the monsters.

"Is it true that you can't be hurt by mortal weapons?"

He coughed. "That rule's for level-ten demons." And, since he was part demon, yeah, weapons forged by man couldn't hurt him—but he didn't make a habit of revealing that fact to anyone.

"So, what? You have to have your heart cut out? Get beheaded?"

The old immortal-killing standbys. Luis sighed. "It's complicated—and I'm not going to explain it now. Wrong part of town for this talk, sweetheart."

But his witch was on the right track. *If* his head was severed and *if* his heart was cut from his chest—*while it still beat*—and *if* his head and heart were burned to ashes, then, yeah, he'd finally die.

"Has anyone ever almost . . . killed you?" The question was softer than the others. Her gaze wasn't on him. It was on the shadows on the opposite end of the street.

No monsters were there.

He'd sensed no threats on the street, *yet*, so he'd let Serena keep up her questions because he knew that she was afraid.

And he'd discovered that when she was nervous or afraid, his witch liked to talk.

A rather cute trait, and one that he'd allow for a few more moments.

Just until the demons came out.

"Yeah, sweetheart, I've almost been killed a few times." Those panthers in South America had actually come pretty close to taking him out of this world. One had swiped at his chest with those razor sharp panther claws and another had gone for his neck, slicing right at his jugular.

He'd bled *too much,* gotten *too* weak, but still managed to rip through the pack.

Then he'd healed, as was his nature. And lived to fight and kill another day.

Or night.

Like tonight.

"Have you ever been afraid?" Her voice was even softer now, and, still, she didn't glance his way. He was angled diagonally behind her, so he could just make out the faintest movement of her lips.

"Once or twice." With her.

And that long ago day when he'd rushed to save his mother, only to arrive far too late.

Her head jerked toward him, "Luis, I—"

"*Quiet.*"

Power was in the air, flickering.

They weren't alone any longer.

His eyes narrowed as he watched Serena take in a deep breath. Her attention turned back to the dark street.

She wouldn't see the one coming for her . . .

But Luis already had the demon in his sights.

6

Damn, damn, *damn,* but this was a bad idea, one no smart witch should *ever* have agreed to go along with in the first place.

Serena hunched in front of the light post, because, yeah, standing underneath that freaking *beacon* was such a fine plan.

Every psycho in the area would be after her.

Just what Luis wanted.

The warmth had seeped from the city with the fall of night, the temperatures taking a serious nosedive from the warmer weather of previous days, and Serena shifted, rubbing her arms together as she tried to stave off the growing chill in the air.

A week ago, she wouldn't have been afraid. She would have used her power to blast any idiot stupid enough to confront her all the way across the street and into that busted building that looked like an old pawnshop.

A week ago.

Now, she had to rely on Luis, and relying on someone else wasn't exactly her strong suit.

But that's why I summoned him—because I knew he could help me.

She just hadn't realized he'd be doing the whole "bait" routine with her.

Immortal jerk.

And just *where* was the paranormal he'd sensed? She couldn't see anyone, didn't hear anything but the crackle of flames—and who had lit those fires anyway? No one was around but—

"Lost, witch?"

The voice came from her left. Whispered into her ear.

Blood of the goddess.

Serena swallowed. Straightened her shoulders. *The boogeyman's got my back.* He'd better.

"I'm not the least bit lost," she answered slowly, proud that her voice didn't shake even a little. She turned her head toward him, lifted one brow. "Are you?"

One glance was more than enough to tell her that this guy—yeah, he was most definitely *lost.*

His eyes were coal black. Every single bit of his eyes—a demon stare. Usually, demons cloaked their eyes with a glamour and made the color appear like a human's. The true black color only appeared when their emotions and passions were high—like when Luis's gaze had flashed black on her during their wild mating.

But this guy—he wasn't bothering with glamour. No, he was letting his gleaming black eyes show to the world.

His face was long and angular. Too pale. Bloodless. His teeth were sharp, when they shouldn't have been. *What the hell?* The guy's teeth were all narrowed to points, like a vamp's fangs.

Serena realized the demon before her had deliberately filed his teeth.

The better to kill?

She balled the hands that wanted to shake into even tighter fists.

Where's my power when I need it?

The answer, of course, was *tied up in a warlock's web.*

"Seems I've just found the thing I was looking for tonight." He smiled at her, showing off those wicked teeth. Then his gaze raked over her body.

Hell.

"I would have preferred a human. They scream so very loudly, you know."

She wanted to scream right then. Scream for the demon to get the hell away from her.

No, not just away. Out. Out of the city. Out of the damn country.

Her skin crawled as she stared at him. He wore a long black coat, dark pants. His hair was slicked straight back from his forehead, and his fingers . . . bony, with long nails no man should have possessed.

Nails that, even in the bad light, she could see were stained red.

"You-you're not from around here, are you?" She hated that the faintest tremble had entered her voice. OK, so every time the guy opened his mouth, she smelled death. No need to freak out about that fact.

Her bodyguard was just a few feet away.

And Luis had been right—the demon didn't sense him, *at all.*

Perhaps the guy was too focused on her to even see the danger that waited.

The demon laughed. "No, this is my first . . . trip . . . to your city." He lifted a hand toward her, and Serena steeled herself. "I think I'm going to have so much fun here . . ."

At the last second, Serena stepped back so that she missed the touch of his gnarled fingers. "What makes you think I'm a witch?" she asked, her mind jumping back to the first words he'd spoken to her. Demons didn't normally have the ability to recognize her kind and—

" 'Cause you're bound," he muttered, and his nostrils flared. "I can smell the marks on you. Every demon and shifter in the city can." Another chilling smile. "Poor witch. No magic, and all alone."

"Not exactly," she snapped and lifted her chin. If that guy tried to touch her again—

"Oh, *exactly.* You're *exactly* what I want." Not a smile any more. "Let's hear you scream—" His claws came at her.

Serena jumped away.

Luis bounded from the shadows. "Let's here *you* scream, demon." He grabbed the demon, spun the asshole around.

"What the—*fuck!*"

"Hello, Jack."

Jack?

Serena stumbled back a few more feet. If Luis knew the guy, the demon had to be trouble. The kind she didn't want.

"What are you doin' here?" the demon snapped. "Last I heard you were huntin' in Mexico—"

"And that's why you thought it was safe to come out of hiding, huh?" He moved then, in one of his too-fast-to-see whirls. When Serena blinked, she found him holding the demon up against the light post. Luis's fingers were locked around the guy's throat. "Mistake, Jack. Big mistake. It's *never* safe for you to be on the streets. Not safe for the humans, the paranormals, and damn sure not safe for *you*."

The demon's eyes began to bulge.

"Luis . . ."

He didn't glance her way. Not that she blamed him. Luis was dangling a bastard demon two feet up in the air and slowly choking the life from him. Kinda busy . . . but they had come out on these streets for a reason.

The terrorizing of this jerk needed to pause a bit.

"You're weak, Jack. Only a level four." Luis made a clicking sound with his tongue. "Is that why you go after the humans? Cause you feel powerful with them?"

Jack tried to gasp out a reply, but the wheezing wasn't much of a response.

When his face started to purple, Serena stepped forward. "Luis, we're not here for this. The warlock—"

Those bulging black eyes slanted toward her.

"Don't fucking look at her!" His roar shook the street.

The demon's eyes flew back to Luis.

Serena reached out, touched Luis's back. Felt the rock-hard, battle-ready tension in him. "The warlock," she repeated. She didn't know what Luis's past was with this guy, and, yeah, the demon creeped the shit out of her, but they had to find out about the bastard after her.

A shudder passed over Luis's body. "You want to keep breathing," he snarled at the demon, "you answer my questions—and you tell me the *truth*." He rammed the guy's head back into the light pole. Metal groaned. "Got it?"

The demon's lips formed "Yes," but no sound escaped him.

"Stay behind me, Serena," Luis ordered.

Fine with her. She wasn't interested in getting any closer to the demon. He knew that she was bound. Well, partially bound. Easy prey.

Slowly, Luis lowered the demon to the ground. Jack's feet touched down with a soft sigh. Luis eased his hold, but didn't completely move his fingers away from the demon's throat. "I'm looking for a warlock."

"L-lot of 'em h-here . . ." the demon said, voice hoarse.

"Blond. Blue-eyed. One that makes a habit of hanging out with charmers."

Jack blinked. "D-don't k-know h-him. J-just got in-into t-town . . ."

Luis laughed and the sound chilled Serena. She was glad that she couldn't see his face.

But over Luis's shoulder, she could see the demon's face—and the fear that flashed over it.

Luis lifted his hand, and Serena saw claws spring from his fingertips— *What the hell? He wasn't a shifter.*

He slashed the demon's face. Left side. Right. Long, jagged marks dripped blood as the demon howled.

"Wrong answer," Luis murmured.

Jack whimpered.

"Now, let's try again, Jack, and, remember, I can tell when you lie to me . . ."

He could tell when the demon lied—oh, shit! The guy was a detector!

The demon started talking then, fast. "H-he's in one of th-those big, white houses, w-with columns, f-fancy, in R-Roswell—"

The name clicked instantly in Serena's mind. *Roswell.* The antebellum homes. Historic district.

"G-got a b-big, bl-black gate, iron. N-name's Michael . . . something. D-didn't know y-you . . . were af-after him—"

"But you knew he liked to hunt witches."

"Y-yes . . ."

Luis shook his head. "You knew, but you didn't care, did you, Jack? Because you had hunting of your own to do."

Jack didn't reply to that.

Serena figured that was probably answer enough.

"Turn away, Serena," Luis said, and his voice was ice cold.

Jack's lips trembled. "N-no, witch, d-don't, he'll—"

"*Turn away, Serena.*"

Her shoulders stiffened. "I'm not your pet bitch, Luis. Remember that when you talk to me."

He finally shifted to stare at her, glancing back over his shoulder. His eyes were as black as Jack's. "Please, Serena, don't watch me do this."

Voice low, but hard.

She spun on her heel.

The fast and desperate cries of the demon rang in her ears.

Almost helplessly, Serena glanced back—

Luis had freed the demon's neck. Jack was shrinking back against the post. Luis lifted his hands, palms up. The flesh of his hands—it glowed and—

She jerked her gaze away when his fingers landed on the demon's shoulders.

The scream that she heard had her choking back her own cry.

Don't look. The order was her own this time.

But she looked anyway. A witch's curiosity was a dangerous thing, and a weakness most of her kind shared. So her eyes flickered back and she saw the darkness of the demon's eyes fade to a stark white. Heard the last rasp of his breath leave his body. Then watched as Luis lifted his hands. The demon dropped to the ground.

"I told you not to watch." Emotionless.

Her gaze jerked to him. "Luis . . ." His eyes were still black and a faint glow seemed to light his flesh from the inside out.

"Witches . . . always curious, just like the damn cats you all used to be so sickeningly fond of." He spared a glance for the demon on the ground. "I hope you're burning somewhere now, asshole."

Then he turned his back on the demon and fully faced her.

Her heart hammered in her chest and Serena realized her palms were slick with sweat. Not cold any longer, she was burning hot.

Fear could do that to a woman.

He lifted his right hand and Serena jerked back.

His mouth tightened. "You knew what I was when you summoned me, Serena."

Yes, yes, she'd known.

"And when you fucked me."

It was hard not to flinch at that one.

His hand was still in the air between them. Regular nails now, thank the goddess, but . . . "I don't understand." She stopped. Cleared her throat because her voice sounded too weak—and she didn't want to be weak. "How—how did your hands change? *Cazadores* don't come from shifters and—"

His fingers balled into a fist. "I've killed shifters. Dozens of them. Demons. Djinn. The ones who stalked the earth, determined to torture and murder, *I* stopped them." Slowly, he uncurled his fist and his fingers, as they extended, had what looked to be about four-inch long claws sprouting from their tips. "Most don't understand. They think all I do is kill, but I'm a *soul-hunter*. I hunt, and I take the powers that lurk in the souls of the *Other*, so that when they leave this world, they go out as helplessly as humans."

I take the powers that lurk in the souls. Oh, shit. *Shit.* "You mean—all the beings you kill—"

"I get their power." A shrug. The claws vanished in a blink. "Think of my touch as a binding spell, sweetheart. Instead of the three marks, it just takes the grasp of my hand, and any *Other* becomes helpless. When the powers drain away, the body dies." His lips twisted. "And my job is done."

No regret. No guilt. "You just . . . kill." No, he drained powers first, *then* he killed. Her gaze darted to the fallen demon. She shuddered.

He killed.

Just like the warlock who was after her.

Her arms wrapped around her stomach. "Why did you kill him?" OK, yeah, the guy had scared the hell out of her, but other than making her heart jump into her throat, he hadn't actually *done* anything to her and—

"Jack fancied himself a modern-day copy of the original."

Serena shook her head and forced her gaze back to him. *Stop looking at the dead guy.* "I don't know what you're—"

"Jack the Ripper."

She blinked.

"He liked to slash his victims apart just like the original Ripper, except he didn't go after prostitutes—he went after humans, or weak paranormals. Then he had a good old time making them scream and slicing up their flesh."

Let's hear you scream.

Serena rocked back. "You-you knew who he was the moment you first sensed him, didn't you?" He'd known, and he'd let her stand there and talk to a fucking sadistic killer.

One who wanted to make her scream.

A grim nod. "You were never in any danger. I would not have—"

"Asshole!" Maybe it was a *good* thing she didn't have her full power right then—she would have tried to fry the jerk. "How many times do I have to tell you, *I'm not bait?*" Her hands were at her sides now, fisted, because she really, really wanted to slug him.

All powerful *cazador* or not.

"Serena—" He stepped forward, reaching for her.

She threw out a spell. Sent the air to swirling around her as a force field sealed her away from his touch.

His fingers slammed into the invisible wall. His eyes slit. "*Serena.*"

Her brow furrowed as she fought to hold the field. It was weak as hell, but she was making a point! "Don't *use* me, *cazador!*"

His fist punched against the field. "I'm trying to save your life!"

"You could have warned me about Jack, you could have—"

"I didn't know that asshole would be hunting here. By the time I realized it was him, it was too late, and he hunts by sensing *fear*. If I'd told you what was happening and how easily I could take him down, your emotions would have changed and he would have sensed it."

Her temples began to throb. The wall was getting even weaker. "I don't want to be bait," she repeated, but this time, she was talking about the warlock. Or maybe she'd been talking about him all along. Her hand rubbed her right temple. "I don't want to be bound."

"*I* am with you, Serena. No one is going to hurt you. *No one.*"

"I want to protect myself." She always had. "I don't want to be weak." As weak as the pitiful spell that wasn't really holding him off. He could have broken through her force field with one push of magic.

But he hadn't.

"You're not going to be weak," he promised and his hand flattened on the field. "We're going to get the bastard, you're going to be safe, and I promise, I'll return you to full power."

Her hand lifted, hovered over his. "Why did you agree to help me, Luis?" She'd summoned him, but he could have left. Could have vanished in a blink.

"Because I wanted you. From the first glimpse through the fog, *I wanted you.*" Power filled his words.

And she'd wanted him.

"Trust me, Serena. Trust me to save you. Trust me to—" He broke off, shaking his head.

For a moment, her gaze again dropped to the body of the dead demon. Goose bumps rose on her flesh.

Luis had spent lifetimes battling demons like Jack. Fighting to keep the world safe.

Fighting alone. Always alone.

"Why do you do it?" she whispered. "The council is long gone. It's not your duty to keep fighting these bastards." Though she'd screamed that it was his *job* the first time they'd met. But it wasn't. He was entitled to live a life just like any other. So *why* did he do it? Why keep fighting the darkness?

"Because someone has to," he said simply. "And I'm one of the only beings strong enough to face those in the dark."

Her heart pounded so hard that her chest hurt. Was it truly that simple for him? And, goddess, but what must his life be like? So many battles. So much evil.

"Serena . . ." A plea was in his voice now, with even a touch of . . . desperation? "*Trust me.*"

She jerked her gaze away from the demon. Met Luis's stare. Her lover with the golden eyes and the touch of death. The man who fought evil, when others would have run.

Trust him? Oh, yes, she did. With her life.

And with her soul.

As her spell faded with a whisper of air, her fingers curled over his. "I do trust you."

He got her off that street and away from the body as fast as he could. Luis didn't worry about disposing of the demon. The cops would find the body, or, if they didn't, well, the other demons who frequented the area would make certain that *no one* found Jack.

Another bastard off his list.

Damn. When he'd caught the demon's scent and realized who was out stalking, he'd nearly lost it. Almost let his power rip out full force.

He hadn't wanted Serena close to that bastard. Hadn't wanted Jack to so much as *look* at her.

But he'd known that if any *Other* in the city knew about the warlock, well, it would have been a piece of shit like Jack. So he'd held on to his control as long as he could. Let Serena lure the guy in, and when Jack had made the mistake of reaching for Serena, he'd attacked.

He hadn't wanted Serena to see him make the kill.

When she looked at him, sometimes, *sometimes,* he'd catch a hint of fear or worry in her eyes.

But she often just looked at him as if he were . . . a man.

He wanted her to keep looking at him that way. Wanted her to *always* look at him as if he were just her lover.

And not the killer she'd summoned.

His body was bursting with energy. The power of the touch ran through him, pulsing in his veins. The demon's energy blended with his own, sending the currents of magic pumping through him.

Usually after a touch of death, he found a woman. Got between her legs and rode hard and fast for the rest of the night.

He felt the same wild need now, the same lust.

But he didn't just want *any* woman.

He wanted the woman who sat so stiffly beside him as she drove her car, streaking down the streets and racing through the darkness.

The woman who had touched him after a kill and said she trusted him.

Truth.

"Luis . . ." Her voice was husky.

He glanced over at her.

"Something's . . . wrong."

He tried to unclench his fingers from their white-knuckled grip on the door handle.

"Are you all right?"

She hadn't lied to him. He wasn't about to lie to her. "I will be." Once the edge of tension wore off.

In about eight or nine hours.

Fuck.

She braked at a red light. Turned to face him. "Tell me what's happening. You're stiff as a board over there. You're sweating, and you haven't moved in fifteen minutes. Are you sick? Are you—"

"It's aftereffects, sweetheart." The only weakness his kind had. The energy from the kill pumped through his body too hard, too fast. The result was a furious tension and a ravenous sexual hunger.

But then, his hunger for Serena was always pretty ravenous.

The light changed to green, but Serena didn't take her foot off the brake. "What does that mean? Do you need to rest? To eat, to—"

"Fuck."

She blinked.

No lies. Not between them. *Not to her.* "To get back to being one hundred percent, I need to fuck. I need to get you, naked, and plunge into that pretty pink sex until the power shock fades and I'm close to normal," *normal for him,* "and I can stop breathing without my cock twitching for you."

Her lips parted. "Ah . . . I . . . see."

Probably not. She didn't understand that he was literally drowning in her scent then, that talking was hard, and that every breath he drew, he tasted her.

And wanted to fuck her so bad he ached.

She glanced around the darkened streets. Gave a nod, then punched the gas and spun the wheel to the left.

"Serena!"

Tires squealed.

She didn't glance his way. "You want me."

Hell, yes.

"You need to have sex to . . . work through this tension."

He needed to have sex because he wanted inside her. But, yeah, getting past the power surge was necessary, too.

"My art studio is a few blocks away. I-I had to get a place to meet with my clients. It's not real big, but if you don't mind the paint and the lack of a bed—"

If he could have her, he wouldn't mind a damn thing.

"Then we can be there in two minutes." She glanced at him, and Luis was caught by the desire he saw in her emerald stare. One that was almost a match for his own ferocious need. "And you can have me in three."

Hell, yes.

7

The scent of paint hit him the moment Serena unlocked the door to the small loft.

"I-I rented here because the light is so good. The clients like the studio and I like to have a separate place for doing their work." She flipped on the lights.

Luis tried to bite down on his hunger. Her art was on the wall. Same dark colors. Same proud passion. "You're damn good, Serena."

Her lips parted in surprise.

He had to kiss those lips. Feel that tongue he could see peeking behind her teeth.

"Ah, thanks. Painting—it's almost like magic to me."

She smiled at him, a sweet, real smile.

His heart lurched.

Ah, hell . . . No way was he going to be able to wait.

Luis dragged her into his arms. Kicked the door closed and took her mouth.

He kissed her with a fury and a hungry need. Started stripping off her clothes. Heard the thud of her boots as she kicked them to the floor.

He wasn't going to take the time to strip. He unbuckled his pants, shoved them out of the way, caught his straining erection and—

"Let me." She breathed the words against his mouth.

Then she pulled back and dropped to her knees before him.

"*Serena*." A few drops of liquid pulsed from the tip of his cock.

Her fingers closed around him. Squeezing. Stroking. She seemed to know exactly how to touch him and make the hunger grow even more.

His knees trembled as his cock jerked eagerly in her grasp.

Her lips curved. Parted.

Then she bent her head toward him, that luscious red mouth open, and took him inside.

His teeth clenched as a ragged groan burst from his lips.

She moved her head, sucked, her cheeks hollowing as she drew on him.

Stars danced before his eyes. His fingers sank into the riotous mass of her curls. So damn soft.

And her mouth was so hot.

She drew him in deep, then pulled back to lick the head of his arousal. Swirled her tongue over his flesh. Another long, deep suck.

Then she swallowed.

His fingers tightened as his control snapped. He started moving her, faster, harder, thrusting his cock, trying to go deeper.

She swallowed again.

Luis came, roaring her name and shuddering helplessly as she drank in his essence.

When she'd wrung every drop from his body, she pulled away from him. Rocked back on her haunches.

Luis stared down at her.

His cock began to swell again.

What looked like white sheets were draped across the floor behind her. Paint spotted the material.

The sheets would be better than the floor.

"Take off the rest of your clothes, witch." The strongest witch he'd ever met.

She'd bewitched him with nothing more than a touch that first night. Enslaved him with a smile.

He knew the truth now. He would never, *ever* get enough of her.

She laughed as she pushed off her panties. "But I wanted more." Her eyes danced with hunger and sensual power.

Because she'd just broken a *cazador's* control.

He dropped to his knees before her. Kissed the delicate inside of her ankle. One, then the other. Licked his way up the silky smooth skin of her leg. "My turn to taste." He wanted to hear Serena scream *his* name.

And what a cazador wanted . . .

He parted her legs. Touched the warm, creamy flesh that had already plumped with arousal. Her clit was waiting for him, and when he touched the button of her desire, Serena's back arched off the floor.

A good start.

He put his mouth on her and *took.*

Her moan was so sweet.

But he wanted more.

His tongue stroked over her. Licked. Fast, hard licks. Then short, slow swipes.

She began to call his name.

But not to scream for him. Not yet.

He pushed two fingers inside her. Felt the delicate muscles of her sex clamp greedily around him. He thrust, driving knuckle deep, then retreating.

Licking.

Her hips rocked against his hand, jerking faster with each move of his fingers.

Luis wanted more.

He pulled his fingers free. Lowered his mouth. Touched her trembling flesh with the tip of his tongue.

Then drove his tongue inside of her.

The scream she gave was pure music to his ears.

Luis thrust his cock into her just as the last tremors of her climax faded.

Serena stared up at him. Lines of tension and need were etched onto his face.

A dark power drove him. She could feel the magic in the air. But there was more.

The hunger she felt for him, the stark lust she'd experienced nearly from the beginning, was reflected in his eyes.

Power to power.

234 / Cynthia Eden

Lover to lover.

Sex to sex.

She locked her legs around him. Held on tight as he slammed into her, driving that thick cock deep into her. Her muscles clamped around him. Clutched tight, and a flash of pleasure had her undulating beneath him.

Then he thrust harder. Curled his hands around her hips and lifted her into his strokes.

His eyes began to darken as he gazed down at her.

The pleasure built again.

She didn't look away from him. Couldn't.

Serena tightened around him and rode his cock as wildly as she could.

When the next climax hit her, she didn't even try to muffle her cry of release.

But then, neither did he.

She slept at some point. After she rode him, breasts bouncing as she took his cock inside. After he flipped her onto her stomach and took her with her hands digging into the paint-stained sheets.

She slept, and he watched her.

His fingers traced the star on her belly. Such a beautiful, simple design. One witches had long used.

I don't want to be weak. Her words played through his mind.

His little witch didn't understand, even without her magic, she wouldn't be powerless. She was smart, resourceful, and brave. Not many would have stood beneath that streetlight and waited for a lost demon to walk from the darkness.

And not many would have risked using dark magic to summon him.

He brushed his face against her curls. Inhaled her scent.

I don't want to be weak.

His head lifted. His mother had been weak, at the end.

Life was too short for so many.

He put his hand back over Serena's stomach. Power and a dark need still filled him.

But his control was back, and it *would* hold. No matter how much his witch tempted him.

Because he had a promise to keep and a warlock to kill.

She shifted against him, and her lashes blinked open. "Luis?"

Bending, he pressed a kiss to her sleep-softened lips. "We have to go, sweetheart." There were only about two more hours of darkness left.

Enough time to finish this battle.

Understanding filled her eyes as the mist of dreams faded. "We're going after him."

"You won't worry another night about the warlock." He pulled away from her, found his clothes scattered on the floor, and began to dress.

Serena sat up slowly. "And then you'll go away. Back to— wherever the hell you were before, huh?" A touch of anger had entered her voice.

Yeah, he'd go back to Mexico. He had a level-nine demon with a death wish to track.

There was always someone to track.

He picked up Serena's clothes, handed them to her. "Our deal will be over."

Her eyes narrowed. "You'll just walk away." The words were bitten out from between her teeth.

Luis frowned. "What do you want of me, witch?" He'd fight with his last breath for her, *kill* for her.

"More than you can give, *dammit*." She swiped at her eyes.

Oh, hell, was Serena crying?

"This wasn't supposed to happen!" She jumped up, jerked on her clothes. Didn't look at him. "You were supposed to come here, help me, leave and not—" Her words tumbled to a halt, and she shook her head. "Forget it. Let's go get the warlock and end this."

End this. The words echoed in his mind.

Not yet. "What wasn't I supposed to do, Serena?" The question was important. He didn't want to have failed her.

Not when she'd given him a glimpse of life. Passion. Warmth. Things he hadn't felt or seen in centuries.

Her hands balled onto her hips. "*Care.* OK, asshole? You weren't supposed to make me *care.*"

He stilled.

"This is stupid!" Another hard swipe with her hand. "Look, just forget it. I'm scared, I'm tired, I'm trapped in some weird

lust-land with you and I don't know what the hell I'm saying."
She tugged on her boots, hopping. "Just forget—"

His hands caught her and held her steady. "I'm not ever going
to forget you."

For a moment, her lips trembled. Then she pressed them together and shook her head.

He freed her, then stepped back.

"You will," she said, voice steady, eyes wide. "When years
pass and I'm nothing more than ashes on this earth and you're
still living, you'll forget me. Just like you've probably forgotten
so many others and—"

"*I've never forgotten.*" The snarl burst from him and the
room trembled. "Not a soul I've taken, not a loved one I've lost."

Her breath hitched. "Luis . . ."

"You're wrong if you think immortality is easy, sweetheart.
It's not. It's not fun, and it's sure as hell not pretty. It's dark and
it's cold. It's finding villages torn to the ground by fucking
killers—and seeing the bodies of innocents left in their wake. It's
tracking murdering bastards—and burying the dead they leave
behind. It's—"

"Stop." Her fingers pressed against his mouth. "Don't tell me
any more."

This life, it hadn't been *his* choice. To walk alone, no, he'd
never wanted that.

To kill forever.

And live in the darkness.

Torture. Hell, for him.

"I'm sorry," she whispered, and her fingers slid down to cup
his jaw. Serena rose on tiptoe. She pressed her mouth against his.

His arms locked around her, pulled her tightly against him.

The kiss wasn't wild this time. Not desperate.

Softer. Sweeter.

Tender.

He tasted her slowly. Savored the flavor of her on his tongue.
He brushed his lips over hers, so lightly.

After a time, Luis forced his head to lift.

She hadn't expected to care. Well, in such a short time, he sure
as hell hadn't, either.

But he cared for her. He exhaled heavily. Why lie to himself? The feelings were a lot more than just *caring*.

Lust. Need. Want. Yeah, he felt all of those things.

He also wanted just to hold her. To watch her paint in the sunlight. To see her smile.

That wouldn't happen. It wasn't what fate had planned.

At the beginning, he'd thought he'd try to take her. To force her into his world so that he could have a bit of the burning light that he saw shining so brightly within her.

But he couldn't do that. He couldn't force Serena to come into his world.

Not when she didn't belong in his life of violence and death. She needed life and passion.

She didn't need him. Even if she had started to . . . *care* for him.

His mother had warned him of this. Warned that the men in his family fell too quickly, could need and want too much.

His father, for all his power, had died of a broken heart. After all, no mortal weapons could kill one such as he.

But the death of his wife, yeah, that had done it.

Luis gazed down at his witch. "Tomorrow is Halloween." A day normally celebrated by witches. All Hallow's Eve.

A nod.

"We have to stop him before midnight. He'll bind you today if he can, and then he'll try to kill you—"

"On Halloween," she finished, voice quiet. "That's what he did to the witches in LA. Binding, then death."

Because the magic was always stronger on All Hallow's Eve. He stroked her cheek. Brushed back a stray curl. "I'm not going to let that happen."

That pert chin of hers lifted. "Neither am I."

It would be the end for them, though. Serena couldn't go with him where he had to travel. She couldn't, *wouldn't* want to spend the years of her life battling the dregs of the *Other* world.

The foolish plan he'd hatched in the heat of his hunger and selfish lust felt hollow now.

He'd just been alone for so long, and Serena . . . she made him feel so alive.

Yet she deserved peace. Happiness. A happy ending, those endings that princesses got in stories, and witches never did.

He'd always hated those stories.

"Are you ready?" He wasn't.

Serena nodded again.

Then it was time. "Let's go take us down a warlock."

Serena drove to Roswell, knowing the area in the northern section of Atlanta well. There was no traffic on the streets—it was far too early for most folks. She and Luis didn't talk as they drove. Luis was tense and silent, and after her stupid confession fiasco, she wasn't about to open her mouth.

Once they reached Roswell, there were several houses that sported the white columns Jack had mentioned, but only one concealed behind a huge, wrought-iron gate.

"He's going to sense us," she warned, but knew Luis must have already realized that fact. She braked a distance from the house. She didn't feel the pull of the warlock's power, not yet, but if she got much closer . . .

"Won't do him any good. A thirty-second warning isn't going to save his ass."

No, it wouldn't. Not from Luis. And not from her.

"You . . . don't have to come inside, Serena. Let me finish this. There's no need for you to see—"

Me kill. He didn't finish the sentence, but Serena knew exactly what Luis meant.

"I'm coming."

His lips parted as if he would speak, but then he merely gave a grim nod.

"Luis . . ." She touched his arm. "I'm not afraid to see you kill. The idea that psychotic bastards are out there and that they might get to keep hurting and killing others—just like this prick has done—that *frightens* me."

His head cocked to the left side.

"When I saw you kill, yes, for a moment, I was scared—but I was sure as hell terrified more when I realized just what old Jack was capable of doing—*and* what he'd already done."

His eyes were so very golden. She loved those eyes, even when they flooded black with his demon power. "Someone has to stop the darkness, and I think we're all lucky that someone is you."

"I-I can't stop it all. I never can."

Of course not, he was one being. And the world was so very big. And so very bad. "You make a difference, Luis. To me, to others, you make a *huge* difference. I-I want you to know that, and to know that I won't be forgetting you, either."

He bent his head. Crushed his lips to hers. "You damn well better not, sweetheart, or I might just have to come back and remind you of exactly who I am."

Then he was gone. Climbing from the car. Shutting the door.

Serena inhaled slowly, then turned to shove open her own door. As she stood, she realized that she wanted him to come back to her.

Hell, she didn't want him to leave at all.

Not enough time.

She began stalking toward the house. She felt the stir in the air that told her one of her kind was close.

One of her kind—one that had chosen the dark magic. So tempting, that magic. Offering untold power and, according to some, eternal life.

"I've got him," she whispered.

Luis gave a slight inclination of his head. "So do I."

Almost in unison, they began running forward. If they sensed the warlock, then he would have to sense them. *His warning.*

They bounded up the wooden steps of the porch. Luis blasted open the door with a wave of his hand. Serena darted after him, ready to face the bastard who had tormented her. She wanted to find him and—

A sudden, fiery pain knocked her off her feet. She fell onto the gleaming floor of the foyer, a sharp cry on her lips.

The burning cut into her muscles, dug down to the bone, and she didn't need to jerk away the sleeve of her sweater to know what had happened.

The third binding mark branded her upper arm.

Bastard.

Oh, yeah, she had him.

But the asshole sure had her, too.

8

Serena's cry iced his veins. Luis glanced back, saw her stumble to the floor. He reached for her—

"No!" Her face snapped up toward him. Tears slid down her cheeks. "It's the bind—*go!* Stop him!"

He didn't want to leave her on the floor, crying in pain, but there was no choice. With a last glance, he spun on his heel and stormed through the house.

He could feel the magical pull of the warlock's power. There, up ahead, to the right—

A wave of his fingers sent the door flying inward.

It smashed into the wall, missing the warlock's blond head by about a foot.

Lucky bastard.

Well, not for long.

The warlock spun around, a small cloth and a black-hilted athame clutched in his hands.

He looked at Luis for a moment, then he smiled.

Luis hesitated. *Not the usual way death was greeted.*

"Where's the little witch?" the warlock drawled, and the knife slashed across the cloth, cutting the fabric into two pieces that fluttered to the floor.

Serena's shirt. It looked just like one he'd glimpsed in her closet. "You're not going to get her power."

The warlock's smile widened. "I've already gotten the witch's power—it's all tied up and waiting for me."

Bound.

Luis stepped forward and tried to block the image of Serena crying out in pain. His legs were braced apart, and he lifted his hands, letting his claws out. "You're going to die here, warlock."

"Michael. Michael Deveaux." The warlock shook his head. "Really, if you're going to hunt, you should at least know the name of the one you seek."

The name was familiar. A Deveaux had attacked a coven of witches back in the 1900s in South Carolina, but word had passed that he'd died in the fire that consumed the coven house and—

The warlock laughed. "Trying to figure it all out, are you, *cazador?*" He shook his head. "Come now, surely you didn't think that one of my kind wouldn't find the secret to immortality, too? Why let the vampires and your sick lot have all the fun?"

Hell.

"Most witches and wizards—those fucking idiots—think the dark path just brings pain, terror. Death. But they're wrong. The dark—it can bring life, and the secret to living forever, it's so simple, really." He tossed the knife in his hand. The blade glinted. "All you have to do is steal a bit of magic . . ." His hand moved in a deceptively slow twist—and then the blade was spinning, tumbling end over end as it flew toward Luis.

He knocked the knife away with a toss of his right hand. The blade clattered to the floor. "I'm not one of your bound witches, asshole. It'll take a hell of a lot more than you've got to stop me." He didn't care how old the guy was.

Or how powerful the idiot thought he was.

Deveaux would die soon.

"I'm stronger than you think," the warlock growled. "And I know what makes *you* weak."

A scream echoed through the house.

Serena's scream.

Deveaux lifted his hand—

Serena flew into the room, fighting, thrashing, struggling against an invisible force that pulled her through the air.

Luis lunged across the room. Caught the warlock in a fierce grip and threw him against the wall.

Serena's body dropped to the floor. She scrambled across the hard wood and—

The warlock slammed his fist into Luis's chest, the full wrath of his magic behind the blow. This time, Luis was the one who rocked back, stumbling and slamming into the side of a chair.

OK, so the bastard was strong.

He wasn't strong *enough.*

"To me, witch!" the warlock screamed, lifting his hands as power whipped through the room. Wind howled inside the house.

Serena seemed to rocket to the bastard. The warlock smiled that sick, twisted grin as she screamed and shot toward him.

Luis lunged to his feet and—

Serena whipped the warlock's knife from behind her back. "Here I am, asshole!" She plunged the blade into his chest.

The warlock shrieked, an earsplitting cry of rage and fury.

Luis grabbed Serena's wrist and yanked her behind him. As fast as he could, Luis threw up a spell to shield her. The warlock wouldn't touch her again—not with magic or hands.

Deveaux pulled the knife from his chest. "You've desecrated my athame, bitch!"

Serena gave a ragged laugh behind him. "Like I give a damn! You've desecrated all of *our* kind!"

Enough talk. Luis grabbed the warlock. Lifted him into the air. "Tell me, Deveaux, have you killed witches? Bound them, stolen their powers and their lives?"

The question of guilt or innocence was always asked before death. Though he *knew* what answer he'd get from the warlock straining in his grasp.

"Yes, yes, *cazador*, I have, and I'll do it again. I'll kill those bitches and—"

Truth.

"Get ready to burn," Luis whispered and the hot breath of his power flowed through him. His hands heated, the magic boiling beneath his touch and—

"You get ready," Deveaux snarled and slammed his forehead into Luis's.

Luis growled at the snap of pain, but never released his hold on the warlock.

The fire of his magic burned brighter. His hands began to glow.

"I'm not some weak demon, *cazador!* I'm the strongest warlock who has ever walked this earth! You won't kill me, you can't—"

A gust of wind sent the pictures flying from the walls and slid the furniture across the room.

Then the warlock managed to snatch his right hand free of Luis's grasp. His fingers went for Luis's eyes.

"Let's see what you fear, *cazador!*"

The dark spell came at him, hard, fast, and too powerful to block.

His mother. Burning. Screaming his name.

His father, lost, dying.

Serena. Three raised slashes near her shoulder. She lay curled on the floor. Fire raced toward her.

"Luis! Help me! Luis!"

"Dream to reality . . ." The warlock whispered as his fingers fell away. With a snap of sound, fire sparked near the curtains behind them.

Then greedily swept across the room.

"Witches burn so quickly. They're so weak . . ."

"No!" Serena's voice. But not afraid. Furious. "Don't let him trick you!" Her fingers dug into his arms. The nails he loved bit into his flesh. "Forget the flames—fight him!"

But the fire burned so hot.

I don't want to be weak.

She would never be.

"Luis, forget about me. He can't be allowed to hurt the coven. We have to stop him!"

Never weak.

The fire was too close.

He gathered his magic, and let the soul-eater loose.

His hands burned through the warlock's clothes. Deveaux whimpered. Denial. Fear.

His eyes widened when his magic was bound.

The fire around them faded into weak tendrils of smoke.

Deveaux's mouth opened in a scream when death whispered in his ear.

Luis pressed all the harder onto him. He felt the surge of all the dark power trapped within the warlock's body.

Power that would be his.

Every last bloodstained drop.

Deveaux began to shudder against him. Spittle flew from his mouth and the warlock choked, gasping for breath.

His death was too easy. For the crimes he'd committed, he should have suffered, writhed in agony.

But that wasn't the way of the *cazador*.

No, it was for another far stronger than he to give final punishment.

His job was just to deliver the souls.

Luis lifted his hands.

Deveaux fell to the floor, body hard as a rock, breath gone.

Heart forever still.

Luis spun to face Serena then. She was staring, lips parted, at the warlock. He grabbed the sleeve of her sweater. Yanked—

"What—"

The seams snapped free and the sleeve fell to the floor. The three slashes lined her upper arm. Red, angry and—

Fading.

As he watched, the binding marks lightened. The raised skin lowered.

"You did it," she whispered.

He touched her soft skin, smoothed his fingers over her flesh. The marks vanished.

Her smile was so beautiful it broke the heart he'd long forgotten.

"You're safe, Serena, and your coven's safe."

She had her magic, her sisters of the blood.

Her life would be just fine.

As for his . . .

It would never be the same.

* * *

He wasn't the type for good-byes. Especially not with her.

They went back to her home, crossed the threshold just as the first rays of the dawn light trickled across the sky.

He knew that he should leave her. Just walk away.

But he couldn't, not without having her just one more time. A final time.

Luis carried Serena to her bedroom. He didn't bother turning on any of the lights. He undressed her slowly, tenderly. Kissed the hollow of her throat. Tasted the sweetness of her nipples.

His tongue laved the soft curve of her belly, teased the piercing that drove him wild.

His fingers caressed her hips. Parted her thighs. Touched the warm cream that waited for him.

Before, he'd known heat and wild passion with her.

This time, it was different.

When he sank into her, the first thrust was slow. Her sex took him eagerly, squeezing his cock and coating his flesh with her slick heat.

Her eyes were open and locked with his as he withdrew, then thrust. The rhythm was slow, but the hunger burned just as fiercely as before in his blood.

Their lips met in a kiss. Mouths open, tongues tangling. His fingers caressed the center of her arousal even as he drove into her.

The bed squeaked beneath them. The scent of sex filled the air, and her taste flowed onto his tongue.

His head lifted. He raised his body, bracing his weight on his arms, and watched as his cock plunged past her plump nether lips.

Her pale thighs trembled.

He withdrew. Drove back into her snug sex.

Felt the creamy clasp of her body from his cock's root to tip.

She came, clenching around him, breathing out his name.

Another thrust. Another slow, deep drive into her body.

It would never be this good again.

When he climaxed, he didn't speak her name.

But his soul did.

* * *

He was gone.

Serena knew that Luis had left her even before she opened her eyes. There was a coldness, an emptiness, in the room. In the bed.

Steeling herself, she opened her eyes. The bright light of the afternoon sun filled the room.

The imprint of Luis's head was still on her pillow, but her *cazador* was gone.

A long-stemmed red rose lay in his place.

She reached for the flower and lifted it to her nose. The soft petals brushed against her skin.

Such a sweet smell.

Such a fucking painful good-bye.

He did his job. He saved you. The coven. He had to go back to his life.

Her fingers clenched around the rose. A thorn pierced her thumb, drawing blood.

He hadn't even said good-bye. Hadn't even asked if she might want him to stay . . . or if she might want to go with him.

"Because he's a damn *cazador*," she muttered, dropping the rose and glaring at the flower. It was either glare or cry, and she was *not* going to cry. "He has to fight the world. He doesn't have time to spend his days with a witch."

But she would have liked to have spent her days *and* nights with him.

Dammit. She hadn't bargained on falling for him.

Not for a second.

He wasn't supposed to be a man that she could love. He was supposed to have been the worst kind of monster.

Not the perfect mate.

She inhaled, catching the scent of the rose, sex, and . . . him.

"No." Serena shook her head. No, she'd just been through hell. She wasn't going to skulk away now and let her dreams die.

Because she'd realized when that third binding mark bit into her skin that she *did* have dreams. Dreams of a home, of a man who loved her.

Dreams of Luis.

Too late. She should have told him how she felt, not that crap about caring, but how she *really* felt.

There had to be a way. Something she could do.

She'd fought the warlock.

She was sure as hell going to fight for love.

What could she do—

Her mother's voice whispered in her ear, *"The cazador, he comes after witches when they're bad."*

A smile twisted her lips as inspiration filled her. "Time to get bad."

Midnight on All Hallow's Eve. The witching hour, as some called it.

The perfect time for her.

Serena pulled out her athame and carefully cast a circle in the dirt. A small tremble shook her hand as she gripped the knife, remembering the last time she'd held such a weapon.

But the athame—it *shouldn't* have been a weapon. It was meant for magic, not pain and death.

There had been no choice.

Serena exhaled and then bent to light her candles. The wind was still this night. No leaves fluttered in the breeze. As if the air itself were waiting . . .

Just as she had waited. *Too many hours.*

The circle was cast. The words of the spell poured from her. Magic blazed in her heart.

"I summoned you once," she whispered, "and I'll do it again."

Luis gazed down into his tequila and realized that if he tried hard enough, he could see Serena's reflection in the gleaming liquid.

His beautiful witch.

He'd kissed her before he left. Pressed a soft kiss to her cheek and conjured her a rose.

Leaving without a word had seemed to be the right choice. Because if he'd stayed and seen her when she woke, he would have broken down . . . and begged her to stay with him. Not for a few days. Forever.

Forever was a very, *very* long time for him.

Behind him, two coyote shifters snarled over a pool table. He didn't spare them a glance. He was far too focused on memories of his witch.

Would she have considered staying with him? Tying her soul to his so that she could share his life?

No.

Shit. Had he really been arrogant enough to think that he could force her into his life? Back at the beginning, for a wild moment, *he had.* He'd taken one look at her, fallen as hard and fast as his father had for his mother all those centuries before, and he'd thought, simply—

Mine.

But no matter how much he craved her, he couldn't force her into his world.

He brought the glass to his lips. Drained the fiery liquid in one swallow.

A soul bond with someone like him—that was no easy undertaking. Serena would have been forced to give up her home. Her coven. His witch deserved happiness, and she wouldn't find that battling demons every day of her life.

She deserved more. So much more.

So he'd given her the only gift that he could.

He'd walked away to let her live a real life with someone else.

Some utterly lucky asshole who would never, *ever* deserve her and—

The air began to swirl around him. A small tornado that separated him from the others.

Luis stilled. This had happened before. Actually, just seconds before Serena had—

He disappeared and his empty glass fell to the floor, shattering.

He didn't look pissed.

Serena slowly lowered her arms and gazed at Luis's face. Such a handsome face, really. Not hard at all. Strong. Determined.

Perfect.

His eyes narrowed. He stepped out of her circle. "You can't keep playing with dark magic."

"I'm not playing." The whispers in her mind as she'd performed the spell had been louder this time—but she hadn't been the least bit tempted by their lures.

She'd done the spell for one reason. *Love.* The dark powers in this world—and the next—couldn't touch that.

"Why, Serena?" Stark. "Why risk the danger?"

"Why did you leave me without a good-bye?" The rose was on the ground near his left foot. Another part of her spell.

"To spare you." He lifted his right hand, and she saw his claws. His left, and she saw a ball of flames. "Tell me, witch, did you really want to wake to this in your bed every day?"

No hesitation. Besides, she now understood that he'd know when she lied. "Yes."

His nostrils flared.

"That was a truth, wasn't it, *cazador?*"

His head jerked.

"Want to hear a few more?"

He didn't move.

"I didn't expect you—oh, I knew I was getting the big, bad, *cazador*—but I didn't expect *you.* You touched me, and I hungered. Pleasured me, and I wanted more. You held me—" By the blood, she was stripping her pride bare before him, but she wasn't letting him go without a fight! "And I wanted to stay in your arms forever."

Truth. She saw the knowledge in his eyes.

"I told you I cared, and that was a lie."

So easy to see the lies now. Waking up alone with hope gone had a tendency to make things crystal clear for a witch.

Or any woman.

"My body aches for you and so does . . . *shit!* So does my heart, Luis. I feel like I've been waiting for you to come into my life for years, and I didn't even know it until I woke up without you." She sounded sappy, and she wasn't the sappy type.

She was the desperate type. "If you don't want me, tell *me.* I'm a big girl. I can take it." Yeah, it would hurt like hell, and she'd miss him for the rest of her days, but she wouldn't stop him from leaving her. "But do *not* just walk away, without telling me good-bye. Give me that much and—"

And Luis had her in his arms, his hold too tight. "I can't walk away again. *I won't.*"

Truth, even she could sense that.

"I need you, witch. More than I need the night. More than breath. More than magic."

Oh, hell, her knees went weak.

"I left you once, because I didn't want to force you into my world." He drew in a ragged breath. "Because if I think you're mine, if I claim you and cross that line, I'll never let you go and—"

"I am yours." Her mother had told her once that souls recognized their mates. Luis was the mate of her soul. "I've been from the beginning." Understanding had just taken some time.

"If I bind us," he whispered, "there will be no going back, don't you see that? I'll lock you to me, forever. Chain your soul to mine—"

"*Cazador*, it already is." That wrenching emptiness she'd felt upon waking—her soul had missed his.

No more. The binding he spoke of—it wasn't something she feared. No loss of powers, only a joining of spirits.

"Tell me, Luis, tell me how you feel—"

"I feel like you're my world. *My damn world.*"

She didn't try to stop the smile that stretched across her face. "Then I think you're going to be stuck with me."

"Sweetheart, forever is a very long time for me—for *us*—if I bind our souls—"

"Good." She'd never sought immortality and, had forever not promised her life with Luis, well, she probably never would have chosen it. But as long as she had him . . . "Then I'll fight by your side. Love by your side. My magic's back and I can help you. We can make this world better—"

"You already have." He kissed her, the touch of his lips so sweet that she nearly cried out. "You already have."

Air swirled around them. Magic warmed the night.

"Luis?"

"Hold onto me, witch. This ride might get rough . . ."

She laughed and held on tighter. "Just the kind of ride that I like."

He kissed her again and the power bloomed between them.

Serena realized that her mother had been right, about so many things. *If only she'd gotten the chance to tell her so.*

Souls did touch others in this world. They looked for their mates.

The big, bad monsters that waited in the dark—they *did* come after the bad witches.

And sometimes, well, sometimes, it was just good to be a little bit bad . . .

And under love's sweet and sexy spell.

Turn Me On

Noelle Mack

1

"SpectraSign," the receptionist said automatically, continuing to type as she talked into the microphone of a headset. "Our creative concepts light up your—whoops, I have to put you on hold for a sec, okay?"

Beth Danforth, who was waiting to be interviewed, watched as the receptionist corrected something on the computer screen, saved it with a tap on the keyboard, and punched the flashing hold button on the phone console, multitasking for all she was worth.

"Sorry about that," the receptionist was saying. "Of course you don't want your whoops to light up. Yes, sir. I can hear how upset you are." She listened to whoever was screaming at her for another minute. Beth, who was sitting on a padded bench not far away from the reception desk, heard a threat to have the receptionist fired come through loud and clear, peppered with curse words.

It was a weird world and getting weirder every day. Nobody could wait five seconds anymore without tempers being lost and rank being pulled.

"Of course, sir," the receptionist said politely. "Yes. Let me transfer your call." She punched a glowing button on a brushed-aluminum console and the faint yelling stopped. "You are now in voicemail hell, sir," she said to the air and took off her headset.

Then she swiveled in her chair, away from the console and her monitor, to face Beth Danforth. "Justin's expecting you," the receptionist said. "Go on in. First door you come to."

Beth stood up and looked into the corridor that led away from the reception area, seeing only seamless walls. She opened her mouth to ask where the door was, but the other woman seemed to have read her mind.

The receptionist winked. "Trust me, there is a door, but it's closed. Right that way." She pointed with a candy-striped pen that she took out of the straggly but pretty arrangement of cobalt-blue hair piled high on her head. Beth would not go so far as to call the arrangement a bun. There were several other items stuck into the blue hair: a painted butterfly trembling on a spring, a striped feather, and what seemed to be a pair of chopsticks.

"Okay. Thanks very much." Beth picked up the laptop, her presentation for the interview safely snuggled inside its hard drive, and headed right that way, wondering a little.

The CEO was referred to as just . . . Justin? Not Mr. Watts? Looked like SpectraSign was a really laid-back place, even by the freewheeling standards of ad agencies and graphic design companies.

She'd already gotten out of the elevator and gotten lost on the floor below before she made her way up here for her interview. The company was bigger than she'd thought. Judging by the drop-dead funky decor and buzz of activity, it was on the cutting edge of its very competitive field. The receptionist returned to whatever she'd been doing again. In back of her, Beth could hear fingertips clicking lightly on the keyboard. The receptionist answered an internal ring on the phone console and Beth heard her talk to someone she assumed was Justin Watts. "She should be at your door in a second. Uh-huh. Yes, the Times Square pedestrian pattern report's almost done."

There was a door with a recessed latch at the end of the long, white, sun-filled corridor, but it was invisible until you stood in front of it. Beth reached out a finger and traced a few inches of the infinitesimally thin crack that separated the door from the wall. Even with that light pressure, she could feel a hum coming from inside, an electronic kind of hum.

Computers, probably. Lots of them.

She wondered what Justin Watts looked like, mentally running through the possibilities at warp speed. Tall or short? Lean or chunky? Cute or not? Cool cat or dirty dawg?

Beth took a calming breath, told herself she could ace this, added a silent rah-rah and threw in a couple of Hail Marys as a nod to her Catholic grandmother. For good measure, she summoned up her comic-book alter ego, Graphic Design Girl, who could rock a website and simplify a layout in a single bound. She was good at what she did, even if she was starting from scratch all over again, beginning with this interview.

Visionary, her former employer, had closed up shop two months ago, leaving nothing behind in their downtown loft but crumpled sandwich bags and broadband wiring sprouting from a lot of holes in the drywall.

She had brushed up her resumé, posted it every place she could, and hit the hiring trail immediately. So far, no takers. Unfortunately, no one, whether they were in corporate HR or an independent client, seemed to care one way or another about the way her creativity had been praised to the skies. By her friends. On their arty blogs. There were not enough adjectives to describe her talent, according to them. Her marketing concepts had been touted as unique, outstanding, and fantastic.

It was just too bad that Visionary, the video game company whose national advertising she'd created, had tanked so fast. The two geek gods who'd founded the company, college pals whose entire wardrobe consisted of sweatpants and funny, funny T-shirts, had burned through a million dollars of start-up capital and gone back to live with their parents.

Shortly after her search for meaningful employment began, Beth had hustled up a few freelance jobs—one for table lamps, one for pickled beets, one for kitty litter—and given each her all, but the money, at least for the first two, was almost gone. Number three, the kitty litter account, had gone up in smoke when the Whizzy Whizkers king ran off to Boca Raton with his mistress and cleaned out the company account. So the company check had bounced, boing boing, and her bank had socked her with a $35 fee just for letting her know. Nice of them.

No, freelancing wasn't going to cut it. She needed a steady job and she needed health insurance and she needed to pay the exorbitant rent on her dreary little studio apartment in lower Manhattan.

So far, there hadn't been one response to her posts, except from SpectraSign. Would she fit in here? The voice who'd called her cell and made the appointment for today belonged to the receptionist she'd just met, who seemed nice enough, but not like the kind of person who was easily wowed. Beth had no idea what anyone at SpectraSign thought of her credentials and she hadn't been able to find out too much about the company or its CEO. Justin Watts didn't even have a picture on Google Images.

She looked around again, stalling just a little bit longer. For a media-biz company, it definitely seemed to be prospering. The corridor—unlike those at the Visionary—did not bear the sneaker marks of postgrad dudes playing foam-football and colliding bodily with the walls. There was no eviction notice posted on a dartboard, either. No, this space was spectacular in an austere way. Every surface was pure white or brushed aluminum; every piece of furniture was high-end modern design.

She put her hand on the recessed latch to turn it, letting it stay there for a second or two. The latch was pleasantly warm and Beth didn't want to give Justin Watts a chilly-fingered handshake.

"C'mon in," a friendly voice said. A nice, deep, male voice.

Beth took a deep breath. She wanted to make a favorable impression from the second she walked in. Confidence was key. Her ex-boyfriends had always told her she was pretty and the reflection in the mirror this morning hadn't been too scary. Eyeliner and lipgloss and a touch of blush had done the trick today. Her skin had cooperated, for once, not presenting her with an evil little surprise on her nose the way it sometimes did when she was stressed. So she looked okay. There was nothing to distract him from her creative genius and her portfolio. And then there were . . . she searched her mind for irresistible physical attributes and drew a blank.

She did have nice knees, she thought desperately and a little irrationally, and the skirt she had on showed them. Above the knees things got a little plump, below the knees were legs that were okay but not great. Work the knees, she told herself. Beth felt like she was picking up a mysterious charge from this place.

Her skirt clung to her thighs, even edged up slightly. She tugged it down. In the store the skirt had been just right. Not demure and not too revealing, either. It didn't wrinkle. That was why she'd worn it. But material that didn't wrinkle had a slithery side, betraying its origin in Satan's Little Tailor Shop, she thought.

"Anyone out there?" The voice from inside sounded even deeper and more male.

Rah rah rah. He was waiting for her. She turned the latch and went in.

"Hello." Beth took a look at the man working away on one of two monitors and her poor, unemployed heart beat faster.

"Hey . . . be right with you. Hold on a sec," he murmured.

The glow from the screen made his face look faintly luminous, which was an interesting effect. His features were on the rugged side, and there was a dimple involved on the left side of his mouth. *Melt me fucking down*, she thought. Justin Watts was hot.

"Sorry," he said without looking up just yet. "I don't want to lose this thought and I don't mean to be rude but—"

"You're not," she said. "I understand." How many seconds had she dawdled on the other side of the closed door? *Way to go on making a good first impression,* she scolded herself. He continued to study the screen, and she continued to study him.

"Thanks. Okay. That'll do it. Let me just input these changes—" he tapped at the keyboard— "and I'll be right with you."

"No problem. Take your time."

She took the opportunity to flat-out stare at what she could see of him while he concentrated on finishing what he was doing. Justin Watts had thick, dark hair that was the opposite of styled. It stuck up every which way and looked like he had been running his hands through it while he pondered layouts on the drafting table he sat at.

"Done." He tapped another couple of keys and glanced up at her at last. The glance turned into a look that turned into a stare. His gaze was intense, but for some reason Beth didn't feel intimidated. Probably because he had nice, really nice, eyes. Supersexy. And beach-glass blue, shadowed by lashes that were as thick and dark as his hair. His smile made his eyes crinkle at the corners.

Save me, she thought weakly. He rose from the drafting table and walked around it to meet her, giving her a warm, strong, almost electrifying handshake that chased away her nervousness. Mmm. On second thought, she didn't want to be saved.

"Okay," he said. "So you're Beth. I'm Justin." He laughed a little self-consciously. "That's obvious, I guess."

She was charmed. Justin Watts might be a big deal, but he didn't act like one. For one thing, he wasn't sitting behind a typical, CEO-style fortress of a desk made of bleached titanium or whatever, but at a real, old-style, honey-pine drafting table with a state-of-the-art double monitor setup, plus scrap paper and layouts and art stuff all over it. He was clearly a hands-on kind of guy.

"It's really nice to meet you," he was saying. She returned her gaze to his face. "I checked out some of your work on your website—I was impressed."

"Oh. Ah, thanks." Now that he had let go of her hand, her nervousness returned. She clutched the handles of her laptop case like it was her third-grade lunchbox and she was guarding the cupcakes in it from the Table Five death squad, then told herself not to be so twitchy. "Which ones?"

"You can set the laptop right here," Justin said, pointing to the drafting table. "Um, the lamp ads were great. And that animated campaign you did with the dancing beets? Even better—genius, in fact."

She gave him what she hoped was a cool, totally professional nod of acknowledgment. "Thanks," she said, thrilled inside that he'd looked at more than just her resume. "I worked really hard on those."

The lamp assignment had involved nothing more than a good layout using the company's photos, but the stop-motion process of putting tap shoes on pickled beets and making them shuffle off to Buffalo had been a bitch. But she wasn't going to say that. Let him chalk it up to pure genius if he wanted to. And she wasn't going to mention the kitty litter gig at all. He hadn't. Anyway, it didn't count, since she hadn't been paid, the way guys said a date didn't count if they hadn't been laid.

She suspected Justin Watts would never say anything so crude. But no doubt there were women waiting in line just to do him.

She imagined him beckoning and her going to the head of that line and smiled inwardly. No, no, no. She needed this job more than she needed sex right now.

Justin leaned over the drafting table and pushed the layouts to one side. She couldn't help looking. One atmospheric, faux Depression-era photo showed a half-naked guy in faded jeans leaning on a 1930s pickup truck out in a field somewhere. Waving wheat. Hay fork propped on the truck. And the faux farmboy was to die for—it was classic prairie porn, all the way.

The model had quite a manly bulge, she noted. Almost as big as the bale of hay his battered workboot was resting on. Then she looked at the model's face. Oh, yeah. He was famous, even if she couldn't remember his name at the moment. Who he was didn't matter, because a well-known logo was splashed across the bottom of the photo. Blue Blaze Jeans. That was a huge company. She breathed an inward sigh of relief. So SpectraSign had at least one major client to pay their bills. Her paycheck wouldn't bounce.

You're not hired yet, she told herself, setting down her laptop case. Quit ogling manly bulges and get back to convincing Justin Watts that he needs you and only you, on staff, with benefits, as a designer.

Beth unzipped the case and took out the laptop, bending down a little to raise the screen and angle it up while she went through the beep-and-boop ritual of starting it.

"Sorry. You need something to sit down in." He brought over a chair that matched his own—gleaming curves of aluminum formed the legs and seat and back.

Beth settled herself into it and put on her best interview smile as she looked up at him. It made her face feel stretched.

"Did you bring a portfolio?"

She shook her head. "Everything's on my laptop. It just seemed like an easier way of giving you a comprehensive overview."

True and not true. Her ancient cat, who did not take kindly to sudden awakenings, had been sleeping on her actual portfolio. Moving him meant a revenge hairball on the bathmat sooner or later. Usually sooner. She hadn't been willing to risk it when she'd been rushing to get here as it was. Besides that, the contents of the portfolio were disorganized and she had a lot of personal stuff—letters and photos and old comic books—mixed in with her project layouts. It needed winnowing and she hadn't had time.

"Fine." He sat back down and scooted his chair over to the end of the table. "Let's see what you've got."

"Okay." Fumbling a little, Beth pulled up the files she wanted. His being so near was a little disconcerting. Justin wasn't trying to lean in or lech or anything remotely like that, and his long legs were tucked back under his aluminum chair, but even so. He radiated warm sexuality. He couldn't help it, she decided.

"Beth, since I've already seen the final versions of the lamps and the beets, could you give me an idea of how you got there? Second thoughts, mistakes, and all."

"Sure." She tapped the touchpad to open a file.

"I'm interested in your creative process."

Beth laughed. "If you could call it that. Sometimes I think what I do is like trying to catch light in midair. Sometimes I can hold on to it. Not often, though."

His face grew thoughtful. "Funny you should say that."

She looked up at him before she turned the laptop his way. "What do you mean?"

"Ah—geez, it's hard to explain." He searched for the right words while she waited politely. "Basically, I guess I feel that way sometimes myself."

"Oh."

"I just bought SpectraSign," he explained. "I have a lot of ideas to grow the company, but I'm not sure where to start. That's why I decided to bring in a really original designer. And by that I mean someone who hasn't hit the big time yet."

That would be her. But not from want of trying. "Interesting. I didn't know that." She made a vague gesture at the door she'd come through. "I understood the company's been around for several years. I just assumed you were the founder."

He shook his head. "The new owner."

"I see."

"And the CEO, of course. SpectraSign seemed like a worthwhile investment and a good fit for my area of expertise."

"And what's that? If you don't mind my asking," she added hastily.

"Electrical engineering. Quantum mechanics and physics."

Mega-smart and super-sexy. Beth sighed inwardly. She was not remotely in his league. With her luck, he'd turn out to have a spandex suit and the ability to fly.

"I won't bore you with the technical details," he was saying. "Because they don't have much to do with SpectraSign. Long story short, I specialized in the study of photons, angstroms, wave energy, things like that."

Spacey things. Even though she'd been tagged as a space cadet for her comic-book habit, Beth wouldn't know what a photon was if one bit her, and she suspected one had in Science 101 back in high school.

"Anyway, I was curious to see what would happen if I could combine that knowledge with a creative approach," he went on, "and right now I want to build the most dazzling sign Times Square has ever seen."

"Is there a contest going on or something?" Beth searched her brain. He must have just made half a billion by selling a tech company she'd never heard of and was looking for something else to do. Maybe he had money to burn. Hmmm. She couldn't very well ask if he did in so many words.

"No."

"Then why—"

"I have a lot of energy, Beth. Running a world-class sign company ought to be fun, don't you think?"

"World-class? Really? I didn't know SpectraSign was at that level." She flinched the second the words were out of her mouth. "Gah. Sorry. I guess I should have known, huh?" *Good going, you bigmouth bass,* she told herself bitterly. And after he did his homework on you.

Justin only shrugged. "They started out in Las Vegas, made a fortune on the strip. Then the company founder moved to Japan for some reason. They did most of the Ginza signs in Tokyo, you know."

"Awesome place. That's very cool."

"Anyway, he retired, and I bought the company just for the hell of it. First I hired the best software programmers in the business, and then got them started developing multiscreen vid displays, light-emitting diode designs, and other new signage concepts."

"Aha. That explains the humming in the air—the worker bees are busy."

"What humming?" he asked blandly. "I'm not following you."

"I felt it when I touched the door."

He rested his big hands, fingers splayed out, on the drafting table. "You know, I think you're right. The IT department is below my office. I stay out of there, but you pegged the hum. Not surprising. It's a rat's nest of cables and computers and guardian geeks."

"I know the type," Beth said, grinning. She had just noticed, with joy, that he wore no wedding ring, and, furthermore, that there was no telltale trace of a former wedding ring indenting his fourth finger, left hand.

He was single. He radiated sexual energy. He was brilliant. A girl couldn't ask for anything more, besides a job offer.

"Let's get back to Beth Danforth. Tell me more," he was saying. "I want to know everything about you."

An executive who didn't just brag about himself and his company? Now that was unusual. She looked down at her skirt. The knees must be working. She looked back up. All he seemed fixated on was her face, as if he thought she was really pretty. Good going. It was almost time to trot out her talent, but if he wanted her life story, he could have it, judiciously edited to podcast length.

"Oh, I grew up on Long Island," Beth began. "Wait a minute. You don't want to hear that."

"Yes, I do."

"You do? Really?"

"Yeah." He looked totally enthusiastic. In fact, he had a born-yesterday quality that she really liked and his interest in her seemed totally unfaked.

Ahh. She felt even warmer all over. Attention, the ultimate aphrodisiac.

She took a deep breath. "I'll make it mercifully short. My father was a comic book artist. He raised me on his own after my mother died of cancer."

"I'm sorry."

"I was really little," she said matter-of-factly. "I didn't know her, but I wish I had. No, it was just me and the Ink Man."

She was not going to tell Justin Watts that she was Graphic Design Girl.

"Anyway, my aunt—his sister—made sure I ate my vegetables and brushed my hair and did my homework and applied to college."

"In that order?"

"Pretty much. Eventually I majored in marketing, but I always cherished the hope that I could make a living doing what I loved."

Justin looked at her thoughtfully. "You can do better than make a living."

"Huh?"

Out of the blue, he named a salary for the job she was interviewing for that made tears come into her eyes. One rogue tear even trickled into her ear. Great. Her ears were crying. But she had heard him correctly.

"Are you kidding? That much?"

He only nodded. "I have a feeling you're exactly what this company needs."

"But I didn't even finish my presentation. You're not offering me the job, are you?"

"Not if you don't want me to." Justin grinned as he leaned back in his chair and crossed his arms in back of his head. "Go ahead and finish."

"Ah—okay." Beth shook her head, a little nonplussed, and got back to her laptop, opening file after file before he could change his mind. She lost track of time as they brainstormed ideas for a sign to end all signs, she was having so much fun. They eventually agreed to disagree on what he called the dazzle factor.

Justin was for it, she was against.

"It doesn't matter how dazzling an ad is," she informed him, "The second it goes up in Times Square, another company will try to out-dazzle you."

Justin grinned. "Bring 'em on. We'll make another one that's brighter and bigger."

Beth shook her head. "Good marketing doesn't work like that. You have to reach people on an emotional level, not just blow their minds with special effects."

"Really. Tell me more." He sat back up, propped his chin on his hand and gave her an encouraging look.

266 / Noelle Mack

She reached down to pick up the photo of the male model in jeans, which had slipped out of the paper clip holding it to the layout. "All right. Take him, for example—"

"Why?" Justin gave the faux farmboy a bored look. "He has better abs than I do. So I wouldn't buy the jeans," he said.

Beth waved the photo at him. "You're missing the point. He's designed to appeal to a female customer in a subtle way."

"I wouldn't call that pose subtle."

"But he's not all lit up. This looks like an old photograph of the bad boy she, meaning our hypothetical customer, used to love. Who she still wants."

"Whoa." Justin held up both hands. "Isn't he selling men's jeans?"

"Women buy jeans for their guys. Or they make their guys buy the right jeans. You know, the nuances of how jeans should hang on a male body and what jeans should do for a male butt are lost on most straight guys, who will go out and buy the cheapest pair they can find unless—"

He was smiling. Beth realized she had gotten off-topic. Way off-topic. And this was a job interview.

"Um, I talk too much. Sorry."

"Not at all," he laughed. "This is great. You just lay it out there. And I obviously have a lot to learn."

"Really." She covered her flustered feeling by talking fast. "About what? I mean, you have a major client already—Blue Blazes Jeans is huge—" She stopped, telling herself not to babble.

He looked . . . eager. If that was the right word. At least his face still had that luminous glow she'd noticed when she came into his office, even though both monitors on the drafting table were off and he wasn't looking at her laptop at the moment.

"Yeah, well, they are. Anyway, Blue Blazes sent over those mock-ups and some others but I'm not sure the concept will work when the model is forty feet tall, in motion, and lit up."

She nodded in agreement, although she wouldn't have minded seeing that particular male model strutting his stuff at any size. Come to think of it, that went for Justin Watts too. She doubted that the model had better abs than Justin. She would guess that they were about even when it came to world-class male abs.

"Your company has at least one sign in Times Square right now, right?"

"We do." He named the brand and the global food conglomerate that owned it. "It's a great big bag of holographic potato chips. The bag rotates and the potato chips float out. The idea is that they're lighter than other potato chips."

"Got it."

"Of course, we don't show the calorie count or fat grams. Both would give a cardiologist a heart attack."

"I understand," Beth said, laughing. "But that's a great account to have."

"But visually not exciting. There's a limit to what you can do with potato chips. Seen one, seen 'em all. That's why I was so interested in what you did with the tap-dancing beets. They had personality."

She smiled. "That wasn't easy."

"I can imagine."

"So . . ." She was curious, and he had asked all the questions. "You really do have the Blue Blazes account?"

"Yup."

She nodded in understanding. "And you want to do a jeans ad that will have everyone talking and stopping to look."

"That's right," Justin said. "But I don't think their approach is going to do it." He flicked the photograph of the male model to one side.

"Hmm." Beth clicked through older folders in her documents. "Let me show you the first sign I ever did—here it is. I scanned in these drawings."

Justin peered at the image on the screen. "What is that?"

"A fried clam. Sammy the Clam, to be exact."

"You've improved."

Beth laughed. "Well, I was only seventeen when I did those. I worked at the Olde Clamme Shacke as a waitress and the owner needed a new sign. So I came up with Sammy. The orders went up right away."

"Why?"

"We printed Sammy on the menus and the placemats, too. He was a goofy little character that stuck in people's heads, I guess. Different from what I usually drew."

Justin shot her an interested look. "Which was?"

"Superheroes. If you grow up reading comic books, it comes kinda naturally."

"I see. Doesn't seem like a girl thing to do, but why not?"

"Hey, I put plastic dinosaur heads on my Barbies. I wasn't ever a girly girl—basically, I was just a weird kid."

"Weird kids usually grow up to be some of the most interesting people, Beth."

Awww. She beamed at him, momentarily forgetting that she was supposed to be in interview mode. "Sometimes I was shy and sometimes I couldn't stop talking."

"I'm not sure that's changed." Justin chuckled in a very nice way. "So keep talking."

Encouraged by his wink, Beth took a breath and continued. "Um, I never really felt like I belonged in suburban Long Island. When I was old enough, I took the train into New York every chance I got. It always seemed like a perfect place for superheroes and it felt like home to me. Lots of comics are set in, quote-unquote, Gotham. Anyway, blah blah, I went looking for the settings I'd seen in my dad's portfolio and I actually found a few."

"I'd like to see them."

Beth gave him a curious look. "They're still there. Maybe not for long. The city's getting ripped up and torn down."

"I know what you mean. An entire YMCA can disappear overnight."

"Yeah. At least in comics, an intergalactic rec center would pop up in its place."

"Sign me up," Justin said with a huge, guy-type grin.

Beth grinned back. They just looked at each other for a minute that didn't feel at all uncomfortable or weird.

"So," he said at last, "how would you define your approach to a campaign like this?"

Beth thought it over. "You have to make people believe that wonderful, impossible things are real. It's all about that."

"Which makes you perfect for advertising work."

Beth smiled. "I hope so." Perfect for this job would be just fine. Had he decided? Evidently not.

"Show me more," he said.

Beth clicked open a few more files with drawings and concepts for all kinds of things. Then she came to one with a title she didn't recognize and opened it without thinking.

The image appeared. It showed a canopy bed with four posters made of neon tubes. Hot pink neon tubes.

"What's that?" Justin seemed more than curious. He leaned in for a really good look.

Holy cow. She never should've clicked on that one. Beth wanted to close it out, but she couldn't quite bring herself to. It would be like slamming a door right in Justin's face.

"Ah—not my work. An ex-boyfriend of mine designed that. Not exactly practical."

Justin was reading the fine print next to the image of the bed. "Says here that it lights up at the moment of orgasm."

Uh-oh. She'd forgotten about that part. Beth gave him a sheepish smile. "He never did build it."

"Great concept, though."

Beth cleared her throat. "Never was more than that. Okay, moving right along—"

She finished her presentation and Justin's attention never strayed. If she had to describe his reaction, she would say that he seemed really excited by her ideas. Maybe even by her.

His energy was definitely contagious. Her initial nervousness had completely vanished by the time the interview was over.

He got up while she shut down her laptop and wandered around his office, looking out the floor-to-ceiling windows.

"You never did mention where you're from," she said, by way of making conversation. She closed the cover with a snick. "New York?"

"Yeah." He waved at the skyline outside. Or the sky. Whatever. She didn't need to pry.

"Still live in the city?" she asked lightly.

Justin turned around. His energy almost seemed to crackle around him, but then he'd said he'd just bought the company, so maybe the carpets were new and full of static.

Beth tugged at her skirt to keep it down, just in case it got electrified and started clinging. The interview had been all about her talent and not her knees. *Good sign,* she thought.

"Yes, I do. How about you?"

She nodded. "I have a studio just off Hudson Street."

"Oh, then you're not far from me. I live in the Bolt Building."

Beth thought a minute. "The Art Deco skyscraper that's way downtown? The one with all the lightning bolts on the façade?"

"That's right. Built in 1935 by Jasper Bolt, the world's craziest billionaire."

"How did he make his money?"

"No one really knows. But the building is great, full of freaky architectural details."

He didn't say anything tacky like *come on up and play in my penthouse*. But given a few weeks of working with him, assuming she had been hired, she wouldn't mind if he did. Was she, then? He had quoted a salary. He just hadn't said the most wonderful three little words in the world. *You have job.*

I love you would've been okay with her too, but that was definitely rushing things.

"I bet it is," Beth said politely.

"Okay," he said suddenly. "Let's get back to business. You do have the job, if you want it."

She inhaled, and tried desperately not to squeak on the exhale. "I do? This job?"

"Yes." He waited for a beat. "Now you say yes."

Beth willed herself to remain completely calm and forced her voice to reflect some self-control. "Exactly what will my responsibilities entail?"

He shrugged. "We'll figure that out as we go along, Beth. You know the salary."

She nodded, rigid with the effort of not jumping around the room. "I think it's commensurate with my abilities."

He stuck his hands in his pockets. "Talk corporate to me. I love it. Is that a yes or a no?"

That damned dimple of his was flashing like a go-for-it sign. "Full benefits, by the way. Dental. Disability. And 401K matching, the whole nine."

Beth fought the urge to throw her arms around him and give him an exuberant kiss on the cheek. But she couldn't resist the excellent offer a second longer.

"I accept. Thank you." She wanted to scream a yes. She hoped her measured voice communicated some enthusiasm. She knew her eyes were sparkling, because her nose was itching. She couldn't scratch it, just couldn't.

Justin nodded, and gave her a huge grin. "All right. See you Monday. Bright and early."

"Okay." She couldn't think of anything else intelligent to say. "Wow. This is so incredible. Thanks again. This is going to be great."

"I agree."

He stayed where he was. She backed out, trying not to trip on his new carpet. Beth clutched her laptop under one arm and gave him a fingery wave. Then she skittered down the long, white hallway, flashed a huge smile at the receptionist, and went out the door. She did dance in the elevator. There was no one in it but her.

Out on the sidewalk, she felt like she was walking on air. She had a job. She wasn't going to be broke. She was ready, really ready to sell blue jeans. Life was good again.

She blew her last bucks on a work-appropriate wardrobe for SpectraSign, shopping until early evening. You deserve it, you need it, you will be able to pay for it in another week, she told herself, lugging the bags home, along Hudson Street, trying to keep the strap of her laptop case from sliding off her shoulder.

It was twilight and the streetlamps were just coming on. A strong westerly breeze was blowing from the river, making a few pieces of litter fly around through the side streets, including hers. Beth went up the stoop of her five-story building, the bags rattling and bouncing against her legs. Her short skirt was a lost cause, flipping wildly.

It was a relief to edge inside the main door. She set everything down except the laptop and peered into the brass grille of her mailbox. There was something white in there. Probably another bill.

Ha ha. She could pay them all now. She could even afford senior-care cat food for old Freddy, and maybe cut down on the hairball count. Beth found her key ring and looked for the tiny brass one that opened the mailbox, pulling out a letter from her father.

She knew it was from him without even looking at the return address. He always drew on his envelopes and letters, something he couldn't do with e-mail. She saved each missive—since she'd moved out of his house on Long Island, there had been one every week for years. She slipped the decorated envelope into one of the shopping bags and continued upstairs.

Four locks later, she was inside her studio apartment. Still struggling with the bags, Beth bumped into the antique dress-maker's dummy that she called Miss Boom Bah and used as a coatrack. The full-figured dummy tipped forward, then stood up-right again when she gave it a shove back. It took a lot to upset Miss Boom Bah.

Beth slung her light jacket over the coat on the dummy's shoulders and looked down at the old gingerbread-colored cat rubbing her ankle. "Guess what, Freddy?"

The cat gave a wheezing, very faint meow. She bent down to give him a chin rub just the way he liked it.

"We're in the money. I have a job."

Freddy wheezed, and she sat down and stroked him for a while. He got bored with it, wandered off, and stuck his nose into one of the shopping bags.

"Stay away from my fabulous new wardrobe," she told him sternly. Freddy glared at her as she got up, gathered all the bags, and hung them on an inside hook in her tiny closet. Then she went into the kitchenette to call her dad.

2

Two months later . . .

"So this is the famous Bolt Building."
Justin was waiting for her, a bulging plastic shopping bag in his hand. He was wearing jeans with a few for-real rips, and a linen shirt, and disreputable-looking sneakers. He looked fabulous. "Yup. And this is just the lobby."

"Wow," she said. The riotous Art Deco ornamentation didn't stop. Every surface she could see was covered with stylized motifs, quite a few of them representing lightning, as far as she could tell.

The concierge, an unassuming older guy, sat at a console, if that was the right word, which would have been a great altar for a pagan god. Huge, freestanding bolts of lightning bolts framed it, done in chrome polished to a high shine. The console itself was also metal, with a huge bronze sun emitting spiky rays adorning the front.

When Beth got done looking at it, she studied the vaulted ceiling, shot through with more bronze rays and zigzagging lines. No matter where her gaze settled, something about the restless design made it move on. She got the dizzying feeling she'd walked into an alternate galaxy and glanced down again, at the floor, hoping it would ground her.

No such luck.

Even the floor was decorated with fanciful planets and stars and comets, done in flat metal and imbedded at random in each of the tiles.

"Welcome to my world," Justin said laughing. "It's a bit much, isn't it?"

"It's spectacular," she said, "but I guess you get used to it after a while, like anything else."

"Yeah, I am by now." He walked toward the bank of elevators, and Beth followed.

"How long have you been living here?"

"I bought my apartment when I bought SpectraSign," he said. He punched the up button, which was in the shape of a very small lightning bolt, and waited with her. "Glad you could come."

"I wouldn't have missed this for anything," she said. And she didn't mean the lobby. He'd taken her out for dinner several times since he'd hired her, and it was clear that his interest in her wasn't all about work.

Though they had been doing plenty of that. The design team, a bunch of thirtyish men and women with eyeglasses so narrow she wondered how they saw out of them, had slaved away on the Blue Blazes account and the software geeks had actually been able to turn their ideas into something that worked.

The resulting sign concept was accepted by Blue Blaze top management and was now being built in Times Square. It would be fifty feet high, thirty feet wide. Beth couldn't wait to see it. They were celebrating the go-ahead tonight.

She'd coordinated the project from her first day on the job, simply because she worked so closely with Justin. At first Beth had wondered if that was wise, but it wasn't like she exactly had a choice. That was how he wanted it.

And it was really clear that he wanted her. Likewise, as far as she was concerned. Which was why she'd bought killer lingerie from Agent Provocateur for tonight. It did wonderful things for her, um, things. If he got that far.

From the way he was looking at her right now, she suspected he would.

An elevator arrived, the door whooshed open, and they went inside. She looked around, wondering why it had glass walls, then figured it was to let the passengers look at the decorated inside of the shaft. Yep, more lightning.

"This Bolt guy was crazy," she said.

"Certifiable." Justin put a keycard in a slot next to the PH button and up they went.

A penthouse. Ooh. She really wanted to see what life was like that high up in the air.

"Do you get vertigo?" he asked.

"Not usually, why?"

"We'll be in the glass part of the elevator shaft in another few floors. It was added much later, about ten years ago—here it comes."

Beth gasped. "Oh my God, what a view!" All of lower Manhattan suddenly appeared. The buildings thrust upward, almost appearing to move along with them, their lit windows turning into streaks of light here and there. She glimpsed details that were impossible to see from the street—on the older buildings, gargoyles and lion's heads and decorative pediments and, on the new buildings, raked angles of glass that glowed strangely in the twilight and even neon outlining the tops.

What a view, she thought. She wasn't going to crow it out loud again, because it was a corny thing to say and he was probably just as used to the spectacular scene as he was to everything else about the Bolt Building.

"Yeah, it's incredible."

There was a note of awe in his voice, which pleased her. She'd picked up on his natural enthusiasm from the first day they'd met and in the eight weeks that she'd been on the job, observed how it inspired the company clients and his employees, her, most of all.

Beth looked at him instead of the cityscape for a moment, observing the way the otherworldly glow of the city at night brought out something that was indescribably wonderful in his face. The color of his eyes seemed to intensify and become a different blue. Call it blue times two.

Justin sighed with pleasure as the elevator came to a stop and he held the button for her to exit ahead of him.

"Hold on. I just want one last look," Beth said. She turned

around to take in the panoramic view of New York's harbor. Even in the semidarkness, she could make out the giant orange ferries coming and going from Staten Island, trailing long white wakes, and innumerable small boats out on the water. The vast shapes of tankers moved slowly, guided by the tugs she'd loved to watch as a kid, heading toward the graceful, gigantic bridge that soared over the narrows before the open sea.

"You can see that from my living room," Justin said, keeping his finger on the open button and letting her look her fill. "And the Statue of Liberty, too. My big green girlfriend."

She thought of Miss Boom Bah and smiled.

"We can drink a toast to her," Justin added. "I have champagne on ice."

"Sounds glamorous."

He chuckled. "It's good champagne. And I made great cheese dip to go with it."

"Is that the gourmet meal you promised me?"

"In the bag." He held it up so she could see it. "The delivery dude got to the lobby just before you did."

"And I thought you came down to meet me."

"I'm willing to take the credit for it."

Beth shook her head. "Nope. And I thought that you were going to do the cooking."

"I made no promises to that effect. Hey, you said you didn't feel like going out to another restaurant tonight. Anyway, we've gone to all my favorites and yours."

She nodded, understanding his unspoken message: I want to get you alone. He probably assumed she had a roommate, although he had never asked. Nothing doing. She wasn't about to invite him over to her place for an intimate dinner with wheezing Freddy and Miss Boom Bah.

The kitchenette wasn't really big enough to cook in, anyway. She could just imagine Justin perched on her rump-sprung sofa with a plate on his lap and a Chinese takeout bag between them, rolling up shredded moo shu cabbage inside those thin pancakes and trying to make small talk while the gooey sauce squirted out the other end.

Too suggestive. Nothing doing. He'd finally asked her over and she'd said yes at once.

He led the way down a hall lined with . . . that couldn't be lapis lazuli. She looked closer and touched a hand to the smooth, floor-to-ceiling panel. Maybe it was. The deep blue stone was speckled with tiny fragments of gold. How rich was he?

Okay, she admonished herself, his apartment, which he owned, was on this floor, but that didn't mean he owned the whole floor and had paneled the hallways in semiprecious stone. Justin Watts didn't seem like the kind of guy who had to show off to that degree. He didn't really show off at all, despite his engaging, boyish enthusiasm. And as far as she knew, he wasn't a billionaire, which would have been fairly weird. No, he was down-to-earth, even if he lived up in the clouds. She couldn't wait to see his place.

"So you didn't do the cooking. Hmm. Any other secrets to reveal, Justin?"

"Not just yet," he said.

Watching his broad shoulders under the linen shirt he hadn't bothered to tuck into his jeans, Beth was willing to bet that all would be revealed—meaning her fabulous new underwear—before midnight.

He used the same keycard to unlock his door and in they went.

Beth looked around. Huge windows gave an even better view of lower Manhattan by night. She almost ran to them. There were the massive gothic arches of the Brooklyn Bridge, joined by the delicate tracery of lights on the supporting cables. She could see for miles, over all of Brooklyn, low but lit up, and out into the harbor and beyond. Beth looked right and there was the Statue of Liberty, looking small and stalwart, her torch raised.

"Oh my God," she breathed. "This is amazing. Just amazing."

"Glad you like it. Haven't been here long enough to decorate much. Walk around, make yourself at home."

He got busy in the kitchen, unloading the bag as she did what he suggested. There wasn't much furniture and it wasn't too different from what any young, successful guy in Manhattan had. Leather sofa, nine feet long. Monster plasma TV. Squooshy leather armchairs with ottomans. In a bedroom she peeked into, a really big bed. There were a lot of rooms but some doors were closed and she wasn't going to snoop.

She realized she was going in a circle, though, and that the apartment was a floor-through. My, my, my.

Beth ended up in the kitchen again, determined to sound casual. What could she possibly say that wouldn't make her sound like a gold-digger or a hick from the sticks?

She was going to keep right on relating to him like he was just this incredibly cute, nice guy she worked with, that was all.

"So what's for dinner?"

"Steak. Salad. Baked potatoes." He ripped off the menu stapled to the bag and read aloud. "From Peter O'Grady's legendary steakhouse, home of the hundred-dollar sirloin."

"How bad can it be?"

He gestured at the foil containers lined up neatly on his kitchen counter, which she was relieved to see was made of mere granite. "Let's eat."

She picked up a fork and speared a piece of salad. "Can't go wrong with the tried and true."

"Is it? I guess food like that is still kinda new to me," he laughed.

Beth didn't really hear him say it. The lettuce she was chewing was very fresh and very crunchy.

He stuck a fork into a piece of sliced steak and ate it. "Fantastic," he said. "Have some. Want a plate?"

"Not really," she laughed, "I'm starving."

He nodded. "Me too. What about the champagne?"

Beth slid the foil container of sliced steak in front of her. "Let's have it with dessert."

"Good idea."

They were both starving and the movable feast disappeared pretty quickly. Satisfied, feeling pleasantly absentminded, Beth licked the tines of her fork when she was done. Justin noticed. Boy, did he notice. What she was doing made him stop eating.

"Are you trying to turn me on?"

She snorted and put the fork down. "No. Does that do it for you?"

"Your pretty pink tongue? Licking? Yeah," he answered boldly. "It really does."

Well, all right. They had gone from zero to sixty in less a second.

"That was fast," she said.

He sighed. "No sense fighting it, then, is there? I really care about you, Beth. And you turn me on like no one else."

She squirmed in her seat. Not as if she hadn't imagined herself in his arms a thousand times already. But being here, alone with him, was different.

"What's for dessert?" she asked.

"You are." He smiled a slow, slow smile that was scorchingly sexy. It melted whatever was left of her resistance.

As it turned out, he knew how to take his time. He'd suggested a move to the sofa and a look at the ever-changing view, and eventually he'd opened the champagne.

Giddy from it, and her own excitement, she was lying on his bed in nothing but stockings attached to a gartered thong and a demi-cup bra.

"Wow," was all he said as he stroked her legs. "You are incredible."

Beth blushed, a head-to-foot feeling of warmth.

"Would you mind rolling over? I want to see what this pretty stuff looks like from the back," he murmured.

"There's not much of it." She smiled, though, and rolled over on her tummy, supporting her head on her folded arms.

Justin's big hands moved in sweeping caresses over her back and shoulders. He took a minute just to play with her hair, running his fingers through it and letting the long locks slide away from her neck.

With gentle pressure, using mostly his thumb, he rubbed her neck and went on down her spine from there.

Slow, small circles. Circles that seemed interconnected in some way, as if he was joining together parts of her that needed to get to know each other again. Beth felt a whole-body sense of profound relaxation. And trust.

"Mmm."

He kept on rubbing. "Moan away. I want this to feel as good as possible."

When his fingers reached the back part of her bra, he unhooked it and pushed the two parts away. Then he continued to massage her spine all the way down to her tailbone and up again to her neck.

Beth sighed with delight. He stopped and she could tell from the sounds of zippers and buttons that he was shedding his clothes.

She wanted to look and almost turned around . . . and then it occurred to her how wonderful it would be to experience him first just through his touch. The feel of his bare skin against hers.

And Justin didn't disappoint her.

She felt him clamber onto the bed, pleasurably aware of the muscular hardness of the thighs that suddenly straddled her bare ass. The prickle of the fine hair on them was stimulating. Little shivers of arousal coursed through her.

Staying up, he continued his luxurious massage of her back and shoulders. Every so often she felt his balls brush against her behind, and she smiled into the tumbling hair that covered the side of her face.

They felt soft but heavy, and tighter each time they touched down. His gentleness held an unmistakable strength, and she relaxed even more as the caressing pressure of his hands grew more intense.

He moved her hair away so that he could come down and kiss her neck and the one ear he could get at.

Then she felt it. His huge, silky-stiff cock rested between the cheeks of her bare ass. Not doing anything, not thrusting, just there.

He was down on his elbows now, his legs folded up, his whole body covering hers.

Justin kissed her neck and treated her to tiny bites on the nape. The sensation traveled down every nerve she had and ended up between her legs. In another few minutes, he licked and nipped at her ear, suckling on the lobe, and had her dripping wet. The soft front panel of the thong was soaked.

Usually she would never get that hot without nipple play and it was incredible to even imagine how good that was going to be.

Beth began to rock under him, savoring the feel of that big, hard body covering her but not weighing her down. He slid down a hand under her, moving it over the front of her hips, until he could slip a probing finger into her wet thong panties.

Her clit just about jumped when he touched it. He sighed with warm satisfaction into her ear. "There it is. You're as hard as I am."

"Yeah?" she murmured, giving a sensual, almost inaudible laugh. "But you've got a good nine inches on me. That feels like quite a cock."

"Like it?"

"Yes," she said.

"Want it?"

"You know I do," she whispered.

"It's almost in you," he whispered back. He continued to kiss and nip her neck while he pressed down a little more and played with her clit through the panties. The sheer size of his rod kept her ass cheeks apart.

Justin withdrew his finger and touched it to her lips. "Taste yourself. I want to see that pretty pink tongue again."

She darted it out and licked his finger daintily.

"You're delicious," he said.

"If you say so," she murmured. She turned her head a little more so she could open her mouth and suck on his finger, letting him slide it in and out.

His breathing got faster and his cock got stiffer.

"I can't wait to taste you myself," was the last thing he said before he rose up again. But he stayed essentially where he was, still straddling her, only lower down.

This time it was her ass that got the royal treatment.

Justin placed a big, warm hand on each cheek and began to alternate strokes and squeezes.

Not quite aware she was doing it, Beth began to moan.

"You like that, don't you?"

"Uh-huh. Oh . . . . ohhhh. Don't stop . . . ohhh."

Now he was pushing her hips down into the soft, ultra-comfortable bed but doing it lightly. Still, the repeated press-and-release motion was incredibly exciting.

He stopped and she held her breath.

Staying on his knees, Justin moved out of the straddle and to the side. Then he got off the bed and she heard him walk around.

She stayed motionless. Whatever he wanted to do was fine with her.

Beth smiled a hidden smile when she felt his hands encircle her ankles and spread her legs with a swift, strong motion that left no doubt in her mind that he was staring at her juicy pussy. The thong front had been pulled between her labia, which were freshly shaved and exquisitely sensitive.

The powder-puff of springy curls she left at the top couldn't be seen in this position. Just plump, utterly feminine flesh split in two, begging to take cock.

He sighed as he looked his fill, holding her ankles more tightly than before.

"I wish you could see yourself like this," he said at last.

Beth raised her head but she didn't turn around. "I masturbate with a hand mirror sometimes, but I can't get this view. Glad you like it."

"Oh, I do." He didn't speak for just a beat. "Tell me about that. Tell me how you do it with a mirror."

He let go of her ankles and kneeled between them, rubbing her ass again, taking a voluptuous pleasure in doing it extra slowly.

"I use a dildo," she murmured. "I hold the mirror in the other hand. It's an antique dildo, made of sterling silver."

He chuckled in a very soft, very male voice.

"And where'd you get that?"

"In London, of all places. In one of those goddess shops."

"Sterling silver, huh? I'd love to see that penetrating your beautiful, slippery, pink pussy."

"It feels really good. And it gets warm quickly, almost hot. It's different from the plastic ones. It's not that big. Nowhere near as big as you."

"Just right for starters, hmm?"

She nodded.

"Go on."

Beth sighed with pleasure. He had begun to push her down into the bed again. She wasn't sure of how much more she could take before she flipped over and begged him to fuck her if he had to shred the thong to do it.

"Where was I?"

"The mirror."

"Right. I hold it so I can see all of my pussy and I get the silver dildo nice and slick on the outside. Then I put it most of the way in."

"Mmm," he said. "I can see you doing that."

"Then I tease my clit. If my pussy gets too excited, the dildo begins to rise and I push it back in. The base is kind of swollen and kind of flat so it can't go all the way in."

"Unlike me. Because I will. When you're ready."

Beth stretched luxuriously, enjoying the absolute best ass massage she'd ever had for as long as he was willing to do it.

"Then I put the mirror aside," she said after a while.

"Yes. And?" He knew better than to quit.

"I hold the base of the dildo and thrust it in and out while I pinch my clit. I try—" She faltered for a moment. Thinking about what she had done for solo pleasure combined with what he was doing to her right now was about to make her have an orgasm. And this was only the foreplay, she thought with wonder.

"Yes?"

"I try to make my fingers feel like tight lips on my clit. Sucking me and sucking me until I come—I want to come—oh!"

Several playful but pleasurably strong slaps on the ass from Justin put that thought out of her mind.

In another second, he had her turned over. And then she saw him naked.

He was much better than her imagination. The solid muscles of his torso were beautifully cut and sprinkled with fine, dark hair that twirled into a narrow trail down past his bellybutton, a sexy innie.

That pointed straight to his gorgeous, thick cock, which he was holding.

He let out a ragged breath. "I'm trying to get a grip. You make it hard, Beth."

He looked down, drinking her in. The bra had fallen off the bed when she turned and her breasts were still bouncing.

Justin let go of his cock and bent over her on all fours, sucking one nipple and caressing the other under his circling palm. He reversed his attentions until both breasts were wildly stimulated. She cupped them in her hands and squeezed to intensify the pleasure he was giving her, squeezed so that her fingernails dug into her own soft flesh, leaving little scratches.

Justin rose onto one hand and stopped her, kissing each mark lovingly and soothingly.

"Your tits are hotter than your ass, if that's possible," he murmured, stroking them next. "All of you is round and gorgeous. You're made for sex, do you know that?"

Beth shook her head. Her hair was tangled, hot underneath her. She was frustrated as hell, but enjoying this to the max.

"What do you want me to do next?"

Beth reached down and ran a finger over the front of his cock, down the part like a seam and up into the split part of the plum-like head, all the way down and then up again, over and over.

Her subtle stroking obviously excited him. He held still, but finally trembled when a pearly drop of precum welled from the head and stayed there on the heated, swollen skin. She swiped it off with a fingertip and popped it into her mouth, savoring the thick saltiness taste while she looked into his mesmerized eyes.

"Get over my mouth," she whispered.

Justin did—the bed was huge and there was plenty of room for them to try a hundred different positions.

She looked up, her eyes half-closed with pure pleasure at the sight of everything he had between his legs but much closer now: heavy, big balls and that unbelievable cock.

She reached for a pillow, rolled it under her head, and began to lick him exactly as she guessed he wanted to be licked—thoroughly and sensually. She gave him long strokes along the shaft, teasing ones over the head, wet, eager laps over and around his balls until he began to moan, gripping his thighs until the veins on his hands stood out just to keep upright in the precise position for her to pleasure him orally like this.

He tasted so good. His smell was a combination of plain clean and pure man. She nuzzled between his legs, breathing it in. Then Beth stopped and encircled her fingers around his cock, pushing him back a little with one hand on his groin.

"I want this," she said. "Get ready."

Never had she seen a man get up, find a condom, and sheathe himself that fast. She got rid of the thong and the stockings in record time herself. Just watching him roll the nearly transparent latex on as his huge rod strained against his hand turned her on. A lot.

In another second Justin was over her on all fours, lifting one of her legs over his bent arm. She could just reach to help him position the head, but her hand was almost caught between their bodies when he suddenly rammed into her with a rough cry.

Oh, God. His eyes widened as he looked into hers, the sensation of that first, deep penetration thrilling them both.

"More," she begged. "Give it to me hard. I want it hard. I want you—"

His thrusts were charged with erotic energy, his body vibrating with it. Bucking under him, taking all nine very hot inches deep inside her pussy again and again, Beth wanted to scream with pleasure, but bit her lip instead.

His hand went around her chin and he gave her a deeply passionate kiss while he fucked her, capturing her moans.

"Go ahead," he growled when he stopped kissing her to take a breath. He didn't stop fucking her, though. He was rolling and rocking now, stimulating her clit with the pressure of his body in between thrusts. "We're on top of the world, girl. Make all the noise you want to."

Lost in the extreme pleasure of what he was doing. Beth let go completely. She brought her hips up to meet every downward thrust of his, clawing at his fine, hard ass, and begging for more.

She got it. She got everything she ever dreamed of from a man who seemed to have come out of her wildest dreams. She screamed his name when he made her come and he shouted hers.

Slowly, slowly, the glorious feeling ebbed away. He pulled out, did what he had to with the condom, turned her on her side and curled completely around her, her bare ass tucked against his groin and her breasts lifted by one of his mighty arms. The other was stretched over the long curve of her hip, heavy with his weariness. From the very male and beginning-to-be-scratchy chin that rested on her head to her toes, which rested on the tops of his big warm feet, she felt protected and utterly satisfied.

On top of the world? Not quite, she thought. She felt more like she was on top of the universe as she drifted off, half in love, blissed out. Somewhere around midnight, they woke up and did it again. Only better.

* * *

The long moan of a ship's horn startled her out of a very deep sleep. Beth eased out of Justin's cocooning embrace—he was in back of her, which made it easy—and wriggled to look at the clock. Five-oh-five a.m. Just before daybreak. There was no light coming from the windows to speak of—they were uncurtained, it was too high up for anyone to see in. But there was a light in the room that puzzled her, an ambient glow that was a deep, indefinable blue. It didn't seem to be coming from anywhere in particular. But what if it woke Justin? They would both have to get up in time to shower and she would have to dash home to change her clothes, she thought drowsily.

Gee. She felt kind of proud. She hadn't had to do the Stayed-Out-All-Night-Wearing-The-Clothes-I-Slept-In Walk of Shame in front of coworkers for a long time.

Beth rubbed her eyes, thinking about it. Maybe it would be best if she left first, got a taxi before the early-rising traders got down to the Wall Street area, even before the coffee vendors arrived in their rattling, quilted-steel carts.

Yeah. Good idea.

She rolled over to look at Justin. He had flopped back into the pillows, still naked, a hand on his balls and one big arm over his head. He was still asleep but . . .

What the hell was going on?

The odd light in the room was coming from him. She stared in wonder. Patterns of shimmering color, moving in waves like the aurora borealis, moved over his skin as if he were lit from deep inside. As if he was hollow. As if he was made of light.

What the hell?

Beth's mouth opened, but no words came out. His eyes opened slowly as if he felt hers on him. Eyes that had been blue times two were now blue times ten.

She looked at him a few seconds longer, fainted, and fell right off the bed.

Dawn was breaking when she came to. She was nestled into the pillows, on her back with the covers drawn up and tucked in. He was sitting beside her, stroking her thoughtfully, a troubled look on his face.

He looked exactly like himself again, wearing a cotton robe.

"Justin!" She struggled to sit up.

"I'm here, baby," he soothed her. "Right here." He took her in his arms and she clung to him.

"I had the weirdest dream," she said. "I woke up in the middle of the night and I turned around and you—you were lit up from inside. The colors of the light kept changing."

"Shhh," he said, stroking her hair.

Beth looked up at him. "Do you have a dream book or something? I know they're ridiculous, but I'd love a little insight on that one."

"I can understand why you would."

"It seemed so real." She searched his face. His eyes were the same as when she'd first seen them: beach-glass blue. Not blue times two or ten. Just normal blue eyes, really beautiful blue eyes. Everything about him was beautiful. His body, naked or clothed. His very male charm. His unpretentiousness. His skill at lovemaking. She was never, ever, going to forget the sex they'd had last night. It must have unhinged her mind a little and triggered that crazy dream.

Justin sighed and let her go. "It was real."

"Come on," she said. "It was not. Just tell me I'm not going crazy. That's all I need to hear."

"No, you're not going crazy."

"Well, then. I guess you fucked my brains out."

He shook his head. "Ugly phrase. Never liked it. Didn't do it."

"Okay, I know when I'm being humored." She pushed the covers aside. "What's for breakfast? I gotta get out of here, get home, and get changed."

Justin rose so she could get up. "No rush. I told the receptionist we were going out early to scout a sign site, and that we would be in late. Let her do the explaining."

"We can't come in at the same time, Justin. People will know."

He studied her for a long moment. "You may be right. Go look in the mirror."

"Tell me what I'm going to see. Pouty, kissed-up lips? Rosy cheeks?"

He nodded.

Beth rose and dragged a sheet from the bed to serve as a robe. Uninhibited as the sex had been, the light of day still demanded a little modesty. She let a couple of yards of sheet trail after her like the train on a wedding dress, and it wound around the doorjamb when she went into the bathroom.

She peered into the mirror. Sure enough, she looked like she'd been kissed, good and hard and often. No surprise there. Her eyelashes were glumpy with leftover mascara and her lids were puffy. Her hair was a hopeless snarl. It was kind of funny, though, that she also looked happy and satisfied and womanly. Beth gave herself a scrunched-up, screwy little smile.

"See it yet?" Justin called.

She stretched her chin out, looking for a hickey on her neck. The skin was smooth and unmarred. "See what?"

A flash of moving light on her face caught her eye. She tried to focus on it, but it was small and kept moving. To her cheek. To her forehead. Shimmering. The colors in it kept changing.

Beth saw Justin standing behind her in the mirror. He nodded. "Full disclosure," he said. "I'm made of light. It seems to be catching."

Beth whirled around and the train of sheet caught on the doorjamb tightened all the rest of it and made her lose her balance. She fell into his arms.

Justin held her, looked at her ruefully and dropped a kiss on her nose. "It wasn't a dream, Beth." Right before her eyes he started turning colors again. Glowing. He felt just the same. Big and warm and strong. But he wasn't the same. She pummeled his chest. It didn't echo and he wasn't hollow. She stopped and looked up into his eyes. They were turning an otherworldly shade of blue, little by little.

"Explain!" she shrieked.

"Like I said, I'm made of light."

She was willing to believe it by now. He had stood stoically in the bathroom while she did her damnedest to beat him up, changing colors on her again and again. When she'd scratched at him, trying to draw blood, he'd glowed red and his eyes had flashed.

Beth had bagged it at that point. She'd run into the living room, collapsed into the sofa and curled up into a ball of misery. His gentle and very real caresses had made her uncurl eventually.

"I wanted to come to earth. The stratosphere was kind of boring. Nothing to do but wave at Swedes and Inuit walrus-hunters and a couple of Canadians now and then."

"How did you end up in New York?"

Justin shrugged. "It's pretty fucking bright. Easy to blend in."

"So's Vegas."

"Yeah, but who wants to go to Vegas? The whole city smells like an ashtray. And I don't like to gamble."

"Gotcha." It did make sense. She hated gambling herself.

"So, I zoomed around in the skyscrapers for a while. This was a few years ago. Lit up a few new ones that hadn't been turned on yet, just for fun."

Beth looked at him curiously. "Is that you?"

"What?"

"When the spire of the Chrysler Building switches on or the Empire State Building turns different colors, is that you?"

Justin smiled. "I wish. No, lighting designers do those buildings. And I guess one of the building crew gets to flip the switch. No, that's not me."

Beth had a point to make but it was kind of escaping her. What he did do was enough to boggle anyone's mind. Oh, yeah. It came back to her. "But that's not me. I may have caught a little piece of your rainbow but I'm still only human. While you're zooming around in the sky, I'm on the sidewalk, just being ordinary. Walking around with the pigeons."

Justin looked interested. "Hey, why is it that New York pigeons hardly ever fly?"

"Because they can't get off the ground with a whole bagel in their beak," she snapped.

He laughed. "Good one."

Beth didn't know whether to cry or howl or what. "I wish I could fly," she said all of a sudden. "I'd be outa here in a heartbeat."

He gave her a sad look. "Don't say that. It's not that big a deal. By my standards, you're the lucky one. I wanted to be inside a real body. I was doing too much zooming around the universe, if you really want to know."

"Doing what, exactly?"

"Causing trouble and raising hell. Joyriding on comets. Kinda got old after a while. I didn't have anyone to do it with."

"Oh."

Justin slumped down on the sofa, looking unhappy, and didn't say anything more for a little while.

What a trip. Even a man with superpowers who traveled at the speed of light—who was light—was just a great big baby when he didn't get his way. "Sulk if you want to." Beth got up, grabbing at the sheet. "I'm going to take a shower."

She went back into the bathroom and looked very, very hard at herself, naked, all over. The moving spot of light seemed to have vanished. Good riddance.

She turned the shower on full blast and stood under the hot, pulsing jets of water, hoping it would wash away all trace of her contact with him.

Then she began to cry. The shower washed away the tears. She didn't want that, not at all. His touch, his lovemaking, his born-yesterday eagerness—born yesterday. From what he'd just told her when they sat on the sofa, it was literally true. And she had to go and practically fall in love with him. She bawled like a baby. From what she remembered of the properties of light, he could be born yesterday and live forever. It was everlasting. He was everlasting.

She was not.

But there was something about him that she had to have. They'd worked together, and been pals; they'd slept together, and now they were lovers. No matter the circumstances, she felt different around him. Brighter. Her heart felt genuinely happy for the first time in a long while. It wasn't just thudding along, it was really beating.

Well, she resolved, as she toweled off, she was going to enjoy this as long it lasted. When she came out of the bedroom to find him, she was dressed in a shirt of his that went down to her knees.

Justin had gotten dressed while she was in the shower and was pottering around the kitchen. He looked at her and ventured a smile.

"Not mad at me anymore?"

She shook her head. "I want some coffee. And more explanations."

"You want milk and sugar with your explanations?"

"No, I take mine straight up." Beth eased on a high stool and leaned on the counter. "First of all, where'd you get the body?"

He poured two cups of black coffee and pushed one over to her.

"Friend of mine at MIT. Brilliant guy but a serious wacko. I used to hang out with him when I was in a photon state. But I'll explain that later."

Beth narrowed her eyes. "Why?"

"I just want to begin at the beginning."

"Okay."

"Beth, you have to understand that light takes a lot of forms. And humans can only see a small fraction of it. Being in a body and having a brain is really new to me. A whole different set of rules applies."

"Uh-huh. I think I understand."

"It's not like I only wanted to roam around the galaxies, you know."

She shot him a not entirely sympathetic look. "Poor you. No comets and UFOs and asteroids to play with."

Justin sighed. "You know, when you said you loved comic books and superheroes, I thought you'd get what I was all about, if it ever came to that."

"I do. In my book, you're not a hero."

He drank half his coffee in one go. "Maybe I'm not. But I felt like I needed to be contained. To be pure light is just so—so amorphous."

"Explain."

"Sometimes I'm wave energy that no one on earth can see—no one human, anyway. I'm not so sure about cats."

Beth thought of old Freddy and how he stared at nothing for a long, long time. "You could be right about cats."

"Who knows? Anyway, getting back to what you were asking about, sometimes I was a sunspot or rays of sunlight that hit the earth."

"Which did you prefer?"

Justin thought it over. "It was kind of cool being sunlight. Every woman who turned her face to me got a kiss and didn't know it. The office chicks grabbing a few rays before they had to get back to their cubicles. The nice old grandmas who just dug being warm and outside. The teenagers with all that glossy hair I could shine on. Swinging, bouncing. And I helped out on a lot of modeling shoots, of course."

"Did you like the models?" Beth asked, disliking the jealous edge in her voice.

Justin shook his head. "They don't do anything for me. Too skinny. They complained that the lights made them sweat."

"Was that you?

He gave her a sheepish look. "I got into big lights sometimes. On photo shoots and movie sets. Not table lamps or anything."

"I see."

"Could we rewind this discussion?"

"Sure. Let the sun shine in."

Justin gave her a bad-boy grin. "Let me explain. I could shine on beautiful girls on the beach, get them to roll over. Glistening butts. Lotioned-up boobs. The more I shone, the creamier they got. It was making me insanely horny. But that was as far as I could go."

"Right. Got it. You know," she hesitated, looking at him with a little more respect, "sometimes when I was sunning myself I could swear the warmth felt like an invisible hand moving over me."

"Yeah," he said with satisfaction. "That's what I'm talking about."

"And when the clouds got in between it used to make me really annoyed," Beth added.

"Then it would have been time for a cloud smackdown. I always tried to dissolve them. Or ask my best friend, Wind, if he wanted to move them along."

"And did he want to?"

Justin lifted up both hands in a who-knows gesture. "Wind does what he wants. If what you want coincides with that, then count yourself lucky. Know what I mean?"

"I don't know him. So, no."

"Depended on what he was up to. You know, if he was playing with summer skirts in Chicago or making a sarong blow open in Tahiti, then he wouldn't bother."

"The two of you are double trouble for womankind."

Justin eased onto a stool next to her. "Maybe. You're cute. Come here often?"

"Once might be enough." She looked into his eyes, which were plain blue again. He slipped a hand under the part of the shirt that covered her thigh and caressed her there, moving up but not too far up.

He came close enough to nuzzle her neck, and she let him. When he raised her head, she'd turned her face to catch a kiss. He gave her one, slow and deep and easy and lightly flavored with coffee. Then they bumped noses and he smiled at her, the dimple flickering in his cheek like he wasn't sure she was going to smack it off him or not.

The smile stayed where it was, though.

God, she could love a guy who was sunny in the morning, instead of grumpy and foul-breathed—oh, fuck me, she thought. How ironic that she'd found him at last.

"Could I have more coffee? And a croissant, if you have one."

"Blackberry jam, or strawberry? How about honey? You look good in my shirt."

"Thanks," she said, fluffing out her nearly dry hair. "I'll try not to get jam on it. I'll take strawberry."

"I don't care if you do mess up my shirt. I want you to be happy and I'm an easygoing guy."

"You and Wind both," she said. "Let me guess. He, like you, fell to earth once upon a time. What name does he go by?" She was beginning to enjoy this. It beat reality, at least for a while.

Justin went about making her breakfast, getting out butter and the jam, and putting a pat of one and a spoonful of the other on a plate. He took out a croissant from a bakery bag—it looked like a real one, with multiple buttery layers and fragile flakes—and put it in the microwave on a paper towel to warm up for a few seconds. Then he leaned across the counter to kiss her again.

"You're so pretty in the morning, with no makeup and your hair off your face. I can't help myself. So . . . where was I? Oh yeah, he decided to go by Windham Devane—" He stopped talking when the microwave beeped.

He took out the croissant and slid it onto the plate, handing it to her. "Don't get me wrong. It wasn't always about chasing women for Wind. Sometimes he was at Birdland with old J.T. Carten when J.T. was playing the saxophone, giving him the extra breath for cool grooves. Sure worked for him. Women just have to hear good music that makes their bodies move and they're, like, all over a guy. Music gets them way down deep, in a secret place. So Wind was getting something I couldn't."

"What do you mean?"

"You ever see the sun in a jazz club? They're like caverns. Most of those guys don't even get out of bed until nightfall."

"You have a point."

"So I could hang with Wind during the day but I was pretty much limited to the great outdoors."

"Hard to believe that a good-time guy—" she stopped in mid-sentence—"or a good-time being or whatever the hell it is you are, didn't go out at night," Beth said.

"I just didn't. No chick was going to throw her leg over a lamp, if you know what I mean. And I didn't have a body then."

Beth giggled.

"Anyway, when J.T. sat out a set, Wind could make his sax moan and whisper and cry just like he did—it was emotional, not just physical."

"Got it. The women went wild for him. You were frustrated."

Justin stole a bite of her croissant and dipped it in the jam, then ate it thoughtfully.

"He and I discussed getting our own bodies, but that wasn't easy. I hadn't met up with the MIT guy yet, so we figured we had to wait for the right ones. And they had to be unoccupied but not dead."

Beth almost finished her croissant before he swiped the rest, just in case he didn't have another one. It was really good. "You should have tried a frat house. It's full of brainless bodies in reasonably good condition."

"We didn't think of that."

"So what happened?" She looked at Justin as the last bite went into her mouth.

"Wind got to know this dancer, a great guy, a real wild man who performed at Birdland sometimes. One night he jumped so high he didn't come back down, mentally speaking. But his body was there and Wind slipped in."

Beth nodded. "Wow. How'd that work out?"

Justin put the dishes and cups into the sink. "Eventually the dancer did come back and Wind got evicted. He did a deal with a basketball player from the West Fourth Street team next. Sometimes he has the body, sometimes the basketball player does. I understand that Wind likes being really tall."

"I bet," Beth said. "So how'd you find yours?"

"The MIT guy wanted a challenge. He called in a few favors, found someone at Harvard, a young guy who was a professor of Eastern religions. He transcended physical reality on his way to nirvana and he didn't want to be saddled with this body or reincarnated so I got it."

"Permanently?"

"Yup. Works really well. Added some custom-built improvements, though."

"So I noticed," Beth said wryly.

"It felt good right from the start. I had to figure out how not to burn it up. I scorched a few shirts when I started, burned holes in my boxers, that kind of thing."

"I'm not sure I want to know how," Beth said.

"What can I say? I'm a man on fire."

She shook her head, but she smiled anyway.

"Are we done with the questions? I actually would like to get some work done today." He slid off the stool.

"Excuse me?" Beth said. "You just announce you're made of light and you used to not even have a body and I don't get to ask questions? You plant your butt right back on that stool."

"Yes, ma'am." He did as she asked.

"Where does all the money come from? You seem to have an awful lot of it."

"Energy futures. I played the market. Did really well, got out while I was ahead."

"That explanation is way too short."

He smirked. "It happens to be totally true. I paid cash for this place."

"Wait until you see mine," she said with a groan.

"I'd love to."

"It's just me and Freddy and—"

"Who's Freddy?"

"My ancient cat. And Miss Boom Bah. She's my coatrack. I'm not bringing you home."

"Have it your way," he said reluctantly. "But it still doesn't seem fair."

"You know what, Justin? Life isn't fair. You being an everlasting being really isn't fair to me. I can't get a new body like you can. If you're mortal, it's one to a customer."

He looked at her worriedly. "You sure about that?"

"Yes!' she said with instant exasperation. "Enjoy me while it lasts."

"Does that work in reverse? Are you going to enjoy me?"

"Yes," she said a lot more slowly. "I had a good cry in the shower about it and that—that's pretty much what I decided. I mean, it's crazy, but I've been crazy before about guys who didn't hold a candle to—who couldn't outshine—I give up," she cried out, "they weren't you. And I want you. For as long as I can have you. I may wake up in Bellevue with a team of shrinks at my side when it's all over, but for right now, I want you."

"That's a start," Justin said.

"When I'm with you, my heart feels . . . light. That's the only way I can explain it."

"Works for me."

Beth patted his cheek. "But please try not to turn colors and glow in public."

"I never have," he said. "That happened after you and I had sex. I don't know why, though. Want me to ask the MIT guy?"

"No way." She looked at him, aghast. A strange man with a pocket protector finding out all the fascinating details of what she liked to do in bed? Absolutely no freaking way. "This is strictly between you and me. No one else is going to know about this."

"Okay," Justin said. "I promise. No one will."

3

"Let's get going. I want to take you to Times Square. Part of the installation is up."

He was done explaining, evidently.

Beth looked down at what she was wearing. "I guess I'd better change."

"Why? You look great."

"Will there be other SpectraSign people there?"

"Maybe." He narrowed his eyes at her. "So?"

"I could just embroider *I'm fucking the boss* over the pocket of your shirt in case they can't figure it out."

"You worry too much."

She leaned in close to make sure he understood. "Listen, Mr. Born Yesterday, you have never owned a real live company before. Gossip travels faster than the speed of light."

"Really?" he said, genuinely curious. "Can I look up the physics on that? I don't think Einstein covered the subject."

Beth shook her head dismissively. "What else can I borrow of yours? Got something that doesn't look so morning-after?"

"Sweats?"

"Okay." He gestured for her to follow him and they headed back to his bedroom, where he pulled open a dresser drawer filled with neatly folded sweatshirts and pants. "I'll find something."

"Have at." Justin sat on the bed, looking around the room but mostly at her. Suddenly he leaned forward and came up with a scrap of feminine lingerie. Her bra, thong, and stockings fit right into his hand, all crumpled up. "Do I have to give these back?"

Beth held up one of the smaller sweatshirts in a nondescript gray. It would do.

"I need the bra right now. You can wash the rest and then give them back."

He grinned wolfishly. "I would be honored to see these dripping from my shower rack. Just seeing that thong on you was enough to blow my mind forever."

"Yeah," she said, unbuttoning the shirt. "That's nice." She put it on the bed and extracted the bra from his unwilling hand.

Justin stared, fascinated, as she clasped it, spun it around her waist, and flipped it up over her boobs. "Mind if I drool?"

"Aren't you the one who wanted to get going?"

He sighed. "Yeah."

She slipped on the sweatshirt and looked in the drawer for black pants that wouldn't look too weird with the dress shoes she'd worn last night. The sweatshirt would fit under her jacket and she could buy a bright scarf from a street vendor on the way. Something in neon green, perhaps. No one would look at anything but a neon green scarf, especially if it had long fringe. And it might be windy up on the roof where the installation was in progress, so she had a reason to be wearing it.

Done rationalizing, nearly dressed, she looked around for her shoes, wiggling her bare feet in his plush bedroom carpet.

He looked at them fondly. "Want your toes sucked?"

"Not right now." She rumpled his hair and he turned his head to give her a love bite on the meaty part of her thumb. Look at us, she marveled silently. Acting like honeymooners. Even after just one night, it felt like that to be with him.

But there was a part of having sex with Justin that was troublesome. What had he said? *It seems to be catching.*

She'd assumed she'd been able to wash off the dash of moving light on her face, but that was a pretty big assumption. True, the dash had seemed more superficial than his full-body light show, but she didn't know enough about the nature of the phenomenon to be totally sure. Versed in useless comic-book lore, she knew it wouldn't come in handy now—hey, it never had, except for on-

line arguments with fanboys and other maniacs. And her marketing degree from Hofstra hadn't required physics.

In a word, she might be fucked if they ever fucked again. So
they weren't going to until she got that aspect of the connection
between them figured out.

Justin was still sitting there, giving her adoring looks, her dirty
underwear and stockings forgotten in his hand. Why oh why did
she have to fall for a cute guy from the wrong side of the asteroid
belt? It really, really wasn't fair.

Beth bent down to plant an absentminded kiss on his forehead. "Let's get going," she said when she straightened up. Then
she spotted her shoes under the nightstand and slipped them on.
"Sweatpants and high heels," she said. "It's a look."

"I love it on you," Justin said loyally.

It was breezy up on the rooftop. Beth pulled a mouthful of
long, neon-green fringe out of her mouth and tucked the ends of
the scarf into her jacket. Justin was checking the installation with
two guys from the SpectraSign tech department, so she was free to
walk around. A New York City roof was an interesting place to
be when you had nothing else important to do.

She went near the edge of the rooftop, looking out over a low
wall rounded with asphalt tiles and decades' worth of slapped-on
tar. There were pigeons perched on it, cooing and bobbing their
heads, stepping to keep their balance in the breeze. One wrinkly,
pink bird foot stepped on another and they all flapped in an irritated way. But basically, they were just like most New Yorkers.
They got along somehow.

Times Square was teeming with people, tourists, office work-
ers, oddballs. It was like watching a very colorful river that
twisted around and doubled back. A river that had yellow taxis
bobbing in the middle of the current.

Justin called her name softly as he came up behind her, and she
turned around. "Hey. Didn't want to startle you so near the edge
of the roof."

"Thanks," she said.

He leaned in a little closer like he was going to give her a kiss,
but she glared at him and shook her head.

"Right," he said, glancing at the tech guys, who hadn't seen a thing. "Almost forgot. Sorry." A sign rigger had joined the two men and was helping them set up panels that would eventually become part of the main sign.

He got closer to the roof edge and looked over. "There's our pedestrian survey person." He waved and Beth looked into the surging crowds. A young woman in a baseball cap holding a clipboard was waving back, a clicker in her hand.

"What does she do again?"

"She counts people passing by and divides them by gender. That way we have an idea who sees the sign."

"Eyeballs are everything," Beth said wryly.

He unrolled the layouts he'd kept under his arm. It flapped wildly in the breeze and he set it down on the curved rooftop wall, pinning it with spread-out fingers. Beth got close enough to help him so he could have a hand free.

She held down a corner and he pointed to the first panel. "The model enters here, in the first video panel, walking from the background. Then," he pointed to the second panel, "he comes in closer and he gets bigger and bigger and starts to fill all the panels."

"Oh, boy."

"Then he towers over Times Square, throbbing with manliness," Justin said. "You can let go. What do you think?"

"It's okay." She raised her hand and the layout rolled itself back up into his hand. "Oughta sell plenty of jeans."

"That's the idea." One of the tech guys called him and he looked over that way. "Gotta go. You good over here?"

"Yeah. I'm having fun. Don't worry about me."

Justin winked at her and turned around.

Beth resumed her absentminded viewing of the panorama of Times Square. This would have to be one hell of a sign to compete with what was already up.

Her personal favorite—the giant, steaming Cup O' Noodles—was gone, replaced by an extravaganza of rippling colors that was eye-popping even in daylight. Half-naked women in high heels seemed to stalk over rooftops, eyed disdainfully or ignored by male underwear models on different billboards.

Giant cell phones revolved like objects of worship; gazed at by the happy customers of online dating sites. Music, candy, Broadway shows, movie posters, an endless digital ribbon of repeating headlines—it all moved, shouted, tickled the eye. If the Blue Blaze sign managed to stand out, it would be a marketing miracle.

Several hours later, they were seated at a table for two at Capsouto Frères. Beth looked around the serene space. Linen tablecloths, pale cream walls that glowed softly, classic menu—this place was posh and nothing like the Cowgirl Hall of Fame on Hudson Street, where she usually ate out if she was going to splurge.

No margaritas in mason jars here. No lethal chili. No vanilla-ice-cream fake potatoes dusted with cocoa for a nice brown skin and topped with whipped cream and peppermint chives.

She slipped a spoon into her onion soup, lifting up the bread and cheese crust to get at the oniony broth underneath, sipping it daintily. Then she looked up at him. "Why are you smiling like that?"

"I didn't know you could eat with utensils," he laughed.

"Oh. Well, I can. And a fork makes an excellent catapult for a roll." She took one out of the breadbasket and positioned it on the curving tines. "Don't tempt me."

"Okay, fair enough."

They polished off their soup and just sat there looking at each other for several awkward moments. Hot soup, good wine, unqualified adoration—a triple threat to her sanity.

"So." Justin set an elbow on the table and rested his chin in one hand. "What do you want to do tonight?"

"I should go home," she said primly.

"And where's that again?"

"Near Hudson Street. Not all that far from here."

He looked really happy about that. In fact, his eyes started to glow.

"Don't do that," she said hastily.

"I'm just sitting here looking at you."

Beth looked around the restaurant. "No, you're glowing at me. Any minute now you're going to look like a sign in Times Square."

The intensity in his eyes faded. "Do you honestly think anyone in New York would notice if I did?"

"They might."

He straightened up. "And is that, like, a bad reflection on you?"

"No, Justin." She fussed with her silverware and took the roll
off the fork, tossing it back in the breadbasket. "It's just that—I
don't know."

"Beth," he said. "You're not exactly making yourself clear."

She took a nice, deep, calming breath. "The light thing just
makes me nervous, that's all. We have to talk about it."

Justin grinned and looked very pleased. "Hey, this is my first
we-have-to-talk moment. I guess I'm a real guy after all."

"That's exactly my point," she said, a little more crisply than
she'd intended. "You're not."

Justin blew out his breath. "Last night you seemed happy enough.
Maybe I don't have a whole hell of a lot of experience, but that
seemed like great sex to me."

Another burning question that hadn't occurred to her until
then. How had he learned everything he knew? He hadn't been in
that gorgeous body all that long, even if it was permanently his.
Beth surveyed him. He sure did look real. Big chest, broad shoulders, ribbed sweater. Tousled dark hair, crinkly eyes, dimple. All
the damn details added up perfectly. She'd seen several women
check him out, cast a disapproving eye at the black sweatpants
accessorized with the neon-green scarf that she still had on, and
go right back to poking at their collapsed soufflés.

There was one at the very next table. Beth smiled thinly at her
and the watching woman returned it, giving her a very small
smile that was even thinner than hers—a trimmed fingernail of a
smile. The woman, who had been eating alone, got up and saun-
tered to the coat check area while the maitre d' fussed over her
and took care of the bill.

Beth turned her full attention to Justin. "How and where did
you learn to make love like that?"

"Um, the look and learn method."

"You perv."

He held up his hands in a whaddya-want-from-me gesture.
"Hey, I was sunlight. Even moonlight, sometimes. That's just a

reflection, really. I was everywhere, all the time. But invisible. You see a lot, you pick up a few pointers."

Beth frowned.

"You weren't objecting to anything I did," he said slyly.

"Okay, granted." She had to concede the point. "It was great. And you are who you are. I can't argue with that."

"So what's bothering you?"

Beth leaned back as the waiter silently set down their entrées. She wasn't hungry at all. Justin picked up his fork and knife and went to work "The light that was on me—or in me—for a little while. You said it seemed to be catching."

He nodded and chewed.

"Is it?"

She watched him swallow and cut another bite. "Dunno," he said before his mouth was filled with food again.

"So is it theoretically possible that I could somehow leave my body the way you entered yours, and become pure light?"

He thought that over, then pushed his food away. "Guess we'd better get this wrapped up to go."

"Fine with me." She hadn't even touched hers.

He motioned the waiter over and made some excuse about having to leave. Then he turned his attention back to her. "Anything's theoretically possible. Whether it would actually happen is hard to say. The sexual connection did seem to trigger it."

Beth nodded, fixing him with a meaningful look.

Justin reached for his wallet and pulled out a credit card. "I think I know where this is going."

"Good."

"You don't want to have sex again. You're afraid you'll dissolve or something. What's that called, having boundary issues?"

"Something like that. Justin, I've never been outside my body and I don't think I want to be. What if I can't get back in?"

He folded his arms across his chest. "Out-of-body experiences are great. We can take an extended vacation in the galaxy while you get used to it. You know, fly to the moon, cruise a nebula or two. Just you and me."

"I don't want to see a nebula. Not up close, anyway."

His eyes got dreamy. "You sure? They're really something. Very female. Pulsing, mysterious, beautiful—"

"No!"

"Okay, okay."

The waiter came back with two containers in a plastic bag and Justin settled the bill. They got their coats and left.

"Can I walk you home, Beth?"

She still didn't want him to see where she lived. Sure, he could Mapquest her address from her resume and find out for himself, but inviting him in was something else again. It was too intimate, somehow.

You let him inside your body, said a little voice in her head. *It doesn't get any more intimate than that.* She decided to ignore the little voice.

"Let's walk along the river," she suggested. "I need to clear my head."

In a few short blocks they were by the Hudson. The usual ships and boats drifted by and there was even a kayaker, paddling in a steady rhythm that made her wish she was out on the water too, bobbing along.

They kept to the pedestrian part of the path, letting the bicyclists and rollerbladers whiz past. Justin shortened his long stride to match her pace, swinging the bag and looking her way. "So where do we go from here?" he said after a while.

"I have to fold laundry and feed Freddy and play with him a little. You can keep the food. I probably wouldn't eat it."

He frowned, not looking too thrilled at playing second fiddle to laundry and a geriatric cat. "Okay, Beth. If that's how you want it."

He seemed to be waiting for an invitation, which she couldn't bring herself to give. "I guess that means I'm going home to the Bolt Building," he finally said. "Alone."

Beth nodded.

He stopped and looked directly into her eyes. She drew in her breath with a gasp. They were a fiery blue, fueled with emotion. "You don't want to make that connection again, do you?"

"Not just yet," she said after a beat. "Not until I know more. I have to be sure that I'm in control of what happens to me. Mortal or not, it's the only body I have and I don't want to lose it."

The fire in his eyes died down some. "I think I understand. You mean no sex for right now. But you don't mean never again."

Beth breathed out a great big sigh of relief. "That's right."

"And we're still going to work together and pal around and talk until one in the morning and stuff like that."

"Well, yeah," she said cautiously. "Unless that gets the light show going again."

"It's fine with me if you want to chill for a while. Although we could try just oral sex. Me doing you."

"Do we have to have this conversation right here? Right now?"

"Let me know the second you want to have any kind of sex again." Justin swung the bag dangerously high, looking really happy. "Then you have a deal."

"Careful," she said. "Your entrée is going to end up in the Hudson."

He turned around in joyful circles, his arms outstretched, whirling and whirling. "I don't care! It's fish!"

"Yeah, but it's filleted. It'll never swim again," Beth said and smiled awkwardly at a little old lady passing by on an honest-to-God giant tricycle. "He's nice but he's nuts," she said to her.

"Enjoy it while you're young, dear." The old lady pedaled away, heading north.

"Stop it," Beth hissed at Justin. "You're so impulsive. Why are you so goddamned happy?"

He stopped whirling and enfolded her in his arms, giving her a huge hug. "Because you gave me a second chance. It may be a snowball's chance in hell, but I'm taking it."

Beth opened her mouth to argue and got herself a sensual kiss instead. She gave into it, half enjoying it and half wondering whether she was shimmering. The sensations racing through her one after another sure made it feel that way.

"Shtop it," she said around his tongue.

He shook his head and kissed her harder, and she gave in. Justin was a fabulous kisser. She could always do a light check on herself afterward with a pocket mirror, just in case. They could probably still do this even if they didn't have sex for a while.

His tenderness and his skill and his being so damn hot for her added up to a kiss that was just too good to stop.

A bicyclist whizzed by, bent way over his handlebars and so close they could hear his chain clicking, and Justin pulled her out of harm's way, right up against him. He lifted his head, about to shout after the jerk when Beth spotted the old lady on the giant tricycle coming back.

"Don't curse," she said.

He heard Beth just in time to yell, "Eff you, you effing eff!" after the cyclist, who was long gone.

The old lady beamed at Justin as she approached, picking up speed. "That crazy asshole almost sideswiped me!" she shouted. "I'm going to run over his skinny butt if I can catch up with him!"

They watched her head south, pedaling madly, bent on vengeance.

"Go, granny, go," Beth murmured. She looked up at Justin again. "Where were we?"

He bent his head to hers and got right back to kissing her.

"Ahhh." Justin eventually came up for air but he wasn't letting her get much. He was holding her very close. "I'm blissing out on you—your smell, your nearness, everything. I can't get enough."

"This *is* a public place," she reminded him.

"But no one stops long enough to see anything."

Beth laughed and pushed him away. "Let's do something else. Walk. Jog. I don't care."

Justin thought for a minute. "Tell you what. How about we watch a basketball game that makes the Knicks look like ninety-eight-pound weaklings? And it's free."

"Okay. You're on. Where?"

"West Fourth Street over in the Village. Not that much of a walk from here."

"Fine." She took the hand that wasn't holding their bagged entrees and they headed that way. Then she stopped. "Hey, wait a minute. Is that where your friend Windham Devane plays basketball?"

"That's right."

"I remember you saying he was on the West Fourth Street team."

Justin squeezed her hand in his. "He's amazing. All the guys are."

"Of course, Wind is the one who's a little bit more than human," she reminded him.

"He only uses his powers for good," Justin said seriously.

Beth snorted. "What, have you been reading comic books out there in the stratosphere?"

"No. But I read some over a few shoulders when I was just pure light. It's fun. I pick up stuff quickly."

"Guess so."

"Ask my genius buddy at MIT. The man knows how to mind-meld. I acquired the equivalent of a college education because of him in one night. It was a long night, but that's all it took."

"Uh-huh." She looked up at Justin, who was humming under his breath. "I sense there's more."

"There is. It involved a bong and Wikipedia. He got high and figured out how to download the whole damn website into my brain."

"Holy cow. No wonder you're such a know-it-all, Justin."

"I am not. I learn something new every day," he said with a little-boy grin.

On his rugged face, it was heart-meltingly effective. Beth didn't feel like arguing the point. It was just too peaceful to do anything but be together and be happy. The streets of the Village were relatively quiet, the old glassed-in restaurant fronts radiating a warm, golden glow onto the cobblestone parts.

She stopped to pet a dog sitting outside one, tied to the tree while he looked inside anxiously at his master, who was paying for an order of takeout.

"Be right there, Beau," the man inside called to the dog.

Beau's tail thumped in anticipation. She gave his ears a final fondle and strolled on with Justin. There were a few other couples out, hand in hand, just like them.

They went down Bleecker Street and walked past the guitar store, stopping to admire what was in the window. A steel guitar was front and center, hand-engraved with a wild profusion of vines and flowers.

"Look at that," she breathed. "I've never seen a guitar like that in my life."

"Want it?"

She leaned on his arm, looking at the glittering beauty of the instrument and laughing. "I can't play a note. But thanks."

"You could learn."

"Not well enough to justify what that probably costs."

Justin bent down, looking for a price tag. "Uh . . . twenty thousand dollars."

"Yeah. Not for me." She sighed appreciatively, gave it one more look, and tugged at his hand to get him to move on.

Bleecker Street still had the small shops that made New York so great, she thought wistfully. The big chains hadn't taken over every single storefront. There were still grocers with fruit piled in neat pyramids on bright green racks, and still a couple of mom-and-pop stores. Okay, so what if mom and pop were selling flavored condoms? Small businesses had to do what they could.

Aglow with nostalgia, she got him to the intersection of Sixth and they dodged the onrushing taxis to cross the wide avenue, ignoring the blaring horns. A block or so up to the left were the West Fourth Street courts and she could hear a raucous game in progress even from here.

A crowd milled around the high chain-link fence, shouting and encouraging the players.

"There's Wind," Justin said.

Beth saw a tall, lanky black guy spring into the air and seem to hover there, the ball spinning on the tips of his fingers. He threw and the basketball went through the hoop in almost the same second.

Below it a bunch of shoving, screaming players tried to take control of it as the crowd roared. Someone she couldn't see passed it to Wind, and he handled it as deftly as before, scoring another point.

They were close enough now to see the game. Great-looking but sweaty guys in headbands, baggy shorts, and loose tanks, all different heights and different colors, slammed into each other, playing with a fierce passion that their audience shared.

Eventually Wind detached himself from the crowd and went over to the corner of the fence to grab a Gatorade, exchanging high fives and more complicated handshakes along the way.

He uncapped it and literally poured a full bottle of liquid down his throat in one go, swallowing smoothly and evenly. Beth was fascinated. She had never actually gotten this close to an athlete, pro or amateur.

Wind licked his lips and looked straight at Justin for almost a minute without saying anything.

Justin didn't look away. Beth realized that the blue of Justin's eyes was intensifying, but it wasn't because he was angry, just in challenge. A guy thing. A staredown.

Which Justin won. Wind burst out in a huge laugh that made her jump.

"A'most had you," he said to Justin. The two of them exchanged a handshake of unbelievable complexity. She couldn't follow the ins and outs of which hand was where. "Justin, Justin. My man. How ya been?"

"Better than ever."

"Uh-huh. I can guess why. And who is this pretty lady?"

"This is Beth." He looked down at her proudly and then back up at Windham. "Beth Danforth."

"Nice to meet you, Beth. Is he—and I do mean Sunny Boy—treating you right?"

"Yeah, he really is," she said with a grin. "He's a great guy." So was Wind, whom she liked instantly. He had the same enthusiasm that Justin did, but it was more like a cool breeze.

"A'ight." Wind capped the bottle and slam-dunked it into a recycling bin. "Gotta get back in the game. See you two around."

"If you're lucky," Justin joked.

"Nice to meet you," Beth said, getting another uproarious laugh from Windham. She threw a what-did-I-do look at Justin, who only shrugged.

"Now that girl has good manners, Justin," Wind said. "Unlike you. Me and the boys and I are taking up a collection to send you to charm school. Take off them rough edges you got."

"Hey, just because I held on to the ball last time I played," Justin began.

"Naw, you didn't just hold on to it. Your hands were velcro'd on to that ball," Wind said. "That's not *po*-lite and you know it."

"Okay, okay," Justin laughed. "Next time I'm down here, we'll play a rematch. I'll be good."

"We'll see about that." Wind gave Beth a smile and jumped back in the game. They watched for a while and then wandered down a side street looking for a coffee shop.

Two decaf flufferinos later, he walked her all the way back to the street off Hudson, waiting on the sidewalk while she climbed the stoop, looking for her keys.

"I'm not going to ask to come up," he said.

Beth shot him a glance from where she was, feeling just a little disappointed. He could, though. They could talk and not have sex. Yeah, right, she told herself, letting her keys jingle on her finger while she looked at him more thoughtfully.

"Why not?" she asked him.

"Because I'll want to make love. And you don't want to."

"It's not that I don't want to, Justin. Oh, geez—I just need to figure all this out. How many times do I have to say it?"

"As many times as you like," he said affably.

A guy walking by looked at her and Beth realized that she was swinging the key ring even harder. "It's not what you think," she said to him.

The guy caught Justin's glare and mumbled, "I wasn't thinking anything," and hurried away.

Justin stayed down on the sidewalk and blew her a kiss.

"Where are you going?" she asked. "Not that it's any of my business."

He stuck his big hands in his pockets and shrugged. "I haven't decided. I might shoot some pool. Go to a bookstore. Maybe I'll check out that charm school that Wind has in mind."

"Is he for real?"

Justin laughed in a low voice. "He's about as real as I am. Will that do?"

"I guess it'll have to," she said. "Okay. Well, good night, then. I had a really good time."

"Me too."

"See ya at SpectraSign." She put the key in the downstairs lock and pushed the door open, her back to him.

"Wow," she heard him say. "You have a great ass."

Beth got inside and ducked her head out. "You keep working on that charm, Justin. Good night."

He gave her a jaunty wave and headed off down the street, whistling. Beth watched him move from one pool of light under a streetlamp to another, until he came to a dark part of the street and stood still for a second. Then she thought he'd moved on . . . but she suddenly realized he'd made his own pool of light and was tying his shoe in it.

He really was one of a kind. Beth turned away and looked in the mailbox, seeing her weekly letter from her father behind the pierced brass grille.

4

A week or so later . . .

Beth was the proud possessor of a vintage drafting table as beat-up as Justin's. It was the same honey-colored pine but a little smaller.

He'd given her a state-of-the-art computer setup to translate her sketches into a multimedia presentation for the Blue Blaze people. She still wasn't happy with the campaign. She uploaded a few images into Illustrator and fooled around with the male model, grafting a goat's head onto his neck and then a kitten's. The goat's head looked pretty good, actually.

Beth was idly rotating the image when Justin walked in. "How's it coming?"

"Not great."

He looked over his shoulder to make sure no one was behind him before he planted a kiss on her cheek. "That's allowed, right? Just have to make sure I don't forget how."

"Ha ha," she said glumly.

"Why, if I didn't know better, I'd say you needed to get laid or something."

"Oh, shut up." He was right and that only made it worse.

"Okay. Let's talk about—" he looked at the image of the male model on her screen—"him. Why is he upside down and where did the goat's head come from?"

"Clip art," she said absently. "He's upside down because I just don't like him."

Justin nodded. "Me neither."

"I know, I know. His abs are nicer than yours."

Justin slapped his belly. "Not for long, though. I've been working out with Windham at the gym."

"Yeah?" She gave him a wistful once-over. "You two are real men. This model is like a Ken doll. I hate the way he just stands there and stares into space."

"Maybe he needs a swift kick in his Blue Blazes jeans," Justin suggested. "He might not react, though."

"That's it." She clicked on her mouse to rotate him the right way and removed the goat's head.

"I seem to be missing the eureka moment. What are you talking about?"

"The model needs something to react to. Or someone."

Justin nodded sagely, coming to stand beside her. "He isn't the only one."

"Justin, please. Not now. Soon, though," she amended. "Do you think we can reshoot this?"

He gave a nonchalant wave. "And go $500,000 over budget? Sure. What the hell. Let's go for broke. The client will scream, but who cares, right?"

"Be serious."

"I could bring it up at the next storyboard meeting, I guess. But give me something visual to go on. Blue Blazes isn't going to pay for a reshoot unless we make it crystal-clear that our new direction is a big improvement."

Beth fiddled with various images, shrinking the model and bringing in a few sultry females from an image-bank folder. She did a quick-and-dirty collage and Justin nodded, concentrating on the screen.

"See what I mean? Even though I'm just slapping this together, he looks a lot more alive now."

"You're right."

Beth felt excited about this campaign. "If you put the right woman in there, you'll have a sign that will make everybody stop and stare. Men and women."

"I see what you're saying, but go on."

"It'd be like a romantic movie. A hot romantic movie. And you could make it a little different every day, so people don't know what to expect."

"Got it. That's great. We could post clips on YouTube and try to get it to go viral."

"And we could track who was watching it online with Adzilla or Phorm. But the original sign in the Times Square location is key. You'd get repeat views. Traffic would come to a standstill."

"Yeah. This is really good, Beth. I think our client is going to eat this up."

Two days later, they were in the middle of a studio photo shoot that involved a rusty old pickup, a bale of hay, and amber waves of fake wheat, lightly stirred by a plastic fan.

The models actually did seem hot for each other, at least at first. They acted like there wasn't even a camera on them. In fact, there were fourteen cameras in all, still and movie. He was really into her and their chemistry came across.

Hours and hours of footage were shot the first day, and hours more were shot on the second day. The models pouted and posed and panted at each other until they got sick of it.

"So much for their chemistry," Justin whispered in Beth's ear when a playful tussle turned into a vicious slapping match.

"Great stuff!" the director shouted. The female model burst into unphotogenic tears and stormed off, refusing to return. The director finally called it a day after a few more close-ups of the male model tensing his abs and unbuttoning his fly until he couldn't take it any more and stormed off too.

"That's a wrap," the director said, like he'd planned it that way all along. The production assistants ran around, frantically breaking down the set and issuing orders to each other.

"Now what?" Beth said. She was exhausted. Her whole body was stiff and her mind echoed with the endlessly repeated dialogue. Making a movie, even a three-minute-long movie, was utterly unglamorous. All she wanted to do was to get out of there.

"Gil and the film editor shut themselves up in a dark room and make movie magic on a digital console. We're not going to see them for days."

"Thank God. I'm sick of looking at them. And everybody else on this set. Moviemaking is boring," she said crossly.

"You're just tired. Come on. I'll take you out for a burger."

"You're on," Beth said. "Fries and ketchup."

"That's my girl."

"Maybe I am at that," she said.

Justin looked at her curiously. "Would you mind telling me what's gotten into you?"

She blew out an exasperated breath. "All this fake lust. It worked in reverse. At first I couldn't take my eyes off them. And then I started watching you. And I wanted the real thing, even though you're not really real. And then they started fighting and I thought about the way you make me feel—"

"Which is?"

She scowled at him. "Lighthearted. Happy."

"So why are you making that face at me?"

"Because I really, really need to blow off steam. I want to get physical. Does that make sense?"

"No, but I can work with it."

He looked around for someone from SpectraSign and realized they were the last two from his company there. He didn't even have to make an excuse. They could just *go*. Then he hustled her out the door of the studio, into her coat and down to the street, where he hailed a cab.

"Where to?" the driver said as they got in.

"Just drive through Central Park, please. We're still trying to figure that out."

"Okay, boss. Whatever you say." The driver started the meter and the red numbers started running.

"So you want to fool around," Justin whispered. "You're tired and frantic and you need release. That definitely calls for oral. Hmm. May I put my hand on your leg while I think about it?"

"Are you going to ask permission for every little thing?"

"No."

"Good." Beth wrapped her arms around his neck and kissed him, rumpling his hair and half-crawling into his lap.

"Mrmmf. Yeah," he said thickly. "More of that. I suggest we check into a hotel. Before you change your mind."

She didn't.

They got checked in and headed for the elevator, eyeing each other heatedly. Once inside the suite, he got her naked in record time and had her spread out on the squooshiest, most luxurious bed ever. But he didn't take his clothes off. He didn't waste a second. That long tongue of his got to work, licking her clit and gently pushing between her labia.

Holy . . . wow. She had never been tongue-fucked. The sensation was amazing. Tender and lingering. She could concentrate just on what she was feeling. Her nervous tension was eased away as he sexed her down like a pro. She could go with this flow forever. Oh yessss . . . yesyesyes.

Justin Watts was a master of this, too. She surrendered to his expertise, running her fingers through his hair, pushing his head down between her legs so he could make her come . . . and come . . . and come . . .

"That was unbelievably excellent," she said when he had her cuddled up. She was still naked and he was still wearing every stitch of clothing he'd had on, but not shoes. "I can't believe you're still dressed."

"Had no choice. I would have rammed up inside you right away," he said. "No, this is fine for a while. It's probably good for my character."

"Oh, please." She reached down and unzipped him. "Allow me to return the favor."

And she did.

5

A month later . . .

Beth was awfully glad she'd given in. He was right about the oral sex not causing her to turn different colors. His magic tongue could practically dissolve her and vice versa, but that was okay. The glow they experienced was no different from a standard-issue postcoital glow.

She'd been just fine afterward, thank you. And she was still fine. Humming as she walked down the street, a relaxed bounce in her walk, she was pretty much walking on air these days. In contrast to everyone else at SpectraSign, now that they were rushing through the last phases of completing the massive sign.

It was being installed under wraps, on top of the building where she'd had the panoramic view of Times Square. Justin spent most of his time there.

He was—the thought made her hesitate—not doing so great. His inexhaustible energy was being drained by his insistence on attending to every detail personally.

Late at night, wrapped in his arms, she would whisper the sweet word, "Delegate," in his ear, hoping he would hear it subliminally while he slept. It didn't seem to help.

His sleep was restless and he usually woke up in a bad mood. Not like him. Not like him at all.

Justin had finally offered an explanation.

"It's the sunspot cycle," he explained. "Every twelve years, there are suddenly a lot more of them and it changes everything. My energy level goes haywire. Up. Down." He seesawed a hand through the air. "I get a little manic and I don't sleep well."

"Is it just you? I thought that happened to everyone in New York."

He'd shrugged. "Could explain a lot of things. It's not all bad, you know. Way up north, the aurora borealis goes crazy—it's much more intense. Turbocharged ions howling in from outer space, woo hoo, and all that. The colors are stronger and the patterns get wilder and it just doesn't stop."

He was talking faster and faster, not seeing her worried look.

"We could go up to Alaska. Or Sweden. Hang out and watch the northern lights and forget all about this crazy sign for a while. Something about it is getting to me. Maybe I wasn't born to sell blue jeans. What do you think? I really want to know."

But he hadn't even listened to her answer. She'd vetoed the all-expenses-paid trip to the tundra he'd proposed and pointed out that she didn't think it was the sign that was making him crazy. He had a whole company full of dedicated geeks and visual freaks to help make that happen.

No, he had to be right about the sunspots. And he was more than a little manic. Beth wasn't happy about that. She was having second thoughts. Even third, fourth, and fifth thoughts. She really couldn't imagine introducing him to her father while he was in this state, although Dave Danforth, mild-mannered cartoonist, probably would be thrilled to have a son-in-law who could harness all the energy in the known universe when he wanted to.

Son-in-law?

Where the hell had that ominous phrase come from?

The great day came. The wraps came off. He didn't want her to see it before it was dark and he insisted on being the one to put it through its paces. The project team from SpectraSign had left him to it, at his insistence.

He stood at a high table in front of the sign, looking a lot like a conductor at a podium. The laptop that controlled the special effects of the enormous sign was on the table and he rested his hands by it, a minute away from switching on the sign. The fact that he hadn't combed his hair for a few days added to the messy air of genius.

"It's finished. My magnum opus," he sighed. "What do you think?"

"I haven't seen it yet."

He started typing on the laptop. The screen lit up and she saw that it was a miniature of the giant sign. Whatever he did on the laptop would be instantly replicated above him.

He summoned up colors first, in shifting, swirling patterns. Then random things. Flying taxis. Sharks in sunglasses. Motifs appeared and disappeared with dizzying speed.

"Fun, huh?" he murmured. His eyes were glowing.

A breeze whipped her hair up around her face and she pushed it away. "Wow," was all she said, looking up at the sign.

In its final, complete stage, it was forty feet high, composed of hundreds of vid screens that fit together like a mosaic. Justin pushed a button. "Enough of that." The sign went dark. "Here comes the Blue Blaze man."

The multiple vid screens shimmered to life again, each showing a piece of the jeans-clad male model for the ad campaign, as if someone had taken scissors and cut up an old photo, then blown it up to building size.

The pieces of the photo came together as the male model strode slowly across the field of waving wheat toward the battered 1930s pickup.

Tinged with sepia, the familiar scene they'd seen being shot in bits and pieces came to coherent life. Edited, it was compelling. It seemed to have come from an authentic old movie, rich with atmosphere and poignant longing.

"What is he supposed to be doing again?" Beth asked Justin. The theme music swelled and reached a crescendo when the male model stopped and looked toward the horizon.

"I forget. Searching for America. Or true love."

"Here she comes now."

The long-legged female model walked toward him, her jeans a more feminine version of his. The camera came in tight on his crotch, then hers.

The models caressed each other's bodies with lingering strokes that the final edit made the most of by repeating endlessly. The result was actually quite erotic.

Beth ran to the edge of the roof and looked down at Times Square to see if anyone was watching.

It was working. There was a knot of people craning their necks and commenting.

She ran back to Justin, who was entering keyboard commands into the laptop that controlled the gigantic array of screens. He played with the color, with the movement of the models, freeze-framing moments and wiping others away in an instant.

There was a rhythm to his improvising that was very sensual and he worked fast. Then faster, intensifying it. Beth went back to the roof's edge. The crowd below had grown much larger in just a few minutes and was oohing and aahing appreciatively.

The images of the Blue Blaze jeans campaign changed constantly, but the concept—a man, a woman, a truck—was so simple to begin with that the effect of the rapid changes was hypnotic. At least Justin seemed to be a little hypnotized. His fingers stayed on the keyboard while he looked up at the sign, as if he was creating music only he could hear out of thin air. He was riveted to what he was doing, his glittering eyes reflecting the brilliance of the display.

Beth tugged at his sleeve. "I think you should stop."

"No," he said without looking at her, "this is a blast."

"But Justin—"

"No," he said again and shrugged her off.

Beth studied his profile, alarmed now by his degree of absorption. It was like she wasn't there at all. It was like he was drunk. On light. On color. The sunspots, millions of miles away, were most definitely getting to him.

"Let's take a trip," he said again without looking at her. He reached a hand sideways, fumbling for hers and missing. "This is great. Yowza. Shazam." He jabbed a button. "Look what I can do. I'm on a sunspot high and I don't want to come down. Everything's moving. I want to move with it. I want to jump right in there. C'mon."

"Nothing doing. I'm staying right here."

"Okay, I'll go in alone." He put both hands on the keyboard and keyed in commands so fast she couldn't tell what he was doing.

And then, in less than a second, he was sucked into the laptop screen . . . and suddenly reappeared in the sign, forty feet high.

"Justin, come back!" she screamed.

He looked down at her, oddly flattened out but very much himself. The models in the movie had vanished. Justin strode through the waving wheat and propped his foot on the bale of hay, having a great time in his own personal movie.

"How do I look?" he asked her, laughing hugely.

"Way too big! Come back here!"

He frowned. "I don't want to." He unbuttoned his shirt and whipped it off. "Women of the world, check me out!" He grinned down at Beth. "Feels good to be gorgeous."

"Don't you think you're getting a little carried away with yourself?"

"I like getting carried away. Being forty feet tall is great. Hey, guess how long my dick is—"

"Be quiet, Justin!" She hoped the crowd hadn't heard that. SpectraSign could kiss the Blue Blazes account good-bye forever if she couldn't shut him up and get him out and calm him the fuck down. "I don't really want to know!"

He stayed inside the sign while she looked at the laptop and tried a few keys. She tapped one, not familiar with the keyboard commands he used to control the enormous sign. Nothing happened.

She tapped another and the sign went completely black. She gasped in horror. What the hell had just happened?

"Beth?" It was just his voice. Disembodied. She looked around wildly but he was nowhere on the roof.

"Beth?" he said again. He sounded kind of nervous. "Where are you? Where am I?"

Oh no. He had to be trapped in that goddamn sign. She had to get him out.

The breeze carried the voices of the crowd below, dispersing. "Show's over." "That was cool." "Who was that guy at the end?"

If you only knew, she thought despairingly. Beth looked up at the black mosaic of screens and wondered if there was a way in.

Suddenly she realized it wasn't just the Blue Blazes sign that had gone black. All around her the signs of Times Square were fading out one by one, some popping off, some fading away.

The streetlights faded out. The ever-present rumble of New York City died away, because the subway trains had stopped on the tracks. The lights in all the buildings winked out.

Somehow, his fooling around with the laptop had started a chain reaction in the city's electrical grid. Justin had caused a blackout. A big one.

The mutters she could hear from the street below confirmed it. All five boroughs involved. No power. Nothing. People stuck in elevators, trains. Traffic lights gone dark. No red, no green, no yellow. Just nothing. Times Square could have been a dark canyon in the middle of nowhere.

Except for the tiny, lit-up screens of thousands of cell phones bobbing in the crowd below, the greatest intersection in the world was plunged into blackness.

"Beth?" Justin said quietly. "You there?"

She looked up. His voice *was* coming from the screen above her. "Yeah," she said. "I'm still here."

"I'm sorry."

"You oughta be, Justin Watts. And when I get you out of there, you're going to be even sorrier."

"Call Wind," his disembodied voice said.

"How?" she snapped. "I don't have a cell phone. And every line out of New York is already jammed. Can't you hear what people on the street are saying?"

She held up a hand to hush him just in case he could see her from inside the screen. "Then listen."

Apparently he was calm enough to obey. They both heard the complaints of no service and the occasional jubilant shout when someone got a call through.

"That's not what I meant," Justin whispered. "Just call him. He'll come, I swear."

Beth shook her head. "You call him."

Justin's voice echoed softly through the air above her, saying his friend's name as if he were breathing it. *Wind. Wind.*

And in another second Windham Devane was standing next to Beth.

"Hey," he said. "Got the word. Is that fool trapped in there?"

Beth just gaped at him. "How'd you know? How'd you get up here?"

"He called, I came. Not the first time I did a favor for him. But this is going to be a big one." He smiled at her, untroubled. Beth couldn't help but smile back, worried as she was.

"We have to get him out." She looked up at the black mosaic. "Fair warning. He's out of control."

"Guess so. You don't sound like you want to get him out, girl."

"He's been acting so crazy!"

Windham nodded. "It's the sunspots. They do it to him every time."

"I don't even want to know. This may not be the time to bring it up, but this superpower crap is getting to me. I want a real man."

"Justin's as real as you want him to be," Wind said.

"Hey, spare me the freaky little metaphysical asides, okay?" She sighed. "I don't know what to think any more. But I guess we'd better get him out of there."

What if he stayed huge? What if he stayed flat? Was it possible to slither through a laptop and blow yourself up to gigantic size and still remain human?

Beth reminded herself that strictly speaking, he wasn't human.

"Step aside, please." Wind took over the laptop from her. "Walk me through this, Sunny Boy," he called up to Justin inside the sign. "And brace yourself on re-entry. It ain't going to be easy."

"Whatever it takes."

"When you come on back through the circuits we can deal with this blackout."

"You mean Justin can fix it?" Beth asked him.

"Maybe. We won't know for sure until we can get him out, though."

Justin's voice issued the keyboard commands and one by one, Wind carried them out. "Is that it?"

"That should do it," Justin said.

Nothing happened. Beth and Windham stood there looking at each other.

"Shit," Windham said. "Okay, one more time. With feeling."

He tapped in the commands again and the huge sign above them rattled. Justin stepped out of it at one corner.

"I created a desktop shortcut," Wind explained calmly. "That's why he didn't come out through the laptop screen. I was afraid he would bust it."

Justin shook his head like he was trying to clear it. He'd left his shirt back in the movie and was still bare-chested, Beth saw.

He looked around, a little dazed, spotted the two of them and ran over. "What happened? All the signs are black!"

"You done triggered a blackout, fool," Windham scolded him.

"Oh my God." He looked searchingly at Beth. "I got a little out of control, didn't I?"

"No, a lot."

"Guess it's time I turned into a hero."

"Beats being a fool," Wind said. "Let's go where we can do the most good."

Justin nodded. "The subway."

"I have a feeling the folks down there could use a cool breeze."

"And some light."

They were right across the street from the entrance to the labyrinth that ran for blocks under Times Square, where twelve subway lines converged. Beth shuddered. She'd gotten lost in the maze of corridors and connections when it was all lit up—it was hard to imagine what it was like in there now.

"Beth, you ever flown without a plane?" Wind was asking.

She backed away. "No. N-no. And I don't want to." Her hands stretched out toward them. What she meant as refusal they took as opportunity.

Wind grabbed one of her hands, Justin grabbed the other, and she was flying between them, soaring over the mass of humanity in Times Square, between the buildings—they scared a few pigeons—and then down to earth by the entrance to the subway station.

The three of them felt their way down, squeezing past the people who were struggling to get up.

They seemed surprisingly calm. Some exchanged tales of the last blackout. Justin worked up the energy to light their way and Wind began to blow subtly, not so anyone would notice.

But it was enough to alleviate the stale air.

"You gotta find a hot connection," he murmured between puffs to Justin. "Use your powers for good."

"So that's where you got that line," Beth said to Justin, who hadn't let go of her hand.

"Yeah. We both read comic books. I'm not much of a hero."

She shook her head. "No. Let's hook you up, light up this place, and help people get out of here."

He glowed more brightly. "There's a transformer around here. Anyone see a Con Ed sign?"

"Shine on, man," Wind said. "We'll find it."

The throng of people moved slowly but surely through the corridor they were in, and Justin got through them to a panel in the tiled wall.

"This is it." He lifted it off.

"You guys from Con Ed?"

"No," said Wind, who was dressed in his basketball clothes, Beth noticed.

"Yes," said Justin, who was bare-chested.

"Whatever," said the man who'd asked.

Justin reached into the wires and fuses, connecting this to that, and ultimately attaching a cord as thick as a finger to his own finger.

"Stand back," he shouted.

No one in the crowd paid any attention. Wind began to blow in their direction, pushing people away without them knowing why.

Justin glowed a brilliant, pulsing yellow.

A lady with two babies in a stroller and an older boy clinging to its handle stopped and stared.

The air was filled with a crackling that made everyone's hair stand on end.

"Justin, be careful!" Beth whispered. She was fascinated, horrified, and totally pissed off at him all at once.

The air hummed and crackled. Justin radiated a light so strong she couldn't look at him. He was turning a thousand different colors in succession.

One guy stopped and dug in his pockets for money to give him. "That's a hell of an act, pal." He smoothed out a paper bag and put a handful of coins on it in front of the three of them.

Justin laughed and the connection broke. The corridor was plunged into blackness again.

"Man, pay attention," Windham said peevishly. "That's chump change. What have I told you about keeping focus?"

"Eyes on the ball," Justin said. "Got it. Okay, here I go." Beth watched as Justin slowly lit up again. He seemed to have less energy than before but for a good reason. One by one the lights that illuminated the labyrinth flickered on. And they stayed on.

People could see their way and streamed toward the staircases.

She heard the subways rumble to life and the doors whoosh open. For the most part, the passengers got off, not wanting to risk getting stuck.

A blackout, in a weird way, was just part of living in New York. Something to dine out on and talk about for years. And this had been a mercifully brief one, thanks to Justin.

But eight million people had been stopped in their tracks, also thanks to Justin. Who'd stopped turning colors and was looking at her sheepishly. "I screwed up, didn't I?"

"Yeah. You did."

"Can we go back to my place?"

"Not on the subway."

"We can take a cab."

"Your wallet's in your shirt pocket. You left it in the movie."

Justin thrust his hands into his pockets and looked at Windham. "Can I borrow twenty bucks, man?"

"Don't look at me," Wind said severely. "You got me off the courts. I wasn't carrying no wallet."

Justin looked back at Beth. "Guess you'll have to pay. I'll make it up to you."

"No!" Beth yelled. All the tension of the last several weeks and the sheer, mind-blowing weirdness of the last hour exploded out of her. "This will never, ever work! I can't be with a guy who can shut down the whole city of New York and hit me up for cab fare home!"

She turned and bolted, looking for the staircase that would bring her out in the heart of Times Square. Justin wasn't far behind her. She could hear his pounding footsteps as she reached the top, panting frantically.

He put a gentle hand on her arm. "Hey, I really am sorry. Whatever was going on with me is over. Turning everything on again took care of it."

She looked away from him, up at the lurid, immense signs that pulsed and glowed and sparkled. It was like the blackout had never even happened.

"Marry me, Beth," he said suddenly. "I love you."

"Hah! The answer is no. Not if you're going to go crazy on me every twelve years."

"I might," he admitted. "Just a little. Lock me in the back bedroom and tell the kids that daddy's watching TV."

"Tell the who? What?"

He reached out his arms and enfolded her in his strength. He was warm . . . so warm. Her temper dissolved in his embrace.

"The kids. Our kids. Someday, when you're ready, I mean. Freddy needs somebody to play with."

"Freddy hates kids."

"So we'll get him a feline friend to perk him up. I'm totally serious. Let's do it. We'll be happy."

She snuffled into his bare, hot chest. It was very satisfying. Her arms slipped around his waist. "How do you know?"

Justin dropped a kiss on her hair. "I just do," he whispered. "I really do love you."

"Will that be enough?" Classic girl-type question, but she couldn't help it.

"You won't have any in-laws."

Beth grinned against him. "You will. Wait til you meet the Ink Man. You'll like him, I think."

"Is that a yes?" He held her away from him and looked at her soulfully. She saw a blue, blue fire deep in his eyes that was close to heavenly. He was radiating pure love.

"Not yet," she said calmly.

A whole year and a lot of couples counseling later . . .

They were sprawled on the enormous sofa in his Bolt Building apartment. He was behind the sports section and she was brushing her hair. Beth looked over at the big feet in clean white socks, which was about all that she could see of him. She patted one fondly.

"Honey, how many superheroes does it take to change a light-bulb?"

"I don't know," he said absently. "How many?"

"One," she replied. "But he has to ask his wife where the lightbulbs are."

Justin rattled the paper. "Ha ha."

Just another peaceful Sunday in their aerie. She was utterly content. She hadn't minded moving in and old wheezy Freddy loved the Bolt Building. He'd laid claim to the sunniest corner and pretty much stayed there all day.

She pulled the sports section out of Justin's hands and threw herself on him to steal a kiss.

He didn't protest. They kept on going from there. Afterward, Beth lay in his arms and thought about how incredibly happy they were, just as he'd said.

No surprise there. The man was the light of her life.

Get in the holiday spirit with
TO ALL A GOOD NIGHT,
A sexy anthology from
Donna Kauffman, Jill Shalvis, and HelenKay Dimon.
Check out Donna's story, "Unleashed."

An hour later, she was quite thankful for the addendum maps, as she'd be hopelessly lost without them. Actually, even with them she'd gotten herself somewhat turned around at the end of the west wing—at least she was pretty sure it was west. Even the dogs had given up on the adventure and trotted off some time back to God knew where. She was sure they'd find her when they got hungry or wanted to go out, so she wasn't too concerned about that. But she was getting hungry herself, and she had no idea how to get back to the kitchen area, much less the garage, or the rooms she'd been assigned to stay in.

She was stumbling down a dark corridor, unable to find the hall light switch, when a very deep male voice said, "If you're a burglar, then might I direct your attention downstairs to the formal dining room. The silver tea set alone would keep you in much better stealth gear for at least the next decade. At the very least, you'd be able to afford a flashlight."

She let out a strangled yelp, as her heart leapt straight to her throat, then froze in the darkness. Except for the animals, she was supposed to be completely alone. Not so much as a valet or sous chef on premises for the next twelve days. Of course the notebook did say that Cicero had a lengthy and amazing vocabulary. But he was at least two floors away. And she doubted he knew how to use the house speaker system. Armed with a notebook and not much else, Emma decided offense was the best defense. "Please state who you are and how you got in here. Security has already been alerted, so you'd best—"

Rich male laughter cut her off. "You must be the sitter."

"Which must make you the burglar, then," she shot back, nerves getting the better of her.

More laughter. Which, despite being sexy as all hell, did little to calm her down. Because though she'd been joking, the idea that she'd been on the job of a lifetime for less than two hours and had already allowed a thief into the house was just a perverse enough thing that it would actually happen to her.

The large shadow moved closer and she was deep into the fight-or-flight debate when a soft click sounded and the hallway was illuminated with a series of crystal wall sconces. Emma's first glance at her unexpected guest did little to balance her equilibrium.

Whoever he was, he beat her five-foot-nine height by a good half foot, which made the fight thing rather moot. Flight probably wasn't going to get her very far, either. He had the kind of broad shoulders, tapered waist and well-built legs that her defensive line-coach dad would recruit in a blink, and charming rascal dimples topped by twinkling blue eyes that her Irish mother would swoon over as she served him beef stew and biscuits.

Emma, on the other hand, had absolutely no idea what to do with him.

Here's a sneak peek at Kathy Love's
I WANT YOU TO WANT ME,
available now from Brava . . .

Just as she raised her hand to knock again, the door jerked open, her fisted hand coming close to bopping him in the nose. In the dim light, Vittorio grimaced at her through sleep heavy eyes. His long hair was tangled and shoved haphazardly back from his face. Bare muscled chest and flat stomach appeared over sweatpants slung low on his narrow hips.

"I'm sorry," Erika immediately said, even as her heart skipped wildly. An image of him lying in bed filled her mind, quickly morphing to a picture of her in bed with him. "I—I didn't think you'd be sleeping," she managed to mumble.

He frowned, blinking, then peering over her shoulder at the evening sky, now nearly leaving them in darkness.

"I keep weird hours." His tone was flat, yet his voice still lent the words a beauty with its deep baritone timbre.

Erika stared at him, unable to keep from studying the shadows emphasizing the muscles of his chest and stomach. Chiseled and perfect. She immediately wanted to capture that perfection with her art.

But she managed to stop gaping and move her gaze up to his face, which was also a study in shadows and beauty.

Clearing her throat, she managed a smile. "I keep odd hours too."

He lifted an eyebrow, but didn't say anything. Instead he leaned on the door frame, crossing his arms over his chest. The movement caused his muscles to come to life. Erika's fingers twitched with the longing to run her hand over them like she would the smooth clay of one of her sculptures.

"I'm guessing you didn't come up here to discuss our sleep habits."

Erika's eyes returned to his, as did the sense of dread she'd been experiencing at the bottom of the stairs. Cool disdain—that was what she was getting. Crap.

"No." She offered him another small smile. "No, I came up to see how your head is."

"It's fine."

Erika nodded at the clipped response that didn't invite further questioning. Yet she couldn't seem to go, even though it was clear he didn't feel the overwhelming attraction she did. She should just give her apology and leave. She'd tested Philippe's theory, and she'd been right all along.

She moved back, preparing to do just that, when she remembered the plate in her hands.

"Oh, I made you these," she said, shoving the plate toward him. "You know as a peace offering."

He stared down at the plastic wrap-covered squares as if he expected them to crawl off the plate and attack. Perhaps sticking in his beautiful long hair.

Her fingers tightened on the plate while feeling a desire to touch the silky looking locks. Was she utterly mad? This man was not interested in her in the least, and she was fantasizing about touching his hair.

"I—" He still regarded the cookies with a definite look of consternation. "I don't eat—sweets."

"Oh." She pulled the plate away from him. "Okay. Well, I did just want to say I'm sorry."

He nodded saying nothing.

"About last night, I mean," she said, watching his expression.

A muscle in his jaw worked as if he was clenching his teeth.

"As you've already said," he stated.

Erika nodded, not sure what else to say. It certainly didn't appear he was any more willing to forgive her tonight than he was last night.

Suddenly that uncharacteristic feeling of irritation swelled inside her again. Why did he dislike her so much? Okay, she had hit him with a cell phone, but it had been in an unusual circumstance. And she did feel truly awful about it.

But instead of just accepting that he wasn't going to warm up to her, she heard herself saying. "I know this is going to sound weird, but I'm actually trying to figure out if you are someone that my psychic told me I'd meet."

Vittorio straightened, and the remote look in his eyes shifted, but it wasn't to an expression she liked any better. His eyes widened with amused disbelief.

"Your psychic?"

Erika had this reaction before. More than once. And she immediately regretted her honesty.

"I'm sure this sounds a little strange to you."

He tilted his head. "What did this psychic say?"

She hesitated. Was he genuinely curious, or did he intend to mock her?

"He's been predicting that I would meet someone who, at least physically, fits your description."

He nodded, his gaze leaving hers as if he was considering the idea. She still couldn't quite decipher what he might be thinking.

"And what else did this psychic say?"

Erika again debated what to tell him. But the lopsided, not altogether kind, slant of his lips made her stop. He thought she was nuts. And he didn't appear to like her any better for her nuttiness.

"Forget it." She raised a hand in a gesture of defeat. "I just wanted to be sure your head was all right."

She started to leave, when his voice stopped her. "Thanks."

And keep an eye out for
Katherine Garbera's latest,
BARE WITNESS,
coming next month from Brava . . .

Justine arched an eyebrow at him. "Are you making fun of me?"

"Never. I was trying—trying to tease a smile back on your lips."

"Why?"

"I like your smile."

"You do?"

"Yes."

"Why?"

Nigel shook his head this time. "You mustn't get many compliments."

She shrugged. "Honestly, I don't trust them."

"Why not?"

"What's with you and all the questions?"

"I'm a CEO. I thrive on information."

"So do bodyguards," she said.

The teasing note was back in her voice and he felt a little thrill of victory at having done that. "Why are you a bodyguard?"

"Well, to be honest, I'm usually more of a weapons expert and marksman. For most assignments we take on, Charity functions as the bodyguard."

"Why is that?"

"She's tall and gorgeous, just the sort of person that makes most assailants think they don't have a thing to worry about."

"And you're not."

She gestured to her short frame. "Height is one thing I've never needed."

"No?"

"No," she said. "I learned early on that if I don't quit, I can take anyone."

"Can you take me?"

"Easily," she said.

He took two steps toward her. The plane rocked and bucked and all the playfullness that she'd had a second ago disappeared as she used her body to take him down to the floor and braced both of their bodies.

When the plane leveled itself out she knew it had to be turbulence and not an engine out or any other danger. But her heart was racing and it had nothing at all to do with the security of Nigel Carter or his daughter.

Justine closed her eyes but that just made everything . . . better. All of her other senses came to life. The feel of his hard body under hers, the scent of his spicy aftershave, the sound of each exhalation of his minty breath against her cheek.

She opened her eyes as Nigel's hands settled low on her waist. This time it wasn't different. His hand was in the exact same spot that had worried her when they'd been standing toe-to-toe. But now it didn't bother her.